TATTERED ON MY SLEEVE

(Lost Kings MC #4)

AUTUMN JONES LAKE

TATTERED
ON
MY SLEEVE
LOST KINGS MC #4
AUTUMN JONES LAKE

Digital Edition ISBN: 978-0-9907945-6-1
Print Edition ISBN: 978-0-9907945-7-8
Copyright 2015 © Autumn Jones Lake
ALL RIGHTS RESERVED.
Edited by: Vanessa Bridges, PREMA
Cover Design: Letitia Hasser , RBA Designs
Cover Photo: Furious Fotog
Cover Model: Jeremy Mooney
Formatting by: AJ Lake

ALSO BY AUTUMN JONES LAKE

THE LOST KINGS MC™ SERIES

Slow Burn (Lost Kings MC #1)– *Free ebook!*
Corrupting Cinderella (Lost Kings MC #2)
Three Kings, One Night (Lost Kings MC #2.5)
Strength From Loyalty (Lost Kings MC #3)
Tattered on My Sleeve (Lost Kings MC #4)
White Heat (Lost Kings MC #5)
Between Embers (Lost Kings MC #5.5)
More Than Miles (Lost Kings MC #6)
White Knuckles (Lost Kings MC #7)
Beyond Reckless (Lost Kings MC #8)
Beyond Reason (Lost Kings MC #9)
One Empire Night (Lost Kings MC #9.5)
After Burn (Lost Kings MC #10)
After Glow (Lost Kings MC #11)
Zero Hour (Lost Kings MC #11.5) - *Free ebook!*
Zero Tolerance (Lost Kings MC #12)
Zero Regret (Lost Kings MC #13)
Zero Apologies (Lost Kings MC #14)
White Lies (Lost Kings MC #15)
Swagger and Sass (A Lost Kings MC Novella) - *Free ebook!*

Rhythm of the Road (Lost Kings MC #16)
Lyrics on the Wind (Lost Kings MC #17)
Diamond in the Dust (Lost Kings MC #18)
Crown of Ghosts (Lost Kings MC #19)
Throne of Scars (Lost Kings MC #20)
Reckless Truths (Lost Kings MC #21)
Rust or Ride (Lost Kings MC #22)
...and many more to come!

BOOKS IN THE LOST KINGS MC WORLD
The Hollywood Demons Series
Kickstart My Heart
Blow My Fuse
Wheels of Fire

Bullets & Bonfires
Warnings & Wildfires
Renegade Path

Paranormal Romance
Catnip & Cauldrons
Onyx Night
Onyx Shadows
Feral Escape

Lust.

Eight years ago, the Lost Kings, MC was recovering from turmoil within the club Wrath and Trinity met. After three perfect nights, Wrath knew she was the one. But Trinity's dark past was about to catch up to her and the Lost Kings MC was her only hope for protection.

Fury.

One misunderstanding led to a mistake that locked both of them into a war to see who could hurt who the most.

Forgiveness.

When long-buried secrets are finally revealed, Wrath will stop at nothing to fix their relationship and make Trinity understand she belongs to him.

Acknowledgments

As always I have to thank a number of people who helped make Tattered on My Sleeve possible.

My faithful critique partners, Cara Connelly, Kari W. Cole and Virginia Frost. If my writing has improved over the last year, I know it's from our weekly Wednesdays. Cara in particular spent many days relentlessly red-inking the mess of pages I handed over and her help was invaluable.

K.A. Mitchell, thank you for your support and belief in me.

Angi J., Amanda, Brandy, Chris, Clarisse, Elizabeth, Iveta, Tamra, and Shelly. Thank you from the bottom of my heart for sticking with me. Thank you for your advice, support, and eagle eyes! Manda, thank you for your expert beta feedback.

Vanessa, I'm so happy we finally got to work together. Thank for pushing me to drill down and focus on the main story. I can't wait for future projects.

Elizabeth, Tanya, Terra, Johnnie-Marie, thank you for the time you spend promoting my books. Krystal, you're the best release day hostess ever-thank you for everything!

My Lost Kings MC Ladies facebook group—you guys are awesome! Thanks for insisting on Trinity Tuesdays and Wrath Wednesdays and for reminding me when I was running late! Now that Wrath has been unleashed, we'll have to figure something else out.

Iza thank you for #propertyofwrath. I think you love Wrath as much as I do.

One thing I've noticed on this journey is that MC Romance readers are some of the most loyal, enthusiastic and supportive readers an author can ask for. Thank you.

There are so many other people I'd like to thank, but I'm afraid I'll forget someone.

Last and never least, my husband. He's the best parts of all my romance heroes wrapped up into one big pain-in-my-ass package and I'd be lost without him. And his "real Wrath" jokes never get old.

Glossary

I first used a glossary in the *Road to Royalty* limited edition boxed set and thought it might be helpful here as well. If you're new to the Lost Kings MC (welcome!) it might be helpful to have some of the things specific to them mentioned ahead of time. If you're new to Motorcycle Club Romances in general, it also might be helpful. If you're familiar with the series (welcome back!), maybe you'll find the refresher useful.

The Lost Kings MC Organizational Structure

President: Rochlan "Rock" North. Leader of the Upstate NY charter of the Lost Kings MC. The word of the President is law within the club. He takes advice from senior club members. He is the public "face" of the MC. No one challenges the decisions of the President.

Sergeant-at-Arms: Wyatt "Wrath" Ramsey. Responsible for the security of the club. Keeps order at club events. Responsible for the safety and protection of the president, the club, its members and its women. Disciplines club members who violate the rules. Keeps track of club by-laws.

Vice President: Zero or "Z". In most clubs, I think the VP would be considered the second-in-command. In mine, I see the VP and SAA on equal footing within the club. Carries out the orders of the President. Communicates with other chapters of the club. Assumes the responsibilities of the President in his absence. Keeps records of club patches and colors issued.

Treasurer: Marcel "Teller" Whelan. Keeps records of income and expenses.

Road Captain: Blake "Murphy" O'Callaghan. Responsible for researching, planning and organizing club runs. Responsible for obtaining and maintaining club vehicles.

Lost Kings MC Terminology

Crystal Ball – The strip club owned by the Lost Kings MC and one of their legitimate businesses. They often refer to it as just "CB".

"Conference Center" – The clubhouse of the Lost Kings MC. It was previously used as a conference center and is sometimes jokingly referred to this way.

Empire – The fictional city in Upstate NY, run by the Lost Kings.

Green Street Crew – Street gang the Lost Kings does business with. Often referred to as "GSC."

LOKI – Short for Lost Kings.

Vipers MC – Rival and frequent enemy MC. Runs Ironworks which borders the Lost Kings Territory.

Wolf Knights MC – Rival and sometimes ally of the Lost Kings.

Other MC Terminology

Most terminology was obtained through research. However, I have also used some artistic license in applying these terms to my romanticized fictional version of an Outlaw Motorcycle Club.

Cage – A car, truck, van, basically anything other than a motorcycle.

Church – Club meetings all full patch members must attend. Led by the President of the club, but all officers will update the members on the areas they oversee.

Citizen – Anyone not a hardcore biker or belonging to an outlaw club. "Citizen Wife" would refer to a spouse kept entirely separate from the club.

Club Mama – A female that is property of all club members. Available to all club members, keeps the clubhouse clean, and meets any other needs a club member may have.

Cut – Leather vest worn by outlaw bikers. Adorned with patches and artwork displaying the club's unique colors. The Lost Kings' colors are blue and gray. Their logo is a skull with a crown.

Colors – The "uniform" of an outlaw motorcycle gang. A leather vest, with the three-piece club patch on the back, and various other patches relating to their role in the club. Colors belong to the club, and are held sacred by all members.

Fly Colors – To ride on a motorcycle wearing colors.

Mother Chapter – First chapter of the club.

Nomad – A club member who does not belong to any specific charter, yet has privileges in all charters. Nomads go anywhere to take care of business usually at the request of the club president.

Old Lady – Wife or steady girlfriend of a club member.

Patched in – When a new member is approved for full membership.

Patch holder – A member who has been vetted through performing duties for the club as a prospect and has earned his three-piece patch.

Prospect – A prospective member of the club. The club needs to unanimously vote him in to become a full member.

Property Patch – When a member takes a woman as his Old Lady (wife status), he gives her a vest with a property patch. "Property of Lost Kings MC" and the member's road name.

Pull a Train – For a girl to have sex with each man in the club, any way he wants it, one after another.

Road Name – Nick name. Usually given by the other members.

Run – A club sanctioned outing sometimes with other chapters and/or clubs. Can also refer to a club business run.

Sweetbutt – A girl who hangs out with the club and is always available for sex. Since my version is a "romantic" take on an MC, they are usually referred to as "club girls" but this term is used once or twice throughout.

DEDICATION

Dedicated to those who've survived their scarred pasts and keep working to create a happy future.

PROLOGUE

Trinity Hurst.

That girl fucking owned me the minute I laid eyes on her. At twenty-one, she already had a cold, calculating wall around her. Porn star hair, angel eyes, beautiful cock-sucking lips. All of it smoothed into an innocent looking package. Well, to anyone else, she might appear pure and innocent. Not me.

She didn't act like any other club girl I'd ever met. Most of them kept their mouths shut and their legs open. She didn't take shit from anyone and made a guy work for every little smile she tossed his way. It was a unique talent that drove me fucking nuts. The walls she built up around herself were designed to keep guys like me away. Underneath her tough-girl exterior lay something sweet and vulnerable.

I had her first.

I fell in love with her.

Then we fucked everything up.

Part One

Our fast love and
furious destruction.

CHAPTER ONE

WRATH

Eight years ago...

A zap of electricity shot through me when the blonde beauty behind the bar turned her head my way. How the hell was this chick planning to keep the peace at the Blue Fox Tavern?

As long as we all behaved, the bar allowed everyone to wear their MC's colors. But it was still a biker bar. If things got out of hand, I didn't have much confidence the little cutie would be able to do much. Girl was gonna get hurt.

Once I got over the shock of seeing the new bartender, I slipped my don't-give-a-fuck face back on. My brothers, Rock and Zero, were right behind me. Brothers by *choice*. As in we belonged to the same MC. But to me, the bond we shared flowed deeper than any blood relation.

The three of us sat at the bar. The sweet, bubbly demeanor the girl approached us with was completely out of place in the seedy hangout. The way her eyes roamed over us, assessing the level of danger we posed, made me rethink my first impression.

"Hey, guys. What can I get you?"

Her gaze skipped to our cuts and zeroed in on each of our patches. She looked me over last, and holy fuck, when our eyes met, my dick perked right up. For just a second, the hard, calculating gleam in her eyes softened into something vulnerable.

The moment passed, and she swung her gaze back to Rock, whose patch read *President*.

"Scotch neat, please, sweetheart," he answered. His eyes were busy assessing her as well, but I didn't get the feeling he wanted to take her in the back room and fuck her like he did with just about every other chick he met.

As the vice president, she took Z's order next. Finally, she returned to me.

"Sergeant-at-arms, huh? The Wrecking Ball."

A slow grin spread across my face. I liked her. "I've been called worse."

"I'm sure you have. What would you like?"

I wanted *her*, spread out on the bar in front of me. "Jack Daniels, neat," I answered.

The three of us were silent while we watched her work. Slapping the drinks down with a tired smile, she glanced at the clock. She turned back to us and cocked her head, checking out our officer patches again.

"You have a shakeup in leadership? Your patches are so squeaky clean," she teased in a husky voice.

"What's your name, sweetheart?" Rock asked.

A short, excessively curvy brunette jiggled into the space behind the bar and yelped, "Trinity! I'm so sorry I'm late!"

The loud chick had herself stuffed into some sort of hot-pink tube top thing that didn't flatter her as much as she probably thought.

"It's okay, Storm," the blonde answered, even though her expression said otherwise.

Storm? Aw, fuck.

As if she heard my thought, Storm turned her big, brown, doe-eyed gaze our way and shrieked.

"Oh, Trinity! These are the guys I was telling you about." She yanked the blonde over to us by the elbow. Her hungry gaze zeroed in on Z right away, which was unfortunate for her because he was strictly hit-it-and-quit-it.

The few times we'd met her, Rock and I had picked up a definite undercurrent of desperation with this broad. Even though we let her party at our clubhouse, we'd both been smart enough to steer clear of her bear-trap pussy.

Trinity seemed less than impressed. I wondered what sort of stories Storm had been spinning about us.

"Can I stop by after work, guys?" Storm asked.

Rock answered quick. "No. There'll be a full house tomorrow. Stop by then, hon."

Her face fell, then brightened at the invitation. I glanced down the bar at Z, who looked ready to choke our prez. I couldn't wait to give him shit later.

I finished my drink and got up to take a walk around the place. Rock's meeting was with a crew we hadn't established a lot of trust with yet. My job was to check things out before they got here. Keep the place secure. Make sure nothing happened to my president.

Back corner booth. That was where the meeting needed to go down. As I pulled a chair over, a breathy voice behind me called out, "Hold on. I haven't cleaned that yet."

Trinity rushed over with a rag and wiped the most recent stickiness from the tabletop. I'm only human, so while she was busy cleaning, I checked out her pleasantly round ass. My fingers flexed as I imagined how perfectly her cheeks would fit my hands. For a biker chick, she was awfully conservative. I spotted what looked like two tank tops. Black on top, bright pink underneath. No thong or tramp stamp peeking out when she bent over—I think I liked that part most.

She finished and spun around. Too bad my eyes were slow to react. She definitely caught me checking out her ass. I wasn't ashamed, though, because shame's never been an emotion I wasted my time on. Besides, now my gaze was fixed on something even more exciting—her tits all pushed up and spilling out of her shirt.

It was difficult, but I looked up into her honey-colored eyes. How had I missed that color before? Or was it just the strange amber lighting we were standing under in the otherwise dark corner? "Is Trinity a road name or your legal one?"

"Real. My mother had me during her Catholic phase."

I snorted a laugh. "How's that working out for you?"

"Well, I'm tending bar at a biker hangout, so what do you think?"

"I think things worked out well. For me, anyway."

Yeah, that one was lame. But it got a genuine smile out of her, which had been my goal.

"So, Wrecking Ball, I don't know your name."

"Wrath."

She fake-shivered and made a *brrrr* sound with her sexy-as-fuck lips. "Scary. Are you an angry fellow?"

Man, I liked this girl. She didn't say a lot, but when she spoke, she was a flirty little bitch. She clearly put up walls to keep guys like me at arm's length, and that made me want her even more.

"Not tonight. You got an ol' man?"

She scrunched up her nose. "Fuck no." Then she looked me straight in the eyes, practically daring me. "And I'm not looking for one either."

Trinity

Wrath. His name should have been *lust*, because that was the deadly sin burning through me when I looked up—way up—into his ocean-blue eyes. I should've gotten the fuck out of there. My shift was up. Storm finally had her annoying ass slinging drinks. But curiosity chained me to the bar.

I should've despised bikers. I should've most definitely steered clear of this one, with his thick, muscled arms and low, sensual voice.

My normally impeccable self-preservation instinct seemed to be on the fritz.

"Well, that's good to hear. I'm not looking for an ol' lady."

"I'm not looking for a hookup either. If you don't mind, my shift is over."

Actually, I wouldn't mind a hook-up with all three of them. Maybe not the president; there was something about him that triggered a warm, brotherly memory. Which was weird because I was an only child. But the other two, yeah, I would definitely be down to—

"Trinity!" Storm yelped from behind the bar.

"Christ."

I forgot about the Wrecking Ball and stomped over to the bar.

"What?"

"I cut my hand, really bad."

As I rounded the corner, her bloody hand came into view, and I swallowed back a tidal wave of barf.

"Ew, fuck!" I whipped around and headed for the back office. "I'll go get Marky. He should probably run you to the ER."

Marky took Storm to the hospital, and I got stuck behind the bar for the rest of the night. Wrath and his friends met with an even scarier group of thugs. But they didn't cause any trouble and they ignored me, so I didn't care.

"Trinity?"

I looked up to find the president staring at me.

"Have you heard from Storm? She okay?"

I shook my head. It was unlikely I'd hear from Storm or Marky. "Nothing yet."

He nodded once and tipped his head to the side. "You hang with any local MCs?"

He was asking if I was club ass for one of his rivals. Surprisingly, I wasn't offended. "No."

"Oh, you just seemed familiar—"

"My dad was in the Silver Saints when I was a kid."

Sympathy shone in his gray eyes. Clearly, he knew their rep. Fuck, why did I even tell him that? I usually kept that shit to myself.

"He still in?"

"He's dead."

He quirked an eyebrow at me as if he wanted me to continue, and for some strange reason, I did.

"He died in prison when I was ten."

"Club take care of you and your mother?"

A shiver of revulsion rippled over me, and I closed my eyes for a second. Yeah, they'd taken care of us all right.

"Not really."

He nodded as if he wasn't surprised.

His VP called to him. He quickly scribbled on one of the napkins. "Here's the address and number for our clubhouse. We're working on moving into a bigger place, but this is it for now. Stop by tomorrow night if you want. At the door, tell them Rock invited you."

"How many patched-in brothers you got, Rock?"

"Ten right now."

"Small."

"Yeah. Like you said—had a shakeup in leadership. Later, Trinity."

I watched him walk away. Like fuck was I going to any club party. I didn't care how "hot" or "nice" they were—according to Storm.

I looked at the address. Right next door to a strip club. Big surprise there.

"You closing soon?" The Wrecking Ball was back.

"Yeah, thank fuck. My feet are killing me."

He threw back his head and laughed, a deep, sexy, rumbling chuckle. Curling his hands over the side of the bar, he swung his upper body over to check out my shoes. "At least you're wearing sneakers and not fuck-me pumps like Storm. Can I buy you a drink, Trinity?" he asked in a much more serious tone.

"I don't drink on the job."

He gave me a curt nod, and I took the trash into the back room. Marky could deal with it later. I wasn't stepping foot in that alley by myself.

WRATH

I'd waited an hour for Trinity to disappear long enough for me to hustle her straggling customers out the door. The three of us agreed we'd stay until closing since Trinity was all by herself. But the poor girl looked ready to drop, so the bar was closing early.

"Oh, did everyone leave?" Her soft voice pulled me away from my staring contest with a bottle of Jack Daniels. I pushed it away.

"Yup."

"Even your guys?"

That bugged me for some reason. I'd seen her chatting with Rock earlier. "Yeah, why?"

She shrugged as if she'd only asked to be polite and didn't really care one way or another.

"Anything else you need to do?"

"No, fuck it, I already worked way over my shift."

I chuckled at that. She punched her time card and stood there watching me.

"Do you leave by the back door or something?"

She laughed. "No, nothing but a dark, dirty, scary alleyway."

"Can I give you a lift home?"

Her gaze drifted to mine and a mischievous little gleam shone in her eyes. "Do you have your bike?"

"Of course." What a ridiculous question.

"Sure, you can give me a ride."

On the surface, her words were innocent, but she made them sound dirty. Or maybe it was my dick's wishful thinking.

My baby was parked right outside. Trinity studied it for a minute before looking up at me. "Do you have an extra helmet?"

"Actually, I do." I liked to be prepared when picking up chicks.

I dug it out and handed it over. She fiddled with it for a minute, then strapped it on like a pro.

The night was chilly, and I wished I had something to offer that would cover her better than the skinny little straps of her tank tops. "You're going to be cold. I'm sorry. I don't have a sweatshirt or something with me."

"I'll be okay."

She got on behind me like she'd done it a million times.

"Have you been on a bike before?"

A soft chuckle and her warm breath swept over the side of my neck. "Yeah, I've ridden."

I started her up, twisted the throttle a few times, and took off. After a few blocks, Trinity's hands moved from my hips to my front as she wrapped her arms around me. The distinctive movement of her hand inching toward my cock distracted me for a moment. What the hell was she up to?

When I finally stopped at a red light, I turned my head to shout, "Where are we going?"

"751 Mason Street."

Mason Street. Why did that sound familiar? "That's three doors down from the bar!"

"I know. I wanted a ride."

I shook my head and took the long way back to Mason Street. Maybe she wasn't as indifferent to my charms as she seemed.

Surprisingly, the spot I vacated was still open, so I slid in there. She handed me the helmet and ran her hands through her hair a few times. I don't think she did it on purpose, but she looked damn sexy. I still straddled my bike because she hadn't invited me in yet.

"Aren't you going to walk me home?"

Hell. Yeah.

I scanned the quiet street, searching for 751. It really was almost right next to the bar.

It was also a shithole.

"That's convenient," I said, nodding at the Blue Fox.

"Happy accident."

She had her keys in her hand, and we stood there staring at each other. She seemed to be trying to come to a decision. I'm a patient guy. I could wait.

"Do you want to come in? I can make you a biker's poison."

I tried really hard not to get all cocky about the invite. "What's that?" I asked, reaching out to tuck a few strands of wild hair behind her ear. Her eyelids fluttered at my touch. I was getting to her. The urge to do some sort of touchdown dance hit me.

"It's Jack and rum. Shake it and shoot it."

My lip curled in disgust. "Gross. Why ruin Jack like that?"

"I knew it. Knew you were a whiskey snob."

She was actually teasing me and joking around. I wanted to kiss her.

"Come on. I'll find something else for you."

If the outside of the building looked bad, inside was a fucking nightmare. This coming from a guy who hung out in a clubhouse with nine other male pigs. Rickety stairs led up to an even more questionable landing.

She opened the first door.

Inside wasn't so bad. It was tiny but clean. What little she had was organized and pretty.

"Do you want a beer?"

"Sure."

My big shit-kicking boots felt strange in her tiny little apartment. But toeing them off might give her the wrong impression. I threw myself onto her couch and sank down so fast, I wondered if I'd ever get out of it.

She returned and handed me a bottle of beer.

"Thanks. I think you're done serving for the night now."

A small smile played over her lips. After a beat or two, she tucked herself onto the couch. Not really next to me, but not so far away I couldn't reach out and run my finger down her arm.

"So, Wrath, what do you do besides the sergeant-at-arms stuff?" She flicked her hand in the air like the topic bored her.

Huh. She was the first chick who hadn't wanted to sit and discuss the MC for hours on end.

"I fight."

She rolled her eyes at me. "So predictable."

"No really. Mixed martial arts style."

"Are you any good?"

"I'm undefeated."

"Doesn't the MC take a lot of time away from your training?"

I considered her question carefully before answering. Yes. Actually, the last two years had been nothing but battle after battle within our club. I'd had little time to focus on training or fighting. I hadn't needed anywhere else to redirect my rage either.

"Yeah, sometimes."

"If you're undefeated, shouldn't I have heard about you?"

"MMA isn't legal in New York. These are underground fights."

"So what else do you do?"

Fuck chicks, ride my bike, knock people out.

"Saving to get my own gym."

Suddenly, she was right next to me. Her hand brushed over my cheek.

"What do you like to do, Trinity?"

"Read."

"That's not very exciting."

"Trust me, I've had enough excitement in my life." Her voice came out more pained than teasing. It held that vulnerability I glimpsed at the bar.

I turned to face her, cupped her cheek, and ran my thumb over her soft skin. She pushed forward and tentatively pressed her lips to mine. I reached behind me to set the beer on the end table, then placed my hand on the other side of her face.

She yelped and bolted backward. "Cold hand!"

"Sorry."

Unruffled, she swooped in and kissed me again. Her hand dropped to my lap and she gave my cock a quick squeeze. Fuck. She had me so hard I didn't think I'd be able to get out of my jeans with a hacksaw. She rubbed harder, pressing her palm into me.

"Trin—"

I slid down a little to relieve the pressure, and she took it as an invitation to work my pants open, running her hands up and down my cock. Still no words from her, though. Just kept looking at me with those fuck-me eyes. Suddenly, she dropped down on her belly, stretching her legs out behind her on the couch, and closed her mouth around my cock.

I hissed out a breath. Fuck, that felt good.

She angled and arranged herself over my lap, licking, sucking, exploring. Christ, it was amazing.

"Babe, wouldn't that be easier on your knees?" I pointed to the floor.

She released my cock with a soft pop and tilted her head toward me, her lips shiny and red.

"I don't get on my knees for anyone. Ever."

Shit. Why can't I ever keep my big mouth shut?

"Okay." I reached out and stroked her hair. My cock really wanted back in her mouth.

Her hand kept lazily working up and down my shaft. Finally, she bent over and took me in her mouth again.

Sweet motherfucking heaven. I couldn't help thrusting up, and she didn't seem to mind. She made happy little humming noises that vibrated up and down my dick.

"Trinity, honey. I'm close. Fuck, I'm gonna blow. Stop now if you don't want me shooting in your mouth, babe."

Please don't stop. Please don't stop.

She paused, and for an awful second, I thought she was going to stop. I froze, waiting, but then she took me deeper, trailing her tongue along the underside of my cock where she apparently realized I was extra sensitive.

My fist curled in her hair. I really wanted to see her fucking eyes but couldn't from this position. Then she took me all the way to the back of her throat. All thought left. White lightning gathered in my sac, streaking up until I came with painful intensity. Trinity didn't stop. She sucked and swallowed while keeping her plush lips wrapped around my cock.

"Ah, fuck! Trin. Shit."

She kept licking and kissing. Finally, she stopped and looked up with a soft smile.

I cupped my hand behind her neck and pulled her to me. "Thank you."

I tried kissing her, but she wriggled away. "Guys don't like to after doing that."

Huh?

She sat up and reached over to take a sip of my beer. Christ, my spent cock jumped when she put the bottle to her lips. She set the bottle down and crawled into my lap. With one hand at the back of her head and one above her ass, I pressed her against me and took her mouth hard. Forcing my tongue in her mouth, I explored every inch. I wasn't nearly done with this little angel. No fucking way. I slid my hands down to cup her ass. Just as I'd suspected, my palms curved perfectly around each cheek. Holding her tight, I powered off the couch. She held on and let out a little squeal.

"Bedroom?"

She giggled and jerked her head in the only possible direction the bedroom could be. Yeah, she'd sucked my brain out through my cock.

I shuffled us in there, even with my pants falling down.

The fuck?

A pink, frilly twin bed and some cheap furniture were all she had in here. I set her down gently, and she scooted up onto the mattress.

I took a moment to zip up, but left everything else undone because I planned to fuck her as soon as possible.

"Get those pants off, babe."

She stood and tried to push past me. I held her with one arm. Tilting her head up, I searched her eyes. "That wasn't enough, Angel Eyes."

Her lashes fluttered and she stood on her tiptoes to press a soft kiss on my lips. Hooking my fingers in the straps of her tank tops, I slid them down her shoulders. Fucking mercy, she had a fantastic pair of tits jammed into a push-up bra. I took a second to admire the black lace cradling her soft, white skin, then reached around to unhook it and slide it off her shoulders.

"You're fucking gorgeous." Her body trembled, and I frowned. Most girls eat that shit up, but for some reason, compliments seemed to freak Trinity out. It made me want to work harder to show her how pretty she was.

I kissed her cheek and her neck, down to her breasts, stopping to suck and tease her soft pink nipples into hard little peaks. My hands started working her jeans off. Kneeling down in front of her, I peeled them down her legs. I finally stripped them off and just stared. Knockout figure, with full breasts and curvy hips. Beautiful curves in all my favorite places. Those soft, rounded hips would be perfect to hold on to while pounding into her from behind. I gripped them and she went still. The skin on her right hip felt textured and rough. I turned her slightly and found red, scarred skin from the top of her thigh to just over her hip.

I flicked my gaze up. "What happened, babe?"

She relaxed a notch before answering. "Fire when I was a kid."

"Does it hurt?"

Her pretty eyes closed again. "No. Just feels weird I guess."

I pressed my lips against her scarred skin, then kissed my way to her belly button.

"Lie back."

She did, and I positioned myself right between her thighs. Hooking my fingers in her panties, I slowly pulled them down, kissing each bit of skin they passed.

"Open for me."

She planted her elbows on the bed and levered up to look down at me. "Wrath, I can't. Um. I've never... I can't come that way."

Challenge accepted.

26

"Okay, baby. Just let me taste you until I'm ready to fuck you. I haven't recovered from the couch yet."

Lie. Big, fat, motherfucking lie.

I was so hard it hurt.

I slipped my fingers between her legs and rubbed her softly, tracing her slick, bare skin.

"Do you have any idea how pretty you are—everywhere?"

She hummed and twisted on the bed. I leaned forward and nuzzled her mound. Her hips jerked, so I grabbed them to hold her still, letting my thumbs slide into the juncture of her thighs.

"Open for me. Put your feet on my shoulders."

It took a few seconds, but she did it.

Spreading her lips, I leaned in and swept my tongue over her.

She let out a sharp little screech.

I glanced up. "You like that?"

"Yes."

I gave her another long, wet lick, and she gasped. I dipped one finger inside her, in and out, until her hips were rocking with me. Taking another lick, I made my way to her clit, licking slow, sucking, more soft kisses.

Her moans were constant, beautiful, raw sounds. Her hips bumped up. Capturing her little nub between my lips, I sucked gently, still sliding my fingers in and out. Her legs shook and quivered.

Almost there.

She screamed and tightened, grinding herself on my face and fingers. I fuckin' loved every delicious second. She was able to let go for me. Because of what *I* did to her. She raked her nails through my hair, holding me where she needed me.

"Please, please, please, don't stop," she begged.

I growled and shook my head. No fucking way. Couldn't stop if I wanted to.

When her screaming died down to little whimpers, I shrugged out of my cut, tossing it on her nightstand. Yanked my shirt over my head and threw it on the floor. Worked my pants off. I needed to bury myself in her that second. I dug through my pocket for a condom and rolled it on.

"You with me, Trinity?"

"Yes." She held out her arms to me. Seeing we weren't going to fit on the bed the way she was positioned, I picked her up and tossed her head-first to the pillows before climbing over her.

Running my gaze over her flushed face gave me a head rush. I fucking did that. She said no one else had ever gotten her off that way.

I did.

Mine.

"You're incredible," she whispered while she reached for me. My fingers curled over hers, and I kissed the back of her hand.

"So are you."

Trinity

Holy shit.

I didn't lie when I told Wrath I couldn't come like that. Or I thought I couldn't. No one had ever put so much effort into pleasing me. Oh, wow, had I been missing out.

He hovered over me. He was so fucking big. Sculpted, massive muscles everywhere. Beautiful. But I wagered he wouldn't appreciate me calling him beautiful.

"Spread for me, baby," he rasped.

Yes, please.

His thick erection prodded against my still-tingling folds. Sensation rushed through me as he pushed in, spreading me so wide. I arched and wrapped my legs around him. In one thrust, he slid in. It was almost too much. *He* was too much, in so many ways.

He shuddered and strained against me. "You feel so good, babe."

He pulled back slow and thrust back in deep.

"Oh my God, that's amazing," I said, gasping for the breath he kept stealing. "Right there."

I arched my hips and he slid over that spot again.

"Yes. Right there."

Again. "Yeah, you like that?" he asked.

Was he kidding? I *loved* him inside me. Never wanted it to end. "Yes."

He grinned a wickedly, devilish smile, then slid over that spot again and again. "You gonna come for me one more time, Angel Face?"

"I don't know."

"Yeah, you are." He grunted as he pressed inside again, and I reached up to pull him to me, crushing my mouth to his. I tilted my hips again, and he kept hammering away.

Fuck, sex had never felt so good before. Hard. Intense. Pleasurable.

"Trin, give me one more," Wrath's strained voice demanded against my ear.

My body shot from pleasurable simmer to overflowing boil. My orgasm hit hard, crashing through me. He kept stroking, working me until I was limp.

"Oh fuck," he groaned. He tensed and thrust deep, holding while he climaxed with a husky roar.

He looked down at me with soft, warm eyes and a big smile. He touched his lips to my forehead, my cheek, and finally my lips.

Then he rolled to the side and right off the bed. "Ow! Fuck!"

I slapped my hand over my mouth to smother any giggles. Leaning over, I found him sitting on the floor, wearing nothing but a condom and a scowl.

"Who the fuck still has a twin bed at your age?" he grumbled while picking himself up off the floor.

"I don't want to encourage my hook-ups to stay." Fuck. I didn't mean that.

He snatched up his clothes. "Message received, babe."

His heavy footsteps thudded over the thin floor, shaking the walls as he headed to the bathroom.

Tears slid down my cheeks. Why, why, why did I say something so stupid after he'd been so fucking sweet to me?

The building's old pipes rattled and whined as he started up the shower, making me cry harder. *Shit.*

My bathroom door had no lock, so I eased it open and peeked in the shower.

"Wrath?"

He jumped a little. "Shit."

"I'm sorry. I didn't mean it." Tears still rolled down my cheeks and this pitiful sniffling sound gurgled out of me.

I glanced up and found him studying my face. "Why you crying? Was the sex that bad?"

His words forced a harsh sob from me. "No. I feel awful. I don't know why I said that to you. I didn't mean it."

Some of his anger melted away, and he tugged me in the shower with him. He wrapped me up in his big, powerful arms, and I slid my hands around his middle. Tepid water beat down his back, but he was so big he blocked the spray, keeping me dry for the most part.

"Don't go."

He squeezed me tighter, resting his chin on top of my head. "You're a strange girl, Trinity." His voice rumbled through me.

I nodded, my cheek sliding along his damp skin. "I know."

He spun us, which, with his massive shoulders and my tiny shower stall, wasn't easy. But he did it. Very gently and thoroughly, he cleaned every inch of my body. I was humming with need by the time he finished.

One arm wrapped around me and the other shut off the shower. He leaned down and traced the outside of my ear with his tongue, stopping to nibble on my earlobe. I sighed and relaxed against him.

"Babe, do you have any condoms? I only had the one."

"Yes," I whispered.

"Good."

WRATH

I was thrilled she had condoms, because I really needed to fuck her again. But after that hook-up comment, the idea she was prepared like some naughty Girl Scout pissed me the fuck off.

After she led me back into her bedroom, she opened her nightstand drawer and handed me an *unopened* box. Just like that, I was a little less annoyed.

I set the box down and pulled her to me. Grinding my cock against her. Even though I was still grumpy about her comment, seeing her crying about it twisted my cold heart. My plan had been to storm the fuck out after I washed her off me.

Instead of leaving, I considered that other challenge she laid down out in her living room.

I gathered her hair in my fist and used it to tilt her head back so I could take her sweet mouth. With my other hand, I worked her nipples, then slid lower to her juicy, tight pussy. She jerked away at first, then leaned into my hand, letting me pump two fingers inside her.

I bumped her with my cock again and used her hair to tug her down.

She wrapped her hands around my forearms, stopping me. "I told you. I don't get on my knees."

I leaned down to whisper in her ear. "Yes, you will. Only for me, though, Angel Face. You'll hate how much you love it."

She glared up at me with bold eyes. Her fearlessness was the biggest turn-on. My fingers worked in and out of her pussy faster, then moved up, spreading her moisture around her clit, circling, and rubbing until she came on my hand, gasping in my ear. Her knees buckled and she grabbed my cock on the way down. Kneeling upright, so sweet and pretty, she opened her mouth.

At first, she tasted me with little strokes, swirling her tongue around, licking. I tightened my fist in her hair.

"Stop being a fucking tease and take me deep like I know you can."

Honey eyes flashed up at me. Stretching her lips to accommodate my thick size, she took as much of me as she could, then sucked her way back up. After repeating the movement three times, her eyes closed and she let out a moan.

"Fuck, you're so fucking beautiful. Look at me. I want to see your angel eyes while you're sucking my cock."

She met my gaze, smiled around my cock, and I almost lost it. I yanked her up, whirled her around, and bent her over the ridiculous twin bed.

I should have opened the fucking box when she handed it over. The way she wiggled her ass and arched her back distracted me. I finally got the box open and strips of condoms went flying everywhere. I tried to ignore that she kept a *big* box of condoms stashed away as I rolled one on.

"Brace yourself," I warned. She didn't giggle though. She waited, patient yet eager.

Positioning myself, I slammed up inside her hard and fast. She let out a startled scream, then started pushing back against me. "That's it. Ride my cock."

I stood still and let her work herself up and down my dick. What a gorgeous sight. But I needed to see her eyes.

She let out the sexiest, neediest whimper as I pulled out. I stretched out on her bed and pulled her to me. "Climb on."

Her sexy red lips curled into a smile as she did exactly that. Positioning herself over me, she eased down my dick nice and slow. She flinched and raised herself.

"You okay?"

"Your dick's really fucking big," she gasped.

A laugh burst out of me. "Thanks, Angel Face. That's the nicest thing you've said to me all night."

I ended up staying over. In the absurd twin bed. With her wrapped in my arms, she made a perfect little armful. Still too worked up to sleep, my gaze wandered around the cramped room, absently wondering if I could at least fit in a double bed.

What the fuck?

One night and I'm planning to redecorate her apartment?

Against me, she struggled and moaned. But not in a sex dream sort of way. A nightmarish way. I gripped her tighter. "Trinity. You're okay. I got you."

Warm wetness slid over my chest. She was fuckin' crying in her sleep. I barely knew her, but it killed me. I ran my hands over her harder. I didn't want to scare her awake, but I hated the misery in her voice. Nothing she said made sense. In the back of my head, I wondered if somehow I pushed her too far and caused her nightmare. Fuck, it's not like I knew a damn thing about the chick.

After thrashing around for a bit, she finally settled down. I watched over her until I eventually fell asleep too.

My phone went off way too fucking early.

Rock: Where R U? Meeting hippies @ prop today.

Fuck, I'd forgotten all about that.

Me: Be there in 45.

Trin was curled up in a tiny ball almost all the way against the wall. I unfolded myself from the cramped bed, slow so I wouldn't disturb her. I stood there staring at her for a few seconds. A completely new feeling washed over me. *Not* wanting to leave after a hook-up. Usually, I was out the door as soon as the rubber hit the wastebasket. Or I pointedly offered the chick a ride home.

Trinity.

Without a doubt, one of the most beautiful girls I'd taken a tumble with. But it wasn't her pretty face or sick curves. Underneath her protective, bitchy shell, something sweet and vulnerable lurked. I actually *liked* her.

My clothes were still scattered in the bathroom. I gathered up everything and got dressed. A quick search located her cell phone. I got her number and programmed mine into her phone. After peeking in the bedroom, I saw she hadn't moved. It burned my ass she might think I took off, so I sent her a brief explanation before leaving.

"Are you sure there's anything up here?" Z asked for the third time.

"Yes, asshole, I'm sure. Ask me again, I'll kick your ass," Rock growled.

That type of exchange wasn't unusual. Normally, I'd join in, but I was pissed I wasn't snuggling with Trinity.

"Can you both shut the fuck up and read me the next direction?" I snapped.

Rock pointed to a small dirt road coming up on our right. "There."

It was a sharp right and the road barely looked big enough for our vehicle. There were grassy fields on either side. "Are you sure? This looks more like an ATV trail than a road."

Rock consulted the printout in his hands. "It's a road."

Not much farther and we passed a wrought iron fence. Most of it was obscured by overgrown grass, but it still stuck out.

"That's it."

The gate was wide open, so I drove right in. "What the fuck?" popped out of my mouth when I spied the giant Buddha statue in front of us.

Rock snorted. "Big, fat good luck charm I guess."

"Didn't do these hippies any good. Fucking IRS is about to take all this shit from them," Z added.

Sparky sat in the back, silently observing everything. I hoped he gave this place his seal of approval. He'd be the one to decide if this was the new MC or not. Personally, I couldn't wait to get the fuck away from Empire, specifically Crystal Ball. Too many of the dancers thought our MC was their second fucking home. Made shit awkward.

"Drive right up to the conference center," Rock directed.

I hung a right and we climbed the hilly, overgrown driveway.

"Gonna need to get some serious landscaping equipment up here," Z muttered. He definitely knew what we needed and how to get our hands on it.

The guy waiting outside the conference center was dressed in jeans and a T-shirt. Guess I expected him to be wearing a long robe or some shit. None of us were wearing colors. Rock was in a motherfucking suit, which made all of us piss our pants before we left the MC.

Before we stepped out, Rock tugged on his sleeves one last time. "God, I feel like an asshole," he muttered.

"You look like one too," Z responded, completely serious.

"Fuck you."

John Polly waited patiently for us at the front entrance. Not that I expected trouble, but I was pissed with myself because I couldn't stop checking my phone. Trinity never texted me back.

Focus. Club business *now.* Trinity *later.*

"Good morning, gentlemen." Now that was fucking funny. There wasn't one *gentle* man in our group. "I pray you had no difficulty finding us?" Polly asked with a small bow. I was eager to move on, not stand around making small talk, so I kept my mouth shut.

He shook Rock's hand but ignored the rest of us. Fine by me.

"I'll give you a quick tour. Then you can wander around. We're very motivated. Most of our members have already relocated, so the place is ready for you to take over now." By "relocated" I think the guy meant "fled the country."

Rock nodded but kept his bored expression in place.

Our lack of enthusiasm seemed to alarm Polly. I guess he expected us to be more eager. We were but would never show it.

The conference center was massive. Huge entertaining area. Polly called it the reception area. There was a front desk that would make a fantastic bar. A fireplace. Two conference rooms on the right. One would be perfect for our war room where we'd have weekly church. The other we'd use as office space. On the first floor, there were dorm-style bathrooms, a fucking yoga studio, a bedroom suite, laundry room, gym, kitchen, and large dining area. It was enormous, and would allow the club lots of room to conduct both business and our degenerate parties.

Upstairs contained enough bedrooms for each member and then some. At least half had their own bathrooms attached. A huge suite was at one end of the hall. More dorm-style bathrooms and another smaller laundry room. Beautiful hardwood floors throughout the place and lots of open woodwork. It was almost too nice for a pack of biker thugs.

As nice as the place was, our real interest lay in what was downstairs. We asked to see the basement.

Polly shrugged. "It's unfinished. We've only used it for storage."

"I'd still like to inspect it," Rock answered using a hint of biker impatience.

Polly sighed as he opened the basement door. The dude must have had a fear of basements, because instead of leading us downstairs, he went outside. We filed down the stairs. Everything was sturdy, clean, and well lit. No creepy-horror-movie-type basement. Nope.

Sparky finally perked the fuck up.

"Fuck, boss! This is it. This is perfect!" He ran through the open space like a little fucking kid.

Whoever built the place must have planned to use it for something. The ceilings were at least ten feet high, which considering my size, I appreciated. At least I wouldn't give myself a concussion if I had to spend a lot of time down here. The basement contained drainage and thick beams. But the walls were unfinished. That suited us fine since we had a serious construction project planned for the space.

Sparky whipped out a measuring tape, little notebook, and started jotting down notes.

"How much are we talking, Sparky?" Rock asked.

"A lot. Almost everything we got. But I swear we'll make it back within two years."

Two *years*. Long damn time to be out so much cash. Especially since the way we earned had been severely limited.

Rock glanced at Z and me with a raised eyebrow.

"Only active members get a vote on it," Z said.

True. No way would the retired guys have voted yea for this. But it wasn't them risking their fucking necks anymore. Sparky and Rock had a solid idea.

"How strong is CB?" I asked Rock.

He nodded and thought it over before answering. "Club Salvatore is the last competition we got, and they won't be around much longer. Earnings are better and better. Getting quality talent in there since we've cleaned shit up."

"Can we live off it for the next two years?" Z asked.

Rock shrugged. "I'll talk to the accountant. We gotta figure out the treasurer position soon. But yeah, I think so."

"Your prospect is good with numbers," Z said.

We both stared at him. "What?"

"Marcel."

Rock glanced at me.

I tried to think over all the stuff I knew about the kid. He'd been hanging around the club for years before he earned his prospect rocker. Finished high school. Knew a fuck lot about bikes. Had a little sister he was super protective of. His best friend, Blake Irish-name-I-can't-bother-to-remember, was also a prospect. Marcel was close to being patched in. Two years younger than his buddy, Blake would have to wait a bit longer before being patched in. For young guys, they were both loyal, hard workers. Came from questionable families just like the rest of us.

"You can't patch a brother in and immediately make him an officer," I pointed out.

"We can do whatever the fuck we want," Rock answered.

True enough. It was time to update our by-laws.

Sparky moved farther into the basement. The space was so big we could barely see him. He was busy muttering and measuring, not paying any attention to us.

"Sparky! Let's go. We still got shit to see," Rock called out.

Sparky jogged back to where we were waiting. "Boss, this is it. This is the place. I'm telling you," he said between harsh, panting breaths. Brother smoked way too much weed. He had the lung capacity of a two-year-old.

"Okay, calm down. I hear you. Let's go see the outside."

John patiently waited outside on a low stone bench against the building.

He stood as we stepped outside and walked us to the garage. Each of us probably got a boner over the size of it. Lots of space inside for working on our bikes during the winter months. There was also a big diesel plow truck John said the cult—I mean spiritual group—would throw in with the sale of the property. The garage even had its own dedicated generator. The center had two.

We hiked through the woods. John pointed out a large stone amphitheater-type area to us. Looked exactly like the kind of place a cult would use to sacrifice virgins, but I kept that thought to myself. We kept hiking, finally reaching a clearing with four windmills. Motherfucking windmills. Unreal. John explained the setup to Rock and Sparky while I wandered around and took in the views. The setup couldn't be more spectacular. For someone like me, who hated cramped spaces, it was perfect.

Was it weird to have an MC out in the middle of nowhere? Yeah, probably. But living off the grid, how we wanted, with no one sticking their nose in our business? That was about as free as one could ask for in this life.

On the way back, we spotted the solar panels lining the roof. Sparky almost came in his pants over the second alternate energy source. John explained they were installed only a year ago and should be good for another eight to ten years. He warned us it would be a big expense when we had to replace or upgrade them.

He led us into the kitchen and handed over the paperwork about the solar panels, generators, warranties, info about their deal with the power company for the windmills—crap that fell under Rock's job description. Next, John handed over a contract. While Rock looked it over, I wandered through the kitchen. Appliances were all new, top-of-the-line shit.

It hit me hard how much I wanted this to work out.

In the truck on the way back, Rock asked Zero and me what we thought. Z was as pumped as me. Sparky was so busy going over his notes, none of us bothered him. We all knew how he'd vote.

"Let's call Glassman and drop the contract off to him. We have forty-eight hours before they go to the next buyer."

CHAPTER TWO

Trinity

Wrath hunkered down at the end of the bar around eight o'clock. He came in alone. Even though he went to the trouble of programming his number into my phone and texting me to explain why he skipped out early, I was surprised to see him again. He didn't strike me as a guy who'd be interested in a repeat performance. Especially since I'd been a bit of a bitch.

Without a word, I made my way to him and set a bottle of Jack and a glass on the bar. His eyes met mine and I winked, then returned to my other customers. The next free moment I had, I brought him a glass of water and took the bottle of Jack away. A corner of his mouth lifted.

As I turned to wait on a customer, he reached out and caught my hand. "What time are you done?"

Shivers worked through me. His voice was such a damn turn-on. "Ten."

A slow grin spread over his face. "Want to go for a ride? Or are you tired tonight?"

Was that some sort of hint that I might be exhausted after our hot night of wild monkey sex?

"A ride sounds good. Any place special in mind?"

"Yeah."

"Are you going to tell me?"

"No."

It didn't matter. We already established last night I'd do whatever Wrath wanted. Someone called me. Well, actually, they yelled out, "Hey, bar wench." Wrath growled and leaned over the bar to catch who said it. I placed my hand over his and shook my head. "I got it."

Storm showed up at ten after ten. Immediately, she headed for Wrath instead of putting on her apron and asking me what needed to be done. You know, her fucking job. They spoke for a second before Wrath pointed at me. Her face screwed into a scowl, but she finally ran over.

"Sorry I'm late."

"It's okay. I'm heading out. Crowd isn't too bad tonight." I ran over everything she needed to do for the night. At the last minute, I remembered to ask how her hand was. She held it up in front of my face. It was bandaged but not bad enough to get in the way.

"I'm surprised you came in."

"Marky said he'd cover the hospital bill if I didn't call in," she said, as if that made him some sort of hero

"Uh, he should cover it anyway since it happened on the job."

"We get paid under the table, Trin. Not like we have workers' comp."

Good point. I patted her shoulder and took off with only a small twinge of guilt.

Wrath waited for me at the end of the bar. As I approached, he held out a sweatshirt to me.

"What's this?"

"So you're not chilly tonight."

Stunned, I stared at him like a moron for a few seconds before accepting it. "Thanks," I said softly as I slipped into it.

He held the door open and fixed my hood when we stepped out onto the sidewalk.

We took the quickest route out of the city. Within twenty minutes, we were cruising through backcountry roads. The cool night air rushed over me. Aside from last night, I felt more alive than I had in a long time.

The bike climbed through the mountain roads with ease. As the road evened out, he let off the throttle and we cruised through an area with sparsely scattered houses. After a while, the houses disappeared and he slowed to a crawl. We seemed to have entered some sort of park.

We coasted over some grass and stopped in the middle of a grove of trees. Slipping both our helmets off, he placed his finger against his lips.

"Where are we?" I whispered.

"It's a surprise. Be quiet though."

He grabbed a few things from his saddlebag and took my hand. "Watch where you step," he cautioned.

We trudged through... the woods I guessed. Crunching over leaves and twigs, ducking under branches. I didn't think we were being very quiet. Finally, our feet touched something more solid and less noisy. Pavement?

"Look up, Trin."

Before me was the most beautiful nighttime view. We had to be looking over the tri-county area. I spotted the city of Empire straight ahead and a little to the right. Ironworks had to be to the left, and much farther right must be Slater City. Hundreds of lights from tiny villages and towns twinkled in between.

"We're at Fletcher Park at night? How beautiful." I sighed.

"The park is closed and does have a patrol person, so we have to be quiet."

"Okay," I whispered back. On instinct, I rocked to my tiptoes and pressed a quick kiss to his jaw. The gesture seemed to take him by surprise, and he glanced down, cupping my cheek and holding me for a full kiss. He dropped whatever he was carrying and wrapped me in his arms, lifting me off the ground. Our kisses escalated until our tongues were licking and stroking. I pulled away, dazed and out of breath.

He brushed his fingers through my hair. "Follow me."

We stepped up and over the low stone wall designed to keep people from falling off the edge of the cliff. Wrath assured me there was a wide ledge and took out his cell phone to shine the light and prove it. Reassured I wouldn't go flying off into the night, I watched as he spread a blanket right up along the wall.

He sat with his back to the wall and pulled me down between his legs. We both faced the breathtaking view.

"Are you warm enough?" he asked, while snaking his arms around my waist, holding me tight to him.

I leaned against his chest and stared up at him. "Yes."

He rustled around in his bag and handed me one of those clear, plastic takeout food containers. "Chocolate or strawberry?"

"What?"

"Cake. I thought most girls like chocolate, but I wasn't sure. There's a piece of triple chocolate cake or strawberry shortcake."

"Oooh, chocolate, definitely."

It was so dark neither of us could tell which was which, so I popped open one of the tops. Inhaling the rich, chocolate scent, I knew I had the right one. He pushed a plastic fork into my hand, and we ate our cake, looking out over the view.

The cake was so rich I could only eat half of it, so I passed it back to Wrath. I'm pretty sure he finished mine off before stuffing the empty boxes back in his pack.

"Milk or water? My drink options were kind of limited," he asked.

"Milk. I hear it does a body good."

"Your body's already good, baby," he teased in his low, sensual voice that made my brain fuzz. He pressed a small, cool bottle of milk into my hand. I uncapped it and took a sip. "Oh, this is whole milk. Can I have the water instead?"

We swapped bottles. "Sorry, babe."

"No, that's okay. Thank you."

One of his arms was still wrapped around me, his hand restlessly moving over my leg. "Did you have a good night at work?" he asked after a while.

"Eh. It was okay. Nothing exciting until around eight thirty when this really hot guy came in."

"Oh yeah?"

I turned and sat back on my knees. "Yeah." Reaching out, I ran my fingers through his hair. "He's got this awesome blond hair and these big, ocean-blue eyes."

Wrath chuckled, low and deep. "Ocean blue, huh?"

"*Mmm-hmmm.*"

His hand circled my wrist, bringing me closer to kiss my fingers. "Come closer."

It would've been hard to get closer without straddling his lap, so as gracefully as possible, that's what I did. Somehow I arranged myself without kneeing him in the groin.

We were almost nose to nose. "I was surprised you came in tonight."

He cocked his head. "Why?"

Because you could have any girl you wanted. "I don't know."

"I told you I was sorry I had to cut out this morning. Rock had an early meeting he needed me at."

"Club business?"

"Yeah."

"Secret?"

He thought about it for a minute. "We're in the process of buying a bigger place for our MC."

"Oh yeah, I think Rock mentioned that yesterday."

Wrath's eyes narrowed and he studied me for a minute. "Really?"

"Yeah, he told me to come to your party tonight. I guess that's the other reason I was surprised to see you."

"Would you have stopped by if I hadn't come in?"

Willingly walk into an MC clubhouse by myself—no fucking way. But I didn't want to offend him. "Probably not."

He nodded, and I wasn't sure if my answer was what he wanted to hear. Did he want me to come looking for him? It was so hard to read him in the dark.

I shouldn't have been falling for this big, dangerous biker, but between the thoughtful date and his focused attention, I felt as if I'd taken five steps forward and jumped right off the ledge.

WRATH

Clearly, Trinity wouldn't have come looking for me at the clubhouse. I didn't mind. She didn't need to be anywhere near my brothers. The thought of any of them getting within ten feet of her triggered a torrent of rage in me. Why, I had no idea yet.

"Give me that lovely mouth, Angel Face," I whispered.

A sweet, breathy sigh fell from her lips, chocolate breath washing over my skin. Threading my fingers in the hair at the back of her head, I pulled her to me. Lips parted and wet, she let me in immediately. My tongue stroked over hers, and she pushed her breasts into my chest. The slow, seductive thing I was trying out would be a massive failure if she kept that up.

"Are you warm enough?" I asked her.

"I'm burning up," she whispered.

Fuck yeah.

Unzipping the hoodie slowly, I set it next to us on the blanket, then carefully worked her T-shirt up. She must have been wearing another one of those sexy fucking push-up bras because her pale skin overflowed and glowed in the moonlight. Cupping her breasts with both my big hands, I tested their weight, kneading, stroking my thumb over her lace-covered nipples. She tossed her head back, exposing her long, graceful neck. Pulling the lace cups aside, I took one hard nipple into my mouth, running my tongue around it and lightly scraping my teeth against her flesh. She jerked in my lap, grinding herself against my stone-hard dick.

"God, you're perfect," I rasped, coming up for air.

Slowly, she lifted her head, looking down at my hands cupping her breasts. "I feel so tiny in your grasp."

"You are tiny next to me," I answered with a laugh.

"I like that. No one's ever made me feel that way."

I wasn't sure what she meant by that, but it sounded good to me. Anything I did to her first made me really fucking happy.

I showed my appreciation by sucking her other nipple into my mouth. Her hands searched for something to hold on to and finally gripped my shoulders. Over and over, I slid my tongue across the hard peak. When she whined, I gently tugged and nipped. Her hips jerked in my lap, her nails digging into my shoulders.

"Wrath..."

Letting her nipple go with a soft pop, I kissed my way up her chest, stopping to suck on her neck before continuing to nibble on her ear. "Yes, Angel Face?"

She ground against my cock restlessly. "Please? I need..."

A slow grin turned my mouth up. "What do you need?" I asked with my lips pressed against her neck.

More grinding, shifting. Christ, I was gonna come in my pants if she kept it up.

"You, please."

Fuck, I wanted to drown in the sound of Trinity begging for my cock. "Where do you need me?"

She pushed out a frustrated breath. "In-inside me."

Running my finger over her bottom lip, I pressed the tip inside. "Inside you here?"

She sucked on my finger while shaking her head no.

Dropping my hand to her lap, I pressed my fingers against her pussy. Through her jeans, I could tell she was hot and wet for me. "Here, baby?"

She made this deep moaning sound before answering, "Yes, please."

That simple "yes, please" fucked me up in a big way. That might be the exact moment she ruined me for any other woman.

Coiled tight against me, she rocked her hips against my hand. It wasn't enough and she was quickly frustrated.

"Sit back, babe."

She leaned back enough for me to work her jeans open. Lifting her ass a little, I tugged her pants down her legs, slipped off her sneakers, then worked her pants off the rest of the way.

My hand immediately dove for her spread pussy. "You're really wet, baby."

She moaned as my fingers glided over her slippery skin. So fucking sexy.

"You know you have to be quiet, right?"

"Oh. Oh, I don't think..."

She couldn't talk because I eased one finger into her snug, little pussy, slid out, then thrust it back in again. When I thought she was close, I eased off.

"You want it bad, don't you?" Even though it was torture on my dick, I loved teasing her.

"Please, I want you. Make me come."

"You'll come on my cock when I say so."

"Yes, okay. Please," she whimpered. With those words, she reached inside my chest and stole a chunk of my heart.

I flicked my thumb over her clit and squeezed one nipple with my other hand.

I shook off whatever I was feeling and decided to stop tormenting myself. My dick hadn't done anything wrong to deserve this suffering. I was ready to fucking explode.

"Lift up, baby," I coaxed.

Her head lolled to the side, but she lifted herself enough for me to work my cock out. Snagging a condom from my pocket, I rolled it on.

"Okay, come here. I'm gonna take care of you." I slid my hands under her ass and pulled her toward me, easing her down my cock nice and slow.

"There we go. That better?" I couldn't help but smirk, but she was so out of it, I doubt she minded.

Her hands settled on my shoulders and she sat up a little straighter. I grunted as the movement pushed her farther down my dick. "Yes. So good," she whimpered.

Fucking love that.

She lifted up a little and her lips parted. I covered her mouth with my own, swallowing her cries. I was vaguely aware she was sliding up and down my dick faster, grinding into me harder on each down stroke. Slicking a finger over her clit brought on another scream I barely caught in time. She was soaking by this point, and I glided in and out faster. She tightened and rocked, her head falling back, teeth sinking into her bottom lip.

Beautiful.

Keeping her hips still, I hammered up into her fast and deep until I shot so hard, all breath left me in a rush.

An unexpected tidal wave of emotion crashed over me. Wasn't that supposed to happen to chicks with amazing sex? Not me. Never before. But there it was.

She bent forward and placed soft kisses along my jaw. "Thank you," she said so sweetly.

Game over.

CHAPTER THREE

Present day...

WRATH

Trinity's trying hard to make me lose it tonight. I grip the bottle of Jack in my hand so fucking tight, I won't be surprised when it shatters all over me.

Fucking Teller and Murphy. I want to smash the bottle over both their fucking heads. My *brothers.*

Fuck.

A voice in my head reminds me *it's not their fault,* because I never opened my fucking mouth.

More Jack should drown out that voice.

I shouldn't be letting a bitch get between me and my brothers. The fact that she is and has been for years pisses me off even more.

Cookie struts over to me and straddles my lap. "You look tense, Wrath baby. Can I help?"

Throwing another glare at Trinity, who is oblivious to anything other than grinding her ass into Teller's dick while Murphy gropes her tits, I nod at Cookie. They're dancing in the middle of the room with a bunch of people. But they might as well be fucking. I'm sure in another twenty minutes, they will be.

Again.

"Yeah, hon." I push her off my lap onto the floor and free my half-hard cock. Not the first time I'll get a blowjob on this couch in front of everyone. Hell, I'm not even the first person tonight to get sucked off out in the open.

Cookie's rubbing up and down my shaft with enthusiasm, but it's not doing much for me. Watching Teller suck on Trinity's shoulder while her arms are looped around his neck is pissing me off way too much. I close my eyes.

Honey eyes peeking up at me.

Fuck, I'm hard as steel now. Eight fucking miserable years later, and that memory still works every time. I snag a condom out of my left back pocket and hand it to Cookie. The fake-chemical scent of cherries reaches my nose as she rolls it down with her mouth. Christ, the tricks this bitch can do with that mouth of hers.

Sweet motherfuck.

Cookie takes me right to the back of her throat and stays for a second before bobbing up and down. Why Rock gave this bitch up, I have no fucking idea.

Opening my eyes is a mistake. Trinity stares at me with wide-eyed pain all over her angel face. I stare back and cock my head in a way I want her to read as: *You're kidding, right?* Teller and Murphy still have their hands and mouths all over her, and she's, what? Hurt I'm getting some head?

Fuck that.

And fuck her too. I flip her off, and she finally takes her wounded kitten face elsewhere.

Twisting my hand in Cookie's hair, I push and pull her up and down my cock. She goes soft and lets me just fuck her face until I come. She looks up at me, and I smile.

"Thanks, darlin'. You're right. I do feel better now." *Lie.* If anything, I feel worse, but that's not Cookie's fault. I give her a quick peck on the cheek, and she beams.

She cleans me up and goes away.

Perfect.

Scanning the room, I don't see the threesome.

Oh, there they are, heading upstairs.

Fuck-fuck-fucking bullshit!

The front door opens, pulling my attention away from the nightmare headed upstairs. Rock, dragging in the bitch he's been hard up for at least two goddamn years. She's skinnier than I remember. Still has a nice rack, though. Must be drunk off her ass because she's swaying and kind of dazed as she looks around the room.

She smiles when Rock leans down and whispers in her ear. I guess she's pretty. Still don't see what all the fuss is about. Why we had to risk a war with the Vipers over her. Why my best friend is so fucking obsessed with her.

Rock sees me and nods over the crowd. He looks like he just won the motherfucking lottery.

Whatthefuckever.

It's good to see him happy. Maybe once he fucks her out of his system, he can get back to nailing club ass and tappin' strippers like a boss.

He pulls her over to my little pity corner, and she's so out of it, I doubt she even notices me.

"Everything good?" he asks, taking stock of my miserable, drunken condition.

"Same old shit." I point my bottle at Hope. "She okay?"

He hugs her tight to his side. "Yeah, had a little too much to drink out with her friends."

She finally shakes her hair out of her face and looks at me with bleary eyes. Suddenly, her lips turn up in a big, dopey smile. "I remember you. You were there the day Rock tried to ruin my life," she blurts out, then falls into uncontrollable giggles.

My eyebrows shoot up at that, but I manage to contain my laughter.

Nice work, prez. All righty then. Good luck with that.

After we talk a few more seconds, he leads her upstairs. I'd like to go upstairs too. My head's pounding and I'd like to go to fucking bed. But I know the three of *them* are up there, and if I run into them or so much as hear them, I might murder all three. And that would be bad.

Why does prez let *her* get away with shit? She wants to be a whore, she should have to fuck in her own damn room. Downstairs. Away from me.

To my knowledge, she's never let *any* of the brothers in her room.

Whipping out my cell phone, I send the guy who schedules my underground fights a text. *Get me something soon.*

After what seems like forever, I get a response. *Thursday. Address TBA.*

Sweet, I'll unleash some of this rage in a nice and nasty underground fight. Hopefully, I can hang on until then.

Trinity

It's hard to think with Murphy pressed against my back and Teller in front of me, nipping at my neck. We stumble into one of the free rooms—neutral ground—and Teller goes straight for my shirt, whipping it over my head and palming my breasts. Murphy slides his hands down the front of my pants, cupping my mound while he grinds his cock against my ass.

I can't get Wrath's furious face out of my head.

Fucking mad at me, when he had Cookie bobbing up and down on his dick in front of everyone.

Jerk.

My pants get kicked to the side after Murphy works them down my legs. After I get Teller out of his clothes, I fall back against him. He wraps his arms around me, sliding his hands into my panties to tease my clit. My hips jerk against him, so he retreats. Murphy kisses me, tangling his fingers in my hair while I work his clothes off. My eyes flicker open. We left the door open. Not the first time.

Murphy works my panties off. I should be embarrassed about how turned on I am, but they love it, so I'm not. He presses in, moving those fingers slowly over my sensitized flesh.

At my back, Teller steps away. The rough and familiar drag of the nightstand drawer opening excites me even more. He tosses some condoms on the bed and stretches out over the comforter, watching Murphy work me over. Murphy has me pinned tight to him but angles our bodies so Teller can see exactly what his friend's doing to me.

"Fuck."

"Yeah." His husky voice vibrates against my jaw, sending heat through me. He grins while pressing kisses over my face and down my neck.

Teller reaches out his hands to me, pulling me on top of him. With one hand behind my head, he pulls me to him for a kiss. A deep, hard, demanding kiss. His other arm bands around me, pinning me tight to him. I'm hyperaware of his cock nestled against me.

"Stop teasing me, Trinity." He groans with a smile.

Taking my hands, he pushes me up and helps me sink all the way down his shaft.

"Fuuuck, that's good, girl."

Ever patient, Murphy waits, fisting his cock as he watches us. This might be easier on my knees with one behind and one in front, but they know I don't do that. Over the years, they've never complained or made me feel bad about it.

Releasing one of Teller's hands, I pull Murphy to me and eagerly lick the head of his cock. I circle him with my tongue, suck, and pull him in my mouth. Teller's hands cup my hips as he starts rocking me up and down. Eventually, we find the right rhythm.

Briefly, my eyes flutter open, and I notice a woman standing just outside the doorway, watching us. That's nothing new. Rock tugs her away, yells at us and slams the door shut.

I wake a few hours later, cuddled in Teller's arms. He's sound asleep. Murphy's long gone. He never stays. I'm an expert at extracting myself from Teller's embrace by now. Wrath's the only man I've ever happily slept beside for an entire night. I tug on my clothes and press a quick kiss to Teller's cheek. Closing the door quietly behind me, a low voice breaks the silence.

"Have fun?"

Fuck.

I turn and find a furious-faced Wrath leaning against the wall opposite the room I just left and want to die. With arms crossed over his chest and anger pinching his face, he looks tired. I want to reach out and touch him, or offer anything besides this angry glaring thing we're doing.

The soft moment sours, and I square my shoulders. "Yes. Did you?"

His jaw clenches and he shakes his head. "No. Not at all." He pushes off the wall and storms down the hall, slamming his door shut without another word.

Whatever. I'm not going to cry. He can't make me cry anymore.

He had his chance. Why does he keep punishing me?

When I get downstairs, I tiptoe over a few sleeping bodies and make my way to my room. Locking the door behind me, I grab a quick shower and then crawl into my own bed.

Alone.

As usual, my eyes pop open much earlier than I'd like. Knowing I'll never get back to sleep, I dress quickly. The dining room's empty, but any minute one or two of the guys will be in there. I should at least get coffee started.

Teller's in the dining room first. He pulls me into his lap and gives me a quick kiss on the cheek. "Where'd you disappear to?"

I ruffle his hair with my fingers. "My room."

"Hmmm."

"What do you want for breakfast?"

"Would you be mad if I said you?"

I laugh off his words and kiss his cheek. "Tell me or it's eggs and bacon for you."

He sighs and gives me a gentle shove off his lap. "That's fine."

Hoot, one of the prospects, is already in the kitchen, gathering supplies for me. He has the griddle going and plates lined up.

"Thanks, kid."

He grunts at me. I don't think he likes being called kid. *Whoops.*

I hear more people out in the dining room and stick my head out to see Bricks. He's almost never up here, so I wave to him. He waves back and sits with Teller. Ducking back into the kitchen, I grab two mugs and the now-full coffee pot and head out.

And stop dead in my tracks.

Wrath's sitting next to Teller.

Squaring my shoulders, I'm determined not to let him intimidate me. I set a mug in front of Bricks and Teller and pour their coffee.

I can feel Wrath's eyes drilling holes in me, but I don't turn to him until I'm finished.

"Do you want coffee? Breakfast?"

For a second, he looks like he's going to say something nasty, but he just nods. I set the coffee on the table, run to get a couple more mugs, and return.

"Breakfast should be done in a few minutes."

I'm hoping some of the other girls wake up soon so they can take over kitchen duty. As much as I'd like to knock Cookie out after last night, she's usually a big help in the mornings. I need to get the hell out of here for a few merciful hours.

Stash calls Hoot downstairs to help him with something, so I get stuck bringing out the tray of food for everyone. I concentrate really hard on not dropping everything all over the place. There's a reason I used to tend bar and not waitress. I see Rock and toss him one of my standard silly greetings and set down everyone's plates.

My breath catches and my cheeks sizzle with heat when I notice the woman sitting next to him. The same woman who stopped to watch us last night. *You've got to be kidding.* Of course she's with prez. The tray rattles and almost falls out of my hands. What a horrible first impression.

Wrath chooses that moment to embarrass me by pulling me into his lap. I introduce myself to Hope. She doesn't seem to remember me, but I'm still freaked-out-mortified. I shouldn't care. Nothing she saw was outside the realm of normal around here. But she's new, and I get the feeling by her squeaky-clean demeanor, she's not familiar with MCs at all. She offers to come help me, which really sets my nerves jittering. No way is the president's girlfriend setting foot in the kitchen. She's nice and asks for something simple. Either she doesn't remember last night or she's too classy to mention it. Both suit me fine.

Just before I open the kitchen door, Wrath's big voice reaches me. "You know how she got the name Trinity, right? All three holes—"

"Wrath! The fuck?" Rock snaps.

The slight good mood I'd worked myself into is ruined after hearing that from Wrath. *Dickhead.*

I'm sure he didn't think I'd overhear it, and somehow that makes it even worse.

WRATH

The last person I want to see this morning is of course in the dining room. *Teller.* My fists itch to knock him the fuck out. At least Bricks is here as a buffer so I don't kill the little fuck.

Make that the second-to-last person I want to see.

Trinity flutters out of the kitchen with coffee and a smile for everyone. Glad she's looking so chipper and satisfied this morning.

Even more fantastic, Rock's girl is still here. She's sober this morning and looks freshly fucked, only adding to my bad mood. Prez fawns all over her so much we all have to pick our jaws up off the table.

I'm barely paying attention to what's being said. Hope's fucking clueless and annoying. Touching Bricks like that with her man sitting right there. The fuck?

Trinity steers clear of me when she returns and sets a giant box of cereal and a gallon of milk on the table. It strikes me funny since Rock's bitch is so fuckin' skinny she probably couldn't eat that much in a month.

"Jesus Christ, Trin, how much ya think she's gonna eat?" Because I'm so fucked up, my lame attempt at a joke just sounds mean. Rock eyes me like he's deciding which boot he wants to shove up my ass.

"It's fine. Thank you, Trinity. I'm starving," she says with a friendly smile, ignoring the rest of us.

I have to give Hope credit. She's a classy girl and not the stuck-up bitch I expected her to be.

Ain't I one big fucking contradiction? Here I am giving Trinity a hard time, yet I'm happy Rock's girl is so nice to her.

Anticipating Trinity's next visit to our table divides my attention. Hope's still yapping to Bricks. He wants to hire her to handle his ex-wife's latest family court drama. Don't see why not.

"It's safe now. Vipers are in the fucking gr—" I start to tell her.

Rock's fist slams into the table, rattling everything on the surface and startling Hope. "Are you fucking high?"

Whoa. I assumed he'd explained some of this shit to her by now. Guess not. I'm just jamming my feet in my mouth all over this morning.

And I know just who to blame for that.

Trinity.

She's got me so fucking messed up after last night and then running into her earlier.

When Hope runs upstairs, I think it's the perfect time to get out of here before I say something else I shouldn't.

"Stop right there, asshole," Rock growls at me.

Asshole, yup. That's me this morning.

"What the ever-loving fuck is wrong with you?" Rock asks.

"Prez, I thought she knew at least a little bit." Even to my own ears, I sound like a whiny cunt.

He continues his rant. "Well, she doesn't. All this shit is new to her, and if it's all right with you, I'd like to break her in slowly, got it?"

I smirk because he's going to have his work cut out for him breaking his little Cinderella into MC life. She's clueless as fuck. But I keep my opinion to myself because I'm not in the mood to take a punch to the throat right now.

"Yeah, sure," I answer.

"And treat Trinity with some respect, would ya?"

My chest tightens at that. I've been a real asshole this morning. The fact that Rock even has to say that to me outlines how awful I've acted.

Next to me, Teller snorts with laughter.

Rock pins him with a hard stare. Good, at least the pressure is finally off me. "What's so funny?"

"Everyone's had a piece of Trinny," Teller says.

What. A. Dick.

Considering he and Murphy just worked her over less than eight hours ago, that's a pretty dickish thing to say. It surprises me coming from Teller. He's not usually such an asshat.

Rock's *not* amused. As much as the motherfucker gets around—or got around—you'll never hear him talk shit about a chick he's nailed. "So fucking what? She tossed your homely ass a pity fuck. Be grateful, not a dick about it." He all but snarls at Teller.

Teller snaps his yap shut. That's the way shit works 'round here.

"Rock's right. She's a nice girl, and she does a lot for the club," Bricks adds.

Oh, shut the fuck up. "Ass-kisser," I grumble.

Rock's clearly done with us and stressed from having Hope out of his sight for five fucking seconds. He gives us all a behave-or-I'll-kill-you stare and takes off.

I'm out next, except I'm not sure where to go. I don't want to run into Rock and Hope in the common room, and I don't want to run into Trinity in the kitchen. But I can't stay here either. I'm a goddamned trapped animal.

Trinity, ironically enough, makes the decision for me as she slowly approaches our table. "You guys need anything?"

Teller flicks his gaze up and smiles. "Just you, babe."

Fucking asshole.

To my utter shock and delight, she shuts him down, moving away to sit next to Bricks.

"Haven't seen you in forever. How's Winter?"

Bricks is one of those faithful types. Won't lay a finger on Trinity. I still need to get away from all of them.

Sparky's in the living room, having a shit fit because Rock hasn't been downstairs to discuss tonight's drop yet.

"Brother, we've got hours. Chill the fuck out."

Sparky huffs and flails his way to the basement door.

Rock *has* been gone a while now. I take a look around outside. His bike's still here. Hope's keys are in my pocket and her car is parked on the side of the building. They've got to be here somewhere.

The sound of crunching leaves alerts me that someone's coming in from the woods. Rock strolling back with his girl. It doesn't take a rocket scientist to figure out what they were up to out in the woods. Her hair's wild and pine needles are sprinkled all over her sweatshirt. I smother a laugh. Surprised the poor bitch can even walk. Prez has a year's worth of fucking to take out on her ass.

Because I've been properly scolded by my president for my shitty behavior this morning, I'm determined not to make any smart remarks that make Hope uncomfortable.

Yeah, we'll see how that goes. There's a first time for everything.

"Hey, guys."

Hope's reddened lips curve into a smile. She really is a nice woman. It's hard not to smile back. I hand her the keys to her car, and Rock glares at me. Goddamn, can't do a fuckin' thing right today.

Careful not to reveal more than I'm supposed to, I remind him, "Prez, we got that thing this afternoon." I catch his warning look and keep my yap shut.

He turns Hope away and they murmur to each other. I kick a few stray pebbles while I wait. Glancing up, I catch the lick of pink flaming across her cheeks.

She finally leaves, and I can tell Rock's pissed about it.

"Tell me again why I put up with these Green Street dickwads?" he asks.

Yeah, maybe a walk down bad memory lane is what my brother needs to get his head in the right space for tonight. "Because they buy everything we grow."

He grunts at me.

"And when we stopped moving stuff for the Mexicans and growing our own shit, they stuck with us." I remind him.

He nods and finally glances at me, a wry smile twisting his mouth up. "Still doesn't explain why that mouthy little punk insists I be there for every damn drop."

"I think he's got a crush on you, prez."

He doesn't seem to find that as amusing as I do.

"So what's the story with the uptight lawyer chick? How was she?" Nope, by the look on his face, he's *not* in a joking mood. If I had to guess—he's considering dismembering me and scattering my body parts around the club's property.

"Do you have some sort of death wish you need to discuss with me?" Yup. My brother's got murder on his mind.

Where exactly does he see things going with this chick? "She your ol' lady now?"

He's quick to answer. "Yeah, she's gonna be."

I swallow down the first thing I want to say, which is—*Are you fucking serious?* "Wow, that's big, prez." We don't got any ol' ladies right now. So that's huge," I say instead.

"I'm sure Trinity wouldn't mind you making her an ol' lady," he says, just to be a dick.

What can I say? We fucked up good there. She's never going to forgive me, and I can't forgive her. "That's never going to happen, prez."

"Why? She's a good girl. She's gorgeous. Knows when to keep her mouth shut. Knows her way around the club."

He just had to say that, didn't he? I know he didn't mean it the way I took it, but it still stings, especially after last night. "That's the problem. She knows her way around the club a little *too* well."

"Oh please, you've fucked every skank within a hundred-mile radius, so what's the difference?" He's right. But none of those skanks were her sisters. Well, I guess the other club girls are... sorta.

Whatever. This isn't the first time Rock's expressed his strong opinion on this subject. He's very much a *What's good for the goose* type of fellow. But since he apparently plans to make a total outsider his ol' lady, I'm of the mindset he should take his self-righteous attitude and shove it up his ass. I'm about to say so, when Trinity's voice comes out of nowhere.

"The difference is, I wouldn't be his old lady if he got down on both knees and begged in front of the entire club." The hurt in her voice shames the shit out of me.

"Fuck, Trinny. I should make you wear a damn bell around your neck," Rock teases.

She walks around the corner with a pained smile. Won't even look at me. I grind my teeth so hard my jaw aches.

"Thanks for sticking up for me, Rock," she says softly, still not glancing my way.

Rock holds out his arms to her, and she hurries over, throwing a nasty glare my way. He gives her a hug and tries to make her feel better. "You're a big help to the club, Trinny, and we all appreciate what you do."

"I know that's not true. But I know *you* appreciate it and that's all that matters."

Rock pats her hip, and white, ragey spots spar with my eyes. I don't know why. I hate how tight the two of them are. Always have. They share secrets the rest of us know nothing about, and it drives me nuts. She was mine first. It should have been *me* she confided in.

"You headed out, babe?" Rock asks as they both continue to ignore me.

"Kitchen's all cleaned up for now. There's still some girls inside, so if it gets messed up again, they'll take care of it."

"Good deal. You coming back later?"

Finally, she looks at me, and I prepare to apologize for my shitty comments.

"No. I've got a date tonight," she announces.

Fuck this shit.

Trinity

I don't actually have a date. But pissing Wrath off feels pretty fucking good after the bullshit he's been tossing at me all morning. After the crack about my name in front of Rock's girl, I gave serious consideration to returning from the kitchen with a knife to slit his throat.

And Teller. Well, at least I know what he really thinks of me. I hope he had fun last night because that's the last time I'm crawling into bed with him for a long fucking time.

As usual, Rock stands up for me. And not just because he doesn't want them saying that shit in front of his woman. Because he doesn't tolerate any disrespect toward me or any of the girls. He knows full well what goes on in his clubhouse, but he's never once made me feel like shit about it.

Nor has he ever made a move on me.

In eight years, he hasn't once treated me as anything other than a friend under his protection.

In return, there's nothing I won't do for him.

Not since my father was alive have I trusted a man the way I trust Rock.

For a brief time, I thought I could trust Wrath that way. Look where that got me.

The door slams shut after Wrath stomps off like a pissed-off toddler, and I can't help laughing.

"That was fun."

Rock smirks at me. "Thanks, babe. He's had it coming all morning."

Yup. Definitely caught that vibe. "I like Hope. Will we be seeing more of her around here?"

Rock seems pleased. "That's the plan."

"Good. It's about time you find the right woman. You do so much for everyone. You deserve to be happy too." He seems embarrassed by my words, but I mean every one of them. I've seen Rock with an endless parade of dancers and club girls. I've never seen him with a civilian woman. I've never seen him this at ease and happy either. That woman better be prepared, because Rock's not letting her go anytime soon.

"Think you can show her the ropes? Ease her in slow?" he asks.

Seems I'll have my work cut out for me on that front. "Of course. You know I'll do anything for you, prez."

My first priority's gonna be keeping her away from Wrath. I know him well enough to know he's not going to tolerate an outsider real well. Especially one so tight with his president.

I keep that to myself, though. That falls under the category of club business, which is not *my* business.

Speaking of business people shouldn't meddle in. "Don't worry about Wrath and me. It's never going to happen. I'm over it," I say, just in case Rock gets the urge to play matchmaker again.

He sighs and rakes his fingers through his hair. "Trinity—"

Nope. Not happening. I can't tolerate pity from him. "Seriously, Rock. I'm fine."

WRATH

The only thing on my mind on the long drive to our drop-off with the Green Street Crew is Rock's unease before we left the clubhouse.

Motherfucker has one hell of an intuition. There was a brief time when he held my position in the club. His instincts have saved our lives more than once over the years.

So if Rock's uneasy, I'm anxious and alert for trouble. Even more than I usually am.

Riverwalk Park is deserted. My gaze sweeps the shadows as we roll in. No hidden cars tucked in any corners, nothing. The park is serene and empty.

While Rock makes small talk with GSC's shotcaller, Gunner, I continue inspecting the area. Any couples looking for a quiet place to park and fuck tonight will be redirected elsewhere.

Thumping bass music from an incoming SUV gets me trigger twitchy, and I keep my hand on my piece while I walk over to Rock.

It's just the other two dipshits from Gunner's crew. Bunch of useless fucking twats, every one of them. Well, the nice, fat duffel bag of cash is useful and the only reason we're here.

After we do our exchange—weed for cash—Gunner and Rock step

aside to talk. This annoys the fuck out of me. These drops should be quick. Get in. Get out. The longer we stand around scratching our asses, the more risks we take.

My point's proven about two seconds later when the distinct sound of Harleys roars into the park.

"Wrap it up," Rock shouts, and that's my cue to get on my hog and lead us the fuck out.

But I don't even get to start her up.

The bikes come into view, two punks who have no clue how to control the machines they're riding or the guns they're shooting.

One of them aims at Gunner. I couldn't give two fucks about the punk, but my president's standing right next to him.

I launch myself at the kid with the gun, punching him clean off the bike.

Somewhere, there's a god who favors angry biker thugs, because *this* is exactly what I need tonight.

The thrill of adrenaline rushes through me. I love to fight, but while I get my kicks by sparring with my brothers from time to time and the occasional underground fight, I always hold back so I don't kill someone.

I don't have to hold back this time.

Fuck yes.

Blood pounds through me as I land one blow to the fucker's face. I drill a second jab into his gut.

The punk doesn't do much in the way of fighting back. Kinda takes all the fun out of it for me. I still punch him a few more times. For fuck's sake, he *shot* at us. He's earned every hit.

Barely out of breath, I stand but keep my foot on the kid's chest so I can keep an eye on Rock. He's no slouch in the fighting department. Trained him myself. He's a big fucker—not as big as me, but then not many men are. One deadly motherfucker too, but he has an incredible amount of self-control, something I've always lacked.

I laugh as the kid lands a few hits, doubting Rock even noticed. When the punk's down, Rock hauls him up. I remove my foot and pick up my prize too.

"What the fuck do you think you're doing?" Rock shouts at the kid who reanimates enough to mouth off and spit at Rock.

Aw, buddy, big mistake.

Rock plants his fist in the kid's gut hard enough to make him puke.

Gunner—not sure what he was doing the whole time we were taking care of this mess for him—puts his gun to the kid on the ground and starts questioning him. Kid's in no condition to answer.

Mine is, and I give him a shake to get him talking.

"You punks lift these from someone?" Rock asks, gesturing at the downed Harleys.

"Yes! We picked them up outside the Green Room."

Holy fuck, that's Viper territory. What the fuck did we step in tonight?

"Are you two suicidal or plain stupid?" Rock asks. Damn good question.

Gunner moves like he's going to shoot them.

Rock halts him with a hand on his arm, lowering the weapon. "Not so fast."

"Grab some zip ties and a Sharpie," he tells Bricks.

Personally, I prefer to shoot them and dump them in the Hudson River. It's only an additional ten feet from the spot we drag them to.

We tie them to a tree and leave a message for the Vipers when they find them.

Whatever. "Should do," I say.

After Rock finishes with Gunner, he sends our crew on their way. One look at him and I see he's still lit up from the fight.

"Where you going, prez?" Our usual routine after something like this used to be hittin' up Crystal Ball, finding a couple dancers, and fucking the living daylights out of them.

Rock scowls at me. He doesn't even have to answer. I know exactly where he's going. "Hope's," he answers.

Ding! Ding! Ding!

"Tell her I said hi."

He flips me off.

Together we leave the park. At the exit, he stops close enough to tap his knuckles against mine. "Shiny side up, brother. You did fuckin' great tonight," he shouts over the combined rumble of our engines. Then he's gone.

I take the long way back to the clubhouse so I can replay everything that happened and see where I fucked up. What a bizarre night. Fuckin' 18th Street Boyz. Worthless punks. The club's been through so much bad shit together that the idea of being taken out by some young thug flashing around a gun he doesn't know how to use seems almost fitting.

Trinity's Jeep clears the gate ahead of me. Back from her date early I guess.

I hang back and ride up the driveway slow.

Suddenly, the events of the day sink into me, and I'm just bone-weary tired. Got no fight left in me. I back my bike into its spot and wait for Trinity to go inside first. She hasn't opened her car door yet. Maybe she's trying to wait me out? Tired of fucking around, I get off my bike and head inside. Behind me, the soft crunch of her smaller feet hurrying over the gravel makes me pause and hold the door open for her.

"Thanks," she says in a breathless rush.

Once we're both inside, I stop and give her a once-over. She's dressed in jeans and a plain T-shirt and carrying a backpack. Not sure what the fuck kind of date she's been on.

"Date over early?" I ask with a sneer.

Her startled, wide-eyed expression makes me feel like shit. "What?"

"You said you had a date tonight." I jerk my chin at her backpack. "Were you planning to spend the night?"

Her eyes gloss over with tears. Holy fuck. Why can't I learn to keep my mouth shut? "Shit, Trinity. I'm just messing with you," I say, reaching out to give her an awkward hug.

"I didn't have a date," she mutters.

Thank fuck.

This particular Saturday night, the clubhouse is quiet. Usually is nights we have a drop-off. Never know what'll go down, and brothers need to be alert and available—not drunk and elbow deep in pussy—in case shit goes bad. Sparky's waiting in the living room, and I flash him a thumbs-up sign. He grins and heads back downstairs.

"Where's everyone else?" Trinity asks.

"Rock took off for Hope's place."

Trinity smiles at that. "She's nice. I'm happy for prez."

I grunt because I'm not so sure about that chick and how good she's going to be for the club.

"Rest of the guys had the van, so I'm assuming they stopped to get dinner or something."

"You hungry?" she asks.

After the shitty way I acted this morning, I'm shocked she's even speaking to me, so I don't answer right away. I mean, she feeds me break-fast and stuff all the time. But she never offers. I show up in the dining room with everyone else, and she throws whatever she's made at me. Just as she does for all the guys.

"Sure."

I follow her down the hallway. "I gotta drop this in my room." I follow her to her door, but she only opens it only wide enough to set her bag inside.

"Anyone ever been in there besides you?" I tease.

"You know the answer to that."

Yes, I do. When we first moved out here, Rock made it abundantly clear none of us were ever to enter her room unless expressly invited by her.

Yes, that's exactly the way he put it.

Chuckling, I follow her to the dining room. It's late, so I'm not expecting her to cook for me or anything. Which is good, because she only sets out cereal and milk.

"Thanks, babe."

We eat in silence, but it's nice being together without all the extra hostility. Suddenly, I'm feeling anxious. When the guys return, all of this niceness between us will disappear. And I really don't want it to. I like being alone with her. This house is always full of people; it's easy for us to avoid each other. I can't ask her up to my room without her getting the wrong idea. She'll never invite me into her room. The war room has a couch and TV set up. Maybe I can talk her into watching a movie with me.

Excited about this plan, I clean up after us and hustle her out of the kitchen. "Wanna watch a movie?"

She gives me the strangest look. "Okay."

When she heads into the main room, I pull out my keys and open up the war room.

"I thought—"

"You're with me. It's fine."

Her eyes dart around the room, taking in the table where we hold church every week and anytime something urgent comes up that requires a vote.

"Which one is yours?" she asks.

I point it out. The chair at the right hand of the president's throne.

"Yeah." She nods absently.

Not sure why she's so solemn all of a sudden, I nudge her to the couch. She tosses me a curious look, like maybe I brought her in here for another reason.

"What are you in the mood for?" I ask with a nod at the television.

Her eyes flick to the screen as I flip it on and key into the on-demand screen.

"Something scary," she answers.

I'm definitely on board with that. From memory, I know she jumps at every little thing.

Maybe she'll jump right into my lap if I'm lucky.

CHAPTER FOUR

Eight years ago...

WRATH

For the third night in a row, I found myself at the Blue Fox Tavern, watching Trinity. All day, I'd told myself I wasn't showing up again. But there I was.

I was so fucked.

She kept glancing at me shyly all night.

Before Trinity, I'd never considered myself an ass man. The snug black jeans she had her perfect little heart-shaped butt stuffed into turned me into a believer. She kept bending over to get stuff from the lower shelves. Once or twice, she tossed a look over her shoulder and caught me staring. A blush stained her cheeks.

Tonight, she'd abandoned her trusty kicks in favor of a pair of fuck-me pumps. I really wanted to know who she was so dressed-up for.

If it was another guy, the possessive, ragey beast in me wouldn't handle it well.

The rest of our date at Fletcher Park had been perfect. After fucking ourselves into exhaustion, she'd fallen asleep in my arms. When the first tendrils of daybreak curled into the sky, I nudged her awake and helped her dress. We watched the sun come up together, the awed expression on her face no match for a simple sunrise. We hurried back to my bike and took off before park security caught wind of us.

I'd planned to drop her off at her apartment, but she invited me inside. For some reason, I couldn't say no to this chick and hated being away from her. We slept until noon, when I got a call from Rock demanding I get my ass to Crystal Ball.

I sent her a text to explain, but maybe she was annoyed to wake up and find me gone again.

Why did I care so damn much?

As I watched her work, I admired the way she'd pulled all her beautiful golden hair into a high ponytail, displaying her neck. I didn't think she realized she had a faint hickey on the left side. *My* mark.

Suddenly, I was rock hard and didn't dare move from the bar. I prayed it was another early night for her.

When things slowed down, she made her way to my end of the bar. "Hey, handsome."

My lips twitched. "Hey, gorgeous. You done soon?"

"Maybe. Why? You got plans for me?"

I risked a glance into her honey eyes. "Depends. Who you all dressed up for tonight?" Fuck. I didn't mean for her to hear all that jealous come out of me.

Her head tipped down to inspect her outfit, and she looked back up at me, eyebrows drawn in confusion. "What are you talking about?"

My shoulders lifted in a careless shrug. "You look really pretty."

She blinked twice, then beamed at me. At least I finally said something useful. "I'm done at ten. If Storm gets her butt here on time."

I wish I knew where Storm lived 'cause I'd haul her ass in here at 9:59.

Storm was only five minutes late, but it was five too many for my brain. As soon as Trin stepped out from behind the bar, I grabbed her hand and pulled her outside.

"What do you have planned?" she asked.

What a loaded question. I wanted to sprint to her apartment and fuck the living hell out of her. She'd probably be fine with that, but for some reason I couldn't identify, I wanted *more*.

"We can catch the second movie at the Jericho," I suggested.

"The drive-in? I've never been."

I cocked my head at her. "How can you live in Empire and not go?"

She shrugged. "Never had anyone I wanted to go with before."

"Wanna go with me?" Was I really *asking* like some high school fuckwad?

The corners of her mouth tilted up in a soft smile. "Yeah, I do."

The drive there was cool, and I was happy I remembered to pack a blanket. The guy in the ticket booth recognized me and waved us in. We timed it just right to hit intermission, so I pulled us up sort of close but all the way to the left side of the field where it looked like we'd have a good view of the big, white screen and a little privacy.

Just in case.

Trinity

I almost fell out of my heels when Wrath walked into the bar for the third night in a row. As soon as he spotted me, his hardened touch-me-and-I'll-kill-you glare lit up in a smile. Not some cocky throwaway smirk, either. No, he flashed me a genuine smile, as if he were pleased to see me.

For the third night in a row.

I didn't know what to make of it.

For an arrogant, sexy-as-sin biker, Wrath seemed to have one hell of a romantic streak. Or maybe I just didn't know the difference.

The fact that he knew he had an all-access pass to get in my panties but still wanted to take me out? It woke something up in me I'd sworn had died a long time ago.

He slowed the bike and tucked us into a nice, dark spot where we still had a good view of the screen. I jumped off and almost snapped one of my heels in the soft grass.

"Fuck, babe. I'm sorry. You okay?"

"Yeah, figures the one time I wear heels it's totally inappropriate."

The corners of his mouth turned up in the cocky grin I'm sure he used to signal most women it was time to drop their panties.

It almost worked on me right there in the middle of the field.

An old-time dancing hot dog cartoon silently played across the screen, and I couldn't help laughing. Wrath glanced at the screen and chuckled, then leaned over to pull a blanket out of one of his saddlebags. After spreading it over the grass, he offered me his hand. Once my feet touched the blanket, I kicked off my shoes.

"Better?" he asked.

"Yup."

"Are you okay if I run and grab some snacks?"

"Yeah, I'll watch your bike," I teased.

He snorted, and I knew why. Anyone would have to be insane to mess with a motorcycle that belonged to a Lost King. Especially this mountain of muscle who was probably the most dangerous man at the drive-in.

He was gone for a while. When the dancing hot dogs started to bore me, I checked out the surrounding vehicles.

"I'm back." His deep voice startled me, and I tipped my head back until he came into view.

"Oh my God. Did you leave anything for anyone else?" He handed me a container of nachos and a giant tub of popcorn, then an equally large soda. His hand disappeared into his pocket and he pulled out a chocolate bar.

"For you."

"That's all I get?"

He smirked and, for a big guy, folded himself onto the ground rather gracefully next to me.

"No, I'll share."

The countdown on the screen sent a hush through the crowd. We were close enough to the projector building that we didn't need to turn Wrath's radio on to hear.

The movie turned out to be a creepy, haunted-house type horror movie. Not too gory, but with plenty of scares purposely designed to make us jump.

The second time I squeaked and jerked, popcorn went flying everywhere. Behind me, Wrath chuckled, taking the container out of my hands. He pulled me against his rock-hard chest and leaned down to whisper in my ear.

"Nothing to be scared of, sweetheart. I got you. I'll fucking massacre anyone who tries to touch you—even a ghost."

It was so silly I giggled and leaned into him.

We watched the movie snuggled together for a bit. Behind me, I sensed Wrath getting restless. It didn't surprise me he was the type of guy who couldn't sit still long.

I shifted and turned to face him, then pushed him on his back. He seemed amused, and I knew damn well he was only on his back because he wanted to be. "Whatcha doin'?"

"I want a kiss."

He raised an eyebrow. "Yeah?"

I nodded.

Threading his hand into my hair, he pulled me down. Even with him on the bottom, nothing about his kiss was gentle. It was consuming, carnal, and wiped my mind clear of everything that wasn't us.

WRATH

There was no way we were staying until the end of the movie. After a few kisses, Trinity moaned and my dick said it was time to go. We got the hell out of the drive-in and went straight to her apartment.

She stumbled a little on the sidewalk. Pressing my hands against her hips to steady her, I took a deep breath. "You've been a naughty girl."

She pouted and spun away from me.

I caught up to her easily. She stared up at me with a knowing smile.

"You got me seriously worked up tonight, Angel Face."

Her smile widened and she looped her arms around my neck to pull me down for a kiss. There on the sidewalk outside her apartment, I lost myself in her sugary scent and hungry kisses. My hands slid down to cup her ass, pulling her against me. "Wrap your legs around me."

Her arms strained against my shoulders, but I placed my hands under her ass and lifted her at the same time. She pressed her thighs into my hips.

Fucking awesome.

Her eyes were closed and she kept kissing me, even though I was trying to focus on walking us to her apartment.

"Keys?"

Keeping one arm hooked around my neck, she searched through her purse and finally pulled out keys. I bent toward the door so she could get it open and kicked it closed behind me once we were inside. She squirmed in my arms.

"Let me down. You can't carry me up the stairs."

Insulted, I glanced down at her. She was completely serious.

"Babe, you wound me." With that, I gripped her tighter and got us up the stairs, barely out of breath.

"Impressive," she said in a husky voice that made my brain fuzz.

We fumbled into the apartment, and I finally set her down. Up went her shirt. Off went mine.

"Turn around," I ordered.

She blinked up at me, confusion in her pretty eyes.

Taking her by the shoulders, I spun her. "Put your hands on the back of the couch," I whispered against her neck.

A shiver worked through her as she complied.

The position gave me a nice view of her sinful curves. "Arch your back." I sucked in air through my teeth as she pressed her ass higher. My hands explored every inch. "Were you trying to drive me nuts with these painted-on jeans tonight?"

"No."

"Well, you did."

She wiggled her butt at me, bumping my thigh. I slid my hands to the front of her jeans, unbuttoned them, and slowly eased the zipper down. Peeling the skintight material down her legs took a minute. Especially since I paused to sink my teeth into one round little ass cheek.

A sharp intake of breath above and more wriggling. Leaving the jeans around her knees, I smoothed my hand over the soft skin of her thighs.

"Wrath."

"Yes?"

"Please."

Oh, fuck yeah. I loved the sound of her sweet begging.

My hands returned to her pants as I stripped them off. She kicked her shoes to the side, and I helped her step out of her jeans, leaving them on the floor.

"Put the shoes back on, angel face."

She searched for them with her toes and finally slid into them.

I ran my hands up and down her legs, admiring her sleek muscles. "Very nice. What made you wear those to work tonight?"

She shrugged.

"Weren't you uncomfortable?"

"It was a short shift."

"Were you trying to look sexy for someone?"

She froze, and I paused. Had she been waiting for another guy?

"You," she finally whispered.

A relieved breath pushed out of my lungs.

"Although, I had no idea we'd be doing outdoor activities tonight," she added with a giggle.

"Babe, you're crazy sexy no matter what you do. And you should always be prepared for the unexpected with me."

"I like that," she whispered.

Good, because I fucking liked every damn thing about her.

I traced my fingers over the delicate peacock feather tattooed down her spine. It curled to the right around her shoulder blade and was the only ink on her body. The vibrant colors were beautiful against her pale skin. This was the first time I'd stopped to take a good look at it.

"This is pretty."

Her whole body quivered under my touch. "Thank you."

I was torn. I wanted to take her hard and rough from behind while she gripped the back of the couch. But I also wanted to make love to her slow and steady while looking in her eyes.

That's new.

No reason we couldn't do both.

Sliding my hand over her belly and down to her mound, I cupped her soaking wet pussy. "You want this bad, don't you?"

"Yes."

The sheer blue thong she had on didn't do a damn thing to cover her, so I pulled it aside. My fingers slipped against her slick flesh, and I groaned. She bucked her hips against me. Arching, stretching, circling her lower body. My cock was in my hand, and I rolled down a condom in no time. Even in her heels, I needed to bend down to get the right angle. Once I sank inside her, everything around us faded to nothing.

"Hold on," I cautioned when she started to move.

Squeezing the curves of her hips, I thrust in deep once and almost lost it.

"Ohhh, *fuck*."

"Take every inch of me like a good girl."

"There's a lot of them." The laughter following her words was low and throaty.

Fuck me. A girl who not only complimented my dick size, but did it with a giggle while I was buried to the hilt inside her? I wanted to switch my road name from "Wrath" to "Lucky Bastard" then and there.

She pressed back against me harder, into it as much as me. I took a few deep breaths. Instead of slamming into her, I thrust with a slow, tortuous rhythm intended to drive us both crazy.

The more she writhed under me, the tighter I pinned her. Kept giving her steady strokes until she clenched tight around me. I paused, then adjusted my angle and started pounding into her.

"Don't stop," she cried.

"No way."

So slick and hot, moving under me, making the sexiest noises.

It was my turn to do some begging. "Come for me." I couldn't take much more.

My fingers worked over her clit, and a second later, she went off. Pulsing, throbbing, gripping my cock so hard I thought I would drown. She screamed so loud I hoped the neighbors wouldn't call the cops. Didn't matter. I kept hammering at her, white lightning seized me, and I came with a shout.

Out of breath, sweat dripping in my eyes, I rested my forehead against her shoulder. "You okay?"

I felt her nod, and then she melted onto the floor at my feet.

"That good, huh?" I teased, struggling with my natural inclination to cover up any real emotion with a joke. "I'll be right back." I needed a minute. For some reason, I felt oddly exposed—which annoyed me. I disposed of the condom and buttoned my jeans back up.

Returning to the living room, I found her still slumped on the floor. I toed off my boots and squatted down next to her.

"Hey."

"Hey," she rasped.

My hand reached out to smooth some hair off her face that escaped her ponytail.

Her lips trembled into a hesitant smile. The thought that she might be feeling as exposed and unsure as I was snapped me out of my fog.

"Come here." I reached out and tucked one arm under her knees and the other behind her back and plucked her off the floor.

She giggled as I raised her in the air. "All those weights you must lift are worth it."

I kissed her cheek for the compliment and carried her into the bedroom. As I set her down next to the bed, she threw back the covers, slid off her soaked thong, unhooked her bra, and crawled into bed.

Naked Trinity. Nice.

Once I gathered her all snug in my arms, my agitation eased.

"What's your real name?" she asked while running her hand over my chest.

"Wyatt," I answered without thinking. Couldn't remember the last time I told anyone my real name. Couldn't remember the last woman who even bothered to ask.

"Wyatt, Wyatt, Wyatt." She rolled my name around in her mouth. "I like it."

"I always hated it."

She pressed her hand against my chest and sat up a little. "Why? It's a good name. Strong. Haven't you ever heard of the fearless sheriff Wyatt Earp? Crack shot, but usually kept order with his fists. Kinda like you I bet."

Stunned, I didn't know what to say. No one had ever had so much to say about my name. Not even my worthless parents who gave it to me. No one had ever nailed me so well either. And here Trinity and I barely knew each other. Or at least that's what I kept telling myself. Because I was starting to think we knew each other a whole hell of a lot better than either of us realized.

I was *falling in love* with this woman. "Trinity, I have to tell you something."

"Uh-oh. Don't tell me you're married."

Her even suggesting I'd be a two-timing asshole, bugged the shit outta me. "Fuck, no. I'm leaving to go on a run tomorrow. Gonna be gone for three weeks at least."

This run had been planned forever. It was important to the club. I didn't have much of a choice. Rock needed to be here to finish the MC deal. Zero and the Irish prospect were coming with me. After all the bad shit our club just went through, this run needed to happen.

Suddenly, I didn't want to go. I'd never hesitated to go on a run before. I'd do anything for my club. I loved the freedom of being out on the open road.

"Oh. Club business?"

"Yeah."

"I understand."

And I realized she was telling the truth. She understood. She also didn't expect anything from me. Any other time, or with any other woman, I would have been thrilled.

"I'll call you when I can."

"Okay."

"We'll talk when I get back?"

"Sure," she answered.

I felt less and less reassured with every word out of her mouth.

"Are you going alone?"

"No, Z, you met him the other night, and one of our prospects are going too."

"Rock isn't going?"

There she was asking about my best friend again. Fucking weird and it irritated the shit out of me for a number of reasons. "No, he's got stuff to take care of here."

"Well, you know where to find me when you get back."

With that, she turned over and went to sleep.

The next morning, I decided I wasn't leaving again without saying good-bye. I snuggled up behind her, slid her hair off her face, and sucked at her neck. My lips made their way down her shoulder, and she turned toward me. "Wrath," she moaned.

I filled my mouth with her nipple while cupping her other breast and running my thumb over the tight peak. I wanted to make sure this good-bye was memorable. It needed to last us both three weeks. Kissing my way down her stomach, I glanced up to find her watching me.

"Spread for me, Angel Face."

She planted her heels in the mattress and dropped her knees to the side.

"Fuck, you're beautiful."

Leaning in, I pressed a soft kiss to her mound. Her breath was nothing but short little pants. My fingers slid through her slick folds, my tongue flicked over her clit, and she arched up. I dipped two fingers deep inside her hot pussy.

Above me, she let out a moan.

Stroking up, I spread her wetness, flicking my thumb over her clit. Her hips shot off the bed.

"Not yet." I thrust two fingers in again, angling them to hit her sensitive spot. Her breathing turned into whining. Her legs shook, and my hand was drenched. I leaned down and sucked her clit into my mouth.

"Oh, fuck!" she screamed.

I intended to draw this out, but I couldn't wait another second to be inside her. After digging a condom out of her nightstand and squeezing into it, I wrapped my hands around her thighs and pulled her to me. I eased her legs around my hips and slid into her.

"There we go. Better, Angel Face?"

"Yes. Please, please, fuck me."

"I plan to. Your wet pussy sliding over my cock feels so fucking good."

She let out a low, guttural groan—pure sex. I stopped to give her a second to adjust. When she relaxed, I drove in all the way, hard and fast. I fell down over her, gathering her in my arms as I pounded her into the mattress.

Her legs slipped against my hips, but she locked them around my back.

Sharp nails dug into my shoulders. I didn't think I could hold back much longer.

"Come for me, Trinity," I demanded.

She went rigid in my arms, moaning like she couldn't get enough. A second later, my own orgasm overtook me with frightening power. Her greedy little pussy pulsed around my cock so tight I was blown away.

I placed a finger under her chin. "Look at me, baby. Let me see your eyes." Her eyelids fluttered open, and she stared at me, soft and gentle.

"Wyatt."

Fuck me. Hearing her say my name in her sweet, awed voice fucking killed me.

How was I supposed to leave her for three weeks?

CHAPTER FIVE

TRINITY

Wyatt had been on the road for about a week. We hadn't been able to talk much. Wherever he was had terrible cell service. Whatever he was up to was top secret. I already knew what guys like him did on a run. My mother cried about it every time my dad left, then drowned her sorrows in alcohol and dick. Married or not, the guys who visited the MC I grew up in tapped every club whore when they came to town.

So I had a pretty good idea what Wrath was up to.

And that was fine. We hadn't made any promises to each other. I had no intention of ever becoming some biker's ol' lady. Except for three spectacular, mind-blowing nights together, we barely knew each other.

All of this was going through my head when a new customer walked in. The bar was jumping. Storm up and quit two days earlier, so I was stuck training a new girl. Basically, my workload had tripled. Most of the customers were a blur.

Not this one.

No, Jug was an unexpected nightmare from my past. In living, hateful color, he sat on a stool as if he weren't a vile piece of human garbage.

I glanced up and we both stared at each other. His hand circled my wrist. "Lizzie." He drawled out my hated nickname with a nasty smirk twisting his mouth.

I jerked out of his grasp, but he yanked me back.

"My name is Trinity," I answered as calmly as my trembling body allowed.

"Whatever you say, bitch. Tyler's been looking for you for years. Got a fifty-thousand dollar bounty on your tight little ass."

Oh my God. The idea that Tyler wanted me back that bad was terrifying.

"I'm done with the Saints, Jug. Get lost."

His evil sneer brought long-buried memories to the surface. "You may be done with the Saints, but they ain't done with you."

"Leave me alone."

"Bitch, you can either walk out of here with me quietly, or I'll call some guys in and we'll take you with us not so quietly."

"You do what you have to. I'm working."

I wrenched myself out of his grasp and walked to the other end of the bar. When Jug was distracted, I slipped into Marky's office and called Rock. No point calling Wrath. He was too far away to help me.

"Hello?"

"Rock? It's Trinity."

"Hey, sweetheart. What's going on?"

"I need help."

"Where are you?"

"I'm at work. Rock, please, there's someone here who's going to hurt me."

He was silent for a minute. "There a door that leads to the alley?"

"Yeah."

"I'm going to send Dex in. You can trust him. Point out the guy to him. Don't be obvious. Once you do that, meet me in the alley."

"Okay. I'm scared."

"It's okay. We're leaving right now, Trin."

I felt bad for bothering Rock and ditching Starla, but Jug wasn't someone I wanted to fuck around with. Whatever condition he returned me to the Saints in would not be pretty. Then, only if I were super lucky, Tyler would kill me.

Maybe ten minutes later, I spotted Dex and another guy. They took seats at the opposite end of the bar from Jug.

"Which one, Trinity?" Dex asked.

"The one in the Iron Saints cut at the end of the bar."

Dex nodded but didn't even glance in Jug's direction. The prospect smiled, instantly reassuring me.

"Get us two Cokes, honey," Dex instructed.

I poured the drinks and handed them over.

"Is he alone?"

"Yeah, he said if I didn't come with him, he was going to call in guys to take me. Their nearest charter is at least five hours away, though. Saints shouldn't even be in this area."

The prospect placed some money on the bar, picked up his drink, and walked away.

Dex checked his phone.

"Where's your stuff, sweetheart?" he asked without looking up.

"In the office."

"Can you grab it without him seeing?"

"Yeah."

"Okay, go get your things and meet Rock out back."

I slipped the money into the register and handed Dex his change. With every fiber of my being shaking, I walked into the back room. Marky was nowhere to be found, thank God. I grabbed my stuff and, without looking back, pushed open the door to the alley. Rock waited patiently, bike rumbling beneath him, and handed me a helmet.

Balancing my hand on his shoulder, I threw my leg over the bike, and we took off.

I was still trembling like crazy when we got to the MC. Rock ushered me straight into his office.

"Trinity, I like you. I know you been spending time with my boy. Not sure where that's headed, and I'm sorry I had to send him on that run."

"It's okay."

"You want to tell me more about tonight?"

"Can you protect me?"

Rock studied me for a second. "How serious is this thing with Wrath?"

Shit, I didn't know how to answer that. "He hasn't said he wants me to be his ol' lady or anything like that."

That didn't seem to surprise Rock.

"Look, we're moving up to the new clubhouse in a week or so. I could use a girl up there to take care of stuff. Cooking, cleaning, that sort of thing. I think I can trust you. You'll be safe up there. You interested?"

From the little bit I'd gathered from Wrath, the place was a large, secluded piece of property at the edge of Empire County. I was extremely interested. "What else will I have to do?" I asked because I wasn't stupid. Any MC providing me with shelter and protection would expect more than a little cleaning in return.

He cocked his head and studied me for a moment. "Nothing you don't want to do, sweetheart. I promise. Now tell me why this guy got you so rattled."

I gave him the most concise version of my life story that would leave me with some dignity yet still convey how desperate I was for his club's protection. Even so, it was an ugly story. Rock remained stoic as I laid everything out for him, but his ticking jaw muscle told me how furious he was about what he was hearing.

As soon as I finished, he said, "Trinity. I give you my word that shit does *not* happen in my club."

I nodded because I believed him to a certain extent. There was something different about the Lost Kings. I sensed I would be safe under their protection and would do whatever I had to do to earn it and keep it.

Rock glanced at his phone. "Dex says the guy's starting to cause trouble. I'm going to have him take care of it so word's not getting back to Tyler about you just yet."

"Okay."

He sighed. "I got a spare room here. Nothing fancy. You can stay there until we figure this out."

"Okay. Thank you so much, Rock."

A couple days later, Dex took me to clean out my apartment. I packed up anything I cared about and stuffed it into my car. He handed me directions to the new clubhouse, and I made my way there.

Rock eyed my little beater car suspiciously when I pulled up to the building. He opened my door and looked the car over. I was mildly embarrassed, but up until a couple days earlier, I tended bar. What did he expect me to drive? It was bought and paid for and good on gas. That's all I cared about. Men—they were all the same when it came to vehicles.

"You'll need four-wheel drive up here in the winter," he finally said.

I opened my mouth to protest, but he cut me off before I got a word out. "Club will find you something, Trinity."

Not sure how I felt about that. I mean technically, I was offering to be a whore for the club, right? It still felt weird to have the club president talk so casually about taking care of my transportation arrangements that way. I'd never heard of an MC that worried about shit like that for someone as insignificant as a club whore.

The space was pretty fantastic. I'd never seen such an elaborate MC setup. Most were rundown, converted warehouses or trailers. Nothing so flashy. Rock explained it belonged to some sort of religious group that used to hold fancy retreats. That made more sense.

He gave me the grand tour. "It's a lot for one person to keep up on, especially with ten guys messing it up, so if you need to hire someone to help you out, just let me know."

"The club has other girls, right? Regular sweetbutts?"

One corner of his mouth lifted in a bit of a smirk. "We've got regular club girls. Good luck getting any of them to help you clean, though."

What the hell? Any girl who wanted to enjoy the benefits of an MC, their weed, booze, protection... dick, ought to be prepared to give back and help out. I told Rock that and he laughed.

"Okay. You want to whip them into shape, I'll back you all the way, Trinny. Any of them give you shit, they're gone."

Lot of power for one club girl to have, but I think Rock knew I wouldn't abuse it.

The last place we stopped was a room across from a partially furnished workout room. My mind flashed to Wrath telling me he was saving to buy his own gym. I wondered if he'd hang out here a lot.

Rock opened the door and stepped inside. It was a decent-sized suite with a little walk-in closet, its own bathroom, and lots of built-in bookshelves.

"This is nice. What are you going to use it for?" I asked.

"It's yours."

My mouth dropped. I assumed I'd be expected to bunk wherever. Couch, floor. Whoever wanted me in their bed for the night. I'd never heard of a club girl having her own room, unless she belonged to the president or something.

Oh.

Rock sensed the shift in my attitude. Two fingers pressed under my chin, tipping my head up. "Trinity, I want you to have your own space, where the guys won't bother you if you want to be left alone. Nothing more."

Oh, wow.

"I'm asking a lot of you. Cooking, housekeeping, running the other girls, and overseeing party stuff. The least I can do is make sure you have your own room."

"Okay."

"That's *all* I expect from you."

"Okay," I whispered, not entirely convinced.

"You want to be with any of the guys, that's your choice." He studied me for a moment before continuing. "Wait for Wrath to get back before you make any decisions. I haven't had a chance to talk to him."

"You think he's going to be mad?"

Rock shrugged. "All the brothers are good guys. I don't expect you to have any problems. But if you do, talk to me."

Surprised, I just nodded my head.

With another glance at the empty space, Rock clapped his hands. "We're going to be ordering furniture for the rest of the house. I'll drop the catalogs off to you. Just make a list of what you want, and I'll make sure you have it."

I was dumbfounded but managed to mumble an okay.

His face broke into a warm smile. "Everything's going to be fine. You'll be safe here."

I wished I believed him.

WRATH

Stopping to take a break would have been the smart move, but I never claimed to be smart. I needed to see Trinity. We'd talked a few times, but she'd stopped answering her phone a couple days ago. Had she gotten fed up with me? Found someone else? I needed to find out.

This run seemed to take forever. For the first time in my life, I hated every second I was away. My first stop, of course, needed to be the MC to give Rock an update. Naturally, he was nowhere to be found.

Dex stopped me with a big, manly bro hug as I came out of Rock's office. "How'd it go?"

"Good. Long trip."

Z and the prospect shuffled in behind me and headed for the showers.

"Anything new?" I asked.

"Naw, man. Got us a club mama installed at the property, though."

That's new.

"Girl was being hassled by some shady fuck at the bar she worked at. Rock brought her in. Total sweetheart."

A bad feeling curled in my gut.

"Prez up there now?"

"I think so."

Christ, the last thing I felt like doing was getting back on the road. But I pushed aside my fatigue and made my way to the center. I spotted the prospect's bike and a couple others, but not the one I was looking for.

Laughter greeted my ears as I entered. Immediately, my gaze darted to the left where someone had placed barstools along the front desk area. A flash of blond hair turned my vision red.

No.

Trinity—*my girl*—was the new club mama, Dex mentioned?

No. Fucking. Way.

"Trinity?"

She turned and almost fell off her stool. Guilt or surprise flashed in her eyes. I couldn't tell which. She certainly didn't welcome me home with open arms.

The prospect shot me a welcome home wave, but I ignored him.

Trinity's mouth opened, but no words came out.

I approached her with slow, precise steps. "Can I speak to you outside, Trinity?"

"You guys know each other?" the prospect asked.

I glared at him. Prospect was dangerously close to being murdered. "Shouldn't you be outside, prospecting?" I growled at him. He hustled out of the building.

Now I could focus all my rage where it belonged. "What the fuck are you doing here?"

She blinked, but still didn't offer any explanation.

"Because someone said something about us having a club girl on a permanent basis, and I just *know* that isn't you."

"Well, I, uh… Rock offered."

Motherfucking Rock. I was going to gut him. My president. My best fucking friend. I'd fucking kill him the second I saw him.

"You are *not* doing this, Trinity."

That finally loosened her tongue. "Wrath. I need protection and a safe place to stay. There are people—"

"You need a place to live, I'll fucking get you an apartment. You're not living here, spreading your legs for my *brothers*."

Those pretty lips I'd been dreaming about wrapping around my cock for the last three weeks screwed up into a pissed-off pout. "You don't understand."

"You're right. I don't. Were you so goddamned desperate for cock while I was gone you decided to do this?"

Her face twisted into a scowl. "I haven't done anything, Wrath. Would you listen—"

Fury and exhaustion overwhelmed me. "No. You fucking listen. You're not doing this, Trinity. I thought we had something. But this? This ends now."

Girl had her own fury going. She crossed her arms over her chest. "You better talk to Rock."

"Where is he?"

"Down at Crystal Ball. Said he had interviews."

Rage that she knew where he was when Dex—a brother—didn't consumed me. What the fuck went on while I was away? "Yeah, babe, *interviews* means he's busy fucking dancers," I said to twist her.

She shrugged. "That's his business."

Shit. Was I reading things wrong?

I stormed out the door, Trinity behind me. "Wrath, please—"

I turned and took her in. All that beauty was mine. Jesus, it physically hurt to look at her.

It was a miracle I didn't crash my bike on the way back to Empire. I was so livid. I barely remembered the ride. One minute I was tearing out of the center, and the next I was storming into Crystal Ball. Throwing my fist against Rock's office door earned me an invitation. Could have done without the visual that greeted me on the other side. Rock was busy pounding into a petite brunette he had bent over his desk.

He glanced up long enough to greet me. "Welcome back, brother."

"We gotta talk, prez."

He waved a hand over the girl's back. "Join in or get the fuck out."

She wouldn't have been the first chick we spitroasted. And since I'd just spent three weeks turning down club bitches from here to Cali only to come home and find my girl had installed herself as club ass at my MC without anyone having the decency to warn me, I could have used the stress relief. The chick on the desk crooked her finger at me inviting me closer.

Neither my heart nor my dick were interested.

I put my back to the wall and crossed my arms over my chest. "If it's all the same to you, I'll wait right here."

"You mind an audience, darlin'?" Rock asked her with a cocky smirk I wanted to punch right off his face.

"No," she grunted out.

Lucky me.

"Why the fuck is Trinity at the house?" I grumbled while I inspected the paint on the ceiling.

"That's what you're so bent over?"

"Yeah, I want her out."

I flicked my gaze down and found the girl watching me a little too intently and considered waiting outside. Instead, I jerked my chin at him. "Hurry the fuck up, old man."

He closed his eyes. "Christ, give me a second, asshole."

That did the trick.

Rock groaned. Slapping Ginger's ass, he pulled out. "Off you go, sweetie." Rock dismissed her with another slap on her ass.

She straightened her nightie and gave Rock a peck on the cheek. "Can I dance tonight?"

"Sure, darlin'. I'll make sure you're on the list."

"Thanks, Rock," she squealed.

I turned away while he fixed himself up.

As the girl walked past me, she paused and brushed her hand over my arm. "What's your name, big guy? I'll wear you down eventually."

Doubtful.

"Honey, that's Wrath. He's a scary-ass motherfucker. You're best off looking elsewhere," Rock joked.

"Well, Wrath, I'm Ginger, and I hope to see you again real soon." Bold little bitch. Normally that turned me on. Today it irritated the fuck out of me. She fluttered her lashes and strutted out the door.

Whatthefuckever.

Feeling... shitty about the scene that just went down, I decided to needle Rock. "She'll make a great ol' lady."

He stared at me before waving a hand in the air, dismissing the idea. "Fuck that. I ever meet a bitch that doesn't drop her panties at the snap of my fingers—maybe."

"Good luck with that. Is there a chick in this joint you *haven't* bent over your desk?"

"One or two. What are you so pissy about? Thought a long ride woulda fixed your attitude."

Dick. "Why is Trinity at the house?"

He cocked his head and narrowed his eyes. "She needed a place to stay."

Same thing she said. What'd they do, rehearse this shit? "I don't want her there."

"You with her?" he asked.

"We were starting something. Can't do that if she's fucking brothers."

"She's there to cook and clean, asshole."

"Bullshit."

He sighed and dropped into the chair behind his desk. "I ain't running this MC the way it was before, so knock your bullshit off." He flicked his hand at the door. "Go fuckin' talk to her."

Trinity

The last night at the old MC, we threw a huge party. It was the first official party I put together for the Lost Kings.

I hadn't seen Wrath in a couple days. Not since he threw a bunch of shitty accusations at me and stormed out of the new clubhouse.

It didn't stop me from looking for him every couple minutes.

Since it was right next door, dancers from Crystal Ball filtered in and out all night. Most of them were fine. A few catty bitches were downright rude to me.

One petite, curvy brunette—who introduced herself as Ginger—caught my attention by asking about Wrath.

"Haven't seen him yet."

It was killing me not to ask how she knew him.

"What's your name? Are you a dancer too?" she asked me.

Going around insulting the MC's strippers would be a good way to get myself kicked out. Good thing I caught the *Fuck no* on the tip of my tongue just in time. "Trinity. No, I... um take care of the clubhouse."

Her eyes went saucer wide at my name. "Oh yeah, Wrath was saying the other day how he wanted you out of the house. That sucks."

The words were almost sympathetic but her smug face was anything but. My breath caught, burning the back of my throat. He asked Rock to kick me out? Even worse, he asked Rock to throw me out in front of this skank?

Embarrassment heated my skin and made me want to throw up.

Of course, that's when Wrath walked in. His eyes swept the room, finally landing on Ginger and me. His mouth twisted and he turned away.

I felt like the worthless trash I'd been called so many times before.

I needed to get away.

"Hey, Trinity." I glanced up to see Marcel, the prospect the guys had started calling Teller. By this point, I'd heard two stories about how he'd earned his road name. One involved fucking a girl who worked in a bank. The other involved him doling out advice chicks didn't like to hear. In the short time I'd known him, he'd been a sweetheart, so I didn't know which story to believe.

"Hey, cutie, anyone break you in yet?" Ginger asked, running her hand over his arm.

He flashed a tight smile at her, then turned to me. "Let me know if you need a ride home," he said before one of the brothers called him away.

"That's what you need to do. Get tight with one of the prospects so he'll patch you right away," Ginger informed me. I almost laughed in her face. That *so* wasn't how it worked.

Sick panic threatened to leave me blubbering on the floor. The guys were getting drunker and raunchier by the minute. The whole scene brought back a lot of unpleasant memories. This had been a mistake. I had to be out of my mind to get involved with an MC again.

Pushing through the crowd, I found Rock in a clinch with some skanky blonde who'd followed him over from Crystal Ball earlier. Looking away, I cleared my throat. Instantly, he pushed her back and straightened up.

"What's up, Trin?"

"Would you mind if I head up to the clubhouse? I'm not feeling so hot." That was an understatement. Between Ginger, Wrath and the ever-growing crowd, I was nearing a meltdown.

"Of course not. You need someone to drive you?"

"Nope, I have the Jeep."

The blonde kept staring daggers at me, and I realized I'd taken up enough of their time.

"Thanks, prez. I'll be back down tomorrow morning to help out."

He reached up and grabbed my hand, giving me a gentle squeeze that oddly calmed me. "Nah, stay up there and chill."

Pushing my way back into the kitchen made me antsy to get out of there. Someone grabbed my arm and I let out a short scream. My anxiety had reached red-zone levels.

"Trinity, where you going?" Wrath rumbled.

"*Home.* Sorry you couldn't talk Rock into kicking me out," I snapped.

My throat closed as I choked back a sob. Blinking back tears, I straightened up and met his confused gaze. He glanced in Rock's direction. "Who told you that?"

As if she'd heard my thoughts, Ginger appeared at Wrath's side. I nodded to her. "Your girl, Ginger told me all about it."

Ginger grinned. I bit my lip, on the verge of tears and stormed away. No fucking way would I cry in front of him. And I sure as fuck wasn't crying in front of *her.* I just had to hold on to these tears until I got to my car.

Everything around me was a blur, and I stumbled into more than one person on my way to the kitchen. Teller was in there by himself, a giant black trash bag in each hand.

He looked up and smiled. "Hey, Trinity. You leaving?"

His simple greeting and smile eased some of my panic. "Yeah, I've had my fill of bitchy dancers." I huffed out a laugh and rolled my eyes.

"Yeah, hopefully none of them will find their way out to the new clubhouse."

I arched a brow at that. "Thought having a houseful of strippers would be a dream come true for a young stud."

He grinned even broader. "Nah. It gets old quick."

"Wow, first guy I've heard say that."

He shrugged. "You know the wrong guys then."

"Guess so."

"Need a ride?"

"Nope. Got the Jeep." I couldn't call it mine yet. Still felt too weird that the club had given me a car. Well, technically, the other prospect, Blake, had been restoring an old Jeep the club had rotting in the backyard. When he finished, Rock turned it over to me.

"Well, at least let me walk you out," he offered. He held up the trash bags. "Got stuck with garbage duty tonight."

I chuckled. If that was the worst thing the Lost Kings did to their prospects, Teller was lucky.

We said good night by my car.

"Drive safe, Trinity."

At least by the time I got on the road, I didn't feel like crying anymore.

WRATH

Trinity's anger made no sense to me. I didn't hide the fact that I wanted her out of the clubhouse.

"Come on, big guy. Show me your room," Ginger shouted at me.

"Later." I brushed her off and went looking for Trinity.

I ran into one of our guys from our downstate charter. "Hey, did you see a blonde go by?"

He shook his head, but before I could give him a more specific description, Ginger latched on to me. "Why are you looking for that girl? I'll take care of you."

Jesus Christ, the bitch wouldn't quit. "I need to talk to her. I'll catch you later."

"She got a ride from one of your prospects." She wiggled her eyebrows as she said it.

"What?" She shrugged and I wanted to throttle her.

"I dunno. Come on, show me what you can do."

"Not tonight." I finally brushed her off for good. She bitched and moaned as I stomped off to my room, but I really didn't give two fucks. Sure, fucking Ginger would have given me a perverse sense of getting even with Trinity—as sick as that was—but I didn't have it in me that night.

A week later, we'd all moved into the new center. At church, we voted Teller in as a patched member. He'd earned his three-piece patch by being reliable and loyal. Did plenty of bitch work without complaint. Most importantly, he'd had our backs when the club went through the change in leadership.

In another year or two, we'd vote his best friend, Blake, in. He was two years younger than Teller but hardworking, smart and knew a lot about not only bikes but cars too. Also one hell of a fighter.

Surprisingly, I hadn't seen much of Trinity all week. I wasn't even sure where she was staying. Asking Rock was as pointless as asking an actual rock, so that was a dead end.

After church, I spotted her leaving the kitchen and followed her like some creepy, lovesick teenager. She ducked into the room across from the gym. Duh, why hadn't I thought of that before? I remembered the little suite tucked away down here. Made perfect sense. Before I knew what I was doing, I raised my hand and knocked.

She took her time answering, and when the door finally swung open, her face didn't exactly light up at the sight of me.

"Hey, I was wondering where you've been hiding. This your room?"

Her jaw tightened and she slipped out, closing the door behind her. "Yes."

"Can I see what you've done with it?"

"No."

Stunned, I took a step back. She folded her arms over her chest. "Rock said it's my space and I don't have to let any of the brothers in there if I don't want to."

"So who's been lucky enough to see it so far?" I kept my tone light, but inside, I dreaded her answer.

She flinched and the corners of her mouth turned down. "No one."

Huh.

Before I had a chance to ask if *I* could see it, she craned her neck, and swept her gaze up and down the hallway. "Where's your little muffler bunny?"

"Who?"

"I should've known. Got so many you can't keep track, right?"

What the actual fuck? By her narrowed eyes and crossed arms, it was obvious she was serious. Seriously pissed.

"Trinity—"

"Hey, Trinity, got a sec?"

Motherfucking Rock and his shitty timing.

Trin's face lit up when she saw *him.* "Sure, prez, what'd you need?" she asked with a genuine smile.

Fuck this.

Trinity

After the guys left church, I scurried out of the kitchen and back into my room. I still didn't feel quite safe when all the brothers were in the house at once. Everyone was surprisingly nice, but I knew from experience how people you trusted could turn on you, so I wasn't about to let my guard down.

I tried ignoring the knock at my door, but whoever it was wouldn't go away.

Finding Wrath on the other side shocked me.

Thank God, Rock interrupted us. I couldn't argue with Wrath again. If he had his way, he would have booted me back down to Empire where I'd live in fear of being found by Tyler or one of his minions.

Rock had a big grin on his face, until Wrath bumped his shoulder and stormed off. Shaking his head, Rock focused on me. "He giving you shit?"

"Nah, we're whatever. Don't worry about it. What's up?"

He didn't seem satisfied with my words, but didn't question me either. "We patched Marcel in finally. Think you can organize something for him on Friday?" He handed me a credit card. "Get whatever you need, okay?"

I met his eyes briefly. "Okay."

"You know what to get?"

"Alcohol and condoms?"

Rock snorted and shook his head. "Yeah, pretty much. Should I ask any of the CB girls to come up for him?"

I remembered my conversation with Teller the night we said good-bye to the old clubhouse. "Nah, I don't think he'd care for that. He doesn't seem that into them."

He chuckled and ran his hand over the back of his neck. "Can't blame him. They give me a fuckin' headache sometimes."

"Doesn't stop you from nailing them though, does it, prez?" I asked with a laugh.

He shook his head, looking almost embarrassed. "No, it doesn't."

Crap, how could I insult Rock so brazenly after he'd taken me in, protected me, and given me shelter?

"Shit, prez, I'm sorry. That was rude."

A corner of his mouth lifted. "No worries, Trin. Let me know if you need anything else, yeah?"

Excited about Marcel's party, I sat at my desk and scribbled down a list of supplies. I'd finally get to put that fancy, industrial kitchen to good use.

Cake. I hadn't baked in forever, but I enjoyed it when I had the money for ingredients and someone to do it for. Now I had a houseful of hungry bikers to feed.

Rumor had it Wrath was making a run to our downstate charter right after church, which was why I'd been so surprised to find him at my door. Would he make it back for Teller's party?

Do I care?

Sure enough, the rumble of his bike reached my ears as it left the club-house grounds.

Yeah, I care. I knew which motorcycle belonged to Wrath by the sound alone. How pathetic.

Shoving Wrath out of my mind would take a lot of effort. To distract myself, I hustled down to the kitchen and took stock of what we had on hand.

I wasn't in there long before Teller strolled in with a huge grin on his face, proudly sporting his new cut.

"Didn't they rub any dirt on your patches?" I teased.

He grinned big and goofy at me. "You heard already?"

"Sure did. Congrats." I gave him a quick hug and a kiss on the cheek. "Gonna celebrate Friday. Got any special requests?"

"You?"

It took a second for his meaning to sink in. "I, uh—"

He blushed and glanced at the door. "Never mind. I thought now…" He ran his hands over his cut. "You're not with anyone, right?"

"No. Not really. No."

His gaze roamed over me for a brief second. "I should get going. I gotta pick up my sister."

"Okay."

"I'll catch you later, Trin."

Friday came quick. I had a mild freak out that I wouldn't have everything ready in time. Ginger, of all people, showed up early to help me out. I had no reason to hate her fucking guts, but I did. I worked hard to be civil to her because it wasn't her fault and I really needed her help that afternoon.

Wrath showed up shortly after, and it made a whole lot more sense why Ginger was here to "help."

"Hey, baby!" she squealed, rushing to his side. Wrath caught me rolling my eyes and smirked. My heart plummeted and bile rose from my stomach as she reached up to give him a welcome home kiss.

That should have been *my* job.

Instead, I was standing in front of a hot oven, covered in flour, batter, and Betty Crocker only knew what else.

Like an idiot, I sighed with relief when Wrath nudged Ginger aside. "Whatcha making, Trin?" he asked, edging closer. It was utterly pathetic how happy his interest made me.

"Cake for Teller's patch party," I answered proudly, then cursed myself for sounding so perky.

His mouth turned down as he took in all my party preparations. "You do all this for him?"

I shrugged, unsure of the right answer. "Well, yeah. Rock asked me to put something together—"

"Motherfucker," he swore under his breath. At his sides, his hands curled into fists.

Ginger had apparently reached her limit of being ignored. She rushed over and grabbed for Wrath's hand.

"Not now. I gotta talk to prez. I'll catch you later."

Based on some tips from Teller's best friend Blake, I chose to make a triple layer chocolate cake with marshmallow frosting. Messy but worth it, judging from the way the guys demolished the entire thing within minutes.

Warm breath on the back of my neck startled me as I set the remnants on the bar top.

My heart actually skipped.

Wrath.

But then two hands that were definitely *not* Wrath's circled my upper arms.

"Got any of that frosting left?" Teller whispered in my ear.

His lips against my skin tickled, and I giggled. "No, why?"

"I wanted to smear it all over you and lick it off." His lowered voice and the slow way he dropped each word set off a shivery sensation over my skin. I twisted around to face him.

Holy fuck.

Mixing food and sex never interested me much, but the fierce expression he wore actually turned me on and made me reconsider.

He wanted me. *Bad.*

The familiar need to feel wanted by someone consumed me.

Over Teller's shoulder, I caught sight of who *I* wanted—Wrath. The crowd shifted and I spotted Ginger glued to his side.

I moved my gaze back to Teller's hungry eyes. "Next time I'll save some just for you."

One corner of his mouth lifted in a cocky smirk I'd never seen on Teller before. It was sexy on him. "I wanna show you my new room, babe."

A voice in my head whispered I better get this over with. And at least Teller had always been nice to me. "Okay."

He grabbed my hand and pulled me toward the stairs. We had to pass Wrath and Ginger to get there. My gaze collided with Wrath's and held. I willed him to say something. Anything to stop me from going through with the inevitable. Because I knew what would happen when I stepped inside Teller's room. I also knew once I slept with Teller, Wrath and I would be done for good.

My heart shattered as he watched me follow Teller all the way up the stairs and never said a word.

CHAPTER SIX

WRATH

I should have stayed in bed. Or left the house after last night. Sitting at the dining room table was just asking for trouble. I'd gotten word from the guy who organized the underground fights that I had a match for Sunday night. I couldn't fucking wait. Every punch and jab, I'd be picturing Teller's smug face.

Z stumbled in holding his head, fell into the chair next to me, and promptly pressed his cheek to the table.

"Whatthefuck?" he mumbled.

Even in my foul mood, I had to chuckle. "Why you even up, bro?"

"Got shit to do," he answered, although it was so muffled he might've said, "I've got shit in my shoe."

"Stop being a pussy."

He groaned and pushed himself off the table. "Fuck. You drank as much as me. How can you sit upright?"

"I'm a bigger man than you."

"Fuck off." Z leaned back and closed his eyes. "Fucking bullshit with Trinity and Teller, man. No one's been able to pry her fuckin' legs open with a crowbar since she got here. All of a sudden, the prospect gets patched and he's up inside that. Ain't right," he said with a snicker.

Cold swirled in the pit of my stomach, and it had nothing to do with the bottle of Jack I downed a couple hours earlier. "What did you say?"

"Trinity, the club—"

"I know who she is."

"So what do you need explained?"

"Nothing, dick." Not a fucking thing.

I pushed out of my chair and went to find Trinity. White-hot fury rose in my chest. Why hadn't I listened to her? The way she got so wound up fixing his party, I assumed... She tried telling me, Rock tried to tell me, and—

Found her.

In the laundry room. With Teller.

Yeah, wished I hadn't seen *that.*

Wished I'd never voted Teller's ass in either.

Instead of beating the shit out of Teller for touching what was mine and staking a claim on my girl like I should have, I stormed down the hall.

And smacked right into Ginger, almost knocking her over.

"What are you still doing up here?" I snapped.

Not deterred by my tone, she thrust her chest out and stuck a flirty smile on her lips. "Looking for you, big guy."

Perfect.

"You found me." I steered her into the champagne room and shut the door behind us. My stomach rolled. I didn't want *her.*

Ginger eyed the shiny new pole in the middle of the room. "You want a private dance?"

"Sure, show me what you can do." My voice came out flat. I couldn't be bothered to fake any interest.

I let her push me onto the bench seat that ran the length of the room. Instead of dancing, she stood in front of me, looking confused—not an uncommon state for this chick. "There's no music," she finally said.

I pointed at the stereo in the corner, and she perked right up. She flipped it on, not bothering to pick out anything special, which was fine with me.

She danced well enough, not a surprise since our strip club only employed top talent. It didn't do a whole hell of a lot for me. I'd seen plenty of this shit before.

Sensing my boredom, she danced closer until she was straddling my lap. "You good at lap dances, darlin'?" I asked, more to break the silence than because I cared about the answer.

"Yeah." Not much of a conversationalist, this one.

She worked her bra off and my hands automatically cupped her tits. They were definitely nice. Fake as fuck, but nice.

"What do you want?"

"I wanna fuck," she said with a straight face. Direct. A quality I usually appreciated.

I jerked my chin in the direction of the door. "Grab a condom."

She slid off my lap, then hesitated. "I'm on the pill..." She trailed off.

Fuck that.

Nothing against Ginger, but bitch got around. Jesus Christ, I fucking *met* her while she was bent over my best friend's desk, getting drilled from behind. No judgment—because I did my fair share of fucking around—but I wasn't interested in catching some sort of dick rot. Nor did I feel like taking her word about the pills and being tied to this bitch for the next eighteen years of my life.

"You wanna fuck or not?" I asked her with a hard stare.

She pursed her lips into a pout but ran over, grabbed what she needed, and returned.

I'd get her off. It was a matter of pride. I mean, why bother otherwise? Sex with her wasn't quite what I wanted. No, who I wanted was busy on the other side of this wall, fucking one of my brothers. It was like wanting a vanilla milkshake and being handed a strawberry ice cream cone. Sure, it would still taste good, but never satisfy my craving.

"Slide those panties off, darlin'."

Trinity

Teller seemed to think we were an item now, and I had no idea how to correct him. The man I wanted might have hated my guts, but I couldn't see myself ever belonging to anyone else. I spent years feeling so disconnected from my body it didn't matter who touched me. For a brief time, Wrath changed that for me. Then he took it away, leaving me completely hollow.

Teller had taken me on top of the washing machine in the laundry room and couldn't hide his smug smile while I straightened my clothes. I gave him a shove and he laughed.

"Sorry I interrupted. It's the smell of laundry detergent. Gets me every time," he joked, settling my nerves.

He walked me down the hall, his hand brushing mine as we passed the yoga studio and the door flew open. A flushed, sweaty Ginger stepped into the hall. Wrath right behind her.

I sucked in a painful breath, grasping for calm, praying I didn't look and smell like I'd just been fucked on a washing machine where anyone could have walked in on us.

The second Wrath's eyes met mine, I *knew* he knew, and I hated myself more than any other moment in my life. He replaced his frown with a mask of indifference and ushered Ginger out of the room. Teller lifted his chin and asked Wrath something, but he kept staring at me. No other acknowledgment.

Oblivious as always, Ginger stopped when she realized Wrath hadn't followed her. She returned to his side, rubbing her hands possessively up and down his arm. My jaw clenched so tight it was a miracle I didn't break a tooth. Wrath raised an eyebrow at me as if to challenge my jealousy. My skin tingled as disappointment, anger, and shame all converged inside me. I had no right to be jealous or even pissed.

The longer the silence stretched, the more awkward the whole thing became. Then Teller placed his hand on my back, snapping me out of my fog.

"I've got some things I need to do," I said, pushing past Teller to head to the kitchen.

"Later, Trin," Teller called after me. I raised my hand in a wave but didn't look back.

Couldn't look back.

CHAPTER SEVEN

Present day...

WRATH

Rock's definitely going to blow a gasket when I show up at his house. From talking to Z, I already know he's had his time with Hope interrupted once this morning. Another interruption might get my ass kicked.

But this shit is important. Club comes first. He's the prez. He knows that.

I try his cell several times and get nothing, so I drive over to his house, praying like fuck they're still there. This Viper problem just never seems to go the fuck away.

I'm relieved to see his SUV and bike in the driveway. I park outside the gate and walk in.

Moaning catches my ear as I open the side door to the house. It's coming from the garage.

Vipers would be out of their mind to pull something smack in the middle of our territory. At our president's house for fuck's sake. Just in case, I pull my piece and creep closer to the garage. When I peek around the open door, I almost burst out laughing. Tucking my gun back into its holster, I lean against the doorframe and take in the live sex show in front of me.

Now I'm starting to understand a little better what Rock sees in this bitch. Nice, plump tits. Honest fucking reactions; no fake porn star moaning. She opens her eyes and catches me watching. She tenses up and tries to warn him, but then he does something to her that sends her over the edge. When she finally finds her brain again, I decide to end the game with a test.

If Rock asks me to join in, I'll know she ain't gonna be around for long. If he rips my head off, the club may just have a problem on their hands. It's risky. But I haven't seen Rock territorial over a piece of ass in years.

"Don't worry about me, darling. Nothing I haven't seen before," I say, giving her my cockiest wink.

Rock stands and spins so fast he almost tosses Hope on the ground. He's actually shielding her with his body, so I can't get a good look at those fabulous tits… or anything else, except his furious face.

I'll be damned. He's in love with her.

"What the fuck!" he yells.

Whoa. Well, this may have been a mistake. I've never seen him *this* crazed over a chick. Ever.

I back up a few steps. He's not fucking around in the slightest. I hold out my hand in a sort of truce gesture. "Sorry. Door was open. I tried calling you."

"Out," Rock barks.

Yeah, I back the fuck out while I still have all my teeth. Even though I shut the door behind me, I hear Hope burst into tears on the other side. I feel like absolute shit. She's near hysterical, and Rock's talking all soft to her, trying to calm her down. Maybe I've been hanging with strippers and club girls too long. I can't remember the last woman I met who had so much modesty.

What the ever-loving fuck is Rock doing with her? No way is this going to end well. For any of us. Even her.

Even with these revelations, guilt jabs at me when she walks inside and I get a look at her face. She's fucking magenta from the neck up, and she's got tearstains down her cheeks.

"Sorry, Hope," I manage to get out.

She recovers enough to whisper something in Rock's ear that makes his eyes flare. Shit, these two have enough heat behind them that even I'm uncomfortable being in the same room.

Rock and I make a plan to deal with the Viper issue. I'll ask Z to call the prez of our downstate charter to see if he can spare any guys and possibly some nomads who might be close by.

Since I'm tight with the sergeant-at-arms in the Wolf Knight's crew, I'll handle bringing them into the meeting. We'll all meet at Crystal Ball to hammer things out.

Our immediate concern is this possible threat from the Vipers. Prez's love life will have to wait. Although, his ridiculous obsession with this woman got us into this mess in the first place. Doesn't matter. I'll back him no matter what, but deep down, it definitely irritates me.

Things are quiet when I return to the clubhouse. It's still early for most of us, so I'm not surprised. I *am* surprised to find Trinity's Jeep in front. Stepping into the office I share with Rock and Z, I sit down and make my phone calls. Z's already talked to downstate, and we've got guys on their way up now. Whisper and Ulfric assure me they have our backs on this one hundred percent.

My job's done until this evening, so I decide to search for Trinity and see what she's up to.

I find her in the kitchen, cooking and singing softly to herself.

"Hey."

She jumps, but relaxes when she turns and sees it's me. "Hey, Wrath."

"Whatcha makin'?"

Her shoulders bounce once and her cheeks redden. "Ravioli. From a package. Nothing special. Are you hungry?"

"Sure."

Her face breaks into a smile, and she turns back to the fridge and starts digging stuff out.

"I thought you were already making it."

"I am, but I'll make it better if you're going to eat with me. No reason to make anything fancy for myself."

"Trin, don't go to any trouble."

She turns, completely deflated. Her lips push into a sad pout. "I don't mind."

"Okay. Want me to help?"

She looks at me like I'm nuts. "I got it."

I kinda feel like a jackass just sitting here watching her cook for me. But it's nice too. She tumbles a bunch of cut-up vegetables through spices and roasts them in the oven, then adds them to some jar sauce she's simmering on the stove and pours everything over a dish of ravioli.

We eat together in silence for a while. "This is great, Trin."

Her cheeks flush. "Thanks."

"How come you don't cook for us like this all the time?"

She shrugs. "Except for breakfast, none of you guys are ever usually here at the same time."

This is true. We all usually fend for ourselves.

Z has to walk in and ruin our moment.

"Smells awesome in here. What're you making, girl?"

Trin's eyes light up at the compliment. "Help yourself."

Z comes over and curls his hands over her shoulders first. Then the fucker leans over and plants a kiss on her cheek.

"Ready for later?" I ask, hoping to distract him.

"Yeah, why the fuck you think I'm here?" He cocks his head at me. "Also heard from Rock. What'd you do to piss him off now?"

My lips curl in a smirk. I'm sure Rock gave him an earful. "Walked in on him and Hope in the garage."

Z gives me a blank look. "So?"

"Fucking."

Trinity ducks her head and snickers.

Z rolls his eyes. "Fuck. He thought I caught a glimpse of her ass this morning and almost lost his shit."

Already bored with this conversation, I just grunt in response.

"You're not feeling her, are you?" he asks.

"No, and I think he's dead serious about her too."

"No shit."

Does he really not see where I'm going with this? "Eventually, it's going to be a problem."

"Bro, I'd stay far the fuck away from that one. You know damn well he's been into that broad since the day they met."

"Don't you have some paperwork to do, VP? Let me worry about this shit."

It takes a lot to offend Z. He gives me the finger and walks over to the stove. Trinity, of course, jumps up to help him.

I've lost my appetite.

Trinity

Naturally, Wrath storms over to me the minute I step out of Rock's office at Crystal Ball later that night. Rock asked me to bring some supplies and girls down with me after he finished his meeting with the

Wolf Knights MC. We've also got Lost Kings members visiting from out of town. I want to help out any way I can, but I'm also hoping to avoid being hit on tonight.

Wrapping his hand around my upper arm, Wrath pulls me to the side.

He leans down enough for his lips to graze my ear. "No, Trinity." His hoarse voice sends a shiver of desire skittering down my spine.

Why? Why after all these years does my body still respond to him like this?

I try to shake him off. "Rock asked for my help."

He loosens his grip on my arm but doesn't release me. "You're not dancing for these assholes."

My chest tightens. He's the only man I've ever been with who asked about my scars. But that's not why he's forbidding me from dancing. Jealousy, plain and simple, is written all over his face.

Some tender emotion I didn't think I still had toward him brings my palm to his cheek. "I'm just here to serve drinks, Wyatt. But thank you."

His face softens the way it always does when I use his given name. One by one, he unwraps his fingers from my arm.

"You know one of them will want... Trinity, there's sixteen girls and forty bikers. They're not all Kings. I don't want anyone messin' with you."

I'd partied with the Wolf Knights before. They were a little more "handsy" than LOKI, but they weren't a bunch of twisted fucks who thought "no" was a code word for "jam your dick in my ass" either. "I'll be fine." I duck behind the bar, leaving Wrath to chew on whatever's bothering him.

The meeting with Ulfric's crew seems to be over, but Wrath still makes the rounds. He really is good at his job. Alert to everything. He watches Rock's every move, which as the sergeant-at-arms is his responsibility. When I guess he's determined there's no threat, he takes up residence at the end of the bar.

I'm instantly thrown back to when we first met. Those few nights he came into the bar to see me, take me out after work. Before everything went to shit between us. Hot tears blur my vision, and I turn away from the room to hide out by the sink while I pretend to wash my hands. Leaning over, I splash some water on my face, not caring what it will do to the minimal makeup I splattered on before leaving the clubhouse. A quick check in the bar mirror shows everything appears okay. Without thinking, I grab the bottle of Jack I'd tucked under the bar just for Wrath.

Call me sentimental. Stupid would probably be more accurate.

I set the bottle and a glass in front of him, then walk away to uncap a round of beers.

The weight of his heavy gaze bores through me, but I fight the urge to turn his way for as long as I can.

Merlin, the VP for the Wolf Knights, sits down a few stools away from Wrath, which immediately sends a bad signal.

"Hey, Trin. How you doin' tonight?" he asks.

With a lot of effort, I paste on a hospitable smile. "I'm good. How've you been?"

I'd have to be dead, or blind, deaf, and dumb not to feel the tension radiating from Wrath's corner as Merlin strokes his fingers over my arm.

Any minute, Wrath's going to lose his shit. I don't know why he seems to have this sudden urge to piss a circle around me. As far as I know, neither of us has declared a truce to the war we'd started with each other eight years ago.

Speaking of war, if Merlin doesn't back the fuck down, this is going to get ugly.

Cookie strolls up to Merlin and runs her fingers over his neck and down his chest. "How come you haven't said hello to me yet, Mer?" she asks in a girlish voice, complete with babyish pout.

Merlin digs that shit, and Cookie knows it. It's right about then that in my head, I forgive her for sucking Wrath off in front of the entire club the other night. Merlin is nice enough but rather unimpressive in the sack.

Wrath perks up and moves down a few seats, when Cookie escorts Merlin to one of the back rooms. Picturing the scene back there sends a shiver of revulsion through me, and I stop to catch my breath.

Concern darkens Wrath's eyes. "You okay?"

I nod once and turn to fill a plastic tub with ice, stick some beer bottles and cans in it, and set it on the counter. The party seems to be winding down. There's more fucking and smoking up than people needing my bar services.

"You done, Angel Face?"

Holy shit. We both kind of stare at each other. He hasn't called me that in a long time.

"Yeah, I think so," I answer, trying to smooth over the awkward moment.

Someone turns up the music. To drown out the moaning and groaning filling the club, I suppose. It's a slow song. A painful duet about being broken. Amazement fills me when Wrath holds out his hand at the end of the bar.

"Come dance with me."

Slipping my hand into his sends a warm shiver down my spine.

He tugs me out in front of the bar where there's empty space and wraps his arms around me.

"Since when do you dance, Wrecking Ball?" I ask, looking up at him.

A soft, pained smile tugs at the corners of his mouth. Tiny white orbs of light dance around the room with us. Leaving us in shadows most of the time. We're not really dancing as much as we're swaying together with our arms wrapped around one another.

Something a little more upbeat comes on next. Although when I listen to the words, it actually depresses me. Whoever wrote it could have been writing about Wrath and me. Or maybe I'm feeling extra sensitive tonight and everything reminds me of us.

Either way, I'm having fun shimmying my hips from side to side and moving to the beat. Wrath keeps his arm around my waist but his body away from me. Pressing back into him, I understand why.

Except for a round of angry sex maybe four years back, we haven't touched each other this much since those three wonderful nights we had together almost eight years ago. Our nights at Fletcher Park and at the drive-in remain the first and last real dates I've ever been on. While I'm content and grateful for my place in the club, there's a part of me that always wonders…

Tears suddenly fill my eyes, and I try to pull out of his embrace. I can't keep doing this same dance with him over and over.

"What's wrong, Trin?" he rasps, keeping his arms around me.

"Nothing. I'm just getting tired." It's not a lie. Since we seem to have called a truce, being near him has a sedative effect on me. I haven't had anything to drink tonight, but my body is relaxed and happy for a change.

"I rode here with Rock—don't have my bike."

I shake my head. "I drove myself. I'll be okay."

"I wouldn't mind a ride home," he says after he finishes the biggest, fakest grizzly bear yawn.

What the heck is he up to? We did have a lot of fun watching back-to-back scary movies last night. He didn't make a single move on me. Wrath acting like such a reserved gentleman is unnerving. I prop my hand on my hip and adopt a schoolteacher tone. "Are you going to insist on driving my car?"

I sense him struggling, and I almost laugh that he's so concerned with not ticking me off. I honestly don't care if he insists on driving, but I can't help messing with Wrath. He's such a caveman.

"No, I had beer before," he finally answers.

"Mm-hmm."

I pull out of his embrace and reach behind the counter to grab my purse.

"You need to let Rock know we're taking off?"

Wrath searches the club. Not seeing prez anywhere, he holds out his hand to me and we head down the back hallway. Wrath's jaw tightens as we get to Rock's office door, but I don't ask why. After two sharp knocks, Rock's tired voice calls us to come in.

He's stretched out on the couch by himself.

"You okay?" Wrath asks.

"Yeah, just waiting for the place to empty out." Rock sits up and eyes both of us. "You two taking off?"

Wrath looks from me to Rock. "I was. But I'll stay and move everyone out if you want to go see Hope."

"Nah. I'll go see her in the morning. You two go ahead. Dex and Teller still out there?"

"Yeah."

"Thanks. Night."

We step back into the hall, and I can tell Wrath is conflicted about leaving. "We can stay."

He glances down at me. "Let me just go talk to the guys for a sec. Stay here."

Naturally, the minute he takes off, Merlin comes stumbling around the corner. I groan when he spots me.

"Trinity, where you been hidin' all night?"

"Behind the bar." *You know, the place where I talked to you maybe an hour ago?* "How you doing, Merlin?"

"Good. Real good." Jesus, what the fuck did Cookie do to him back there? "You leaving so early, baby?"

"Yeah, I'm waiting here for Wrath."

Merlin isn't so high that he misses the implication of my words.

He gets into my personal space a little more than I care for by pressing me up against the wall opposite Rock's office door. "You with him?" He throws his arms against the wall behind my head, caging me in.

I'm saved from answering.

"What's going on?" Wrath growls from the hallway entrance.

Merlin's slow to turn away from me, but I slip out from underneath his arm and hold my hand out to Wrath. "Nothing. I was just telling Merlin we were about to head out."

Wrath's face registers a second of surprise before he takes my hand, tugs me to him, and slips a possessive arm around my waist. Okay, that's overkill, but I'm not complaining because it feels really good to be up against him.

Merlin straightens up and away from the wall. "Have fun, kids," he says with a wink and heads back into the club.

"Come on, Trin."

Yup, I'm ready to bolt.

WRATH

I'm still shaking with rage when Trinity pulls out onto the highway. Fucking Merlin thinking he's going to what? Fuck her in the goddamn hallway?

"You fuck him?" I blurt out. *Smooth, real smooth, jackass.*

Trinity throws me a cool glance before focusing on the road. "Who?"

"Merlin," I manage to grind out.

"Why are you asking?"

Fuck. Why *am* I asking? I can already sense the answer is a big fat *yes.* So why do I need her to confirm it?

"Never mind, Trin. I shouldn't have said anything."

She glances at me again. I can tell I've shocked her. I'm furious at myself for ruining the good mood we had going on at the club. Dancing with her erased any lingering bad feelings. Having her in my arms again left me certain I needed to fix things between us.

"Do you need me to stop anywhere?" she asks after we've put some miles between us and Crystal Ball.

The longer I'm in her presence, the calmer I feel. I almost forget I wanted to slit the throat of one of our allies not fifteen minutes ago. "Sure. I'm out of beer. Do you mind stopping at Ward's?"

The small grocery store is the last thing we'll pass before taking the long country road to the MC.

"Nope."

The parking lot is almost empty this time of night. I arch a brow when Trinity grabs a shopping cart. "I need to get some things too," she explains.

I gotta admit this is fucking weird. Doing something so ordinary with Trinity. What's weirder is how much I enjoy it. She cruises up and down the aisles, searching for a bunch of stuff. It cracks me up how particular she is about everything she buys, from pasta sauce to her chocolate bars. I know she's in charge of ordering supplies and food for the clubhouse too, but I've never gone on any of those trips with her. A lot of times, I think she just has stuff delivered. But this trip is personal, and it's intriguing.

"Anything else, babe?"

She pauses and a slight flush creeps over her cheeks. "No, I'm good."

She squawks when I pay for everything, but I just laugh.

"Wrath, that was stuff for me, not the club." She protests on the way to the parking lot.

I just shrug. "It's not a big deal. I didn't feel like waiting around for two separate orders."

She hesitates while I'm loading the bags into the back of the Jeep.

"I gotta run back in. I forgot something." She thrusts the keys at me and runs inside before I can get a word out.

Nutty girl.

Arranging the seat so I can drive is a pain in the ass, but by the time I fix the mirrors and pull up to the front door, she's walking out.

"Hey, little girl, want some candy?" I rasp in my creepiest perv voice.

"Oh my God." She laughs and stuffs her bag in the backseat before getting in.

"What did you get?"

"None of your business."

Well, of course now I really want to know. Can't be condoms. We keep the clubhouse so well stocked we should ask Trojan to sponsor our parties.

"More candy bars?"

"Knock it off."

She's blushing furiously and I finally get it. *Girl stuff.* "Sorry."

Even out of the corner of my eye, I can tell my apology shocks her. "Why are you being so nice to me tonight?"

"Have I been mean?"

"Are you serious?"

"Sorry."

"What for?"

"I'm sorry I've been such an asshole that you're shocked when I'm nice to you."

"Wrath—"

"I mean it."

"Okay." She's quiet for a while. Out of the corner of my eye, I see her twisting her hands in her lap. Obviously, there's something she wants to say. "Thanks for worrying about me… before."

I'm not sure which time she's talking about. It seems like I'm always worried about Trinity.

"When I got to CB. I can't believe you think I'd ever get up and take my clothes off in front of a room full of people. I mean, in the dark, you know, with one or—"

"Trin, stop, please."

Christ, I don't need the threesome reminder. It hits me—she means the scarring on her hip. I've always thought she was one of the most beautiful women I've ever known and don't give her scars a lot of thought, so yeah, I thought she came down to CB to dance. It never occurred to me the scars bother her that much.

"You're one of the most beautiful girls I've ever seen, Trinity."

"That's sweet, Wrath."

I can tell by her tone she thinks I'm just blowing smoke up her ass, and I hate it. "Trin, I'm not just saying that."

"Thanks," she says softly, this time sounding more convinced.

For the second night in a row, we're basically alone in the house. All the guys are either downstairs or at Crystal Ball.

"Wanna finish watching those movies?"

We'd only managed to make it through two of the *Paranormal Activity* movies. Just as I remembered, Trin is still a fuck lot of fun to watch scary movies with. She jumps at the scary stuff and pretends to cover her eyes. A lot of the time, she giggles. Maybe originally I'd picked them because I'd been hoping she'd want to cuddle up during the scary scenes, but what ended up happening instead? No contest.

Tonight, she does snuggle up against me, resting her head on my chest. She reaches behind us and pulls down a blanket. I settle my hand on her hip and wait for her to say something or move away, but she stays. After a while, I realize she's asleep. My hand inches under her shirt to stroke her soft skin.

Skin I've really missed touching.

We'd had what turned into an angry hookup the night of the party I held to celebrate the opening of my gym. Fantastic, explosive sex that ended badly because of my stupid mouth. But I hadn't been able to hold her or touch her like this. Not since our first three nights together.

"Wrath, I can't," she whispers, halting my exploration.

Right. The secret supplies she bought. At least I comfort myself with the fact she won't be sleeping with any of my brothers for the next few days either.

"Thought you were asleep, babe."

"I was. You're tickling me."

Oh. My fingers twitch over her ribs, and she giggles. "Stop."

"Okay." Pure lust burns through me, but I rearrange her shirt and lay my hand on top of the blanket. "Go back to sleep, Trin."

After a while, she drops off. I flip on the weather station and mute the television. Throughout the night, the sounds of my brothers and whatever girls they've brought with them infiltrate our quiet little bubble. Eventually, I fall asleep too.

In the morning, I wake up alone.

CHAPTER EIGHT

WRATH

Because I'm a lucky fuck and shit always seems to go my way, Z and Teller are the two brothers who ride with me to the fight. Rock would normally be here, but he's somewhere balls deep in his bitch.

Teller's acting like a nervous mama around me. Considering he's one-third of the reason I'm here, I find that perversely funny.

The guy I'm fighting came in from the West Coast, where supposedly fighters take shit more seriously? Don't know; don't care. What I do know is I have a fuck lot of rage to unleash on someone. Since it can't be my brother, it's gonna be Cali.

"Just worry about your end, Mr. Treasurer. Let me handle the gritty stuff."

He storms off in a toddler-worthy fit.

"What crawled up your ass?" Z asks.

"Gee, I don't know, maybe him questioning my ability to win a fight about an hour before I have to go in the ring?"

"He didn't say that." Z cocks his head and studies me for a minute. "When did you schedule this fight anyway?"

"Last weekend. Why?"

"Just curious. Seemed like it came out of nowhere."

I hadn't been given the name *Wrath* at sixteen because I knew how to hold back, so little welterweight Teller, of all people, questioning me fucking pissed me off. Fighting gave me the outlet to unleash all my boiled-up, held-in, blistering rage. Rage that this time Teller unknowingly has caused.

The only form of fighting I could do was underground, where the rules were bendable. All the people who participated understood the need to keep their mouths shut.

I can't stop thinking about last weekend, after Trinity and I left Crystal Ball together. Time seemed to reverse, leaving us where we were eight years ago. Fuck, if I'm not dying to recapture that. Recapture *her*. Let go of the past and do shit right this time.

Once I get this fight out of the way, I plan to concentrate on her. Our two little movie nights hadn't been enough. I'd only seen her here and there all week. Although, she made a point of stopping to wish me luck before I left tonight. Her honest encouragement and soft smile shredded me inside.

All thoughts left my brain as I stepped into the makeshift ring and focused on my opponent. The rage I kept locked down bubbled through me, further narrowing my focus.

Glaring at the punk-ass bitch who'd flown in from Cali to fight me, I follow him around the ring, assessing his skill. For his heavyweight frame, he moves with grace and speed; I'd give him that. I'm also surprisingly quick for a guy my size. I've got strength and power.

And a fuckload of fury.

Tired of fucking around, I move to take his ass down for good.

Kicking out, I land a solid hit on his thigh, then connect my fist with his chin. A fist to the kidney and punch to his temple, and he hits the floor. After a few ticks, the ref blows the whistle and calls the match in my favor.

I shake off the tingling in my hands and limp out of the ring, barely out of breath.

"Waste of a fucking plane ticket," I growl at the ref, who laughs back.

Z and Teller meet me with grins on their faces.

"Nice job, bro," Teller says with a slap on my back. I suffer a minor bit of guilt for being so pissy with him before.

Couple people in the back room give me shit about how quick the fight ended. Fuck 'em.

People bitch about the money they lost because they bet against me. Fuck them too.

I stay in lethal shape. My life and the lives of my brothers depends on it. Not that any of them are pansies. Every one of my brothers could fight. Even dickhead Teller who used his smaller size to his advantage.

I'd trained them all to some degree. It's in our by-laws that everyone needs to keep in fighting shape. No fat, beer-bellied, sloppy slobs allowed. That was a good way to get yourself killed. I never understood how any true outlaw could let himself get soft. We shunned society's conventions, so our fists, our strength was sometimes all we had. Something these punks never understand—I would fight to the death to protect what belongs to me.

So some little underground match like this?

Bitch, please.

Trinity

The clubhouse is in an uproar when Wrath walks in. Arms stretched over his head, cocky grin in place, he asks for a Jack and Coke the minute he sees me.

Raising an eyebrow and cocking my head to the side, I answer, "Only if you won."

Grinning back at me, he winks. "I always win, babe."

"Cocky fucker," I tease, handing him his drink.

He downs it quick. "Fuck, that's good. Missed ol' Jack."

Club girls swarm around him, and I swallow down my jealousy as he turns around to talk them up.

Prez stays long enough to congratulate Wrath, then takes off. To see Hope, I assume, and the thought makes me happy.

After watching him spend time with skank after skank for years, the way he pants after good girl Hope is pretty adorable.

Teller slides up next to me and runs his fingers up my arm. "You okay?"

"Yeah."

"Should'a seen him. He made it look like it was nothing."

I suck in a painful breath. Wrath has never wanted me to come to one of his fights. "I can imagine."

"Want some help back here?"

Glancing up, I see Wrath and Roxy getting cozy. God, I hate that little bitch. Cookie slides up to him next, and he slips an arm over each of their shoulders.

God-fucking-dammit. After hanging out last weekend, I thought maybe he was willing to let the past go and we might start again. But I see now how fucking stupid that was of me.

His head turns slightly and his eyes narrow. Suddenly, I'm overly aware of how close Teller is standing next to me and what it must look like to Wrath.

I step back to put a little distance between us. But it's too late. Wrath's leading the two of them to the couch. I know what's about to go down, and I just can't watch it again. He's still paying me back for every time I fucked one of his brothers.

But I can't do this anymore.

"Actually, yeah. I'm not feeling too well. I'm going to go to bed."

Teller cocks his head with concern. "Do you need me to get you something?"

A gun so I can put a bullet in Roxy and Cookie would be nice.

"Nah, I'm just exhausted."

"Okay."

Fighting tears, I push my way through the crowd. I'll still be able to hear the party, but at least in my room, I can be alone. I've got some things to work on anyway. If I slip in my headphones while I'm working, I'll never know what's going on out there.

I'm in the bathroom washing my face when someone knocks on my door. Ignoring it, I slip on my nightshirt.

Whoever's out there is a persistent asshole, though, because they knock again.

Opening the door a crack, I find Wrath looming in my doorway. I poke my head out, looking left and right. "Where's your fan club?"

"You in there alone?"

I close the door and step into the hallway with him. "You know I am."

He eyes me up and down, and suddenly, I'm self-conscious in my pink nightshirt with the little gray poodles dotted all over it.

"Cute," he says with a cocky smirk.

"So what did you want?"

His face turns serious. "Teller said you didn't feel well. Do you need anything?"

I'm not sure what to do with that. "I'm okay. Thank you, though."

He looks like he has more to say but isn't sure about it. I wait for a second, but his head drops. "Night, Trin."

"Night, Wrath."

WRATH

I only catch a glimpse of Trinity leaving the bar area. Her head's down as she pushes her way down the hall. Roxy and Cookie are busy making out in my lap and trying to draw me into their clinch.

I'm not feelin' it tonight.

Pushing them onto the couch, I rise and stalk over to Teller. "Where'd Trin go?"

With a pinched expression, he jerks his head toward her room. "Said she wasn't feeling well and wanted to go to bed early."

I don't like that answer at all. Girl's been running herself ragged 'round here.

Not giving a shit what Teller thinks, I head down the hallway. Faced with Trinity's closed door, I hesitate. She might already be trying to rest and now here I am buggin' her.

On the other side of the door, I hear water running, so she's still up. I knock and get nothing. After the second time, the door opens a crack. When she sees it's me, she opens the door a little wider and sticks her head out, making a big show of searching up and down the hall.

"Where's your fan club?" she asks.

She's got her jealous up. Cute.

Good, 'cause I got questions of my own. "You in there alone?"

She closes the door behind her, jiggling the knob to make sure it's unlocked I guess. "You know I am," she answers softly.

When she steps into the hall, I get a good view of her and I'm over-come with how friggin' cute she is. Hair's all messily knotted on top of her head, face scrubbed clean. Christ, if she doesn't look younger than when we met eight years ago. My gaze stops on what she's wearing. Pink sleep shirt with little fucking puppies on it. How fucking adorable is she?

I can't help it. The corner of my mouth curls into a cocky smirk. "Cute."

She crosses her arms over her chest, and suddenly, it's obvious to me she's not wearing a bra.

"So what did you want?" she asks, making me tear my gaze away from her chest.

Reminding me why I'm here.

"Teller said you didn't feel well. You need anything?"

The astonishment on her face sends shame slithering over my skin. "I'm okay. Thank you, though."

I want to ask why she left the party early and if it has anything to do with me. I want her to invite me into her goddamn room or come upstairs with me or something.

Finally, I tell her good night.

"Night, Wrath," she answers back.

But she doesn't go inside. She's still standing there watching me. Her hand reaches back and jiggles the knob again.

Her eyes flutter shut for a second, and she whispers, "I just couldn't do it again."

Confused, I take a step closer, and her eyes open. Glossy, like she's about to cry.

"Do what, honey?"

She takes several deep breaths before finally answering me. "Watch you with them again." She flicks her hand in the direction of the living room. "Any of them."

My first thought is, *Good, now you know how I feel*. Thank fuck I don't blurt that out, because the next thing I think of is what her words mean.

She still cares about me.

I'm too dumbstruck to say anything. I want to tug her in my arms and kiss the fuck outta her.

This is huge.

She still cares about me.

When I still haven't said anything, she shakes her head and opens the door.

"I'm sorry," I finally manage to get out.

"Me too." And she shuts the door behind her.

CHAPTER NINE

WRATH

"You guys all good?" Trinity asks as she clears our breakfast dishes away.

"Yup. Thanks, babe," Teller answers while tickling her side.

My fists clench under the table. Trinity's eyes skip to me, but she doesn't say anything.

Murphy and Z watch her walk all the way back to the kitchen. "Christ, the fucking ass on her," Murphy grumbles.

Teller's mouth kicks up, and my stomach lurches. I'm really not in the mood to sit here and listen to them discuss all the depraved things they've done to Trinity over the years.

"Best thing that ever happened to the MC," Z says with a chuckle.

"Hell yeah." Teller just has to join in. "Mouth for fucking days. Even with her weird 'not on my knees' thing."

My gaze snaps up at that.

"Fuck, right?" Murphy jokes. "We been hittin' that for what, seven years on and off, and not fucking once. Not even doggy. Makes things kinda limited."

"Whatever," Teller mutters. "She's game for anything else. Ain't ever heard you bitch about it before."

"True, she's a spinner," Murphy says. Whatever the fuck that's supposed to mean.

"Except goin' down on her," Z reminds them.

Murphy flashes a smug smile. "Fine by me."

Something painful clenches in my chest. The memory of the first night Trinity and I spent together. Her sweet, trusting honey eyes staring up at me, her coming on my tongue. I'd give pretty much anything to go back to that moment and do things over again. Fuck, I'd give anything not to be part of this conversation right now too.

The guys finally notice I haven't bothered to add to their disgusting gossip session. They turn to me expectantly. I want to keep my mouth shut, but something vicious inside me speaks instead.

"Not the way I remember it at all, boys."

Although I get up quietly and push my chair in with a precise shove, rage blows through me. I *hate* the way my brothers talk about Trinity behind her back. I fucking despise the intimate details they know about her. *She's mine.* Don't give a fuck if we haven't touched each other in years. *Mine.*

Storming up to my room with the intention of doing I'm not sure what, I stop dead in my tracks. Trinity's at the end of the hallway, cleaning. Guess she went out the back door and circled around? Briefly, I wonder if she overheard the guys talking about her and decided to avoid us. Something painful twists inside me at the idea of her overhearing that shit. As furious as she makes me, she doesn't deserve that.

A soft chuckle eases out of me as I watch her dancing at the end of the hall. She's got a mop or some shit in her hands and ear buds. She's so fucking cute wiggling her rear and singing as she cleans.

My fists clench and unclench. She turns and stares at my door, her mouth screwing up into a sad pout. Her hand lingers on the doorknob, but she doesn't knock or try to go in.

My patience snaps seeing her staring at my door with such a serious expression.

I make it to the end of the hall in a few quick strides. She never hears me coming as I grab a fistful of her ponytail and shove her against my door. A short, startled scream is the only sound she makes. Hooking my index finger around the wire, I pop her ear bud out and put my mouth against her ear.

"I'll give you something to polish," I whisper in her ear. Instead of getting pissed or fighting or even laughing at the absurd line, she *relaxes* into my hold when she realizes it's me. Her response stokes the fire burning inside me even brighter.

"We need to talk." Sinking my teeth into her earlobe draws a moan from her, and her knees sag.

My arm bands around her waist to hold her up. With my other hand, I throw my door open, pushing her inside.

I kiss and suck my way down her neck hard enough to leave marks.

"Do you remember when you got on your knees for me?" I ask against her throat.

Breathless, she hums a negative sound and shakes her head.

My foot kicks back, slamming the door shut behind us. Her body jumps at the sharp sound.

"Bullshit. Don't lie. You loved it. No way you forgot."

More head shaking until I grip her tighter.

"You haven't done that for anyone else since me, have you? Tell me the truth, Trinity."

"No," she gasps.

"Why?"

She only whimpers and shakes her head.

I rattle her harder. "You going to do it again if I ask you to?"

"Yes."

"Anytime I want it, babe?"

"Yes," she cries.

"Why? Why me?"

"Because you cared about me and made me trust you," she bursts out with a sob.

Her words hit me like a fist in the gut, and I loosen my grip on her hair.

"What?" This game I'm playing with her might have just gone too far.

Her voice is husky as she lays it out for me. "You asked about my scars. You... kissed them. You made me feel pretty."

I swallow hard. "You're fucking beautiful, Trinity. You know that."

She shakes her head sadly, breaking me.

"What else?"

"You went down on me until I came, even though I told you I couldn't. No one else had ever bothered to try before."

Christ, the memory of the sexy sounds she made, the pure awe on her face as I took the time to learn what her body needed. "Sweetest fucking thing in the world, babe. I would'a stayed there all damn night. What else?"

She sighs and relaxes farther into me. In a defeated voice, she answers,

"You asked before you came in my mouth. I knew you'd stop if I'd asked you to."

Fuck me. What the hell had gone on in her life before I met her? No wonder she's so fucking messed up.

"No one ever asked before?"

"No," she whispers.

I can't dwell on how disturbing this admission is, so I change the course of the conversation a bit. "Did you like it?"

"Yes."

Slowly, I turn her in my arms, releasing her hair and crushing my mouth against hers. She reaches up and grips my shoulders, clinging to me in a way that scares me senseless.

Breaking the kiss, she eases down. Kneeling in front of me, staring up at me with those soft, sweet eyes that drive me nuts. I hurry to free my cock and shove it between her beautiful lips. Her fingers graze the sensitive skin of my balls, then tighten around the base of my dick. She pulls back, the pink tip of her tongue slicking along the head of my cock. Finally, she engulfs all of me. A breath of air hisses out of my lungs and my fingers twine in her hair. Her lush lips circle my cock as she takes me deep. Her sweet mouth a wet, warm paradise. Pleasure jerks my hips forward. She sucks her way back up, cheeks hollowing. Such a beautiful sight. I trace my fingers along her cheekbones.

"You're so pretty with my cock in your mouth."

She releases me with a soft pop, then slurps at the sensitive underside, pushing her tongue into my slit. Fuck, it takes every ounce of self-control not to blow.

Anger still simmers through me as I pick her up off the floor. My hands reach out to grab her face and kiss her. When I pull away, she's staring at me with a dazed expression. So compliant as I turn her to face the bed.

I jerk her pants down her legs, past her knees, and leave them around her ankles. Bending her over, I slam my cock inside her. She yelps and scrabbles on the bed, throwing blankets, sheets, pillows.

"Wyatt, you're hurting me," she finally gasps.

No. Fuck no. I never want to hurt her. I don't know why I'm so fucking angry. I pull out, completely ashamed I'd gone after her like a rutting beast.

Nudging her into the bed, I yank her pants and shoes off, turning her over. She lets out a needy whimper as I kiss my way down her belly, then drop to my knees beside the bed. Gripping her thighs, I slide her to the edge, throwing her legs over my shoulders. Very much like the first time she let me do this.

I run my tongue up over the soft pink lips of her pussy. I glance up to find her watching me. "Who else has done this for you?"

She reaches down and runs her fingers through my hair. "No one. No one since you."

Holy motherfuck.

Slowly, I make my way to her clit, tonguing and rolling it in a tight circle, then sucking. Her back bows off the bed. I grip her hips and hold her in place for my mouth. When she stops squirming, I move my hand to her soft belly. With my other hand, I tease her entrance, then slide one finger inside her, seeking and stroking that special spot I remember can make her go nuts.

She lets out a sharp cry, and I smile against her pussy. I suck the tight peak of her clit into my mouth once more, and she rewards me. Shudder after shudder wracks her body as she thrashes around on the bed.

"Wyatt," she whispers.

Fuck yes, the way she says my name unravels me. I kiss my way up her body, pausing to work her shirt and bra off. She won't be needing those any time soon. My fingers trail over the tips of her nipples, then my tongue. I can't stop touching every inch of her, kissing my way up to her neck and finally her mouth. Her hands fly into my hair and she drags me against her. Her legs wrap around my hips.

I slide my hand between us and down her flat stomach with painstaking slowness. Payback for all the times she's teased me. As I inch closer to her sweet little snatch, her head falls back and she sighs. Cupping her pussy tight in the palm of my hand, I thrust two fingers inside her, slide them out, then thrust deeper.

A louder moan drags from her throat, so I reward it by stroking her clit with my thumb. I keep up the steady pressure until her entire body shakes with need.

I can't take any more.

Slipping my fingers out, I grin like a devil when she whines in protest. The raging caveman inside me isn't satisfied yet. I'd pushed her in here to finally fucking own her the way she's owned me since the first time I laid eyes on her. I snatch a condom out of my pocket and kick off my pants.

I kiss her cheeks, her eyelids, her chin. "You ready for me now, Angel Face?"

"Oh, yes."

I roll the condom on and drive into her with one powerful thrust. She contracts around me, squeezing my cock so fucking tight. I throb, eager to pound into her, but wait. When the tension melts from her body, I pull out and sink back in.

"Trinity."

She quivers as I roll my hips down and start frantically pounding into her. Sweet sighs and moans fill my ears. She nips at my earlobe, and I lose it. Mindlessly, over and over, I thrust into her. I need her to recognize she belongs to me.

"Open those angel eyes. Look at me."

She tips her head forward, her glazed eyes searing into me. "This isn't enough, angel. You better be ready for a whole lot more."

Her inner muscles clamp down. "Yeah, you like that, don't you? Your pussy's strangling my dick."

She bobs her head up and down as a sort of dazed acknowledgment of my filthy words. I keep driving into her at this wild, frantic pace. While she writhes and shakes under me, I lean over, burying my face in her neck.

"Fuck, you feel good." I can't get out any more words. Guttural grunts fill the air around us until I come like a fucking rocket.

Waking up alone the next morning is unexpected. We spent the day and night together. Working each other over. I planned to wake up with a naked Trinity in my arms and do it all over again.

But she's gone.

Checking the bathroom, I find no sign of her.

I dress quickly and open my door. Hallway's empty. It's still early.

Marching downstairs, I'm surprised I don't pass anyone.

I find Trinity coming out of her bedroom. Headed to the kitchen, I suppose.

Words to beg her forgiveness well up in my throat, but I'm not even sure what I did wrong.

Then the anger takes over. I corner her, pushing her against the wall. "Why did you leave?"

She cocks her head and stares at me as if she has no idea what I'm talking about.

"Trinity, I thought we finally had our shit figured out."

"We do. We're friends again. I'm glad. I hate fighting with you."

Friends?

"I've always been your friend." Okay, maybe not entirely true. But I've always loved her. Except how would she know that from my shitty behavior?

"You know what I mean."

"No, I don't. What we did yesterday was anything but friendly," I sneer.

She flushes bright pink. "Yeah, it was a good time."

A good time? A good fucking time? I pause. She's trying to piss me off. Push me away. Why?

Trying a softer approach, I tuck a few strands of hair behind her ear, "Trinity, I thought we could—"

She cuts me off. "Wrath, whatever's going on in your head, just stop. Neither one of us is capable of it right now."

What. The. Fuck?

How fucking dare she tell me what I'm capable of? I've tortured myself. Agonized over this woman for eight fucking years. Just when does she think we'll be *capable*?

"How much more time would you like, Trinity? It's been eight goddamn years."

She's got no answer for me. Before I do something stupid, again, I walk away.

I jog upstairs to grab my phone and text the guy who arranges the fights. There's no way I'm gonna be able to contain this rage. He can't get one scheduled right away, but he promises me something big.

I'm going to need it.

Trinity

The tears I'd been holding on to all morning finally let loose as I'm folding laundry, of all things.

Yesterday with Wrath? Un-fucking-believably amazing. Yet also a complete mindfuck that threw me into the past with a painful thump. Admitting how much I trusted him cut me deep.

Telling him I only wanted to be friends this morning?

Bleeding-out-on-the-floor painful.

I let him believe I thought he was the problem. When deep down, I know it's me. I'm too fucked up. Too damaged to ever be anything more than I am now. A club whore.

Maybe no one calls me that here. But we all know that's what I am. Wrath's kidding himself if he thinks he can change that.

A few more of those thoughts and I'm sobbing into the clean towels.

Warm, fresh-scented terrycloth soaking up my tears.

"Trinity, what's wrong?" Rock's voice behind me startles me out of my sobfest.

Straightening up and willing away the tears, I turn and face the only man—besides my father—who's protected me without expecting a damn thing in return.

I can't burden him with my emotional meltdown. "Nothing. I'm good."

Concern etches his face. His shrewd eyes take me in, lingering on my neck. "Did someone hurt you?"

Fuck. I forgot the hickeys Wrath left all over me. Jackass.

Sniffling the last of my tears away, I shake my head. "No. I'm fine."

"Trinity. Talk to me." He reaches out and gently takes the towel out of my hands and sets it on the washer. After a second, he pulls me into his arms.

The floodgates open. In between all the tears, I'm fucking mortified. I hate crying or showing vulnerability in front of anyone. A long time ago, I learned showing weakness gives people a weapon to use against you.

Although, if I had to cry in front of anyone, at least it's Rock. He won't make fun or take advantage of me.

"Wrath hates me," I mumble against his shirt.

Rock's body stiffens for a moment. Then he rubs my back. "Honey, ever since I've known him, he's carried a fuckload of rage inside. Got nothing to do with you."

"I don't know what he wants from me."

Rock sighs. "He cares about you. Always has."

A hiccup jumps out of me.

"You care about him?"

"Yes," I answer miserably.

"You love him?"

A fresh river of tears flows down my cheeks. "I don't know how."

"Honey, did you ever talk to him? Tell him about your past?"

"No. He was so angry with me and kept trying to push me out of the club. I never tried."

Above me, Rock curses. "I'm sorry, Trinity. I was in a shitty place myself back then, and didn't realize how serious he was about you. I should have done things differently."

His words scald. "You would have kicked me out?"

"No. Of course not. I would have locked you two in a fucking room and made you sort your shit out, though."

I can't help laughing at the image that pops into my head.

"That's better."

I risk a glance up at him. "Is Hope here with you?"

"No, I stopped by to catch up on a few things. Why? Would you feel better talking to her about this instead of me?"

I'm startled by the offer. "Oh, no. She already probably thinks I'm trash. I couldn't—"

His hold on me tightens even as the hard lines of his face soften. "Hey. I don't ever want to hear you say that about yourself again. And I know for a fact she likes you very much."

Something about that makes me happy. I don't have many girlfriends in my life. Club girls don't really count, as they all see me as competition. "I'm sorry. I know you have more important things to deal with."

Rock pins me with one of his serious stares. "Trinity, you *are* important to me. If you need something, I want you to tell me. Always."

"Okay."

"Why don't you finish this later? Guys need towels, they can walk their lazy asses down here and grab them. Go for a walk outside and clear your head."

It's a perfect suggestion. Rock knows me well. I can happily get lost walking through the trails on the property for hours sometimes. Rock and Wrath have always insisted I take a pistol with me in case I run into trespassers or a bear. I grab one I'm familiar with out of the safe. As I'm locking it up and grabbing a jacket, Z and Wrath come in the front door.

"Hey, mama," Z greets me with a peck on the cheek. Wrath's nostrils flare. Any jealousy he's feeling is pointless. Z and I haven't been more than friends in a long time. The only thing we do these days is bitch to each other about our shitty love lives. He keeps moving past me and walks into the office, closing the door behind him.

Wrath lifts his chin at me. "Where you going?"

I'm still so fucking messed up I can't meet his eyes. I'll lose it if he sees that I've been crying over him. Over us.

"Just for a walk. Don't worry. I'm armed," I say, trying to lighten the gloom around us.

That brings a smirk to his lips. "Good." His gaze darts to the closed office door. "I gotta take care of something, but if you can hang on a couple minutes, I'll go with you."

"That's okay. I want to be alone."

His jaw ticks, but he doesn't ask again.

CHAPTER TEN

WRATH

I'm still fuming from Trinity's rejection—actually, make that *two* rejections; she wouldn't even take a damn walk with me—when we sit down to church this week. I finally got my fight scheduled earlier in the day and drop it on the club right before we finish.

"Gonna be a fuck ton of money if we play it right. Three fights. I go last. Kid they want me up against is coming from professional MMA."

"No shit," Z says.

Smug grin firmly in place, I agree with my brother. "Yup. Fucker won't have any idea how to fight dirty. Piece of cake."

Teller stares down at the notes he brought to the meeting. "We could use an influx of cash." He glances at Rock. "How much is the club comfortable parting with?"

"Fuck you," I growl. How dare he suggest I might not win?

Rock holds out his hand. "Simmer the fuck down. It's Teller's job to be risk averse with our money. Nothing against you."

Teller nods. "Sorry, brother."

Everyone approves the rather large amount Rock suggests, and we break. Guys stream out into the clubhouse.

Rock motions me to sit back down. Before I do that, I walk over and swing the door shut. Judging by the grim look he's wearing, I have a feeling he's going to want privacy for whatever he's about to unload on me.

"This fight have anything to do with why I found Trinity crying in the laundry room yesterday? Did you hurt her?"

Shocked because I had no idea, I bristle at Rock sticking his nose in my business. *Especially* where Trinity is concerned. "Leave it alone, prez."

His eyes turn violent. "*No*, you don't listen. I told you to leave her—"

"She said yes."

Rock slams his fist into the table. "Motherfucker, she'll always say yes."

"Good, that's what she's here for, isn't it?" I shoot back.

"You're such an asshole."

I've been holding this back for years, and the words explode out of me as I jump out of my chair and get in his face. "You fucking *knew* how I felt about her."

Rock has never been intimidated by anyone in his life. He gets right back in my face. "You're lucky I got so much love for you, brother, or I'd knock your fucking head off your shoulders."

I sneer back at him. "Love to see you try, *brother*." A little calmer, I add, "You knew I didn't want her up here as club ass. Yet you chose her over me."

"Are you serious right now? Do you have any idea what kind of people were after her?"

What? "No! Because no one told me a fucking thing."

"It wasn't my story to tell." He points at my abandoned chair. "Sit the fuck down."

I yank my chair out so hard it bounces off the wall, leaving a dent in the plaster. Rock pulls the chair next to me around and leans on the back of it. "She told you she grew up around an MC, right?"

"Yeah, anyone can tell within five minutes of meeting her."

"Her father was a member of the Silver Saints."

Fuck. Anyone who knew about the Silver Saints knew there was nothing saintly about that crew. A bad feeling crawled over my skin. Whatever he was going to tell me would be horrible.

"Her father—Ryan "Bishop" Hurst—was one scary fuck. Grinder took me out there once when I was a prospect." He raises an eyebrow at me. "Bishop was their sergeant-at-arms." I'm not sure what to do with that information, so I nod for Rock to continue. "Shortly after I met him, he got put away on some bullshit charge. Should have been a three year stint at the most. His 'brothers' kept asking him to do so many 'favors' on the inside, he had years added to his sentence."

That's not an uncommon scenario in our world. "Fuck."

"Yeah. Trinity was eight when her dad went away. Her mother started earning her keep with the Saints on her back the day Bishop went inside." I don't bother asking how Rock knows this. Motherfucker has an uncanny way of collecting information when he wants to. "When Trinity's ten, someone burns down their trailer. Incidentally, this is right around the time her dad carried out his first 'favor.'"

"Payback?"

"Probably, or the mother trying to get insurance money. Her mom's not all there. She... Fuck, after the dad went away, her mom started tying Trinity to her bed at night so she didn't accidentally see something she shouldn't."

"Jesus Christ."

"So the fire starts. She can't get out 'cause she's tied to her fucking bed. Someone, I'm assuming the assholes who started the fire, hear her screaming and get her out. I don't think torching a kid was on their agenda."

"Where the fuck was her mother?"

"Oh, she made it out fine. 'Forgot' about Trin."

"Cunt." I may be crude, but that's a word I reserve for special occasions. Women who leave their little girls tied to beds are most definitely cunts.

"Yeah. So the Saints' president takes them in. I'm sure you can guess why. Her dad gets shanked not long after. She's got no protection at all. She's club property."

I shake my head, knowing what he's going to say next.

"They turned her out at sixteen."

All my life, I've lived with a fuckload of rage inside. It's how I got the name Wrath. It's why I indulge in underground fighting. To unleash all that anger I carry with me. But knowing exactly what those words mean, I realize I'd underestimated myself. Because every bit of fury I'd ever experienced up until today was a slight flicker of irritation compared to what races through me hearing the woman I love—

"They rape her?" I choke out.

Rock's eyes close and then open. "I don't think that's how she sees it. She went along with things so they didn't hurt her even worse. I think she has it in her head she's at fault somehow? But we both know she wasn't in any way able to consent to that shit."

"How many?" I whisper hoarsely, staring at my best friend.

Rock tilts his head and gives me a sad look. I see it in his face. They made her pull a train. The entire club would have gone at her. At six-motherfucking-teen. She was a kid, for fuck's sake. The same age Teller's mouthy little sister is now.

Christ, the daily beatings I took from my drunken father seem like a trip to Disneyland compared to Trinity's childhood.

"Let me finish. You understand what an MC like Silver Saints is going to do to a beautiful sixteen-year-old girl with no one to protect her?"

I nod because I'm too sick to speak. I've seen adult women pull that shit, and it ain't pretty. And I've been in some fucked-up shit myself. Half those fucked-up things were with the man right in front of me. But never someone unwilling or a kid—just, *no*.

"She got away at eighteen and worked her way here. You and I both know crews like the Saints don't enjoy losing property, especially property that can go to the cops and spill secrets. She grew up in that club-house, hearing and seeing all sorts of shit. Their president wanted her back—bad."

"They put a bounty on her."

"Yes—a big one. I don't think she understood the risk she was taking working the Blue Fox, even if it wasn't Saint's territory."

"Shit."

Rock nods sympathetically. "Yeah. While you were on that run, one of them spotted her in the bar. He threatened her—told her he was taking her back to that hellhole. She knew what was in store for her if she went back. She was terrified. She called and asked for my help." He pins me with a hard stare. "I couldn't let her get hurt. We needed someone to take care of the clubhouse. I offered her the job and our protection. Nothing more. She's the one who made herself available to the club, not me."

Fuck. "Why?"

"You lay claim on her?"

"No. But I told her I'd take care of her."

Rock looks at me in his special *Are you stupid?* way.

"Where is this sick fuck—"

Anger twists his face and his hands curl into the back of the chair he's leaning against. "Shut up," he spits out. "For once in your fucking life where she's concerned, listen to me. Are you going to step the fuck up and own her ass or not? 'Cause if not, stop wasting my fucking time reliving this shit." He shakes his head, then pins me with another glare. "I'll never forget the look on her face when she told me this story."

"If she'll let me, but Rock, you gotta know it's hard to forget she's been with some of my brothers." What the fuck? Why did I even say that? That's been my go-to excuse for why I'm a dick to her for so long, now the words fucking fly out all on their own.

"If that's all you're worried about after what I just told you, then you don't fucking deserve her, you asshole."

He waits for me to say something, but I shake my head. He's right.

"Trin has watched more girls go down on you over the years than I don't know what, so you'll just have to shut the fuck up about who she's been with. 'Cause it must have hurt her every time."

Every time I did it, I did it to piss her off because she fucking hurt me. *Holy fuck.* We're so goddamn dysfunctional and twisted. I don't know if I can ever fix us.

But I want to try.

"Tell me the rest."

He shrugs in his dickish manner he's perfected over the years. "What's to tell?"

I grit my teeth, because I know the fucker's going to make me work for every scrap of information.

After a brief staring contest, he finally continues. "That charter of the Silver Saints no longer exists. I put Tyler in the ground to cancel that fucking bounty and then slowly helped Stump's crew dismantle them. She and I haven't spoken about it since the day I told her the bounty was done and she was property of Lost Kings, free and clear."

"Why didn't I know? Why didn't you tell me? I would've wanted a piece of that."

"You were gone all the time, sorting shit out for the club. The club wouldn't have survived without you."

Yeah, and I know Rock was back here cleaning up the mess our last president and VP left. And apparently working side-by-side with Stump. Doesn't matter, I'm still fuckin' pissed.

"When you were here," he continues, "you two were too busy going to war and trying to see who could hurt who the most. I didn't think you gave a fuck."

"That's fucking bullshit and you know it."

"I thought I was protecting her. She'd been through enough." His shoulders lift in a careless shrug, and the urge to knock him the fuck out returns. "You gonna cry about it or move forward?"

"Fuck you."

This time Rock stares me down and I can see the misery on his face. "I've never seen that girl cry once in eight years. Not even when she told me this horrible story."

"You should have told me."

He doesn't react to my raised voice at all. "Can I finish?" he asks with a solemn expression. I know damn well Rock takes responsibility for everything bad that happens to any of us. I'm just so fucking furious and he's the most convenient place to direct my anger.

I nod for him to continue.

"Yesterday I found her crying, so whatever you did—"

"I didn't do anything, we—"

He shakes his head, cutting me off. "I don't want details. I didn't realize she never told you, until yesterday."

"So that's why you're finally coming clean, eight years later?"

"I was trying to protect her the best way I knew how."

He's right, we're a houseful of hustlers and thugs, not psychiatrists. "Fine. What do you suggest?"

He cocks his head in a way that lets me know I'm working his last fucking nerve. "Do I look like Dr. Fucking Phil to you?" he asks, echoing my thoughts.

I stay silent. I can wait him out.

A heavy sigh. "Fine. First of all, wipe that look off your face. She's a *survivor*. She doesn't need your pity. She sees it, she'll freeze up. Second, stop fucking around, or at least stop doing it in front of her."

"While she keeps fucking my brothers? Sounds legit," I say with a great deal of sarcasm.

One of these days, I should reevaluate my need to flirt with death. Rock cracks his knuckles like he's thinking of knocking *me* out. "I'll help you however I can. But you're going to have to lay claim on her sometime this century."

Whoa. "One step at a time, brother."

Rock's face turns a little less murderous. "You're going to have to cut her some slack. Understand the only value she thinks she has is for sex. From the time she was eight years old, she watched her mother earn her keep by spreading her legs for the club. And even though Trinity didn't have a choice in the matter, she's been doing the same since she was sixteen. It's the only way she knows how to feel accepted. She doesn't know anything else. You upset her, make her feel like shit, she's gonna jump on the first cock she sees. She thinks you're mad at her, she'll try to fuck you out of it. Try giving her something besides sex to feel good about."

Fuck me. I think of all the things I like about Trinity. Sex is very high on the list, but it's not the only thing. "Thanks for the psychology lesson. Smart move installing someone with her issues as club ass here."

Rock's eyes darken as he throws a scowl at me. "Fuck you. Would it have been better for her to get torn up and killed by the Saints? Let her find her way to some other MC that wouldn't give her an ounce of respect? That's what would have happened."

I think about how much Trinity hates being on her knees. Here, the guys accepted it. Maybe joked about her odd behavior behind her back a little, but another club? She might not be so lucky.

A flashback to the night we met grips me and fills me with disgust. What I thought she'd said as some weird challenge had probably been a result of the abuse she suffered as a kid.

Rock sighs. "At least she's safe here. She can say no if she wants to. Not one guy here will force himself on her, or drug her, or any of the other shit she went through."

I swallow back the tidal wave of guilt threatening to crash over me. "I want to make things work. I don't know what the fuck I'm doing though."

"Do any of us? Think about all the fucked-up shit she's been through. Her parents, the fire, her time with the Saints. Any one of those things would make some people give up. But she didn't. Fought her way out of that cesspool. Think about the person she is—sweet and smart. Loyal to the core. Always has a kind word for everyone. Always eager to help out. Can't imagine what this place would look like without her."

Every word's the truth. We all take Trinity for granted.

Rock raises his voice, in case he doesn't have my full attention. "Somehow she managed to finish high school in that fucked-up place. I know she'd been accepted to college but never got to go." Rock slaps the table to get me to look at him. "When she's testing you, set your massive ego aside and focus on those things."

"I will." And I meant it. We'd wasted too many years already.

From now on, I would do better for Trinity.

There was no other option.

CHAPTER ELEVEN

WRATH

I find Trinity in the downstairs laundry room, folding sheets, towels, and crap like that. It strikes me hard how much I hate she's basically a maid some of us use for sex. The biker thug in me knows that's what a club mama is, but the caveman obsessed with Trinity wants to burn the clubhouse to the ground and carry my woman off into the woods.

Shaking the awful feeling that settled over me after my conversation with Rock has been impossible. I see Trinity in a different light. *Not* pity. Admiration? I feel like such an asshole for ever being jealous of the way she fawns over the other guys. Fussing over them for their birthdays, the parties for Teller and Murphy when we patched them in. It's her way of showing appreciation for our shelter and protection.

Clearing my throat to get her attention, I relax my jaw and actually think about what I want to say.

"Hey, Wrath."

"Hey."

She sets down the towel and focuses her attention on me.

"I, uh, wanted to apologize for the other day."

She drops her gaze to the floor. "There's nothing to be sorry about. We had a good time."

My jaw clenches again. It was more than a good time for me. It fucking shattered me into a million pieces hearing her say how she trusted me from the second we met. Knowing the full extent of how badly I fucked up afterward doesn't sit well.

I want to make it up to her. "Well, how would you feel about spending more time together?"

She tilts her head and folds her arms over her chest. "Why?"

Because I need you.

"Well, you know I've got that big fight coming up, right?"

"Yeah," she answers slowly.

"I could use your help training, getting ready."

"I don't know anything about fighting."

"Not the fighting part." Shit, I have to make this up as I go along. "Like a personal assistant. Um, organizing my schedule of classes. Helping me with meal plans. That kind of stuff."

By the excited gleam in her eye, I know I've got her. Warming up to this plan, I start spouting off more nonsense. "I'm just worried 'cause the last fight was a little harder." By harder, I meant I actually broke a sweat, but she doesn't need to know that. "Gettin' older. I need to take this shit more seriously or I'll get hurt."

Her eyes widen as if the idea of me getting injured never occurred to her, which pleases me no end. I also know what a dick I'm being by using her concern to my advantage.

I'm completely confident in my ability to beat the shit out of whoever they put me up against. But this time, Trinity isn't slipping out of my grasp, so I'll use whatever weapons I have at my disposal.

"What would I do?"

"I've got a meal plan, but it's complicated." My lips curve into my best meathead smile. "You know, small meals every two hours with a balance of proteins, fats, and carbs according to when I work out. I'd love your help keeping it all organized."

"Okay."

"And I'll be working myself to exhaustion at the gym, so a ride, would be helpful too."

This serves two purposes for me. Keeping Trinity away from the other guys and spending lots of time together where she can watch me in all my sweaty glory.

"What about my stuff around here?"

"This is a priority, Trin. I already talked to Rock about it." That's not true, but I'm headed to talk to him next. "He's gonna talk to some of the girls and the prospects about pitching in more. Ordering supplies or whatever for the house, you can do from my office down at the gym."

"I'm not a nutritionist or anything."

"I know, but you're smart. If I give you some articles and stuff, you can make sense of all of it for me."

The corners of her mouth twitch up but she's still watching me with suspicious eyes. I guess over the years, I've given her the impression I don't think highly of her. When the exact opposite is true.

Even though I have ulterior motives, I'm excited about my plan. Trinity's smart and knows how to organize shit. Having her help while I condition myself for this fight excites the fuck out of me. I'm already in damn good shape, but I'll be the motherfuckin' Terminator by the time this fight rolls around.

Trinity

I'm not sure what to make of Wrath's proposal. Part of me is flattered. Part of me is cautious. We don't exactly always get along.

Can I tolerate spending days at the gym, watching Wrath punch things? Preparing himself to take punches? As complicated as our relationship is, I can't stand the thought of him hurt. If he thinks I can somehow help him, of course I want to.

And the hint of vulnerability Wrath showed when he asked me to help him went straight to my heart. His faith that I have some sort of skill that will be useful in helping him win his fight, makes me proud. From what he said, a win will mean a lot for the club.

There's no way I'd turn him down.

"Okay, I'm in."

A grin splits his face. "Fuck yeah, baby." He grabs me around the waist, yanks me to him, and crushes his mouth against mine.

He releases me so fast I wonder if I imagined it. The sweet burn of his kiss still lingers on my lips. My pulse is in overdrive.

He catches my eye. "We'll start Monday."

Settle down. This isn't about sex. It's about helping the club.

I can't get carried away and let myself fall into bed with Wrath again.

CHAPTER TWELVE

Four years ago...

Trinity

Wrath finally managed to open the gym he'd told me about when we first met. Every member of the Lost Kings came to Furious Fitness for the grand opening. They even included me. None of the other club girls were invited. A flicker of panic settled over me, but I knew Rock would never let anything bad happen to me. Once I had the invite, I began planning what to do. If left up to Wrath, I knew there would be no refreshments or anything.

I arrived at the gym at four to set stuff up. Just before six, Wrath's voice startled me out of my preparations.

"Trinity, you didn't have to do this."

My shoulders sagged. I knew he'd be pissed.

His hands gripped the tops of my arms and turned me around. "Thank you. This looks really nice."

I beamed at him. "I'm so happy for you. The place looks great. I know you've wanted this for a long time."

His face clouded over, and I regretted mentioning our time together four years ago. It was still a sore subject between us. Since the few fights back then, we'd barely spoken to each other, even though we lived in the

133

same house. He took every long-distance run the club had, so he wasn't around much.

I suspected it had everything to do with not wanting to see me. Not wanting to see what I'd become. After our last fight, it sank in how badly I'd fucked up. No one had ever loved me or given a shit about me before. So it was hard to understand Wrath's feelings might have run deeper than a few nights of hot sex.

Besides my generous rack and my willingness to spread my legs for him the night we met, what on earth could a guy like Wrath possibly like about me?

I couldn't figure it out. But it didn't matter because he was done with me. Especially once it spread through the clubhouse that I had also taken up with Z. He was fun in bed. Always made sure I came first, respected my boundaries and most importantly kept Teller from getting too close.

A few years later, Murphy joined in on my hook-ups with Teller. All of it good, but meaningless sex that helped me regain control and feel alive instead of the constant deadness I carried around inside. I had no clue what love was, but I *liked* them. Teller and I were closer. Murphy pretty much enjoyed getting off and getting gone. All things considered, I shouldn't have had any complaints.

Every few weeks or months, I'd run into Wrath. We'd stare knives at each other, and later I'd fall face down on my mattress, crying my eyes out. When I cleaned myself up, I'd find one of the brothers to help me ease the pain.

It worked.

In our really fucked-up world, it worked.

Sometimes he'd catch me upstairs, leaving one of the bedrooms. Those times were the worst, because shortly after, I'd catch him in the living room, getting a blowjob from one of the other club girls. Or worse, find him with one bent over the back of the couch while he rammed into her from behind. His accusing eyes always found mine. As if I'd done this to us alone.

The fact that he even wanted me at his gym the night of the grand opening meant a lot to me.

"You want to see the whole place?" he asked with a slight smile.

"Sure."

Wrath showed his place off with pride. Two classrooms, two locker rooms, a weight room, cardio room, and a fighting ring. It wasn't huge, but everything seemed to be top of the line. We ended the tour at his office.

"I'm going to grab my stuff from the car and change."

He tilted his head, glancing up and down at the jeans and sweatshirt I wore.

Heat streaked across my face as I scooped up my car keys. Pushing through the back door, I jogged out to the parking lot. I never dressed up for anything. Didn't really have much of a reason to. But tonight, I wanted to put a little more effort into my appearance.

The colors Wrath had chosen for the gym were royal blue and black—shocking, right?

I chose a royal-blue dress that straddled the line between sexy and classy. At least I thought it did. I didn't have a lot of experience with the latter.

After twisting my hair into a knot, I applied a bit more makeup than I normally bothered with. Then I slipped into a pair of black heels and checked my reflection in the full-length mirror behind the bathroom door.

I looked ridiculous.

Before I could chicken out and change back into my jeans, Wrath rapped his knuckles against the door.

"Trin, you okay?"

"Yeah." *Shit.* Avoiding the mirror, I stuffed everything back in my bag and opened the door.

Wrath staggered backward when he saw me.

"Don't," I growled.

"What? You look amazing. Beautiful. You dressed up for me? For my..." He trailed off.

At the time, I hadn't thought of it that way. But I guess, yeah, I had.

He held out his hand, and unsure of what he wanted, I hesitated, until he slipped my bag out of my grasp. "I'll put this in my office for you."

"Thanks."

"The rest of the guys should be here soon, and there are some other people I invited."

"Okay."

A slow, warm smile spread over Wrath's face. "I'm really happy you're here."

So was I.

WRATH

I couldn't keep my eyes off Trinity as she nervously floated around the room. She mainly stuck to hanging with my brothers, but I caught her talking to a couple of the other trainers too. I couldn't get over the sight of her all dressed-up. The bright-blue dress made her honey eyes and gold hair even more beautiful. The blue of the dress matched my gym's blue, and I wondered if she'd done that on purpose. Absurd as it was, she stunned me, and like a pathetic puppy, my eyes followed her everywhere.

To make this gym work, I went to people I knew outside the club—with the club's blessing, of course—for both investors and trainers. I knew enough about underground fighting and street brawling. I'm plenty lethal, but I knew fuck-all about professional regulations and shit like that.

Most of the guys I chose to work with me bordered the line between civilian and outlaw. Types who kept their mouths shut. Except for Whisper, the sergeant-at-arms of the Wolf Knights MC, there wasn't another biker involved.

A guy I'd known for a long time, Jake "Snake Charmer" Wallace, approached Trinity, and I struggled to focus on the conversation in front of me. Jake's call name would have been "pussy charmer" except no one wanted to announce that in the ring. I was familiar enough with his reputation that my blood started to boil watching him with his game face on, talking to my girl.

My girl. Ridiculous.

It was bad enough I knew she hooked up with my brothers on the regular. *This* ain't happening. Especially not in my gym.

"Excuse me, Marshall," I blurted out before stalking away.

Trinity glanced up as I approached. Her thankful expression calmed me down a notch or two. She had no interest in what Snake Charmer was selling.

"Hi, Wrath," she said with a nervous giggle while wrapping her fingers around my forearm. "Your friend Jake was telling me he's going to teach a self-defense class for women. That's pretty cool. Maybe I'll try it."

"No," I answered flatly.

Jake's lips quirked. Trinity flinched against me. Meeting her hurt eyes, I explained how things were going to work here. "Anything you want to learn, *I'll* teach you."

The tension eased from her face and she smiled. "Yeah, but Jake said we get to punch him. Are you going to let me punch you?"

"Yeah, baby." Any way I could get her hands on me was okay. The idea of training her appealed to me. A lot. So I slipped my hand around her waist and pulled her against me. She melted into my side, and just like that, the last thing on my mind was business.

Thankfully, the party was winding down. Every class for the next month had a full roster. We signed up a lot of new members and many other people said they'd be back. Overall, it was a success.

Teller offered Trinity a ride home, but to my surprise, she declined.

After locking up, I found her cleaning and packing stuff away.

"Stop, Trin. You've done enough tonight."

"I don't want to leave you a mess to clean up tomorrow," she huffed over her shoulder as she bent to pick up a discarded napkin.

In that position, her dress rose a few inches, giving me a glimpse of her sleek thighs. Thighs I hadn't seen in way too long.

"You're going to get your dress all dirty," I warned her. My voice came out low and scratchy, so I took a sip of water from the bottle in my hand.

She straightened and turned. "Oh yeah. I'm not used to wearing anything nice. I should change back."

"Don't."

She flicked a surprised glance at me, and I shrugged. "You look pretty."

A soft smile brightened her face. "Thank you."

She started walking toward my office, so I followed.

"What'd you think of Jake?" *Fuck.* Why the hell did I ask her that?

Her sexy laugh floated back to me. Husky enough to remind me of what it had felt like being wrapped up in the dark with her that night we spent up at Fletcher Park.

Instant hard-on.

"Good-looking guy. Cocky fucker though," she answered.

I deliberately ignored the "good-looking" part. "Thought you liked cocky guys?"

She slanted a look at me from under her lashes. "I don't have room in my life for any more."

I didn't know what to make of that. Was it her way of telling me she had no interest in anyone outside the club? Or that she was tired of us and wanted to leave?

I cocked my eyebrow at her. "You think he's good-looking though?"

She gave me a curious stare. "Jealous?" When I didn't answer, she sighed. "Geez, Wyatt, you know you're better than good-looking."

A jolt of arousal quickened my blood. The idea that she still found me attractive made me hard as steel.

My hands tingled with the need to touch her. So I did. I trailed my finger over her cheek and down to her shoulder. Her skin was as fine and silky as I remembered. I wanted to put my mouth all over her and see if she tasted as sweet as I remembered too.

"What are you doing?" she asked in a soft voice.

I yanked my hand away. What *was* I doing?

"I miss you, Trinity."

Her whiskey eyes widened in surprise. "You hate me."

Shit, that hurt. I'd spent so much energy being mad at her and, okay, pissed at myself too. But, "I could *never* hate you."

"You hate what I've become. You can't even stand to look at me half the time."

"That's not true."

She cocked her head. "How are you going to manage this place with all those long runs you take?"

Okay, weird shift in conversation. Those runs had been necessary for our club's survival. Especially in the early days. But it was intricate club business I couldn't explain. I hated her assumption that they were an attempt to get away from her.

"I'll probably scale them back a little. Teller and Murphy can take over."

A pained look flashed across her face when I said their names, and it pissed me the fuck off.

"Don't worry. I'm sure you'll find other fuck buddies."

She sucked in a deep, ragged breath before knocking me sideways with her next question. "Do you want me to leave the club?"

"What? No." Fuck, as much as I hated seeing her with my brothers, the idea of not seeing her at all scared the piss out of me.

"Because Whisper said—"

"No. Fuck no. You wouldn't leave four years ago when I begged you to. Why the fuck would you leave now? And to go whore for the Wolf Knights? What the fuck is wrong with you?"

"That's not what I was going to say, but thanks a lot, asshole." She grabbed her bag and tried to shove past me. My arm shot out and wrapped around her waist, pinning her in place. Girl had quite the temper. It was sexy as fuck.

"Let me go."

"No." I yanked her bag out of her hands and dropped it on the floor, then walked her backward until her ass bumped the wall. Her breath hitched and her eyes lifted to meet mine. Fucking hell, those goddamn honey eyes sparked with a fire that had me ready to violate her in the filthiest way.

Filling my hands with her perfect little ass, I lifted her, keeping her pinned to the wall. Her mouth opened to moan or protest, I wasn't sure, so I bent down to kiss her.

She responded immediately, curling her hand around the back of my neck, pulling me closer. Fingers wide, she raked her nails through my hair, sending tingles down my spine straight to my balls. My cock was so fucking hard, throbbing to be inside her.

Her legs rose and tightened around my hips. The movement pushed her dress up around her thighs. My hands slipped under the edge of the material, gliding over satin. My fingers traced the edge of her underwear while my hips kept her in place. Losing control, I snapped the thin strips of material at her hips and dropped the scrap to the floor.

Her head thunked against the wall. "Wyatt," she moaned.

Oh fuck. It'd been way too long since I'd heard my name from her sweet mouth.

I set her down.

"Get your dress off."

She stared up at me with dazed eyes. Slowly, her hand moved to the hidden zipper at her back. With painful slowness, she eased it down, then pulled the dress up over her head and tossed it on my desk.

"Bra too."

Again, she just stared at me while doing what I asked.

When I finally had her naked before me, I took a moment to absorb every stunning inch of her. She cocked her body to the side, trying to hide her scars from my gaze, but I turned her to face me and tipped her head up.

My mouth slammed down over hers. Her hands immediately went to my shoulders as she struggled to get my shirt up. We broke long enough for me to get it off. Then I was on her again. Tongue deep in her mouth, hands full of her tits. She moaned into me, and once again, my hands slid to her ass. I lifted and pinned her against the wall, my cock grinding into her hot center. She clung to my shoulders and wrapped her legs around me.

I released her long enough to roll a condom down my dick, then bent to suck at her nipples. She squirmed against me, but I stilled her with one deep thrust. I set a sharp, frantic pace. Cupped her ass harder. Fucked her harder. All my energy focused on driving into her slick, tight cunt. Her head rolled back against the wall, and I ducked my head to nip at her breasts.

It didn't take long for her to go over the edge. She gripped my shoulders harder, ground her hips into me, buried her lips against the curve of my neck, and screamed.

"Eyes on me, Angel Face."

Dazed, it took her a second, but then she met my gaze. I slowed my frantic thrusting. "I want you to come again."

She shook her head. "Can't."

I slammed into her. "Yes, you can. Keep those eyes on me while you do it."

Relentless, I drove into her as she stared into my eyes. It didn't take long for her mouth to open and let out a sharp scream.

Staring into her eyes, I was so fucking close. Close to coming. Close to breaking.

I pulled out and released her. She sagged against the wall. "Wyatt?"

Grabbing her hips, I pulled her with me and bent her over the edge of my desk. Wrapping my big hands around her waist, I tilted her the way I wanted and slammed up inside her again.

This was better. Grunting like an animal, a few strokes later, I shuddered and fell against her back. My mouth found its way to her neck and sucked on her sensitive skin, making her wriggle against my spent cock.

"Fuck, Trinity." I eased out of her and tried to gather my scattered thoughts. "Thanks for helping me christen my desk."

Her body stiffened. Fuck, that came out colder than I intended.

She straightened up, tugged her dress on and smoothed it over her hips. "Yeah, no problem," she said without turning around.

"Trin—"

"Can I go now?"

What the fuck? Like I'd held her here against her will? "Sure, babe. Whatever."

She dipped down to pick up her bag and keys. A soft sniffle drifted back to me.

Then she was gone.

CHAPTER THIRTEEN

Present day...

Trinity

It's been four years since I set foot in Wrath's gym. The place looks pretty much the same as it did then. Someone has done a good job keeping the place tidy, which doesn't surprise me. Wrath has always been a rather precise guy.

He leads me into his office, where I set my purse in the bottom drawer of his desk. Heat streaks through me when I remember him bending me over and fucking me on the desk. I flick my eyes up and find him watching with an intensity so deep I know he's remembering that night too.

"How many other chicks have you bent over this desk?" *Fuck. Why the hell did I ask him that?* I don't want him to think I'm jealous or that I even remember that night.

Beyond those thoughts, I don't think I can handle hearing the answer.

"No one since you, babe."

Oh, wow. Totally not what I expected him to say. He's probably lying, but I appreciate the effort not to hurt my feelings.

Unsure of what's next, my hands fidget. Wrath watches me for a few long seconds before meeting my eyes.

"It's okay if you don't believe me right now. You will."

Yeah right. Maybe I'll sprout some wings and fly home later too.

Except Wrath doesn't lie. You would think that's an admirable quality in a man, but it can be pretty fucking annoying. People lie to avoid hurting other people's feelings—Wrath doesn't give a fuck about feelings. People also lie to avoid getting in trouble—Wrath fears nothing.

"Do you want to look around?" he asks, startling me out of my thoughts.

"Sure."

I'm shocked to run into Jake, the trainer I met when Wrath opened the gym. His flirting was charming and nonthreatening.

"Trinity, right? Wow, took you a long time to come in for those self-defense classes."

Wrath is quick to shut Jake down. "She's here to work with me to get ready for the fight."

One corner of Jake's mouth slowly curls up. "Sure. Good to see you."

When Jake pushes through the locker room door, Wrath shakes his head. "That fucker never quits."

"Well, at least I've still got it."

He tilts his head to the side, watching me with a curious expression. "Babe, you don't got it. You *are* it."

Maybe one day I'll believe it. Today isn't that day.

I spend my afternoon in his office, doing research and working out meal plans. I'll need to do some grocery shopping later.

In the middle of the day, when it's quiet, Wrath pops in the office. "Do you want to try those self-defense moves?"

"Now?"

He shrugs. "Yeah, we got another two hours or so until it gets busy in here again."

"Okay, give me a minute."

I meet him in front of one of the heavyweight bags. He's got a man-shaped dummy waiting for me too.

With calm patience I wouldn't think Wrath capable of, he talks me through a bunch of moves. Each one involves him touching me or, worse, pressing himself tight against my body.

Desire swirls through me like a tornado. Wrath, warm, solid, sexy, and lethal, is too much to take. I want him so much. Want him to want me just as much. Despite the soul-shattering sex we had a few days ago, he hasn't made a move on me. Can't blame him after I made a big fuss about how we were "friends" again.

What else could we be? I'd fucked up any chance of ever being his ol' lady. He didn't seem to be in a hurry to find one anyway—and dammit, when I thought of him with someone else, it left me tattered inside. Our only option was to be friends.

If we could be friends who fucked from time to time, that would be even better.

"Trin? Are you paying attention?"

Dammit. His mouth is so close it's taking every bit of willpower I have not to taste him. I want him so much it hurts.

His brows furrow, and he brushes the hair off my sweaty forehead. "You okay, Angel Face?"

Why? Why do tears threaten to embarrass the crap out of me when he uses that old term of endearment? I never understood what he found so angelic about me, but I always loved hearing him say it anyway.

My heart thuds as I struggle to come up with an answer. "I'm okay. I just... I don't have your endurance I guess." Wow, is that the truth.

Concern darkens his eyes from ocean to marine blue. He pulls away from me, and instantly I miss his body heat.

"I'm sorry. I got carried away. We're supposed to be working *me* to exhaustion. Not you."

Almost dizzy with the rush of emotions he stirs up, I drop my gaze to the mat.

"Let me get you some water."

When he steps away, I'm finally able to look up. Sweet mother mercy, he's ridiculously sexy. What the hell was I thinking agreeing to accompany him every day? I've done lots of stupid things in my life. This has to be one of the worst.

He returns with a guilty smile and passes me a bottle of water. My heart's still pounding, and of course, he notices. He reaches out and traces his finger down my neck and over my collarbone. "You sure you're okay?"

This time it's more than concern I see lurking in his gaze. For much longer than I'm comfortable with, he studies me, and it makes me wonder.

WRATH

For the second day in a row I've got a happy buzz stirring inside me. I enjoy having Trinity in my gym with me.

Of course, a lot of lustful urges are also stirred up watching her bend over and store her purse in my bottom desk drawer.

I made a stupid decision once she agreed to help me. After thinking about my conversation with Rock, I decided Trinity and I wouldn't be having sex. Unless she initiates it. Yes, I gave myself that out. I'm not completely insane.

It seems like the best way to show her how I really feel. That she means more to me than a way to get off. That I like her and want to be with her no matter what.

Against my will, my eyes track her every movement in my office. Going through those self-defense moves with her yesterday had been a mistake. It put my "no sex" rule to the test. I spent half the night jerking off under the cold spray of my shower.

She bends at the waist and picks up the bag she brought with her. "Can I use the locker room?"

"Yeah, why?"

"Well, you brought me to a gym. Am I allowed to use it?"

Inwardly, I groan. Just what I need. "Sure. You want to wait until later?" When the gym will be clear of my nosy pervert colleagues.

"Uh, yeah. I can wait. Can I use your computer today to do a few things?"

"You don't have to ask. You can use anything you need, Trin."

Her lips curve into a smile. "Thanks."

She drops into my chair.

I like the way she looks behind my desk. Why didn't I think of this sooner?

We don't see each other much after I leave her to do her thing in my office. I spend my time in the gym going over moves with Jake. As much of a pain in the ass as he can be, he's a great trainer. He's smaller and quick on his feet, so he's a good sparring partner for me to work on a couple issues. He also knows exactly how to needle me to keep me motivated but not kill him.

"Trinity's a pretty girl. She still single?" he asks while I'm busy hanging from a pull-up bar with a stability ball tucked between my ass and ankles.

"No," I huff out. The reason I'm not dropping the ball and kicking his ass is I know he's just fucking with me. If he were serious, he wouldn't have described Trin as a "pretty girl." Something along the lines of "hot piece of ass" would be more his style.

Trinity wanders over while Jake's unleashing his inner sadist by pushing me through "one more set" of bear crawls. My skin prickles the second she's within reach, and I power up off the mat.

"Everything okay?" I ask.

Jake raises an eyebrow at me. "Did I say you were finished, son?"

Now he's asking for an ass kicking.

Trinity snickers but runs her hand over her mouth to hide it. It's an endearing gesture and makes me want to grab her and kiss her.

"He's training you?" She glances between the two of us, and I shrug.

"Don't worry. I'll spar with him later and knock his ass out."

Her eyes widen in surprise, and she glances at Jake again. "How can you go up against each other? You're not evenly matched."

The corner of Jake's mouth curls into a smirk.

"Go ahead, Snake Charmer, lift your shirt."

Jake loves showing off his abs and how cut he is.

"It's not always about size, Trinity," Jake explains, dropping his shirt.

"Yeah, I know." She glances at me. "You ever have him spar with Teller?"

I can only guess why she's asking, and it burns my ass. "Yes."

Jake nods in agreement. "He's a scary little prick. So's his Irish buddy."

Trinity laughs, and I understand why. She's only ever really seen one side of them.

My attention is finally drawn to the papers Trinity has in her hands. "What's that?"

"Oh, it's nothing. I didn't realize Jake was already… You asked me to put some stuff together… So never mind."

She folds the papers in half before I snatch them out of her hands.

"Ow! Thanks for the paper cuts, asshat."

Jake chuckles and grabs her hands to look them over. I can't wait to get in the ring with him later and kick his ass while Trinity watches.

I'm impressed with what she printed out. I knew she'd be good at this. She's got a week's worth of circuit training exercises broken into different ones on each day. Each circuit includes a balance of strength and endurance exercises. I glare at Jake, and he takes the hint to get lost.

"You've done your homework," I say, handing the papers back to Trin.

The corner of her mouth twitches down in disappointment. "You don't think it's any—"

"Is that what I said?" I hate snapping at her, but sometimes it's the only way to get through her self-doubt.

"No."

"Where'd you find some of these?"

"Are they too advanced for you?"

I tilt my head and stare at her. "Seriously?"

She chuckles. "Good, then call me when you're going to try the Front Lever. It looks sexy." She spins away and heads back to the office.

I'm stopped from following her by a rush of kids filling up the place.

Three o'clock is our busiest time. Lots of guys and a few girls from the local high school stop in. Some are punks. Some actually have potential. All their parents have deep pockets. There's a reason I stuck my gym in this suburban armpit.

Jake works with most of them.

At five today, I have a class of kids that come from downtown Empire. Each one of *them* has potential. None of them have a spare dime. Am I training them for free out of the goodness of my heart? No. It's an effective way to find potential prospects. Whisper's here by this point and usually helps out, when he's not seeking out lonely housewives to stick his dick in.

Maybe ten minutes before class ends, I glance up and find Trinity standing in the doorway, arms crossed over her chest and a solemn expression in place.

Unfortunately, Whisper notices her too.

When the class ends, I still have to spend some time talking stuff over with a few of my kids. Normally, I don't mind. Out of the corner of my eye, I see Trinity approaching and wrap things up.

"I had no idea," she says.

I take the towel out of her outstretched hand and rub it over my face. "What's that, babe?"

"You. Teaching kids. Being civil."

Whisper chooses that exact moment to join our conversation. "Lookin' good, Trinity. What're you doing here?"

"She's with me."

Trinity turns pink. "I'll be in the office."

When she's gone, I poke my finger in Whisper's chest. "Stay the fuck away from her."

His eyes widen and he steps back, hands in the air. "Chill. What's up?"

"Nothing. She's helping me out with some stuff. That's all."

Trinity

Nerves have been rattling through me ever since I handed Wrath those exercise drills. He knows what he's doing. I don't. I probably insulted him.

I don't know what to make of the ten kids I caught Wrath teaching self-defense moves to. With his impatience and general dislike of most of the human population, he's the last person I'd expect to spend an hour a week with a bunch of sullen teenagers.

Who knew?

A thump against the door makes me glance up. Jake's filling the doorway, a mischievous grin curving his ridiculously sexy mouth. "How's Wrath's girl doin'?"

Stunned, I sit there with my mouth hanging open. "I'm not Wrath's girl. Why would you say that?"

He stands straighter and enters the room. "Come on. It's so obvious."

"How? Did he tell you that?"

Jake chuckles and shakes his head. "He doesn't need to say anything. He's never brought a woman to work with him. Never threatened to dismember me over one." He jerks his chin at the desk. "Never lets any of *us* use his office."

Wrath's a quiet, sneaky fucker when he wants to be. One minute, Jake's standing in front of me sharing his asinine theory, and the next, Wrath's behind him with an elbow around Jake's neck. "You've got your own office, dickhead," he growls at him. Jake's apparently as stupid as he is good looking because he laughs.

I shoot out of the chair so fast it hits the back wall. "Wyatt, stop before you hurt him."

"I can get out anytime I want, Trin," Jake assures me.

Wrath tightens his arm, and Jake's smug face vanishes. "You sure about that, Snake Charmer?"

Jake gasps. "Don't. Want. To. Embarrass you in front of your girl."

"Keep telling yourself that," Wrath grumbles, releasing him.

Jake stumbles forward coughing and laughing.

I cross my arms over my chest and glare at Wrath. "What's the matter with you?"

His eyes widen into this boyishly innocent face he makes when he knows he's been up to no good. "What? Just practicing my choke hold."

Jake flashes a thumbs-up at me as he leaves.

"Feel better, caveman?"

"Much. Why was he bothering you?"

"He wasn't. We were just talking."

He stares at me in disbelief. "About what?"

"How to get a quickie in without you noticing," I snap. "I'm getting tired of you acting like I'm going to jump on every guy I see."

He drops the cocky smirk. "That's not what I was thinking at all, Trin."

He's full of shit, and we both know it. "How come I never knew about your soft side?"

He makes a big show of patting himself down and checking over himself. "Nope, nothing on me's soft."

"No? So what do the kids in your kiddie class call you?" I prompt with an exasperated sigh.

His forehead wrinkles. "Mr. Ramsey, what else?"

I don't know why, but I find that insanely funny.

As I keep laughing, he smirks at me. "And they're hardly kids. Most of them are an arrest away from prison."

"Please. One of them looked barely old enough to shave."

He chuckles. "That's Twitch. He's very skilled at lock-picking and breaking into safes."

"People still do that?"

"It's a dying art." He shrugs his massive shoulders.

I finally get it. "You're looking for potential prospects."

"Ding, ding, ding." He grins at me. "How do you think I found Birch?"

Never gave it much thought, honestly. I still don't buy it. He was enjoying himself way too much. "Still, that's a lot of time to devote, hoping to find one or two prospects."

His face lights up in his favorite cocky smirk. "Anything for the club, babe."

WRATH

I nearly trip Saturday morning when I enter the kitchen and find Trin bent over with her head in the refrigerator. She's shoving what looks like ten dozen cartons of eggs inside. Or trying to.

"Whatcha doin', Trin?"

"Can you help me?"

I cross the room in a hurry and take the cartons from her. "What's all this?"

"For you. I found this great website with meal plans during pre-fight training. I haven't had a chance to shop all week, so I got up early today and did it. You'll be eating lots of egg whites, lean protein. I got these from the farmer down the road, so there's no nasty antibiotics or anything."

I'm so stunned I don't know what to say. This is Trinity though. If you give her something to focus on, she fucking runs with it. Just like she did with the circuits she put together for me. My core's still burning from the Front Levers she thought were so sexy.

I manage to mumble out a thank you. While I'm waiting for her to do whatever she's doin' in the refrigerator, I spy a box of what looks like chicken breasts on the counter.

"Chicken?"

"Mm-hmm." She nods absently while she's rearranging stuff to make room for the eggs.

I've always been a clean eater before a fight. No drinking. No weed. I guzzle a gallon and a half of water every day. I don't tend to eat fast food even when I'm not training, so that's never an issue. But Trinity? Girl's taking things to a whole new level for me. I'm impressed and some other emotion I can't really put my finger on.

Touched?

"I went to the farmer's market too. Kale." She shakes a bunch of the dark, leafy greens at me. "Lots of kale. It's supposed to be super good for you."

Of course Z has to walk in at that exact moment and ruin everything.

"Looking good, Trin," he says to her ass.

Without turning around or taking her head out of the fridge, she calls out, "Hey, Z."

Z makes a what-the-fuck face at me, and I shrug. "Uh, brother, why you holding like a thousand eggs there?"

Trinity tsks at us. "It's only five dozen, asshat. Okay, I think I got room. Can you hand them to me one by one?"

Actually, it's awkward to juggle them all. Z makes himself useful for a change.

She grins at us when she's finished. "I'll make up a bunch of stuff and pack it up so it's ready during the week."

"Damn, Trin. If I take up fighting, will you feed me all my meals too?" Z asks.

I hate the way she giggles and shoves him away. It's just a goofy friend gesture. Still fuckin' hate it.

When they're done messing around, she takes a folder off the counter and hands it to me. "Here's the meal plan we're following this week."

Z plants a quick kiss on her cheek. "Gotta go, mama. Later, bro," he says, waving at me.

Happy he's finally leaving, I have trouble focusing on the papers Trin handed me. When I glance up, she's nervously chewing on her thumb.

"Do you not like it? I got it from—"

"No, it's great."

"You're okay with the fish?"

"Yup, that's fine. There's not much I won't eat, Trin."

Her mouth curls into a wicked grin. "That's not true. You never eat my ginger cookies."

That makes me laugh because she bitches every Christmas about how I won't even try one. "Okay, this year, I promise I'll try *one*."

My promise puts a smile back on her face.

CHAPTER FOURTEEN

WRATH

I'm not sure how the bitch standing in front of me managed to find her way to our clubhouse again. She's been here once or twice before with Roxy or Ginger. Tonight she was bold enough to come up and introduce herself. Cherry. Probably as fake as her hair, which is like something straight out of a circus—red, wide, and curly.

She leans into me and in an ear-splitting whine asks, "What's your name, big guy?"

Why am I doing this? My eyes skip through the room, seeking Trinity, but not finding her.

"Wrath," I finally answer.

"What? Like the thing you put on your door at Christmas?"

Christ this bitch is dumb.

"That's a wreath, babe. Wrath."

"What's that mean?"

Seriously? Where do these chicks come from?

The memory of the first time Trinity and I met comes rushing back.

"Brrr. Scary. Are you an angry fellow?"

Jesus she was so fucking cute.

Cherry's still yapping away, but I barely hear a word passing her tacky red lips. I scan the room again for Trinity.

A few months ago, my plan would have consisted of something designed to keep Cherry's mouth full, eliminating her endless yammering. But I can't call up an ounce of interest tonight. My dick's begging me to stick him anywhere but in this dumb bitch. There's only one girl I want.

"Want me to show you how I got my nickname?" she asks with a flutter of her eyelashes.

Please. Every MC I've ever heard of has at least one club whore named Cherry. She's not the special snowflake she thinks she is.

She blinks several times, waiting for my answer. Except, one of her spidery lashes must be fake, because half of it's hanging at a weird angle. *Gross.*

There's not one fake thing about Trinity.

"'Scuse me, Cherry, I gotta go find someone."

"Okay. Come back and see me when you're done." She trails her fingers over my bicep and I give her a curt nod.

It's a small party, more girls here than guys. The perfect set up to indulge in some of my usual favorite filthy activities.

Not tonight.

Kitchen seems like the most logical place to find Trinity.

And that's exactly where I find her. Sitting on the counter. With Z between her knees. They're not naked or anything. They seem to only be talking, but their pose is awfully intimate for some chit chat.

Trinity and I have been spending every day together. We've argued a couple times, but it seems to blow over quick. Body-wise I feel better than I have in years and I attribute it to her hard work. We haven't once spoken about her relationship with any of the guys. We haven't fucked again either. I'm starting to wonder if that old superstition about no sex before a fight is true. I'm coiled so tight, I might explode any second.

I clear my throat and they glance over. Z lifts a corner of his mouth in a smirk. "What's up, brother?"

What's up is, *Why the fuck you two all up in each other's shit?* is what I want to say. Instead, I jerk my thumb toward the hallway. "The chick with the clown hair's fuckin' annoying."

Z chuckles and steps back. I notice Trinity staring at a bandage wrapped around her hand.

"You okay, Trin?" When the fuck did she hurt herself? Why is Z the one fixin' her up instead of me?

She tips her head up and gives me a tired smile. "Yeah. I cut myself."

"Just patching her up," Z explains.

"Wrath! Brother, I need you." Dex calls to me from outside. God dammit. With a lingering glance at Trinity, I storm out the back door.

"What?" I snap the second my boots crunch down on the gravel. Dex points at two hangarounds trying to bareknuckle box or some shit in the driveway. "Why is this my problem?"

"Come on, one of them's gonna get hurt."

They both look old enough and no one seems to be forcing them, so it ain't my problem at all. "So?"

Stalking back inside, I find the kitchen empty. The fuck? Pushing through the crowd in the living room, I catch a glimpse of Trinity heading upstairs with Z. *Motherfuckinghell.* This can't be fucking real. We'd been doing real good lately. What did I do now?

A soft touch on my arm stops me from tearing upstairs after them. "Hey," Cherry says, her freshly glossed lips curling into a smirk.

Well, at least I have a way to get even.

If this is getting even, it's pretty fucked up. Because it feels more like punishment. Except I did it to myself.

Cherry's eager enough. Drops to her knees the second I close my bedroom door. Doesn't bitch about the rubber I hand her either. Her eyes are still freaking me the fuck out though. She fixed the one lash, but they're still all spidery and creepy. Each time she glances up with what I assume she thinks is coyness, I feel skeeved. Maybe that's my own doing because I know how wrong this is.

Her hands work my belt loose and I close my eyes pretending I'm anywhere else. *With* anyone else, so I can get this over with, and get her out of my room. Revulsion burns the back of my throat like fire.

I'm hating every second of this whole thing. Not even my suspicion that Trinity's across the hall doing something similar, makes it any better.

My hand intercepts Cherry's as she dives for my dick. "Stop."

She blinks and stares up at me.

"Come on, get up." I wrap my hand around her bicep and pull her off the floor.

"Wait. What's wrong?"

"Nothing. It's not you—" It is absolutely her. She's not Trinity. But I don't see a reason to be cruel to this chick I barely know.

Her hand reaches for my crotch again. "You probably just drank too much. Give me a second."

I block her easily and squeeze harder. "That's *not* the problem."

Since she can't seem to find the door, I open it for her. At the same time, Z's door swings wide. Trin pops out, laughing and thanking Z for something. Both of their gazes lock on Cherry leaving my room. Trin's jaw drops. The devastation on her face cuts me deep. I slam the door.

Fuck.

Dropping on my bed, elbows on my knees, my head falls forward into my hands. She's not going to care that I didn't go through with it. Hell, she's not even going to believe me if I explain myself.

What the fuck did I just do?

Trinity

Sharp pain throbs in my chest at the sight of Cherry leaving Wrath's room. I can guess what happened on the other side of that door. I glance back at Z. He only brought me up here to re-bandage the cut on my hand. It wouldn't stop bleeding so he wanted to use some liquid bandage he had stashed away. Obviously Wrath thought Z and I were up to something more.

We've been spending every waking moment together training for his fight. Stupid me thought maybe it meant something.

Clearly it didn't.

First chance he got, he brought one of the newer girls up to his room. I get it. We've been working hard but haven't slept together. But why didn't he ask me up here?

Once Cherry's out of sight, I cross the hallway and rap on the door.

"Trinity, don't bother," Z warns.

Inside, Wrath snaps. "What?"

The sight of a condom wrapper on the floor assaults my eyes.

He's sitting on the edge of the bed with his head down. Looking as close to broken as I've ever seen him.

Hardening my heart, I sharpen the blade of my tongue. "Have fun breaking in the new girl?"

He slants a look at me. "You're up to your old tricks, so why not?"

Holding up my injured hand, I quietly inform him, "Z had some liquid bandage in his room he wanted to use, because my cut wouldn't stop bleeding. But it's good to know what you really think of me."

Disgust, horror, self-loathing all flash across his face. Or maybe that's my wishful thinking. I want him to hurt. Because he's crushed me and made me feel pathetic and stupid. Whatever lines we'd blurred these last few days of working together to get him ready for his fight, he just replaced with barbed wire.

I want to shake off the feeling of betrayal. We were after all, trying this friends thing out. Obviously, it's not working. The idea that he could ever want me to be more was ridiculous. Foolish. I'm nothing but another Cherry or Roxy to him. It's time to accept that.

He did me a favor, really. Clearly I needed to be reminded of what my place in the club really is.

Choking back a sob, I back out of the door. Heat radiates over my face, burning my eyes, blurring my vision. Like a fucking moron, I just spent ten minutes downstairs telling Z how Wrath and I have been getting along so well and maybe...

Dammit, I'm such an idiot!

I refuse to cry in front of either of them. Z will look at me with pity eyes and try to cheer me up with a joke. I can't stand the thought of it.

Nope. I'll suck those tears in until I'm alone in my room, where no one can see me. I can't afford to show weakness around anyone in this house.

Stumbling downstairs, the sickening images of what just happened in his room invade my imagination. What I *should* have done is brushed it off. I should have spun around, grabbed Z's hand, shoved him into his room and fucked him loud and hard. I should find Teller, or a prospect or anyone with a dick to help me ease this pain.

I pass Cherry on the way to my room. Everything in me screams to take her to the floor and choke the ever-living shit out of her. But I hold my head up and ignore her. It's not her fault.

The fault's all mine.

Part Two

Our rocky road
to forgiveness.

CHAPTER FIFTEEN

WRATH

One idea after another flips through my brain as I sit in my room staring at the floor. How can I make this up to Trinity? Nothing I come up with seems appropriate. The doorway is empty. She'd gone without closing the door. Z stands across the hall staring at me.

"What the hell is going on with you two?"

My fists clench at my sides. "Don't know, brother," I answer.

Shaking his head like I'm the stupidest fucker he's ever known, he heads back downstairs.

Physical pain burns through my chest. My fucking temper and inability to ever stop to think things through fucking ruined things. Again.

The next morning, Trinity's waiting for me on the couch in the living room. The same way she's done every morning since we started training together. Relief floods through me. I fully expected her not to show.

She glances up when she hears me. A slight smile curves her lips, but I can tell it's forced.

No reason to play games. "Trinity, I'm sorry."

She cocks her head to the side and arches an eyebrow. "What for?"

I take a few steps closer to her. "Last night. I didn't mean—"

"You didn't mean what? To stick your dick in a girl that minutes before you said was annoying? Or you didn't mean for me to catch you? Or you didn't mean to have such a low opinion of me? Which is it?"

Shit. I want to tell her nothing happened. Except it's a fucking lie. I had every wrong intention when I brought Cherry into my room. Stopping her before she closed her mouth over my dick doesn't exactly make me a saint. "Don't. It's not like that."

Trinity rolls her eyes and flings a hand out. "You tried out one of the new whores. Good for you. I know how you like to break them in first. It's what you do. I'm a big girl. I know the rules."

I'm actually getting a little turned on seeing her all fired up, because it means she actually gives a fuck. Except I hate that I hurt her. *Again.*

"Trinity—" I take a step toward her, holding out a hand, but she bolts off the couch and backs away from me.

"Are we going to the gym or not?"

Hold up. What? "You're still going to help me?"

She glances around the room before answering. "Yeah. I promised to help. I owe it to *the club* to follow through. We're nothing to each other. It's none of my business who you fuck."

My eyes close trying to block out her flat voice. As much as I don't want her mad at me, it kills me that she thinks she means nothing to me, when she means everything.

This indifference is horrible. I'd rather she go back to angry. I'd rather she punch me, kick me, scream at me. Anything but this flatness.

"It's okay. We can take the day off."

She holds my gaze for a minute and nods. "Fine. I'll see you tomorrow."

CHAPTER SIXTEEN

WRATH

Our president is a no-show for yet another party. His *own* birthday party, no less. Sending him a reminder text gets me nothing.

Fucker.

Trinity and I have reached a truce since the Cherry incident. We're not quite back to where we were—yet.

I've been trying to make things up to her. Show her how much she means to me. Make her happy. Some days it works. Then others, she seems to remember what an asshole I am and puts her guard up.

If Rock ruins this party Trinity's been planning all week, I'm gonna give serious consideration to kicking his ass.

"He'll be here," I reassure her.

"Do you think he's gonna bring Hope with him?" Trin sounds eager to see Rock's woman, and that surprises me.

"To a club party? Fuck, no. No way is he gonna expose his precious Miss Priss to this shit."

That's exactly why I think it's a perfect time to remind Rock of what he's been missing. When Z calls and asks if it's all right for Dex to let Inga and some skank friend of hers up to the clubhouse as a birthday surprise, I say hell fuckin' yes. Rock thinks it's some sort of secret that he hasn't nailed any of his regulars in the last year or so. Been saving himself like some sort of fuckin' virgin for his weddin' night. Although, I gotta give him credit, I've never had that sort of self-control.

Never wanted to before.

Without his delicate little flower around, Inga should have a shot.

Trin touches my arm, thankfully pulling me away from my thoughts. I've been obsessing over my brother's sex life more than I care to think about tonight.

"Did he answer you?"

Fuck me, I don't think I've ever known anyone in the life who wears their heart on their sleeve the way Trinity does.

"Not yet, babe."

My phone buzzes.

Rock: Be there in 20.

I nod at Trinity. "He's on his way."

She's grinning from ear to ear, and while I understand their relationship a little better since Rock and I had our sit down, sometimes it still annoys the fuck out of me.

"You gonna put this much effort into my birthday?" Shit, I didn't mean for that to come out so harsh.

"If you let me, yeah."

"I ain't ever stopped you. You've always been too busy fawning over everyone else—"

"Are you fucking serious? Why are you doing this tonight?"

I don't want to fight with her. "I'm going outside."

I storm out the back door before that sexy fucking pout of hers changes my mind.

Fuckingfuckfuckfuck!

Rock's bike pulls into the parking area stopping me dead in my tracks. Hope's on the back.

Shit's gonna get awkward tonight.

Maybe Inga will be enough to scare Hope away for good. Because this bullshit with him not paying attention and dropping his work in my lap is pissing me off to no end.

And it's *this* chick's fault.

Jesus Christ, he can't keep his fucking hands off her for a minute. I whistle as I walk over to get his attention.

"Prez," I greet—you know, just in case he's forgotten what his fucking role in this club is.

I say hello to Cinderella with a sneer and then ignore her. Rock glares at me. Hope ignores both of us and pulls something out of the pack on Rock's bike and he takes it from her.

"What's in the box, prez?"

"Birthday present from Hope," he answers as he slips his arm around her.

Huh.

I follow them in, convinced she'll lose her shit when she steps inside and witnesses what's going down. Parties have gotten significantly raunchier in his absence.

Rock gets attacked at the door. Hope should freak out any minute.

But she doesn't. Rock sits her down in a far corner and motions me over.

I meet him halfway and he slaps my shoulder, holding on harder than he needs to. "Watch over Hope. I'll be right back." He tightens his grip. "Watch your fuckin' mouth and treat her with respect."

"Oh, ab-so-lute-ly, prez."

"I'm not joking, fucker. You're the only one in this room I trust with her right now."

Okay, that sticks in my throat a little.

As I approach her, something resembling guilt touches me. She looks completely forlorn and out of place.

"Didn't think this would be your scene," I shout over the music as I drop down next to her.

She hesitates. Good, I want her to be afraid of me.

"How long have you and Rock known each other?" she asks.

Long enough to know you won't survive in our world. "Long damn time."

"Did you meet through the club?"

Her question surprises me. "No. We knew each other before." I nod at Z who's across the room auditioning potential fuck-n-gos. "Knew Z too. We all prospected together. Very different time," I add.

"Oh."

"You know much about MCs, Hope?" I don't even have to ask, I know the answer.

"No. I mean, only what I've learned from Rock."

Sounds about right and I can almost guarantee Rock has given her a carefully edited version of what the club is about. I let my gaze wander over her in a way designed to make her uncomfortable and I'm rewarded with her turning pink.

"What are you doing here then?" I ask.

She tilts her head, confused. "I'm here with Rock."

No shit. "What's a woman like you doing with my president? You guys got nothing in common."

Her eyes gloss over. Great, she's a crier. Girl ain't gonna last a minute here. I've barely gotten started. She blinks rapidly and sits up a little straighter. "I like him, and he likes me."

Is she fucking blind? *Like?* So fucking obsessed with her he almost pulled us into a war with the Vipers because he couldn't stay away from her, is closer to the truth. Never mind the club. She'll destroy my best friend. He's fuckin' in love with her and I bet she's one of those good girl types looking to satisfy her bad boy fantasy, but has no interest in him long-term.

"You're just as clueless as Cinda-fuckin-rella aren't you? He doesn't 'like' you. He's fuckin' *in love* with you. As in droppin' responsibilities and getting us into bad shit in love with you. And you're just over there in your little preppy, lawyer world, thinking what exactly? You'll take a walk on the wild side? Throw on some leather and be one of us? You ain't ever gonna be one of us, sweetie."

She recoils in surprise. But this is only a taste of what she's in for if she keeps hanging around here. No tears—yet. Nope. Girl sits up straighter—which pushes her tits out, distracting me for a second—and nails me with what I'm sure she thinks is a tough stare. "Are you sure *you're* not in love with him, Wrath? You sound like a jealous boyfriend," she spits out.

Well now. Bitch has some backbone.

"Well, fuck if you aren't a spitfire." I can't help laughing. That whole jealous boyfriend comment was completely unexpected.

"Well, fuck if you're not a big jerk."

All right then. "That I am, sugar."

A painful thud against my leg draws my attention up.

"That did *not* look like a friendly conversation, asshole. I told you to look after Hope, not terrorize her," Rock shouts at me before motioning Hope to move and then pulling her into his lap. She cuddles right up to him and he props his chin on top of her head.

That's new.

I nail her with a look, daring her to tattle on me. "We're solid. Right, Hope?"

By that expression screwing up her pretty face, she wants to tell me to fuck right off.

"Yup. Wrath was just giving me the lay of the land," she answers while staring me down.

Interesting.

Rock's already got his hand up her shirt. This should be good.

Hope struggles to sit up and I sense Trinity just out of my reach.

"Hi. Trinity, right?" Hope asks. I only hear the question, because I'm focused on Trinity, who clearly ducked into her room and dolled herself up after our argument. She doesn't normally waste a ton of energy on spackling on makeup and shit like all the other chicks. Why the fuck did she do it tonight? I'm also distracted by *her* tits. She's covered, but the tank top fits like a second skin and while her tits aren't quite on display, they definitely grab my attention.

"Yeah. Good to see you again, Hope."

Trin reaches over and taps Rock. "You want a drink, Rock-around-the-clock?" This is some weird thing the two of them have done for years, so it doesn't faze me. Hope, on the other hand narrows her gaze for a second.

Join the club, sweetheart.

"Will you bring me a Crown and Coke, please, hon? Hope, what do you want?"

"I'm okay. Um, maybe just water with lime?"

I snort. Figures.

Trinity finally spares me a look.

Rock talks his girl into a drink. Then Hope straight up stuns me. "Hold on, Trinity, I'll help you."

Of course the idea of the president's girl helping her serve drinks freaks Trinity the fuck out. She darts away, while Rock keeps his girl anchored to his lap.

And then they're going at it again. Good, maybe I'll get a better look at her tits. A whiff of unease settles over me, knowing Inga might drop in at any moment.

The two of them are so wrapped up in each other they don't notice the giant fucking cake, blazing with a crapload of candles, coming their way, until someone dims the lights.

Cookie and Swan help Trinity carry the blasted thing. It's obvious Cookie's going to be a problem tonight. Trinity warned me a while ago that Cookie did not take Rock's whole revirginization thing too well. And now the reason for it is perched in Rock's fucking lap.

Christ.

"Okay, now I really need you naked, Hope." Yes, please, for fuck's sake, *get a room.*

Instead of letting her man take her upstairs and fuck her brains out like she's clearly dying to do, Hope protests. She doesn't want Trinity to feel bad if Rock leaves before having the cake she made him.

Woman barely knows Trinity, but she's worried about the same fuckin' thing that's been pissing me off all damn week. *Shit.* What the fuck did I do? Now I feel even worse knowing Inga's on her way.

Rock—arrogant fuck that he is—doesn't give a shit about the cake or anything else besides getting his dick wet.

Thank fuck for his arrogance. Crisis averted. He picks her up, and carries her to the bar to grab a slice of cake.

Yes, get her upstairs before Inga shows up.

The gods have apparently decided to punish this angry biker thug tonight.

"Happy Birthday, Mr. President!" Inga shouts as she struts in the door.

Hope drops her cake, bits of it smoosh and fly everywhere.

Fuck me.

Inga isn't going to let a little thing like Rock's girlfriend get in her way. She gets as close as she can to him. Hands him one of her porno films and tells him she's going to do a private dance for him.

Now *that* bitch has balls.

I should probably try to fix this clusterfuckin' mess I made.

Trinity

Who the *hell* thought it was a good idea to allow that skank in the door?

One glance at Wrath, and I know exactly how that bitch got here. I can guess why too.

Poor Hope looks like she wants to puke. Please God, if she does, let it be all over Inga's trashy slut costume.

"Did you do this?" I ask Wrath in a low voice.

He ignores me.

Yup. Guilty as sin.

Jerk.

I poke him in his side and he glances down. At least he's not smirking for once. I raise an eyebrow at him and his mouth curves into a sheepish grin. There's no time to prepare myself before he drops down and tosses me over his shoulder.

"Put me down, you big jackass!" I yelp as he carries me down the hall, but I'm laughing and slapping his ass as I say it.

Everyone's crowded into the champagne room, and honestly the idea of watching Inga and Peach do their lesbian-whore routine—that I'm sure will be an insult to lesbians *and* whores everywhere—is very low on my list of things to do. But maybe Hope will feel less awkward if I stick around, and I promised prez I'd try to help her fit in here.

I step out in the hall and spot Rock having a serious talk with her. Wrath's right behind me—because he hasn't caused enough trouble tonight.

"Rock! Show's about to start," Wrath shouts behind me and I jump about ten feet in the air.

"Let her know she should come too," Wrath says in a low voice.

Trying to fix your mess a little late, jackass.

"Come on, Hope. Hurry," I yell to her.

Wrath was right. She grabs Rock's hand and drags him down the hall.

Inga's pissed to see Hope and that Z's taken over the "throne" she arranged for Rock.

Ha. Too bad, bitch.

Rock settles Hope into a darker corner of the room. Probably a good idea. While I grew up around shit like this—and worse—I don't really picture Hope frequenting many strip clubs.

Inga is a straight up whore—oh, excuse me, adult film actress. I've only had a few run-ins with the skinny cunt. Those few times were enough to know that if Rock had ever decided to make her his old lady, I'd seriously consider joining a different MC.

Wrath pulls me into his lap. His lips brush my ear. "You okay?"

Leaning back I whisper in his ear. "No. I really hate this bitch."

His brow wrinkles, but he doesn't laugh like I thought he would. Before he questions me, the speakers blare to life.

Showtime.

I keep my eyes anywhere but on the disgusting duo and laugh my ass off when I see Rock's not watching the show either. Nope. He's strictly focused on his woman and it's a beautiful sight.

Unfortunately Inga also notices she's not commanding all the attention. Her moves become more desperate, until she stalks over to them like the dirty, predatory animal she is and drags Hope into the middle of the room to "dance."

What Inga and Peach do to Hope is closer to molestation than dancing. The guys of course love it. Well except for Rock. When the two start trying to get Hope's shirt off, that's when I decide enough is enough.

I pretty much muppet flail my way into the middle of the dance floor, but it distracts the two bitches long enough for Rock to carry Hope out of the room. Like the dick that he is, Wrath shouts, "Take it off!"

I'm sure he thought I wouldn't. But it's dark enough that I take the dare, whipping my tank top over my head and flinging it at his shocked face.

Poor Dex over in the corner looks pretty fucking miserable. He keeps his gaze fixed on Inga.

Really Dex? You can do so much better.

Dex has always been good to me and I hate to see him unhappy, so I dance over to him and bump him with my leg. His head tips up and the corners of his mouth curve into a smile.

"What are you up to, crazy girl?"

"Nothing." I jerk my head at Inga. "Don't tell me you've got a thing for her."

He shrugs. "We talk a lot when she's in town."

I wasn't aware that bitch knew how to actually hold a conversation. At least Dex looks a little less miserable. I pat his shoulder and he gives me a smirk, lowering his gaze to my tits.

Oh yeah. Forgot I was running around without a shirt there for a second.

Where the fuck did it land?

Oh.

Wrath's glaring at us. Well, me.

For fucks sake, can't I talk to any of the brothers without him going Fred Flintstone on me? After that bullshit with Cherry, he has a lot of nerve. Besides, Dex and I have never been anything more than friends. He helped save me the night Jug showed up. I'll always be grateful to him for that.

Inga and Peach have given up the pretense of a strip show and are just making out on Z's lap now.

I walk over to Wrath and grab my tank top, slipping it over my head.

He won't look at me, but he does snap his fingers at Inga.

"Are you fucking kidding?" I snarl at him. After I just told him how much I hate that bitch?

"Hey, Wrath," she coos. Not so subtly bumping me out of the way.

Fuck both of them.

I'm not sure why I head back to the party instead of my room, but I do. Pissed off must be written all over my face, because Rock motions me to join him right away.

"Where's Wrath?"

Oh the usual, being a jackass. "Trying to fuck Inga or Peach."

He lifts an eyebrow.

Whatever.

"Wrath! Get over here," Rock shouts.

I feel him next to me, but refuse to acknowledge the big jerk.

Rock's clearly pissed. Whether it's because Wrath was trying to hook up with his ex or because of me, I don't know.

I do think it's funny as fuck when he tells Wrath to ride down to Crystal Ball.

Prez asks me to stay with Hope while he has a word with Wrath. I imagine it will be more than one word. I'm more than happy to say yes.

Waving my hand at the degenerate crowd in front of us, I ask, "You doing okay with all this?"

"Yeah."

"I don't know what the guys were thinking bringing Inga here. I swear we don't have porn star entertainment every weekend."

Hope laughs. "Yes, I got that it was a special occasion," she says with a wry smile.

Yeah, she was planning to fuck your man. But I think Hope knows that, no need to point it out to her.

"Listen, don't let Inga or any of these muffler bunnies give you shit." I wave a hand at the room.

Hope looks over the crowd. "A few of the girls have definitely had interesting...stories for me."

Yeah, I bet they have.

She gives me a curious look and I have the urge to clear the air with her. "I've never slept with Rock, if you're wondering."

Yup. That did the trick, she relaxes a little and gives me a warm smile.

"I can only imagine what you've heard."

"What's your role here?" Her tone is neutral and I figure it's best to get this out of the way now.

"Well, club took me in about eight years ago. I have a room here. Club pays my expenses. I kind of take care of the place, clean up after these pigs. And I make myself available to the guys on an as-needed basis."

It's obvious she doesn't know what to make of that. "Why?"

Christ, as if I could ever put it into words. But I try anyway. "I dunno. I grew up around MCs, so I guess I just feel safer around one." As the words come out of my mouth I realize how fucked up that is.

"Safe?" She's not being judgmental. I sense she's honestly curious.

I think about a way to explain it that makes sense. "Have you seen these guys?" I point at Wrath who's storming over with a fierce expression. "Wrath is a dick, sure, but he'd never let anyone hurt me." Well, at least physically. Emotionally he's ripped my heart out too many fucking times to count, but Hope and I are not at the girl-talk stage of our relationship yet.

"I wouldn't let anyone mess with you either, mama," Teller remarks. Jesus. He'd been so fixated on his phone, I forgot he was sitting next to us. I punch him in the arm and he smiles.

Hope wants to get into details about the club that I can't help her with. But I tell her as much as I can. She seems confused but satisfied with my answers.

Wrath, impatient as ever, weasels in between me and Teller, yanking me into his lap.

"How did you find these guys?" Hope asks.

How to answer that one? I wave my hand in the air and then automatically rest it against Wrath's arms, which are somehow wrapped around my waist. "Club girls know how to find bikers."

"Fuck yeah, baby," Wrath says in a low, rumbling tone that sends a quiver of desire through me.

Bastard.

As if that's not bad enough, he nips my ear and flicks his tongue over it.

Oh dear God, why is he doing this to me now? Is this his way of embarrassing me in front of Rock's girl again? I slam my elbow into his chest until he stops fucking around.

"But honestly, I was tending bar downtown with this girl." I twist so I can see Wrath and I hope he reads the *Don't fucking do that again*, in my expression. "You remember Stormy?"

He smirks in response. "Yup. Poser skank."

Yeah, that about covers it.

WRATH

Even though I'm sitting next to what has to be the most clueless woman I've ever met, I've got a fucking boner.

From having Trinity in my lap, not from listening to Hope.

I gotta move my legs to get some of the pressure off. As I stretch, she rolls and struggles to stay upright.

Nope. Trinity wriggling against my dick just made the situation in my pants worse.

"Watch it, woman," I growl in her ear.

I really want to take Trinity upstairs and pay her back for the way she's been tormenting me all night. Fucking dancing around in that sorry excuse for a bra, dancing for Dex, when she's never—

"Thug life," Teller says, jerking me back into the stupid conversation he's having with Hope.

She smiles like it's a joke. "You're not *thugs*." She glances at me and teasingly says. "Well, *you* probably are."

Is she fucking serious?

"I definitely am," I say, staring her down.

"Anyway," Teller continues, because I think he senses I'm about to lose my temper with this chick. "Stormy-girl found herself a nice citizen husband."

She has no idea what that is. Now since Rock just took me in the war room and explained that not only is he planning for this broad to be his ol' lady, but he also wants to marry her and I risked a throat punch by telling him she would be better off as a citizen wife, I find that funny.

"She was one of those good girl types, lookin' to take a walk on the wild side. You know, spice up her dull, sheltered life? Attaching herself to outlaws made her feel special," I explain to her slowly, so maybe this time the message sticks.

Trinity knows me well enough to sense I'm not done mouthin' off.

"That's not entirely true," she says with a shake of her head. "She got tired of being passed around. No one was gonna claim her back then, and she really wanted to get married and start a family."

Oh please, the idea of that lazy cow having children with some miserable bastard is a joke. "No one was claiming club ass. *Back then.*"

Shit. I realize how that must have sounded to Trinity.

She leans as far forward as I'll allow, which ain't much. "From what I hear, Rock hasn't been with any of the club girls in like a year or something," she tells Hope in a conspirator voice. I almost snort. What the fuck —is where Rock sticks his damn dick national news for these chicks?

"All the girls gossip about the guys," Trinity says with a snicker.

Of course.

Welterweight chuckles. "Boys compare notes too."

Teller can fuck right off. His comparing notes about Trinity days are over.

"Anyway, I just wanted you to know. Me and Rock. Never." Trinity slashes her hand through the air.

Holy fuck.

"He's more like a big brother or father figure—"

"Fuck, Trinny. I am *not* old enough to be your dad," Rock grumbles, having overheard the last part of that conversation. I choke back a laugh.

He shares a moment with Hope, and I'll admit the adoring way she stares up at him makes me feel shitty. She may not have wanted to admit it to a scary thug like me earlier, but she's clearly in love with my brother.

All right, I better get this over with. "Uh…Hope, I'm sorry about Inga coming here tonight. I gave the okay for it. I didn't think Rock would actually bring you to a club party."

Trinity's jaw drops and I'm mildly insulted.

She presses the back of her hand against my forehead and I fight the urge to lean into her touch. "You feeling okay, Wyatt?"

She's teasing me, but God dammit for a second I can't even breathe when she says my name.

Because of Rock's meddling, Teller asks Hope for some legal advice. She's clearly stressed about involving herself in Teller's case and I wonder about Rock for sticking his nose in her business. I figure a lawyer woman will go ballistic over something like that, so I sit back and wait for the fireworks.

But they don't come. Her jaw locks and she keeps her mouth shut.

Interesting.

Murphy ambles over looking like shit warmed over. I'm about to say so, when Teller introduces him to Hope.

"Hi, first lady," he says to Hope with a chuckle.

For fuck's sake.

Of course Rock thinks that's hilarious. "First Lady—I like it."

Trinity shifts again and my dick's begging for mercy.

"Geez, why don't you just piss on his leg, girl. Damn. You been in his lap all night. We get it."

Cookie. Been waitin' for this scene to go down all night. Bitch has been obvious about how much she dislikes Princess Clueless.

Hope's nose wrinkles, but she tries hard to act normal. "Uh, hi. I'm Hope."

"Uh, hi. I'm Cookie. I'm you two years ago," Cookie snarks back.

That's too ridiculous to ignore. "Hardly."

Cookie glares at me. *Watch it sweetheart.* She keeps mouthing off like this, ain't nothing I can do to save her fuckin' ass. Bitch has been in the life long enough that she should know better.

"Cookie," Rock warns. "You're being rude to my woman."

That's one.

She finally backs down, but not long enough.

"Well, she ain't gotta be so uppity. Bragging about being a lawyer and shit. I saw her leave the champagne room before. Thinks she's too good to hang with us?"

While I still don't think Cinderella has any business hanging out here, she hasn't once thrown attitude or acted better than anyone else. This is chick shit though, so I keep my mouth shut.

Trin sits up straighter—again making my dick freak out.

"Are you fucking stupid?" she snaps. "Rock carried his woman outta there. We all saw it. Bitch, go sit down," she finishes flicking her hand at Cookie.

I lean down, pressing my forehead up against Trinity—mistake, she smells fucking awesome—and laugh.

"You ain't got nothing to say?" Cookie snaps at Hope. I can't believe she's not letting this go. Has every bitch here lost their mind tonight? Hope stays silent, which only seems to piss Cookie off more. "See? Uppity."

"Maybe she's freaked out that you're acting like a psycho-bitch?" Teller offers.

"Cookie, simmer the fuck down," Rock warns, in a low voice that should be scaring the piss out of Cookie.

That's two.

She's done. Just waitin' for Rock to give the signal.

"Fuck you too, Trinity. You wanna suck up to this uppity cunt, go ahead, but don't forget you're a whore like the rest of us."

If Rock doesn't throw her ass out, I will. No fucking way is she is gettin' away with calling Trinity a whore. I fuckin' hate when Trinity calls herself a whore, but this bitch saying it? *No.*

I glance up at Hope who seems shocked. Doubt she's ever been called a cunt before. And while she annoys the shit out of me, she's been nothing but nice to everyone all night long.

Rock all but throws Hope into the couch, he's up so fast. He gets right in Cookie's face. "You're done."

Finally, asshole.

I loosen my hold on Trinity, because my help is definitely needed to end this situation.

"Rock. I been with the club almost five years. You really gonna pick her over me?" she whines.

Exactly, you've been here long enough to know how this shit works.

"Cookie, you were warned multiple times." He reaches back and flicks his hand. "Wrath."

"On it." I pat Trinity's ass, and she slides off my lap onto the couch, next to Hope.

I stand and roll my shoulders. "Let's go." I grab her arm.

She starts sobbing. "I'm sorry, Rock."

Too late.

I keep moving to the door, Rock following behind. "You're banned, Cookie. You can see if one of the other charters will take you in, but you ever show your face back here, I'll end you."

She stumbles as I tug her outside and then the waterworks flow. "Wrath, don't let him do this. Talk to him."

I hate being around crying females. I snap my fingers at Hoot. He and Birch hustle over, probably thrilled to have something to do besides stand guard over our bikes.

Placing both hands on her shoulders, I look down into her tear-streaked face. "Cookie, come on. You know that kind of disrespect won't stand."

"But what's he doing with someone like her? I don't…I don't get it."

Neither do I. "Yeah, but it ain't your call, darlin'. You been around long enough to know better. Mouthin' off to Trinity like that didn't help your cause either."

She finally shows a hint of genuine remorse, then shakes it off. "Yeah, but why's she gettin' all cozy with that bitch? She always acts like she's better than us and now—"

"False. Trin takes her responsibilities seriously up here. She doesn't stop by to party and fuck. She works her ass off to keep this place running. And Rock *asked* her to spend time with Hope, so she was *doing what her Prez told her.*" I emphasize that last point, so she understands. Had she listened to Rock's multiple warnings we wouldn't be doing this right now.

"Shit." She looks down at the ground. "What do I do now?"

"Leave."

Her eyes tear up again.

"Go down to Sway's compound. Those guys like you."

Defeat's written all over her face. "Yeah, okay."

I motion Hoot and Birch over. "Drive her home."

Hoot ushers her to the van and I wait until they drive off before turning around.

Rock's waitin' in the doorway. "You make it clear?"

"Yeah, she knows."

Rock shakes his head. "Fuck. I shoulda given Hope more warning shit like that might happen."

Ya think?

"She did okay." We both glance over to where Trinity and Teller are clearly trying to cheer Hope up. He snorts. "Thank fuck for Trinny. Don't know what we'd do without her," he turns and glares at me.

"Yeah, she's been talking you up all night too."

Rock raises an eyebrow, silently asking me to continue. "You know, the usual, letting Hope know you're only parking your dick in her garage. Shit like that."

Rock snorts. "Fantastic."

I drill him with a stare. "She also made a point of telling Hope she's never fucked *you.*"

Rock's expression doesn't change. "Good."

I run down to check on the champagne room and duck into the kitchen. No fights. No one drowning in puke or anything else unsavory.

Finding Trin and Teller cozy together when I return is the definition of unsavory.

I'm not gonna play games or compete with anyone for her attention. I kick Teller's foot. "Swan's looking for you."

I'm not above lying though.

Trin gives me a look. She sees right through my bullshit. I sit next to her and casually drape my arm over the back of the couch.

"We were just talking," she says.

When I don't respond, she falls back against the couch and closes her eyes. "What are we doing?"

Good fucking question. A hundred different answers run through my head. I want her to be my girl and I'm tryin' hard to figure out how to make that happen, short of kidnapping her and having "property of Wrath" tattooed on her forehead.

"Takin' the weekend off from training," I answer.

She smirks, turns and opens her eyes. Even with all the black shit smeared around them, her honey eyes are the sweetest things I've seen all night.

"What's with all the eye shit tonight?" I ask, pointing at her face.

Her mouth turns down. Fuck, I didn't mean to hurt her feelings.

"I thought you liked the plastic slut look? Peach set her make-up shotgun on whore tonight and you couldn't wait to get on her."

Fuck it. I'm gonna lay it out for her. "I didn't want Peach."

She rolls her eyes.

"I was pissed seeing you dancing for Dex like that." *You should be doing that shit for me.*

"Dex and I are just friends. For some stupid reason, he seems to have a thing for skank-a-rella."

I snort at that. "What's your deal with Inga? I didn't realize you guys even knew each other."

Trin sits up, turns to face me and tucks one leg under her. "Sure, I've run into her from time to time down at CB. She made it clear that she wasn't a *whore* like me." Trin twirls her hair and makes an airhead face. "She's an adult film actress," she says with a phony voice and snotty attitude I can definitely picture Inga using.

"You tell Rock?"

"No. She's a good stripper. What's he going to do, fire her because she's a bitch to me?"

She's right, but it still pisses me off.

"She fucks on film for money. I fuck to keep a roof over my head. No different in my book."

"Jesus fucking Christ, would you stop with that shit? You're a part of this family, Trin. Doesn't matter who you do or *don't* fuck."

She glances down at her hands resting in her lap and shakes her head.

Placing my hand over hers I ask her to go for a walk with me.

"Where?"

"I don't know. Let's walk down the hill and visit the big Buddha guy."

The corners of her mouth lift and she laughs. "Okay. Let me go grab a sweatshirt."

I'm waitin' by the door for a while and I start to wonder if she changed her mind. When she returns, she's got a LOKI sweatshirt on that's about two sizes too big for her, and a freshly scrubbed face.

Reaching out, I brush my hand over her cheek. "You didn't have to do that. I was only joking around."

She shrugs and takes my hand, leading us outside. Our feet crunch over the gravel as we make our way around the clubhouse and down the long driveway.

Once we get some distance between us and the clubhouse, it's easier to appreciate our surroundings.

"I love it up here," she hush-whispers. She's walking so slow, I stop to see what she's doing and find her staring up at the sky.

"Watch your step, babe."

She drops her head and we continue our walk. Z's got a bunch of motion-detector solar lights installed along the driveway, so we can at least see where we're going.

When we finally get to the statue, we sit on one of the low stone benches. Trin tips her head back to stare at the sky again.

"It's so pretty."

"Yes." But I'm looking at her, not the stars.

"Do you ever look up and wonder if somewhere out in all that blackness is another planet full of people?"

This time I do lean back and take in the oil-black sky and stars. "Not since I was a kid."

She hums in agreement. "Do you think we'll ever know?"

"Maybe." I glance over at her, but she's still gazing up at the stars. "You okay?"

She doesn't answer for a while. "I'll be thirty soon."

I guess I knew that. "Yeah."

"There was a time in my life I didn't think I'd live to see twenty-five, let alone thirty."

Given what Rock's told me about her past, I understand. I've certainly felt that way once or twice in my life. "I know what you mean."

She finally stops staring at the sky and turns to face me. "Yeah, you probably do."

She's close enough to kiss, but I also want her to keep talking.

She sighs. "I've concentrated on survival for so long, I don't even know what I'm doing with my life. Or what I should do."

Her tone. Her words. The lost look on her face. All of it scares me. "Do you want to leave the club?"

"No. It's the only real home and family I've ever had."

I slip my arm around her and pull her against me. Her head drops on my shoulder. "I think that's true for all of us."

Trinity

To be honest, I'm shocked to be having this conversation with Wrath. I don't know what's gotten into me.

Ninety-nine percent of the time, I'm happy with my life here. But there's that one percent of me, always questioning. Is this all there is to life? Warming one bed after another? Parties? Do I want a family? Could I raise a kid in the life, the way I was? If I wanted to leave, where would I go?

"Want to head back?" Wrath asks.

"Not yet."

He stands and stretches. "That bench is killing me," he says as if he's apologizing for leaving my side.

"Sorry."

"You're not the only one getting older. Been abusing this body for years."

If by abusing, he means working it into sinful perfection then, yeah, he's right. "Think you should give up fighting?"

He stares down at his hands, opening and closing them into fists. "I need it."

Yeah, he needs to unleash his anger the same way I need to have sex to feel good about myself.

Admitting what he probably thinks is weakness must have left him feeling vulnerable. He jumps up, grabbing a thick branch and hangs from it. Then starts doing chin-ups.

"What are you doing? You're going to kill that tree," I scold.

He lifts himself up a few more times, and yeah, I definitely admire the flexing of his arms, then he drops down. "Don't want you to think I'm getting soft."

I knew it. "You're the hardest man I know."

He doesn't get all cocky, just nods.

An unexpected yawn escapes me, and I realize I've been going all day. I'm tired.

"Come on, babe. You've had a busy day and it's a long hike back up the hill." Wrath holds his hand out and I take it. He pulls me up on my feet and yanks me against him. Without thinking about it, my arms wrap around his middle and I lay my cheek against his chest. He holds me like that for a while. That's it. His hands don't slide down and grab my ass or anything like that. He does kiss the top of my head, though.

Pulling away, I take his hand and we head back to the clubhouse. I don't think much about the fact that we're holding hands, but I am grateful for it a minute later, when I stumble over a rut in the road. My ankle twists, but I don't fall because Wrath's there to catch me.

Sucking in air through my teeth, I bend over and press my fingers against my foot and up my leg. "Fuck."

"You okay?"

"Yeah. I'll be fine. Just need to shake it off." I'm proved wrong a second later when I try to step on it and yelp in pain.

"Come on." Wrath scoops me into his arms, one arm behind my back, one under my knees.

"You can't carry me back the whole way like this."

"Babe, we're not that far. It'll be a good workout."

That makes me chuckle and smack his chest. "You're crazy."

He's barely out of breath by the time we get inside. People have disappeared to more quiet locations, because the living room is almost empty. Wrath sets me on the couch.

"Stay here, I'll go grab an ice pack."

"Okay."

He pauses briefly as if he's surprised I didn't argue with him. How can I argue? My ankle's throbbing. The thought of hobbling to the kitchen makes me cringe.

While he's gone, I slip off my sneakers and socks. The ankle looks a little puffy, but not horrible.

"Let me see," Wrath says, startling me.

He drops next to me, gently pulling my feet into his lap. With a tenderness you wouldn't expect from such a frightening guy, he inspects both ankles. Finally, he reaches over to the coffee table and grabs an ace bandage. He unwinds it and wraps my foot and ankle with a skill that suggests he's done this before.

"I think it's just a sprain, but if it keeps swelling, I'll take you down to urgent care in the morning."

"Okay," I whisper.

He glances up. "Tired?"

Yeah, that's it.

I nod and he places an icepack on my foot. "I'll hold it here for twenty minutes, then take it off. Why don't you close your eyes?"

I sit up a bit farther, and trace my fingers over his cheek. "Thank you for always taking good care of me."

For a second he leans into my touch, then snorts and looks away. "I don't seem to do a very good job."

"Yeah, you do."

WRATH

I'm fucking pissed with myself for lettin' Trin get hurt. It feels good to take care of her though. Even better that she didn't put up a fuss. After twenty minutes, I set the ice pack to the side. Things look okay. The swelling isn't getting worse. Her foot hasn't turned any weird colors. Hopefully she's better in the morning.

She sighs and turns over, then sits up. Bleary-eyed, she blinks at me a few times.

"Come here, babe." I hold out my arm, and she ducks under it, snuggling up against me.

After a while, she slides down, until she's sleeping on my leg. I'm pretty sure she's drooling on me too, but I'm so happy, I don't care. Resting my hand on her hip, I try to lean back and close my eyes.

"Wrath?" A whiny voice startles me awake. Trinity's still tucked against me sound asleep. No, it's Cherry in front of me.

"Wanna go upstairs?" she asks with a raised eyebrow and freaky fish-pout.

"No. I'm good, thanks."

She wrinkles her nose and glares at Trinity. "Doesn't look much good to me. Come on." She holds out her hand to me.

"No." I pick up the now warm icepack and hand it to her. "Go toss this back in the freezer for me."

She snatches the pack out of my hand and flounces off in a huff. *Whatthefuckever.*

My arm tightens against Trinity and I manage to fall back asleep.

Way too fuckin' early, Murphy walks in, looking like hell again.

"What up, brother?" he whispers, with a chin lift at Trinity.

"Twisted her ankle. Where you been? You look like shit."

The corner of his mouth lifts, but he doesn't give me an answer. "Teller around?"

"Last I saw him, he was headin' to the champagne room. Not sure where he ended up, though."

His gaze skips to Trinity again. "She need anything?"

Me. "No, I got it."

"All right." He heads down to the hall. I don't even want to think about what kind of mess is waiting down there.

Murphy returns a few seconds later. "Can't find him. I'll catch him later."

"Okay."

No sooner is he out the door, Rock and Hope float downstairs, looking disgustingly in love.

"Hey, prez," I greet in a whisper, so he doesn't wake Trin up.

Hope does this princess-finger-wave thing at me and I smirk at her.

Of course within five seconds, they've got their tongues down each other's throats. Couldn't they have just stayed upstairs to do this shit? A sarcastic sigh slips out of me as I wait for them to finish.

"You're up early," Rock says with a grin. "She okay?" he asks, lifting his chin at Trinity.

My gaze skips to Hope, who's taking all of this in. Trinity's eagerness to be friends with Hope prickles my memory. I feel compelled to let her know we didn't fuck last night. Especially after Cookie called her a whore in front of everyone.

"I didn't get any ass last night, thanks to you," I grumble. What the fuck is wrong with me? I don't give a fuck what Cinderella thinks of me.

But it's not me I'm worried about, it's Trinity.

Rock snorts. "Yeah, it's all my fault you're such a prick."

I can live with that. I earned it after last night.

Z pounds down the stairs like a five-year-old. "Morning, fuckers. Oh, hey, Hope. I'm surprised you're still here."

Rock grunts at him and I'm pretty sure he calls him an asshole under his breath.

Heh.

"Where's Peach?" I ask him. I'm hoping she and Inga cleared the building sometime last night and I just missed it.

"Upstairs," he answers.

"You nail her?" I couldn't give a shit less, but I feel like the question is expected of me.

Z shrugs before answering. "She's a shit lay. Mosta them strippers and porn stars are. They act like they're doing ya a favor and just lay there. Fuckin' boring."

There's a ninety-nine percent chance Rock wants to kick both our asses for having this conversation in front of Hope.

Surprisingly she snorts and then giggles. "But you still did her anyway?"

Z widens his eyes. Guess he wasn't expecting that from her. "Well, yeah. Of course." He flashes another smile. "It's my duty to fuck as many women as possible."

I know my brother well enough to know he honestly believes that and that he's trying to get a rise out of Hope.

She doesn't take the bait. Actually, she laughs even harder. "You and Lilly really are kindred spirits."

Oh, that's fantastic. The goofy grin on his face slips. "What?"

Hope chuckles. "She has a similar theory on dating." I know it's just killing him not to pump her for more information.

Unfortunately, Inga joins us next. "Fuuuck." She throws herself on the couch next to Trinity, jostling her awake. I've never hit a woman in my life, but I could choke Inga out right about now and not suffer an ounce of guilt. The two girls glare at each other for a second.

"Morning, Trinny," Rock greets her with a slow grin.

Dick.

Trinity glances at everyone and mumbles good morning, before pushing off the couch and hurrying down the hall.

I still want to smack Inga. Instead, I follow Trinity, catching up to her outside the bathroom.

Grabbing her elbow to stop her, I ask, "How's your ankle?"

The corner of her mouth lifts. "Oh." She glances down and wriggles her foot. "Much better." Her hand reaches up, brushing over my cheek. Fuck, I love her hands on me.

"Thank you for taking such good care of me."

"Any time, babe."

She squirms a little. "I gotta pee."

Chuckling, I swing the door open for her. After it shuts, I return to the living room. Inga's unfortunately still hanging out, being a useless twat.

When Trinity returns, she perches on the end of the couch near Rock, and again I wish Inga would get the fuck out of here.

Hope turns and gives Trinity a sweet smile.

"So, I get how Dex got his nickname now," Inga says even though no one asked. Like the disgusting bitch she is, she wiggles her fingers in the air. "Real good with his hands." She turns toward Trinity.

Hope makes this grossed out face that's pretty damn funny.

Trinity's gaze skips to me. "That's what I've *heard*."

Shaking my head, I answer. "That's not how he got his road name."

I guess if Inga can't embarrass Trinity, Hope will do. "So, how did you like our show last night, Hope?" Inga asks in her casual-bitch voice.

"You're very talented," she answers with a straight face. Fuck me, Hope should get an award for that.

Inga's not finished. "Rocky took you away from us before we got to the good stuff. You actually move really well, once you loosen up." The way she says it does *not* sound like a compliment.

"Uh, thanks."

"If you ever want lessons—I mean, you're a little on the old side—I can teach you how to work the pole."

Rock finally wakes the fuck up. He wraps his arms around Hope and throws a glare at stripper-Barbie. "Knock it off, Inga."

"Yeah, she knows how to work Rock's pole just fine," Z adds. I quiver with laughter. He's such an asshole.

Hope straightens up and gives Inga a haughty look. This should be interesting.

"Inga, I get that you *used* to fuck my man, but if I wanted to hang out with a bitch, I'd get a dog. Keep your thinly veiled insults to yourself, you're not fooling anyone."

A bit wordy, but she *might* just survive being a biker's old lady after all.

Trinity

Once the fireworks are over, I slide off the couch and head to the kitchen. "I'll get breakfast started."

"Hang on, Trinny," Rock says, stopping me in my tracks. "After Ing and Peach get the fuck out, round up whoever's awake, and we'll go down to Hog Heaven."

Awesome. I love that place. They have the best friggin' blueberry pancakes and one of these days I'll sweet talk Frank into giving me his recipe.

I trot down to my room, stepping carefully on the foot I rolled last night. Amazingly my ankle feels fine.

After calling Hog Heaven and being told the best Frank can do is a corner table, because he's got a huge wedding party coming in, I change and freshen up in my room.

When I return to the living room, Wrath and Z are bullshitting while they wait for Rock.

"They're probably fucking again," Z gripes.

"Shut up," I giggle and smack him on the arm.

Inga and Peach clomp down the stairs in their hooker heels. Their outfits are downright garish in the harsh light of day. Like the gentleman he's not, Z walks them both out to the parking lot. As soon as they're gone, he bounds up the stairs. We can hear him banging on Rock's door from downstairs and I giggle some more.

Even Wrath smirks.

When Z returns, he wraps his arms around my waist, lifts me up and spins me around. "Ride with me, mama?"

Laughing, I smack him until he sets me down.

"Okay, okay."

Wrath lifts an eyebrow and tilts his head. I shrug and follow Z out the door.

Z's either starving or has something on his mind, because he takes the absolute fastest route to Hog Heaven. We pull into their unpaved, gravel parking lot ahead of anyone else.

While we're waiting for the others, he leads me over to one of the outdoor picnic benches.

"What's up, Z?"

One corner of his mouth lifts. "You know me too well, Trin."

"Probably."

"You think Hope's gonna tell her friend about last night?"

Nothing about Hope seems gossipy, but who knows. "I have no idea. What do you care, anyway? Thought you were both casual?"

He grinds his teeth but doesn't answer.

"Why'd you do it, then?"

He runs his hand through his hair, actually looking remorseful for once. "I don't fuckin' know. Wasn't worth it, that's for sure."

I laugh and then snort, which makes me laugh even harder.

"I'm glad you think it's funny."

I hiccup and then sit up straight, holding in any more giggles. "Maybe you should enter some sort of sex addiction program."

Now it's Z's turn to laugh. "Thanks, you've been a huge help this morning."

I tip my head at him. "I do what I can."

We're cut off from any more silliness by the sound of Wrath's bike approaching. Rock's not too far behind.

"What'd you rush down here for if you weren't gonna go get a table, jackass?" Wrath says as he approaches. Guess he's cranky I rode down with Z.

WRATH

After breakfast, Z took off. Rock and I decide to take the girls to Fletcher Park.

The idea of taking Trinity up there gets me all kinds of excited. We've visited the park over the years, but usually with a group of people. I ride in the back way and slow down as I pass the first parking lot. Gotta be twenty or so members of the Devil Demons MC taking up one of the private picnic areas.

What the fuck?

If Trinity notices, she doesn't say anything.

I pull into the parking lot for the overlook. Fuck if I don't park right in front of the exact spot where we spent the night eight years ago.

Time for subtlety is over.

Trinity's a smart girl—one of the things I like about her. She misses nothing.

"Is this a hint?" she asks as she takes in the view.

"Hint about what?"

She shakes her head as she walks over to the low stone wall. "Nothing."

For a while she stares out at the view—I was right, it's a perfect day to come up here. Then she drops her gaze to the ground on the other side of the wall and stares at it like she's tryin' to see eight years into the past. Hell, maybe that's what I'm trying to do myself.

"You bring a lot of girls up here, Wrecking Ball?"

What the fuck? "No. Only you."

She snorts and I place my hands on her shoulders to turn her around. "You're the only girl I've ever wanted to impress."

"That's pathetic."

"Knock your shit off."

Her eyes widen and she takes a step back. I'm kind of surprised myself, but I'm tired of this bullshit arguing thing we're always doing.

"I don't know what to do with that," she finally says.

"Yeah, I know you don't."

She stares out at the view again and slips her cell phone out of her pocket. "I wish I had a better camera."

"Why don't we move over there? Less trees in your way."

She tilts her head to the side. "Help me up?"

"You're gonna get us kicked out," I tease. The park has stern signs all over the place that state not to step on or over the wall. But I dare some park ranger to come say that to my face.

My big hands fit just right into the curve of her waist as I pluck her off the blacktop. She squeals and laughs as she gets her footing. There's no danger of her falling off the cliff or anything, but I wrap my arms around her legs just in case.

After what seems like forever, I hear the rumble of Rock's bike cutting through the parking lot behind us. Trinity turns and waves.

Hope wants to snap a few pictures of Trinity and me sitting on the stone wall. I'm more than happy to remember this day. I want it to be a turning point for us.

When the girls are done with pictures, they check out the view, while I give Rock a head's up about the Demon get together.

Rock's eager to get his woman alone, so they split. Trinity and I stare at each other awkwardly for a few seconds.

"What do you want to do?" she asks.

"Let's go for a ride." I point west. "We can follow the back roads out to Roscoe Valley. Should be some pretty views."

She seems surprised. "Okay. Can we stop at one of the farm stands out there?"

The corner of my mouth lifts. "Any one you want."

With Trin at my back and the clear day, it's hard to remember any of the bad stuff between us. The steep mountain roads require a lot of coasting and braking, but we finally roll into the valley, and the views are worth the smell of my brakes burning up.

I take a right and after a few miles a huge, orange barn comes into view. Trin taps my left shoulder, so I assume this is where she wants to stop.

She's laughing and smiling as she hands me her helmet. "That was fun." Her happiness is infectious. She grabs my hand and tugs me inside.

Farm stand doesn't really describe what they have going on here. It's a big operation. A slight older man, who I assume is the owner, stops over to ask Trinity if she needs help. She's got a bunch of questions for him, which amuses me. I'm not really paying attention though, until he mentions they grow tomatoes hydroponically year-round and offers to show her their set-up.

Now, *this* is much more interesting. It's time to drag Sparky out the basement for a field trip one of these days. Trin must know where my mind wandered off to, because she smirks at me.

After our tour, she asks me how much room I've got in the saddlebags.

"As long as you're not getting a pumpkin, we should be fine," I tell her, nodding at one of the big orange gourds that's as tall as she is.

While we're at the register, she makes a face. "Is there a restroom?" she asks.

The old guy points her in the right direction. Before she leaves she reaches up on tiptoes and plants a kiss on my cheek. "Be right back."

I'm so stunned, I stand there like an idiot staring after her while she dashes to the back of the store.

The old guy chuckles. "Your wife?"

My gaze swings back to him. Wife? I can't even get her to admit she's my girlfriend. Can't imagine the fuss she'll kick up when I give her a property patch—because yes, that's definitely happening—but wife? Never gave that much thought. Taking an ol' lady seemed like enough of a commitment. But listening to my best friend so casually mention last night that the woman he's barely been with for a few months will be his wife...made me wonder. And now, this guy asking. It's like a big fucking, neon sign blinking "Wake the fuck up, jackass."

"Not yet. She will be."

Trinity

Wrath's so serious after we leave the farm stand. Did he get annoyed with how much time we spent there? Or is he itching to get home and tell Sparky all about the hydroponic set-up?

I nod at the bags he's stuffing in his pack. "I'll make us dinner when we get back."

Finally, a smile out of him. "I'd like that."

He takes a different, but no less stunning, route home.

Teller's leaving as we pull up to the clubhouse, but stops to talk to us.

"Swan asked me to pick her up," he explains.

The corner of Wrath's mouth lifts, but he doesn't say anything.

"That's good, she's usually a big help."

As soon as Teller leaves, Wrath faces me. "Are you jealous?"

"Of what?"

He shakes his head. "Nothing."

Confused at his change in attitude, I follow him inside. We find Ravage and Stash sitting on the living room floor, busy getting high and playing video games. Rav calls me over immediately and hugs my legs when I get near him.

"Where you been, girl?" he asks, looking up at me with red eyes.

"Out. It's a nice day. You two should check it out. Maybe get some sun."

Rav peers around my legs and lifts his chin at Wrath. "Got any munchy food in there?"

"Nope, all veggies," I answer and laugh when he scrunches up his nose.

"We don't all need to be on his fighter diet," Stash complains.

"God forbid," Wrath snarks from behind me.

Stash flips him off.

Ruffling my fingers through Rav's hair, I untangle my legs from his grasp and follow Wrath to the kitchen.

"They're like two overgrown babies," Wrath bitches as he sets everything on the counter.

"You're *all* a bunch of big babies."

Instead of getting pissed, he chuckles. "Please, I've at least reached the maturity of a toddler," he says, leaning over and setting his hand out knee high.

"I'll give you that," I agree with a head shake.

Opening one of the cabinets, I dig around for a couple of bigger bowls. "What are you doing?" he asks as I walk over to the pantry and return with a couple bags of chips.

"Bringing the munchy twins some snacks." I grab a box of snack cakes from the pantry, and sling a six-pack of mountain dew from the fridge under my arm.

"I thought you were making us dinner?" He's not trying very hard to hide the cranky toddler in his voice. Once I've got everything in my hands and arms, I turn to face him.

"I will, but if I don't go bring them something now, they're going to bother and interrupt us. So give me five minutes and then I'm all yours."

I don't wait for an answer. The surprised and happy grin on Wrath's face is enough.

The guys don't even realize I've returned until I set the bowls in front of them. "Oh, Trin, you're the best," Stash gushes as I hand him the snack cakes.

"You two are gonna be hitting the treadmill hard on Monday," I tease. That of course, prompts Rav to lift his shirt and show me his abs. "Yeah, I see your gut."

That gets an outraged snort out of Rav. "Get out of here, woman."

Wrath's got all my veggies laid out on the counter when I return. "I'm scared to ask what you're planning to make," he jokes.

I falter a bit. Maybe he's getting tired of me telling him what to eat all the time, even though he did ask for my help.

He reaches out and takes my hand, pulling me closer. "Why so serious? I'm just kidding. I know whatever you make will be awesome."

"Thanks."

"Want me to help?"

Normally, I'd say no. But I bought a lot of root vegetables and squashes that need to be cut up into cubes. "You're stronger than me, so can you cut those into one inch pieces, please?"

I hand over my favorite vegetable cleaver and he stares at it for a second. "Christ, Trin, this is serious hardware," he jokes.

"I know. Try not to cut any of your fingers off."

We work next to each other quietly. His idea of one inch cubes isn't quite up to my standards, but he's working so hard at it, I don't comment on the slivers and hunks he passes over. Once the veggies are roasting in the oven, I wave him away and start on the chicken.

"Thank God. Meat. I thought you were only feeding me vegetables for dinner."

Laughter bursts out of me. "Yeah, as if I'd get away with that."

Dinner turns out well. There's barely anything left. We eat in the kitchen and no one bothers us. Our discussion turns to the fight and some of the things he still wants to work on before then.

He taps his arm and my eyes are drawn to his inked skin and defined muscles. "...any progress I've made is because of you."

Since I was distracted, I missed the first part of what he said. Reaching, out I trail my fingers over his arm. "You've made a lot of progress."

Even though I shut the oven off before we sat down, my skin simmers with heat. It's the look Wrath's giving me.

He turns his head and goes back to talking about the fight. This whole friends only thing we've been doing is nice, but also confusing as hell.

"Come on, aren't you afraid of pain?" I ask when he mentions one of the moves his opponent is famous for like it's no big deal.

His ocean-eyes swing back to me. "No babe. The only thing that scares me is the thought of losing you."

That can't be true. "Why?" I stand and clear the table, bringing the dishes to the sink. When I turn, Wrath's standing right behind me.

"You don't get it. I want you. I just don't want to fuck this up again."

He says he wants me. But for what? And how can I be sure if he won't speak the language my body and brain understand—sex?

I'm about to blurt that out when he leans over and presses his lips against mine. His hand cradles the back of my head, holding me still, while he takes his time exploring and tasting my mouth.

After I'm not sure how long, because I lose track of time, he pulls back. His lips curl into a crooked smile that makes my knees weak. "You know the last time I tried to kiss you in the kitchen, you almost barfed on me," he says low and teasing.

My cheeks burn at the memory of that miserable Christmas Eve. "That's not fair, I had the flu."

Without warning, he wraps his hands around my waist, picks me up and sets me on the counter. "You feeling okay tonight?"

"Yes," I whisper.

"Good." He barely gets the whole word out, before his hands are on my face, holding me still. He covers my lips with his, taking charge. Hot and hungry, his tongue brushes against mine. Sweeping into my mouth, reminding me of what he's capable of doing. His hands drop to my hips as he deepens the kiss. I hook my legs around him, drawing him closer. Almost frantic to have him, my fingers fiddle with his belt. One big hand covers mine, stopping me.

He bends and nuzzles my cheek. "Not yet, Angel Face. Not here."

Surprised, I draw back. "Why?"

He doesn't get to answer, because we're interrupted by whoops and shouts coming from the hallway.

Wrath and I stare at each other and he raises an eyebrow.

Pushing myself off the counter, I head to the kitchen door.

Wrath grabs my hand as I pass. "Wait." He peers out of the small square window in the kitchen door. "Looks like a party in the champagne room," he says.

I don't want our moment to end. I'm so close to asking Wrath—no begging him—to come to my room with me.

Except I've never let any of the guys in my room. Wrath's not just anyone. As stubborn as I can be, even I know that.

He shoves the door open hard, and I see Rav and Sparky moving one of the dining room tables.

"What the fuck you two doing?" Wrath shouts at them.

Rav gives him a bleary smile. "Inga. Train. Champagne room."

A shiver of revulsion works over me, and Wrath's hand reaches behind him to pat me on my side. As if he knows why I find this so disturbing.

The door swings shut as he steps back inside. He shakes his head and mutters "fucking disgusting" under his breath.

"You can go. I won't be mad."

Why the hell did I say that?

Wrath cocks his head, and his eyebrows draw down. "Trust me, that's the last fucking thing I feel like doing."

My breath catches and I struggle to fill my lungs with air. "I didn't mean that, Wyatt. I...I'd be hurt, if you—"

He leans down and presses a kiss to my forehead. "Stay here. I'll be right back."

He's only gone long enough for me to finish washing a couple dishes. The door swings open as I'm turning off the tap.

Wrath shakes his head. "Fucking Dex. I don't know what the hell he was thinking."

That sucks. I feel bad for Dex, but I'm not sure how he expected things to turn out any different.

Wrath takes my hand and tugs me toward the back door.

"Come on, let's go outside. Hopefully Rock will be back soon. Let him kick her skank ass out."

He sits on the low stone wall opposite the clubhouse and pulls me down next to him. "We can go for a walk if you want, after Rock gets back."

"I'd like that."

He wraps his arm around my waist and I lean into him like it's the most natural thing in the world. Every now and then muffled shouts can be heard from the house and each one brings back very unpleasant memories for me.

Each time I shiver, Wrath's arm hugs me tighter and a little bit more fear ebbs away.

WRATH

I'm proud of myself for the way I'm keeping a lid on my anger tonight. Fucking Dex. I'm partially to blame for this situation, since I allowed Inga to come up last night.

Normally, I wouldn't be so bent over this sort of thing, but I sensed right away how much it bothered Trinity. Raising bad memories, upsetting her—absolutely not okay.

While it probably falls under my job description to break that party up, I know Inga will throw a monumental hissy. I'd rather not leave Trin alone right now. Plus, the brothers have the right to do what they want in their own fucking clubhouse—even if the rest of us are thoroughly disgusted. Rock's the president for a reason. I figure he can decide how to deal with it.

I'm about to take out my phone and text him, when I hear his bike making its way up the driveway. Trin turns to me and smiles.

"You're going to make him deal with this, aren't you?"

My shoulders lift. "It's his ex."

She bumps her body into mine in a teasing gesture. "Yeah, but you're the one who gave her the okay to come up last night."

True enough.

I get up and walk over as he's backing his bike into his spot. The minute he shuts it down, I'm on him. No need for Hope to walk in on that cumfest.

"Inga's back."

His face twists. "Who the fuck brought her back here?"

"Dex has it bad for her." I glance up at the sky for a second. "Or at least, he did."

Trinity's hand touches my back, so I know she followed me over.

Another wave of shouting can be heard outside.

Rock's eyes narrow as he studies the clubhouse. "What's going on?"

Fuck. I'm not really sure how to explain it in front of Hope. "She wanted to play choo-choo?"

"What are you, five?" Rock snaps.

Well excuse me for not wanting to freak Cinderella out, jackass.

"Who's in there?"

"Everyone except you, me, Bricks, and maybe Z."

Z chooses that exact moment to step outside. Guess the asshole joined in after all. "Dude, your girl, Ing, is playing a serious game of Chinese Fingercuffs."

Oh, that's priceless.

"She's *not* my girl," Rock spits out.

Trinity steps forward a little. "I think she's trying to get you jealous," she says softly.

I can't help snorting at that. "Yeah, that's not the way to win a guy back."

Hope tugs on Rock's arm and he glances at her. "So, your ex-slampiece is in there taking it in every hole from your 'brothers?' Is that what I'm getting out of this conversation?"

Holyfuckingshit!

Seems Cinderella isn't so clueless after all.

Rock chokes and clearly has no idea how to respond to that. Z and I can't stop laughing.

"No one made her," Rock explains, which only makes me laugh harder.

"What, is she hoping you'll go get in line?" Hope spits out.

I'm going to die from lack of oxygen if she keeps this up. "Probably," I gasp.

Trinity attempts to diffuse the situation. "She must have run home and watched one too many *Law and Order* episodes. They don't make girls pull a train to hang here," she explains to Hope.

"What a relief," Hope snaps.

Nope, not liking her tone toward Trinity at all. Z and I both stop laughing and glare at Rock.

Control your woman.

The look on his face clearly says *Fuck off*. He puts his arm around Hope's shoulders. "We're going upstairs."

It'd be nice if it occurred to him that this whole situation might upset Trinity. I put my arm around her waist and tip my head at Rock. "Trin and I were going for a walk."

"I'll take care of it," Z volunteers.

Yeah, Rock's done with this whole situation. "I don't care who does what. Make sure things don't get too out of hand, and make sure she gets home in one piece. Make it clear she's not welcome back. Wipe her GPS if you have to. That bitch can't find her own ass without it."

Hope snorts and rolls her eyes. Whether it's because she doesn't like how well Rock knows the competition or something else, I don't know.

"Oh, some of the guys are filming it," Z decides to finally mention.

Rock's about to blow a gasket. "End that now. She'll lose her contract if that shit gets out. What the fuck is she thinking?"

Z glances at Hope, and I bite my lip so I don't start laughing again. "Uh, you might want to be the one to take care of that," he suggests.

"Are you fucking serious? What the fuck are you wearing this for then?" Rock pokes at the VP patch on Z's cut.

"I'm just saying it will be better coming from you."

All of us clomp into the clubhouse together. Rock runs his hands through his hair, obviously stressed about having to deal with Inga. I suffer a minor twinge of guilt over the whole situation.

The girls join Teller, Murphy, and Swan in the living room. I find my attention divided between what Trinity's up to and Rock pulling me to the side.

"Stay here with Hope and Trinny. Do *not* under any circumstances let the girls take a step in that hallway."

As if I'd let the girls anywhere near that cumguzzling skank show. "Yeah, sure. Why, you gonna slip in a quick one?" I ask, 'cause I'm pissed he thinks I have no common sense.

Someone's not in a joking mood. Rock smacks me and I snicker. "No, fuckface. Just do what I ask," he snaps.

"Come on, chickenshit," he yells to Z.

"Not cool," Z bitches back.

They carry on like that down the hallway and I decide to go join the girls.

Trinity seems to have recovered from whatever was bothering her about the whole situation. She's trying to reassure Hope, who seems pretty pissed off.

"Really, Hope. This almost never happens here. Rock doesn't run the club that way."

Hope arches a brow at Trin, but doesn't respond. Her attitude is starting to tick me off.

It's not long before Dex and Z carry Inga out of the house kicking and screaming. I should probably help with that, except I don't want to.

Rock returns in one piece. He throws himself on the couch and runs his hands over his face like he's trying to erase whatever he just saw. "Jesus Christ, that was disgusting," he mutters.

Hope's lips twitch into a smile. She takes Rock's hand and squeezes it. Her touch seems to calm him down pretty quick.

I'd like to get back to the evening Trin and I were having before we were so rudely interrupted. "Now you know why we were outside, prez," I remind him. I glance at Trinity, and she sits up and flashes a nervous smile at me.

Before we can get away, the front door flies open. I start laughing the second I see who it is. This night just keeps gettin' better and better.

"Marcel!" Heidi yells.

Teller jumps off the couch and grabs his little sister. "What the fuck are you doing here?"

And Heidi's off babbling about teenage nonsense. I try to catch Trinity's eye again, but she's giggling at the family drama unfolding in our living room.

"Hi, Uncle Rock," Heidi says when she finally winds down.

"Hey, Heidi-girl. How'd you find your way up here?"

She rolls her eyes. "I'm sixteen, not stupid." The attitude on this kid is something else.

Rock stares at her until she continues. Heidi lets out one of her famous dramatic sighs. "My boyfriend, Axel, brought me. He wants to prospect for you guys. He's eighteen. I thought you could talk to him," she adds.

Oh boy. Here it comes. Up until this point, Murphy has been doing his best to ignore Heidi. But as soon as the word "boyfriend" comes out of her mouth, he perks right the fuck up.

"Hey, Heidi-bug," Murphy calls.

"Don't call me bug, Blake," she snaps back at him. For fuck's sake they've been having this same argument for about a hundred years now.

Rock snaps his fingers in front of Heidi, clearly losing his patience. "Heidi, we don't allow prospects up here for the first year."

She pushes her lips into a pout. "Oh." Her gaze narrows on Rock's hand resting on Hope's leg. "Who are you?" she asks.

Rock makes the introduction. "Heidi, this is my girlfriend, Hope."

"Oh, wow. That's so cool. Uncle Rock's never had a girlfriend before." *Nope, just lots of slampieces.*

Rock gets Z to go talk to Axel. Teller and Heidi follow him out and again, I raise an eyebrow at Trinity.

"She's fun," Hope says with a laugh.

Fun doesn't begin to cover Heidi. "Well, at least in two more years she'll be Murphy's problem." I smirk at Murphy, who looks like he wants to punch me.

He shakes his head. "Fuck that, man. I'm just like another big brother to her."

Rock grins. "Please—she's been trying to take that ride since she was twelve." I find it amusing he would say that in front of Hope. Even funnier when she gets all pissy about it.

"She's a kid," Hope says.

Duh. "Yeah, which is why when she's *eighteen*, Murphy will sack up and put them both out of each other's misery." Why do I have to explain this to her?

She sits up and glares at me. "Are you serious? Murphy has to be what, ten years older than her?"

"Eight," Murphy says quietly.

She turns and pats his leg. "Sorry."

He flashes a grin and strokes his chin. "It's the beard."

Trinity taps Hope's arm to get her attention. "I think you're misunderstanding."

"What am I missing?"

Good grief. Mind your own business, woman.

Trinity glances at me and Murphy before answering. "They're not saying she *has* to be with Murphy. Or like she's promised to him or anything like that. Is that what you're thinking?"

Hope lifts her shoulders. "Well, yeah." She glances over at me, and I roll my eyes at her. God damn she's dense.

I lose track of the conversation for a second when Trinity has to put her hands on Murphy. "Although Murph will deny it, he's sweet on her too. But he won't do anything about it while she's underage," she explains to Cinderella.

"The age of consent is actually seventeen in New York." Hope educates us with her brilliant legal mind. I can't help snorting in disgust. Trinity's nose wrinkles and I'm seriously getting pissed about this entire conversation, because I gotta imagine it's fucking with Trinity's head.

"What if she's still with Axel?" Hope asks.

Murphy lifts his shoulders and lies through his teeth. "They're more worked up about this than I am. You met her, right? She's a pain in the ass. Not interested."

My hand connects with the back of his head. "Keep telling yourself that, buddy."

Hope runs out of the room and I focus on Rock who responds with a *Don't start* face.

"Did you know she had a boyfriend?" Murphy asks Trinity. Yeah, so much for not being interested.

Trinity's mouth curls into a smirk. "Heidi and I aren't that tight. You *know* that."

There I go getting all rage-y again, because I strongly suspect the reason Heidi dislikes Trin so much has something to do with walking in on something no teenager should ever witness her brother and crush doing to some chick.

Trin and Murphy are busy laughing about something—further sending my blood pressure through the roof. I turn to Rock. "You can't have your ol' lady questioning the club like that, brother."

Rock raises an eyebrow at me. "Simmer down, asshole," he growls at me.

Murphy pipes up. "It's your fucking fault. Why you always gotta hassle me about Heidi?"

Trinity finally leaves Murphy's side and sits next to me. "Wyatt, look at it this way. Heidi's club family. After meeting her for five seconds, Hope was ready to stand up to your scary ass in defense of her. Sounds like perfect ol' lady material to me."

Aw fuck, she's right. As much as she bugs me, Heidi's family, and I'd do pretty much anything to protect her.

"Yeah, I guess," I answer, not quite ready to concede all the way.

Hope returns and we all stop talking for a second. Way to be obvious guys.

Rock stands and stretches, holding out his hand for Cinderella, who eagerly runs to his side. Christ, they're enough to make you vomit. "I've had enough drama for one night." Rock points at me with his free hand. "Wrath, tell Z I'll talk to him about Axel in the morning. Someone make sure Heidi gets home. She can't stay here."

No shit.

CHAPTER SEVENTEEN

Trinity

Wrath and I are alone again.

He stands and holds out his hand to me. "Come stay with me."

I blink up at him in surprise. "Why?"

His mouth twists in annoyance, but his voice is gentle when he answers. Well—gentle for Wrath. "Tonight was kinda crazy. I want to make sure you're safe."

I tilt my head to the side. I *am* jittery, but he has no idea why that whole gangbang thing bothered me so much. "None of the guys will hurt me."

His jaw clenches. He points at the couch. "You slept on me last night and survived. This time we can actually be comfortable in my bed."

"You haven't wanted me in your bed in a long time."

His voice takes on a harsher edge. "Trinity, don't push me tonight."

I *want* him to order me up there. Boss me around like he's so good at doing sometimes. Let me know that he wants me.

But I sense he's struggling with something. Curious, I take his outstretched hand and follow him to his room. He closes the door behind us and I lower my head waiting to see how he wants things to happen.

The sound of him shuffling through drawers gets me curious and excited. What's he up to? I peek up in time to see him toss a T-shirt and pair of boxers on the bed.

"I'm going to take a quick shower. Get dressed for bed," he says without looking at me.

Huh?

Moving over to the bed, I plop down and run my fingers over the faded Harley T-shirt. Bringing it to my nose, I inhale—detergent, mixed with Wrath's unique scent.

I glance up at the bathroom door. He didn't invite me in. This is all too fucking weird. Especially after our kiss downstairs. Balling the clothes in my fist, I perch on the side of the bed and wait for him to emerge.

He finally does and my mouth goes dry at the sight of him. Bare-chest, water droplets still clinging to his inked skin. His blond hair is darker from being wet and frames his face in a way that should be captured on film.

When he notices I'm still dressed, he quirks an eyebrow at me.

My shoulders lift and it takes a second to untie my tongue. "I wanted to take a shower too."

"Sorry, I should have let you go first."

Yeah, or invited me in with you.

My fingers trace the inside of my arm, pinching lightly to make sure I'm still awake.

"I left a toothbrush on the counter for you."

Too stunned to speak, I scurry in the bathroom. As promised, there's a brand new-in-the-box toothbrush. Boy, he really didn't want to let me out of his sight. It's not like I couldn't run downstairs and grab my own toothbrush or nightclothes. I rush through my shower, quickly pat myself dry and toss on my borrowed jammies.

Wrath's already in the bed when I emerge. He turns and smiles. My breath catches. He doesn't smile a lot, but when he does it always levels me. Tonight's no different.

"Come on, it's been a long day."

I approach the bed and wait to see what he wants.

"What are you doing, get up here."

He takes up so much space, the only spot open is a sliver of mattress against the wall. He holds out his hand. When I take it, he yanks me to him, hooks his arms around me and spins me into the space next to him. Then he pulls the blankets up over us, and shuts off the bedside lamp.

"Wrath?"

"What, Trin?"

"You really just want me to *sleep* with you?"

"Yes, Trin."

This sleeping next to each other thing is giving me serious emotional itchies. We were close to something happening downstairs earlier. What changed his mind? Inga? Did he remember that I'm a whore just like she is? If only he knew the truth. Turning over I press up against his solid, comforting body. Everything seems to be in working order.

"What's wrong now, Trin?" he rumbles.

"Nothing." I shift again trying to get comfortable.

"Do you need to get fucked?" he offers without opening his eyes.

I scoot away so fast my ass bumps into the chilly wall. "No."

"Then go to sleep."

I roll over on my stomach. When that doesn't work, I sit up and punch the pillows.

I turn to face him. "Wyatt, if I had said yes, would you?"

He sucks in a deep breath and lets it out slow before answering. "That's not why I wanted you here."

"Then why?"

"Fuck. I told you why. I liked waking up with you this morning."

"Oh."

He holds his arms out to me. "Come here."

Finally, something I'm familiar with. But he just arranges me so my head rests on his chest. His arm curls protectively around me settling on my hip. It makes me feel cherished and protected. And *weird*.

Eventually, his breathing turns deep and even. I manage to drift off too.

WRATH

My poor, confused cock stands at full attention the next morning. Not his fault. We haven't slept with a woman without fucking her in a long damn time. This makes two nights in a row, with the woman I want more than anything. It's not that I *don't* want to fuck her—one glance at the tented sheet confirms that. I just want *not* to fuck things up more. I can only imagine what sort of bad memories last night's events brought up for her. My plan was to make her feel safe and let her know that she means more to me than sex.

This morning, with Trinity still tucked firmly against my side, her warm breath tickles over my ribs. I inhale her fresh, soapy scent and my cock's even harder. I take a few more deep breaths and calm myself before drifting back to sleep.

Not sure how much later it is, but I groan and arch my hips up before I'm even fully awake. Soft fingers stroke my cock harder pulling me fully out of sleep. *Holy fuck.* If she keeps this up, my balls are going to be bluer than my fucking eyes.

I clear my throat, but my voice still comes out all rough and raspy. "Trinity, what are you doing?"

Instead of answering, her warm, wet mouth closes over my dick.

My muscles tighten, jerking me upright. "Oh, fuck!"

Nothing has felt so amazing in a long time.

"Trin...babe...oh," I babble like an idiot, as I'm falling back against the pillows.

She keeps happily bobbing up and down my dick, driving me nuts. Using one hand, I grab her leg and pull her closer to me. From this angle, I can run my hand all over her plump little ass. I need the distraction or I'm going to blow in the next two seconds. By feel alone, I find what I'm looking for and slide one finger deep inside her, searching for the right spot. Her hips jump and I've got her. I add another finger and work them slowly in and out. My thumb finds her clit and gently brushes over it until she moans around my cock.

"Wyatt."

"Don't stop, babe."

Her mouth closes around me again and my brain stops. She wriggles her hips, making me realize my hand has also stopped moving. I really can't take any more of this. She started it, so I'm not going to feel bad. My free hand reaches over to my nightstand and drags out a condom. I've got it out and ready to go, before she even realizes what I'm doing.

"Come here, Angel Face."

She sucks harder and shakes her head. Sweet motherfucking heaven. My palm connects with her ass and she lets out a startled yelp. It's enough to get her attention, and give me some room to squeeze into the fucking rubber. My hand settles on her hip, kneading her flesh.

"Get on top of me."

Her lashes flutter and she hesitates.

"*Now.*"

All her skin from chest to cheeks flushes pink. But the no-nonsense tone was what she needed to get her to straddle me and sink down onto my cock.

"Fuck, angel," I groan as she slides down, then back up. Christ this is better than I'd been imagining since the last time we'd fucked. And I have one hell of an imagination when it comes to Trinity. "Don't stop," I rasp out.

She shakes her head in a determined way. "No. Can't."

"Good." She keeps at it slow and steady, every single time she grinds her hips into me, I bite my lip to keep from blowing. "You feel amazing," I praise, while arching my hips up.

Her throat works, and she looks down at me with wide eyes. "You too."

"Too much?" I ask easing back down.

She nods and I can't take any more, I sit up and pull her tight against me, taking her mouth. Her legs wrap around me, and I gently lower her to the mattress. "You with me?"

"Yes."

That's all I need to hear. I take full advantage of our position and pump into her strong and steady. She throws her head back and I plant my face in the curve of her shoulder, licking and sucking. Her nails rake over my back and the need to come slams into the base of my spine.

"Are you close, baby?" I whisper against her ear.

She mutters a few words that sound like "It's okay."

Uh, hell no. I push up shoving my hand between us, brushing against her clit. She lets out a startled gasp and lifts her hips, seeking more. I keep sliding my fingers over her nub until she trembles and her pussy convulses, squeezing me so fucking tight it steals my breath.

"Good girl." She's so out of it, she doesn't even respond. I push her knees up and hammer into her. Seconds later, the pressure increases, squeezing my balls into a mind-blowing release.

Fucking hell.

I drop down a bit, nuzzle her throat, lick the sweat from her skin and finally kiss her.

This is perfect.

We're quiet as our breathing returns to normal. I hate to move away from her, but I sit up and get rid of my condom. She's limp as a noodle when I pull her up on top of me. My lips press against her forehead, and my hand strokes over her hair.

"Babe. You know that's not why I asked you up here, right?" I want her to understand that while the sex blows my fucking mind, I want all of her.

Trin settles next to me, pulling the sheet up to practically her chin. Her nose scrunches up as she turns to face me. "Why then?"

Is she kidding? "I like spending time with you. We're more than that, don't you think?"

"More than sex? Sure, I guess."

Well that's not encouraging. "We're friends again, right?"

I hate the way she hesitates. "Yeah."

"So maybe we explore that for a while."

"What are you trying to say, Wrath? You want me to be your girl-friend?" Disbelief drips from every word.

Girlfriend. No.

Old Lady. Wife. Soul-stealer. Yes, yes, and yes. "Would that be so horrible?"

She shoots up so fast, my head spins. The fuck? She inches her way down the bed and jumps down to the floor before I can wrap a hand around her ankle to stop her.

"You've gotta be kidding. Club whores don't become ol' ladies."

I swear to fuck if she calls herself that one more time... "Says who? And stop calling yourself a whore."

I gotta say, I'm pretty insulted at the way she's jumping into her jeans with both fucking feet. She can't get away from me fast enough and it's starting to piss me off.

"Where are you going?"

"To my room." She holds out a shaky hand to me in a stop gesture. "Don't. Just don't. We'll talk later."

We'll fucking talk all right.

Trinity

Wrath's clearly lost his fucking mind. I try not to slam the door on my way out of his room. Thank fuck no one's in the hallway to catch me leaving.

My heart skips as I pass Teller's door and Swan steps out. He hasn't asked me into his room in a long time. We always use one of the unoccupied guest rooms, and I don't know what to make of it. I must startle her too, because she jumps when she sees me.

"Morning," she whispers.

"Hey."

She follows me downstairs. "Were you with Wrath?" she asks.

I toss her a look over my shoulder. She's usually not very talkative about who we bag. I just nod.

Her mouth curves into a smile. Swan's a pretty girl. Tall, lean, and graceful. Awfully delicate to be tossed around by a bunch of bikers, when you think about it, but she doesn't seem to mind. She's also fond of using the champagne room here to practice her ballet moves, which I find amusing.

"What's so funny?" I ask.

She startles and holds out her hand. "Nothing. Just the trio of terror was bitching about how he hasn't been with any of them in a long time now."

That stops me. "What?"

"Ginger, Cherry—"

"Yeah, I know who you're talking about." The memory of Cherry leaving Wrath's room a few weeks ago is still enough to spike my anger. And Ginger, I've wanted to choke that bitch out for years.

I refuse to examine why I'm suddenly feeling all violent.

"Cherry's been bitching up a storm since he tossed her out of his room before she got to suck him off," Swan adds.

What the hell?

She barely takes a breath. She definitely doesn't notice my jaw hanging. "They're worried he found some citizen girlfriend, like prez did."

I snort at the very idea of Wrath taking up with a woman like Hope. Nothing against her, she's perfect for Rock. Wrath, not so much. "Unlikely."

"Well, duh. Any girl in this house with half a brain knows he's been in love with you for years," she says with a giggle.

What. The. Fuck.

Her eyes widen at the expression on my face. "Oh." She quickens her pace, probably to get away from me.

I follow her into the downstairs bathroom, a thousand questions burning on the tip of my tongue. She turns the corner and lets out a shriek.

"Those bitches!"

Shaking myself out of thoughts about Wrath, I step up behind her to see what she's so upset about. The bag of stuff she keeps tucked under the bathroom vanity has been emptied, all its contents dumped into one of the toilets.

Jesus Christ. I've been meaning to talk to Rock about getting lockers in here for a while now. Even though I'm not the one who stuffed her leotards and tights in the makeshift porcelain washer, I feel guilty.

Wrinkling my nose, I take a closer look. "Tell me it's just water?"

"Yeah, I guess. They're still a bag of filthy twats, though."

I snicker at her description. "Oh yeah. No doubt. Hang on, I'll go grab a plastic bag. You can wash them downstairs."

I'm livid as I walk down to my room. Those three are getting bolder. I suspect Roxy's one of the girls who tossed some bullshit at Hope the other night too. Swan's sweet, soft-spoken, and never has an attitude. Even though we've never talked about our pasts, I suspect she enjoys hiding out with a bunch of bikers because she's running from something similar to what I left behind. Fucking around with her stuff that way really pisses me off.

Once we take care of her clothes, she runs back upstairs to ask Teller for a ride home. Can't blame the poor girl. I pocket a small box I've been saving for a special occasion and head to the kitchen.

I'm almost giddy when I spot the toxic trio—Roxy, Cherry, and Ginger—at the table hanging all over Ravage and Stash. As soon as Rav spots me, he holds out his arms. "Where you been, baby girl?"

Ignoring the glares from the three bitches, I give him a quick hug. "Around."

"I'll say," Ginger mutters under her breath. That's rich coming from her. I ignore it because I have something so much better than a witty comeback in mind.

Smiling brightly, I ask if everyone wants coffee. Of course none of the three bitches offer to help me in the kitchen, although Roxy takes great care reminding me that she only drinks decaf.

I'm very aware of this fact.

The other two nod along. They pretty much do whatever Roxy says or does.

Breezing into the kitchen, I find Hoot already has a pot of coffee going. "Morning, Trin."

"Morning. Can you hand me the orange carafe?"

He frowns but plucks it off the shelf and hands it to me. "Can you go check if Sparky needs anything?" I ask, to get him out of my way.

His eyebrows draw down again, but he leaves the kitchen.

Perfect.

I have no intention of making a separate pot of coffee for those three cunts. Well, not a pot of decaf coffee anyway. Dumping the entire box of laxatives in the coffee pot, I muse that caffeine will be the least of their concerns in two to four hours.

WRATH

After Trinity stormed out of my room, I tried hard to go back to sleep. I considered going after her, but I actually want things to work this time. Chasing her down when we're both pissed off isn't going to accomplish much.

I've got another two weeks until the big fight. Two more weeks of close quarters with Trinity. My dick gets hard just thinking about her in her tight little workout clothes, helping me out at the gym.

My door slams open, banging off the wall, and I bolt upright.

Trinity storms in, kicking the door shut behind her.

"What the fuck, Trin?"

She plants her hands on her hips and stares me down. "I know you haven't been fucking any of the other club girls."

My jaw drops. "What?"

"I know I'm the only girl you've been with in a while, so what's going on?"

Where is this coming from? What'd she do, go question every chick in the house while she was gone?

Crossing my arms over my chest, I glare right back at her. I'd get up, but I'm still naked from earlier. Trin seems a little unpredictable at the moment, so I prefer to keep my dick safely hidden beneath the sheet. "Why are you so concerned about who warms my cock all of a sudden? You hate me."

Her bottom lip thrusts out in an irresistible little pout. I hate when she makes that face. Every single time, it makes me want to give her every-thing, kiss her, snuggle her, whatever the fuck she has going on in her nutty little head, I want to do to make her smile.

"I don't hate you," she whispers. "Why would you say that?"

"Oh, I don't know. Maybe because I suggested we try being together and you ran out of here like I tried to set you on fire." Fuck, as soon as the words leave my mouth, I wish I could take them back.

She shrugs off my thoughtless comment. "Well, you haven't always been super nice to me either, you know."

"I fucked up. I'm trying hard here, Trin."

"Why are my fuckups still topics of conversation?"

"What are you talking about?" To my knowledge, Trin never admits to fucking up. She's a tough little bitch.

There's that fucking pout again. This time she glances at the floor. Something's weighing on her. "The way you're always telling everyone what a slut I am."

Aw, fuck. "What are you talking about? I've *never* called you that."

"No, but you've implied it and worse." She lifts her gaze, piercing me right down to my soul. All my shitty behavior over the years and especially the last few months comes rushing back.

Then she spills what's been bothering her for the last eight years. What we've never acknowledged or spoken about. "You know what MCs normally expect of girls like me. But here, you could have said I was off-limits and they would have respected it. But you said nothing. I didn't expect a property patch or anything more than what you were capable of giving me at the time. I didn't think you wanted me. It wasn't fair for you to be mad at me when you never said anything."

Each one of her brutally honest words burns like acid. I'm not sure if we're getting somewhere or if this will end up pushing us further apart. "Trinity, you know that's not entirely true. I asked you not to do that for the club. We both know no one pushed you into being club ass." I say it as gently as possible, because I'm really not trying to hurt her feelings. "I told...I'm not going to lie, it fucking hurt, Trin."

My mind flashes back to the night all this shit got fucked up between us for real. All I can see is Teller pulling her up the stairs. Trin's questioning eyes. And I sat there like an asshole and let it happen because I was too proud and pissed off. After my spectacular display of how little I cared, she went with Z not long after. That stung, because we've been friends forever. Still I said nothing. She and Teller got tight for a while. Then she, Teller and Murphy. I stopped paying attention after that. It hurt too fucking much. Because it was my own fault. I couldn't be mad at my brothers because of the reason she said. I never opened my stupid mouth to stop it.

These last few weeks, working with her has been fucking awesome. I love getting up and finding her waiting for me downstairs every morning. Love having her around at my gym all day. We're finally getting back to where we were before things went to hell. No. Actually it's better. I don't want to lose her.

I can't fuck this up again.

Tears silently track down her cheeks. In the past I would have said something nasty to cut her even deeper. Never again.

Pulling her into my arms, I use my thumbs to wipe her tears away.

"I'm sorry," she sobs against my chest. "I didn't—"

"Shhh. It's in the past now, okay?"

Her head tips back. "Is it? Can it ever really be in the past? Because sometimes I can't close my eyes without seeing you and Ginger together. Or Cherry, or—" I place my hand over her mouth to stop her.

"I understand what you're saying." I pin her with a hard stare. "I do. I'm sorry I tried to push you into something you're not ready for. But I want you to understand, you mean more to me than just sex."

She shakes free of my hold but perches next to me on the bed, keeping her feet on the floor. "That's how I felt when we first met. You kept coming back and I didn't understand why."

Laughter rumbles out of me. "It surprised me too. But I couldn't stay away."

"Then, it hurt the way you...didn't care enough to—."

"I'm sorry." Using two fingers, I press them against her cheek and turn her to face me. "You don't trust me yet."

Her hand reaches up, grasping mine and pulling it away from her face. "It's not just you. I don't trust myself."

I know exactly what she means and it doesn't piss me off the way it would have a couple years ago. I understand her better now. Hell, I don't trust myself either.

I bring her hand to my face and brush my lips over her knuckles. "We'll work on it together, okay?"

Instead of giving me the answer I want, she blows me away with a question I'm not expecting. "Why didn't you tell me nothing happened between you and Cherry?"

Fuck, how long was she gone? What'd she do, play dick detective the entire time? "What?"

"You never told—"

I sit up straighter and put my back against the pillows. "I didn't want to make excuses. I still fucked up. I brought her up here intend—"

"But you didn't? Why?"

Because I don't want to get it up for anyone else. "She's not you."

"Yeah, but you thought I was across the hall with Z..."

"It wasn't worth it."

She stares at the wall as if trying to make sense of that.

"That night I spent like ten minutes gushing to Z about how you and I were getting along so well…and…I ended up feeling like such an idiot."

It takes a second to absorb all that information. "Wait. What did you tell him?"

She shrugs and refuses to look at me. "I don't know. That it was like when we first met."

Reaching out, I brush my hand over her cheek. "Is that bad?"

Finally she looks at me with so much hurt in her eyes. "Yeah, because too many bad things have gone down for it to ever be like that again."

She's wrong. She doesn't know it yet. But she's *wrong*.

CHAPTER EIGHTEEN

WRATH

As the fight approaches, the days we spend at the gym get longer and longer. I'm fine with it, but I sense Trinity's getting tired. It's not that I'm worried I'll lose—I'm not. But ever since Rock told me he's bringing Cinderella to the fight, I can't stop thinking about having Trinity there as well. And if she's going to watch, I want to make sure I'm one hundred percent.

"You can go home, babe. I'll ask one of the guys to come pick me up."

She pierces me with a hurt expression. "You want me to leave?"

"Well, it's late and I'm sure you're tired."

"I'm okay. How much longer do you think you'll be?"

"Let me finish this set of drills, I'll grab a shower and we can go, okay?"

"Sounds good. I'm going to use one of the ellipticals if you don't mind."

Do I mind? Trin getting all nice and sweaty in her tight little yoga pants and fitted T-shirt? No, I don't mind one bit.

So much for finishing any drills. I basically stand there hugging the heavy bag drooling over Trinity. Watching the gentle sway of her tits gets me stone hard, something that's hard to conceal in my loose gym shorts.

"Christ, you've got it bad for her," Jake says behind me.

I'm pissed that he managed to startle me and at how obvious I am.

"Why are you here so late?"

"Forgot my fucking cell phone. Can't function without it." He glances at Trinity again. "You gonna make this happen with her, or not?"

"Who are you, dear fuckin' Abby now? Get lost."

Jake isn't offended at all. He knows what a moody prick I am. "Why do you even know who Dear Abby is?"

I don't think explaining that my mother religiously read that column for years is going to make him go away fast enough. "Did you find your phone?"

He waves it in my face. "Yeah."

"Good. Lock up on your way out."

He laughs and slaps me on the shoulder before finally leaving. I approach Trinity slowly and get on the machine next to her. She glances over and smiles, then pulls out her ear bud. "Want me to finish up?"

"Take your time. I'm good."

She glances down at the timer. "I've got ten minutes left."

I nod and set my own clock, taking up a lazy pace next to her. We don't speak for the next ten minutes and when she finishes, she hops off, flushed, sweaty and so fuckin' pretty, I have to look away.

"I'm going to shower and change. Meet you in your office in twenty?"

"Sure."

I can't concentrate knowing there's only a door and a flimsy shower curtain between myself and naked Trinity.

On autopilot, I stalk over to the women's locker room. My hand flattens against the door and I take a second to consider what I'm doing. But then I catch Trinty's voice. Singing. She's singing in the shower and her voice pulls me inside.

She jumps when I push the curtain aside and peers at me over her shoulder.

"What are you doing?" she asks.

"I thought we should conserve water."

One corner of her mouth kicks up. "Oh, really?"

"Yup."

"Is this the new 'Earth friendly' Wrath?"

"Yeah, sure." My hands go to the hem of my shirt and yank it up over my head, dropping it on the bench outside the shower stall. Trinity quirks an eyebrow at me.

"Am I supposed to be impressed?"

She's trying to act cool, but I definitely notice her breathing picking up. I keep my eyes on her as I kick off my sneakers and ease my shorts over my hips. "Not yet. The impressive part's coming right up."

Laughter bubbles out of her, bouncing around the tight confines of the shower stall. "God, you're cocky."

"You have no idea."

I make a good show of sliding my hand up and down my cock. "This is what you do to me."

"Me?" she asks with an innocently raised eyebrow.

"Yeah, you," I answer, taking a step into the shower. She backs up and I reach out to pull her to me.

"I thought you're not supposed to have sex before a fight?"

"That's an old superstition."

"You're not superstitious? Not even a little?"

Instead of answering, I wrap my arms around her slick little body and pick her up, pressing her into the wall. Her legs squeeze my hips, and her head falls back. My mouth finds hers and I kiss her until the air is knocked right out of me. She's panting when I pull away, soaking wet, with water falling down her face, droplets clinging to her plump lips.

I'm stuck. I want to fuck her hard and fast against the wall, but I also want to take my time and taste every inch of her. There's not enough room in the shower for the second option.

"What's wrong?"

"Nothing. I just want more than a quick fuck in the shower."

She cocks her head to the side like she doesn't believe what she's hearing. Slowly, she unlocks her legs from around my waist and holding onto my thighs, she kneels on the shower floor.

"What are you doing, babe?"

Instead of answering, she wraps her lips around my cock and swirls her tongue around the head.

"Fuck," I groan out and almost lose my balance. She grips my legs tighter and I lean forward, bracing myself on the wall so I don't fall. And because I need to watch her. My teeth sink into my lip as she keeps stroking, taking me deeper each time.

"Angel, I'm really close."

She nods and hums, only making things more desperate for me. Her hands squeeze tighter and move faster.

"Fuck. You're killing me."

The corners of her mouth turn up in a devilish smile and she peeks up at me.

That's it. I'm done. She takes me deep one last time, and I'm coming down the back of her throat. She keeps sucking and licking until I can't take another stroke of her hot little tongue, then giggles at me when I pull her up into my arms.

"Why'd you do that? I wanted to come in your tight, fucking pussy, babe."

"Maybe later. If you're good."

Trinity

Wrath's quiet on the way home. Is he mad at me? He shocked the hell out of me in the locker room. I'm still worked up over our encounter.

"Wyatt, are you mad at me?"

"What? No, babe. Why would you think that?"

"You're so quiet."

He reaches over and squeezes my leg. "I'm exhausted, that's all."

"Oh." Now I feel stupid.

"Trin, can I ask you for a favor?"

"Hmmm...I don't know. Pretty soon, I'm going to need to collect on all these favors I'm doing for you."

His hand tightens around my thigh. "I haven't forgotten I owe you an orgasm. Trust me, I plan to bury my face in your pussy as soon as we get home."

I burst out laughing. "Okay."

My hand drops off the steering wheel and curls around his for a minute.

"Will you stay with me until the fight? Up in my room I mean."

Surprised, it takes me a second to absorb that and form an answer. "Okay. Why?"

"I *am* superstitious, and you're like my good luck charm."

I snort at that. "You're full of shit."

Out of the corner of my eye, I catch him grinning. "I know. Will you still stay with me?"

"Okay." I give it some more thought. "What are you going to tell everyone?"

"What does it matter? It's no one's business but ours."

Huh. Okay. Now he doesn't want anyone to think we're together? After the big talk we had, his indifference stings and I hate the little pang of disappointment thumping in my chest.

It's only ten o'clock when we arrive at the clubhouse. Still pretty quiet, even for a weeknight, though.

"Where is everyone?" I ask as we walk up the steps to the clubhouse.

He shrugs. "You know as much as I do. We've been gone all day."

Inside, we find Z sprawled out on the couch smoking a joint.

"Can't you get a vaporizer, so you don't stink up the whole place?" I scold him.

He turns, his mouth curling into a smirk. "You know I'm old school." He holds his arms out. "Hey, babe. Where you been all day?"

I jerk my head at Wrath. "Working with our fighter."

"Yeah? He gonna destroy the competition?"

"Fuck yeah." Wrath shouts so loud my ears cringe.

They give each other one of their man-bro-high-five handshake things. I hang back enjoying Wrath being a little looser. Only took twelve hours at the gym to get him like this.

Z offers to share his smoke. Wrath shakes his head, but I pluck it from his fingers and take a hit. It's strong and I choke as I blow it out. "What the fuck is Sparky up to now?"

Z grins. "Good shit, right? I dunno. He got these new ultra-violet lights he's been messin' with." He sits up. "It's his special project," he adds with finger quotes.

I giggle. "He's got a million special projects."

We catch up about stuff going on at the house. Eventually Wrath yawns.

Z slaps him. "What's wrong old man? Past your bed time?"

"Fuck you. I'd love to see you stick to my routine."

They banter back and forth like that for a few minutes and I just sit back and enjoy the show. Eventually, Wrath turns and raises an eyebrow at me.

"I'm gonna go grab a few things," I say, slapping his leg.

The few things I need to grab include sitting down at my computer to answer a bunch of e-mails I've been neglecting. I figure Z should keep Wrath busy long enough for me to do that.

I was right. When I return to the living room, they're still goofing around. Wrath jumps up when he sees me and salutes Z.

"Night, kids," Z calls out with a smirk.

"What took you so long?" Wrath asks, as soon as he closes the door behind us. "I thought you changed your mind."

Inside I melt at how vulnerable he sounds, then brace myself as I wait for him to get defensive.

But he doesn't.

"I just needed to do a few things."

He lets out another yawn and shakes his head.

"Come on, fighter. It's time for bed. I drop the nightshirt I brought up on the bed and take my shirt off. Behind me Wrath sucks in a harsh breath.

"Shit. Trin, your back."

Twisting and turning, I can't see what he's talking about. "What?"

He comes closer and runs his fingers over my shoulder blades. "Does it hurt?"

"What?"

"In the shower, I must've slammed you into the wall harder than I realized. You're scraped and I'm afraid it's gonna bruise."

"Oh. It can't be that bad. I don't feel anything."

"You might tomorrow." He runs his fingers through his hair, looking so damn upset. "I'm so sorry."

"I'm fine. I know you didn't do it on purpose."

"Hang on. Let me get something." He stalks into the bathroom and returns with a small, white tube. "Arnica gel, it'll help." He thrusts his chin at the bed. "Lie down for me."

I stretch out and the bed dips as he sits next to me. The gel is cool as he slicks it over my skin, and I jump a little. He spends so long rubbing and caring for me that I end up falling asleep. Vaguely I'm aware of him slipping off the rest of my clothes and tucking me under the blankets.

WRATH

Since Trin passed out on me last night, I didn't get to bury my face in her pussy like I promised.

I like to think I'm a man of my word.

The serious case of morning wood I woke up with demands I wake Trinity up in a special way.

She's curled on her side, and I run my hand down the length of her spine. I'm relieved I thought to put something on her back last night, because there doesn't appear to be any bruising this morning. One glance at my big hand against her delicate body is a punch in the gut. A visual reminder to be more careful with her. A soft moan drags out of her and she rolls to her back. Beneath the sheet, I get a glimpse of pretty pink nipples hard from the morning chill.

The insatiable need to bury my dick in her claws at me, but I hold back. I brush my fingertips over her nipples, then use my tongue. Another moan gets me moving, kissing down her body, nuzzling her hip.

Above me she gasps, coming fully awake.

"Morning, angel."

"*Mmmm...*" Her fingers rake through my hair. "Wyatt, what are you doing?"

"Keeping my promises."

Her eyes widen in surprise and her teeth nibble her bottom lip. "Wow. Good morning to you too."

I'm too worked up to laugh. Instead I wrap my hands around her thighs. "Open."

She lies back, arching her hips up, legs falling open.

"Wider."

Her hand tugs on my hair a little, but she does as I ask, closing her eyes.

She sucks in a quivering gasp as I hover over her. "So fucking beautiful."

She's already trembling all over and I haven't even put my mouth on her. My hands move up from her thighs, feathering over her slick folds, massaging up to her clit, until she falls back with a harsh sigh.

With deliberate strokes, my tongue caresses and toys with her, driving her hard and fast to the brink. "You taste so fucking good."

"Please, Wyatt." I can barely hear her soft, begging voice. My thumb slips over her clit as my tongue darts inside her. Any additional words she planned on are lost to moaning.

Easing back, I slide two fingers into her silky heat. "Look at me, Trin."

Forcing open her heavy lids, she blinks and a soft smile curves her lips.

"That's it. Keep your eyes on me while I make you come."

Her eyes penetrate right down to my soul and I falter for a second. Then my thumb twitches and she jolts. My fingers drag in and out of her with measured strokes, making sure to rub right over the spot that will set her off. Watching her struggle to keep her eyes open because I asked her to rips away my restraint.

Her breathing turns ragged, her entire body tensing up. Close. She's so damn close. My mouth finds her clit again, sucking, as my fingers keep working inside. She can't keep her eyes open any longer. Her back bows off the bed and the sweetest screams tear from her throat.

This is torture. I fling my hand out, desperately reaching for a condom while she rides it out.

"Wyatt, please," she begs. "Please, please…"

"What do you need? I'm right here."

"Please fuck me."

It's not the first time she's said those words to me, but the impact slams into me with furious force.

Finally, my fingers brush against a condom. I'm ripping it open quicker than I've ever done before. Trinity's eyes follow my every movement.

"I don't think my dick's ever been so fucking hard, babe," I mutter at her. Her mouth drops open. But it's the loving way her eyes keep following me that excites me the most.

I want to fuck her so hard, so deep, and so thoroughly, she never leaves my bed again.

My lips find hers, drinking in her gasp as I press into her. My dick's screaming at me to move faster, sink into her harder but I hold back, afraid I'll hurt her.

"More, Wyatt."

I find the tender spot between her neck and shoulder, kissing and nipping. Beneath me, she goes nuts. Writhing and meeting every one of my thrusts. Christ, she's surrounding me. Her scent filling my nose, her voice filling my head, her body under mine.

This is it.

She's it.

Stop fucking it up.

The voices in my head are not helpful.

Balancing my weight on my elbows, I'm able to watch her as I ease back, then thrust deep again and again. Her eyes widen and her sexy fucking mouth opens.

"Come for me again, Angel Face," I growl against her ear. "Give me everything."

"*Mmmm.*"

Nope. She's got no words left. I pound into her, loving the way she moves and rolls with me. Her fingers dig into my shoulders as a hard orgasm sweeps over her, taking me along for the ride.

How have I ever denied that this woman owns a piece of my soul?

Always has. Always will.

CHAPTER NINETEEN

WRATH

"I want you to come to the fight with me tomorrow," I whisper in Trinity's ear, hugging her tighter to me.

She tips her face up, cocking her head like she heard wrong. "You've never wanted me at one of your fights before."

That's not entirely true, but we're still wrapped up in my bed together. I'm not ruining the moment by arguing with her. "Well, I want you there."

She keeps staring. Hmm, maybe I need to be more convincing. "You've been such a big help getting me ready for the fight, you deserve to see the rewards." I flash my cockiest grin.

She nibbles on her lower lip.

"Hope will be there," I say, trying to encourage her.

The corner of her mouth twitches, a brief sign of disappointment. "Oh, did Rock ask you to bring me to keep her company?"

She would think that wouldn't she? "No, he didn't. I want you there as my good luck charm."

She chuckles and the sound relaxes me. "What's with you needing a good luck charm lately? Are you nervous?"

I snort. Christ, I've been taking and throwing punches my entire life. Compared to the shit I've lived through, some underground fight barely registers on my give-a-fuck meter.

Pulling her tighter to me, I look into her eyes and lie through my teeth. "I'll be so amped up after, I'll need to fuck you to come down from the adrenaline rush."

A spark of interest flares in her eyes. Of course. As much as I try to change our dynamic, sex is the best way we relate to each other.

"Me?"

Fuck, she's a pain in my ass.

"No one but you." The words come out so easy, I realize they're the absolute truth. Can she tell?

No. Trinity seems shocked and I try not to be insulted.

"Okay," she whispers.

I stand to make a fuckload of money off this fight. For myself and for my club. People will bet against me heartily. As long as I have Trinity there watching, it won't bother me a whip.

Trinity

"What time do you want to leave today?" I ask, because it seems Wrath has no intention of getting out of bed.

"I don't. I think I'll do some light cardio and stuff here, and chill for the afternoon."

Surprised, I turn and peer up at him. "Are you sure?"

"Yeah, I usually do a rest day before getting the shit kicked out of me."

My breath catches and I have to sit up so I can get air in my lungs.

"What's wrong, babe?"

"It just...it just hit me. You could get hurt."

The bed shifts as he sits up next to me. One of his big hands slides over my lower back, soothing me. "What did you think I was getting ready for, a flower arranging contest?"

I can't summon up any laughter. "It's not funny."

"Hey, come here." He pulls me into his arms. "I've done this before. I know you think I'm a cocky asshole, but I really do know what I'm doing."

"I don't think you're an asshole," I whisper.

"Just cocky?"

"Oh, yeah."

He chuckles and kisses the tip of my nose. "How about this. I promise, I won't even let him get a shot in."

He seems so sure of himself. And I have to remember, he's been fighting for longer than I've known him.

"Okay."

"Good." He tickles my side. "You know what I do want to do today?"

"Oh, I can guess."

"Not that. Maybe later."

I punch his arm and he pretends to be seriously injured. "First, I want to eat breakfast. I'm *staaarving*," he says, like a dramatic five-year-old would.

"Yeah, okay. Then what?"

His gaze bounces around the room before settling on his closet. "Why don't we go out to the gun range?"

Typical. "Sounds good. I'd love to kick your ass at some target practice."

He leans over and kisses my cheek. "I'll enjoy watching you try."

After breakfast, Wrath runs upstairs to grab his range bag. I stay in the kitchen and pack lunch into a backpack, then hurry into my room to throw on a sweatshirt.

He's waiting for me by the front door when I return. "Got your gun?"

I nod to the closet where the one of the club's gun lockers is tucked away. "In there."

He cocks his head. "You should keep one in your room." He grumbles to himself and scowls down the hall.

"What?"

"Nothing. I'm just pissed I never thought of how unprotected you are down here."

"What are you talking about? You guys have this place wired better than a doomsday bunker."

My characterization makes him laugh.

"Come on, Angel Face." Warmth prickles over my skin at the familiar endearment. He opens the door and loops his arm over my shoulders as we walk to the garage. I soak up the crisp, fresh air and squint at the bright light. Inside the garage he stares at the ATVs and UTVs for a second. "As much as I enjoy you snuggled up at my back, let's take the Ranger. More room to store our shit."

The UTV he picked is a serious piece of equipment with six wheels and more towing capacity than most on-road vehicles. The guys use it around the property a lot in the spring.

"Give me a sec," Wrath says, holding up a finger. He jogs to the end of the garage and grabs a stack of paper targets, and a staple gun. The club keeps an arsenal stored beneath this garage, so it's not strange to find targets and ammunition stored out here. He returns, drops the stuff in the dump bed and tosses the keys to me. Surprised, I stare at them for a second. Glancing up, I catch his shrug. "I've gotten used to you driving me around."

Cute. Okay.

"Z's only let me drive this beast once," I tell him as I fire it up. He responds with a tight-lipped smile. Wrath compliments me on the way I navigate the trail with the unfamiliar vehicle. The simple, sincere comment means a lot to me. Once or twice he asks me to stop, so he can knock back branches blocking the path.

The range is no joke. Wrath and Z supervised while the prospects built the open structure last year. There are five shooting stations with benches and tables facing targets set up at twenty-five yard intervals all the way out to three hundred yards.

"What did you bring?" I ask.

His lips curl into a grin. Wrath loves his guns.

"A new Glock I picked up and a twenty gage semi-auto I wanna show you how to use."

"I know how to use a shotgun." My dad taught me when I was barely big enough to hold one.

"Good, then it'll be easy for you."

He lays out our weapons on the counter behind us. Everything lined up precise, because that's how Wrath is. He's also a stickler for range safety.

"Clear," he shouts before jogging over to the fifteen yard berm, even though we're the only ones out here. He staples a target up and jogs back.

"We'll just work on getting a pattern down on paper."

My mouth twitches in amusement. I'll humor him for now. He cracks the gun open and loads in five shells.

He jerks his head toward the gear behind us. "Grab some ear plugs and safety glasses out of my bag, please."

Of course he's well prepared. He has dozens of little packets of single use earplugs, a fancier set of professional earmuffs, and protective eyewear.

Even with the earmuffs, the shotgun blast makes me jump. At least it doesn't kick as hard as I'd expected.

Wrath runs down range to grab my target and bring it up. "Good job," he says before showing it to me.

Once I'm comfortable loading it and shooting by myself, we move on to the handguns.

Wrath pulls out a small black pistol. "This would be a good carry gun for you," he says as he hands it over.

"What do I need to conceal carry for? Going to Ward's? I hardly ever leave the property."

Wrath shrugs. "You never know."

I put a few rounds through it and hand it back to Wrath. "I don't like the aggressive texture on the grip." I flex my fingers in front of his face. "It bit into my hand a little."

He frowns, then grabs my hand, kissing the spot where the gun dug into my skin. "It fits you well otherwise. I can swap out the grip."

The simple sweet gesture tangles all my emotions. For a second I can't speak.

"Are you hungry, babe?" he asks, nodding at the picnic backpack I brought with us.

"Uh, yeah." Sure that's it.

WRATH

I'm baffled by Trinity's change in mood after lunch. I thought we had a pleasant, non-sexual afternoon. She's always been a lot of fun at the range. Actually knows what she's doing, but always listens to instruction. Plus, there isn't a single weapon she's afraid of handling. If we ever ran into trouble, I'd be confident having her covering my six.

She yawns when I pull up to the clubhouse.

"Go on, I'll put everything away. Why don't you take a nap? I'll come get you around five and we'll go out to dinner."

"Hmm, that almost sounds like a date."

"Would that be so bad?"

"No," she says softly and pushes out of her seat.

I reach over and grab her hand. "Hey. Give me a kiss."

Her mouth turns up and she stretches over to give me a quick peck on the cheek.

"That wasn't enough, Angel Face. I'm going to collect later."

She chuckles and dashes up the steps.

At five sharp I'm throwing my knuckles against her door. Can't wait another second to see her. She opens it with a smile.

"Ready?"

"Almost. I, uh…had some stuff to do."

Okay. I guess that makes sense. She's been so busy tending to me she probably hasn't had a moment to do her own stuff. Whatever that might be.

She's still standing there, staring up at me. "Can I come in?"

"Uh." She hesitates then steps out, closing the door behind her. "You still want go out to dinner?"

No, I want her to let me in her fucking room "Yes. Been looking forward to it."

She hesitates. "I—"

"Meet you by the front door in half an hour."

The corners of her mouth quirk up. "Okay."

Don't know why, but I half expect her not to show. I rush through a shower and throw on some clothes, fully prepared to drag her out of her room if I need to.

I'm pleasantly surprised to find her waiting by the front door. She took the time to squeeze into some painted-on jeans, and twist her hair into two braids.

"Cute," I say, twirling the ends of one of the braids.

Her shoulders twitch in an embarrassed shrug. "Figured we were taking your bike."

"Yeah. I like it, babe."

Her cheeks flush a pretty shade of pink. It reminds me of her turning pink—

Yeah. Best not to go there.

I want tonight to be about showing her how much I appreciate her help and how much I like being with her. Not about fucking her.

Hog Heaven does a special dinner menu on the weekends, so that's where we go.

"So this is what it feels like to be on a date," Trinity says with a snort after the waitress takes our order.

Words to respond fail me. Can't name one chick I've ever taken out to eat. I flirted, fucked and moved on to the next. All because I'd screwed things up with the one I wanted more than anything.

"Are you happy you'll be rid of me after tomorrow night?" she asks.

"What are you talking about?"

I caught her mid-sip and she stares into her water glass. Obviously, I've done a lousy job proving how I feel about her.

"No. Fuck no, babe. Why would you think that?"

Her shoulders jerk up and her gaze skips away. "Sorry I kicked your ass at target practice today," she says with a smirk.

Way to change the subject.

"You're good, babe, but not that good."

Her eyes widen and her mouth drops in fake indignation. "Liar. What'd you do with those targets? I want a rematch."

Laughter explodes out of me. "Yeah, we should pick you up some fancy pink camo gear on the way home. Maybe it will help you shoot better."

She plants one hand on her hip and leans over the table. Her eyes sparkle with amusement and all I want to do is close the distance between us and kiss her. "I never understood the point of pink camo unless you're hiding out in Candy Land."

The silly comeback makes me laugh even harder. "Fuck, I love you."

We both stop laughing and just stare at each other.

"Which one of you had the barbecue sampler?"

Trinity shakes herself out of our staring contest first and signals the waitress.

"Guess you're the chicken Mykonos, sir." I nod and wait for her to go away so I can tell Trinity that may have sounded off the cuff, but I mean it. She ducks her head and pokes at her coleslaw.

"Thought you'd be tired of chicken by now," she says as soon as the waitress leaves.

Huh? "No. I've got no complaints." I should wait until after the fight tomorrow. Take her someplace nice and lay everything out for her. "I hope you know I appreciate all your help these last few weeks."

"Of course."

"I like all the time we've been able to spend together."

Finally, she looks up at me. "Me too."

"Babe, you look like you're gonna cry. What'd I do?"

"Nothing. I'm fine." She tucks a loose piece of hair behind her ear and attacks her dinner. The rest of the meal we're quiet. When we finally step outside, I snag her around the waist and spin her around until she's shaking with laughter.

"Put me down before I barf!"

I press a wet kiss on her cheek before letting her go. She's laughing and wiping her face. "You nut."

"At least you're smiling. I hate when you're unhappy."

She stops and stares as if no one's ever said that to her before.

Trinity

"I had a nice day with you, Angel Face."

"Me too." I snuggle up closer to him and kiss his cheek, then trail my lips down his neck.

Party noises filter in through the door, but in here, it's quiet and just us. "Not tonight. You're right. I want to conserve my juices for the fight."

Thinking he's kidding, I brush my hand over his chest. He captures it in his hand and brings it to his mouth, kissing my fingertips. "Seriously."

Burning with want, I almost sob while asking, "Do you want me to go sleep in my room?"

"No."

"Well, what if I can't control myself in the morning?"

He kisses my forehead. "I'll fight you off. Get some sleep. Big day tomorrow." With that, he releases me and turns over.

This is it. He's trying to push me away slowly. After the fight, he won't want me staying in his room anymore. I knew all along this was short-term, so why am I so sad? I snuggle up against his back, enjoying his warmth while I still have it.

CHAPTER TWENTY

WRATH

The address for the fight came in around three, a familiar location in Ironworks. I forward it to Rock and Z. I'm still not convinced the girls should come. Spoke to Whisper about it and he said his crew would have some of their ol' ladies with them, which made me only a fraction more comfortable.

But Trinity's enthusiasm went straight to my head. Like the conceited prick I am, I want her to see what I can do in the ring. She's told me a bunch of times, in words and actions, how much she likes seeing me train. The cocky fucker inside of me wants her to see me unrestrained.

I want her to see me win.

Then afterward, we're going someplace nice and quiet. Just the two of us. There are things I need to explain to her.

We spend the day watching YouTube videos, including a few that Jake and I already watched of the kid I'm fighting. I call up a few now and watch them, while Trinity sits on the floor painting her nails. It's nice and domestic.

Well, as domestic as we get.

Every now and then, I reach out and run my fingers through her hair and she turns and smiles up at me. Each one of those smiles fuckin' wrecks me.

As soon as I tell her I've got the address and we should get ready to go, her smiles turn anxious.

Sitting up on the couch, I grab her hands and pull her between my knees. "What did I tell you?"

"You're not going to let him touch you?"

"Yeah. So wipe that worried look off your face, or I'm gonna get insulted."

That makes her laugh softly and she runs her fingers over my cheek. "I don't want anything to happen to this handsome face."

My chest warms and tightens at the way she says that. "I promise you, I'll keep my ugly mug intact."

She leans over and kisses my forehead. It's sweet, but it also puts her tits right in my face. I kiss the bit of cleavage she's flashing, making her giggle.

"No boom-boom before the big fight, remember?"

"Yeah. I remember. Go get ready. Wear something comfortable, though."

She cocks her head at me. "No, I was going to wear a crotch-shot skirt and hooker heels."

Her description makes me laugh. Yeah, that's not Trin's style. Something else I like about her. She makes me work for everything—every smile, every peek.

She meets me at the door, looking cute as fuck in her LOKI tank top and jeans.

I motion her over to the bar and show her an ankle holster and the Glock G43 I had her test out yesterday.

"You want me to carry?" she asks.

"Yeah. Just in case. They're gonna wand people coming in the front. They probably won't check anyone coming in the back and the guys will be too busy staring at your tits to bother checking for an ankle holster."

"Okay."

Fuck, I love how much she trusts me.

Squatting down in front of her, I lift up her right pant leg and attach the ankle holster. "Should probably get you one of those belly band ones so you can carry at your six, but for tonight, this is good."

"Okay," she whispers, leaning on my shoulders for balance. She shivers and I glance up.

"You all right?"

"Yeah. You done?"

Snapping the Glock into place, I roll her pant leg back down and check for any printing.

"Shake your leg."

She scowls, but complies.

"How does it feel?"

"Not bad."

"Draw for me."

Giving me an exasperated sigh, she bends over—shoving her tits in my face for the second time this hour—and whips the gun out pretty fast considering the rig is new to her. She tucks the gun away and quirks an eyebrow at me. "Satisfied?"

"Yes." I stand and give her a peck on the cheek. "Thanks for humoring me."

I toss her a sweatshirt and we get on the road.

Even though we have the okay to be in Ironworks, I'm fucking twitchy being in Viper territory. Trin seems to sense it, and squeezes her arms and legs around me tighter.

Circling the building, I find a hole in the fence that surrounds it and drive right through, parking my bike in the shadow of the old warehouse. Trin must still be nervous. She doesn't hesitate when I take her hand and lead her inside.

I was right about the security. No one even blinks in our direction when we enter the back room. Makes me even happier Trinity's carrying.

We don't get anything fancy like a room. It's just a big open area. Fighters have staked out random spots. Most have their girlfriends as well as some sort of entourage with them. Well aware of my anti-social tendencies, Jake and Whisper are waiting for me in the back corner away from everyone else.

Jake lifts his chin at us. "Hey, Trinity. Ready to see your man kick some ass?"

She seems startled. I'm guessing because of the *your man* comment. But then she laughs. "Yup."

With no small amount of pleasure, I notice she's still holding my hand.

Whisper also notices, but remains quiet. That is, after all, how he got his nickname. He nods and gives me a fist bump.

This operation doesn't bother with bullshit like ring girls running around in their underwear flashing signs at the crowd. No, these fights are purely about money and violence. Vipers have a crew here overseeing things. Wolf Knights have guys besides Whisper here as well. 18th Street and Green Street Crew have some of their punks around. A lot of enemies hanging out in one spot, holding a truce in the name of some quick cash. Most of the spectators have no gang affiliations or club ties. Just degenerate gamblers we'll all make some money off.

Rock and the others should be here soon. I check my phone and see Rock sent me a text when they left—about ten minutes ago. Should take them another twenty to get here and probably fifteen more to make their way inside.

I've never gotten involved in the gossipy shit that goes on in the back room before a fight. Yes, men—hardened criminals—can gossip more than the mouthiest woman. Half the time the lies and bullshit start up needless trouble in already precarious relationships.

We end up standing around talking about nothing in particular. Trinity melts into my side and I like how natural she feels in my arms. You'd think I'd be anxious about the fight that's coming up. But in my head, it's something I need to get through so I can have my conversation with Trinity. I can't wait to lay it all out for her.

She's mine. I'm hers. No more fucking nonsense.

Trinity

Wrath keeps checking his phone. The backstage area continues to fill up with people. Considering there are only six fighters going in the ring tonight, there seems to be an awful lot of activity back here.

"You should have had more of the guys come with us," I say when he finally glances up from his phone.

His forehead wrinkles. "Why?"

I nod at Jake and Whisper. "We're not much of an entourage."

"Oh." He laughs, deep and hearty. "Don't give a fuck about that, babe. Teller or Z usually stay back here with me too."

Wrath glances around the room and scowls, then checks his phone again. His face softens for a second in relief. "Good. They're here." He pushes away from the wall and pulls me over to the open entrance. The cavernous room where the fight ring is set up is packed tight.

"Wait, I want to stay back here with you."

His face locks down cold and hard. "Absolutely not."

"Wrath—"

"No. As much as I trust Jake and Whisper, I want you with Kings. I need to focus, get myself centered, and I can't do that if I'm distracted by you."

My eyes sting and he seems to notice, because his hand curls over my shoulder and he uses a gentler tone. "I can't keep you safe and concentrate on the fight. Remember, I promised you I wouldn't get hurt?"

"Oh." Glancing at the guys assembled back here, I understand his concern. He's right. I like Jake and Whisper fine, but I trust Rock and Z with my life. I open my mouth to apologize, but Wrath nudges my shoulder.

"There's Z. Let me watch you walk out."

I want to give him a good luck kiss, or something, but he pushes me out into the crowd.

Z and the others are easy enough to spot and I squeeze my way through the wall of people. Every inch of me is trembling in fear by the time I reach Z, who pulls me against him and walks me the rest of the way to our group.

Hope breaks out of Rock's iron grip and wraps her arms around me. "You have no idea how happy I am to see you," she gushes.

I can only imagine what's going through her head, and my lips twitch in amusement.

"How's our boy?" Z asks.

My shoulder still burns from where he shoved me into the crowd. "Cold as ice."

Rock tugs me to his side and puts his arm around my shoulders. Secure against him, I'm able to let my guard down a smidge.

"He'll be fine. He's always like that before a fight. That's why we're out here," Rock explains. I know he's trying to cheer me up and I appreciate the effort.

Glued to Rock's other side, Hope peers over at me and raises an eyebrow.

Teller interrupts by butting into the group, waving our betting slips at us. He hands them out and we tuck them away.

It suddenly seems to dawn on Hope what's going on. "Why would anyone bet against Wrath? He's the scariest guy I've ever met."

Everyone laughs. If I wasn't so worried about Wrath backstage, I'd probably laugh too. I make a mental note to tell Wrath Hope finds him terrifying. He'll think it's the funniest thing ever.

The guys keep us protected as we walk to the bleachers and stake out our seats.

Z moves so I can sit next to Hope, but my mind is elsewhere. Wrath didn't think I was paying attention while he watched videos of Irish's old fights. But I saw what the guy is capable of and it starts to sink in how scared I am that Wrath will get hurt. I want to jump up, run to the back and drag him the hell out of here.

"You okay?" Hope asks, breaking into my freak-out.

"Yeah, just nervous." She squeezes my hand and I end up clinging to her, which is so fucking weird, I don't know what to think.

At some point, Z leans over me to talk to Hope. "Unlike most of these guys, Wrath has no interest in getting an MMA deal or something. He just enjoys unleashing his fury on people," he explains. Hope's jaw drops a fraction and my stomach rolls.

The lights blink and the noise drops to a hushed roar. I barely hear the announcer or register when the first fight starts or ends. I keep glancing through the open doorway to the back room hoping to catch a glimpse of Wrath.

The second fight is also a blur.

The quick blast of an air horn silences the crowd.

"Five minutes 'til the blood bath you've all been waiting for. Get those bets placed now. Windows close when the opponents reach the ring."

Oh dear God, I'm going to be sick. I can't stand this. Why the fuck did I ever want to come to one of Wrath's fights? This is torture.

Hope's hand tightens around mine.

Blood thunders through my ears when the horn goes off again. I don't even hear the introduction given to Irish. I do look up in time to watch him bouncing up and down in the ring, scanning the crowd like he's curious who all stopped by to see him get his ass whooped.

He's plenty big, but I'm a little less scared seeing him in the flesh. Wrath's got this.

"Our next fighter scares the shit out of even me. Undefeated in the underground, he doesn't come out of hibernation often, but when he does, it's scary as fuck! Hope you were careful placing your bets because they say the last thing to grow old in a man is Wrath!"

It's a cheesy introduction, and I gotta imagine Wrath's pissed about it. The crowd loves it though. The room detonates into cheers and shouts.

One of his favorite songs is used as his intro music and it makes me chuckle.

Another laugh spills out of me when Wrath strolls into the room as if it's no big deal. At some point he stripped down to the shiny athletic shorts he favors for working out.

As he turns in our direction, my mouth twitches into a smile and I'm about to raise my hand to wave, when Z leans up against me.

"How fast you think he's gonna take that fucker out?" he whispers in my ear just loud enough for me to hear him over the crowd.

I catch the dark look that crosses Wrath's face as he watches us, and I want to clock Z for being such a dick.

Rock notices it too and leans over to scold him. "Knock it off, Zero."

"What? Just making sure—"

"You're wrong," I spit out. Wrath will win all on his own. He doesn't need Z to stir up any jealousy.

Z's not finished. "Yeah, that why you been up in his bed every night for the last two weeks? I don't remember you *ever* spending an entire night with me."

What the fuck? I grind my teeth so I don't end up punching him. "Shut. Up." The thought of Hope overhearing that warms my cheeks with shame.

"Don't break his concentration, Z," Hope snaps at him. The fact that she's worried about Wrath—even though he's been so mean to her—makes me like her even more. Wrath's wrong about her. She'll be an asset to the club—eventually.

Z chuckles and sits back. I jam my elbow in his ribs and he laughs even harder.

The bell goes off and my stomach drops. I can't stand to watch, but I can't look away. My body flinches with every punch Irish throws at Wrath, even though each one misses.

Wrath fucks around with the kid for a while. Tiring him out. Irish moves to throw a right hook, but drops his other hand. That small opening is what Wrath seizes on to go after Irish for real. His fists fly in a brutal flash that my eyes can't keep track of.

Around us is total chaos as the crowd rushes the ring. Our view is blocked and I can't get up on the bleachers fast enough. Air rushes out of my lungs when I finally see Wrath again. He's beating Irish to a pulp and this time I flinch for different reasons.

I understand what a sergeant-at-arms does. Enforces rules. Protects the club—with force when necessary. I also know Wrath's capacity for violence. It's still terrifying to see him in brutal action.

He goes in for the kill, smashing his knee into Irish's face. There's blood everywhere and I'm thankful I didn't eat dinner before we left or I'd be barfing it up by now.

Next to me, Hope starts screaming. Rock pulls her off the bleachers and calms her down quick.

Wrath's declared the winner. Duh, poor Irish is barely able to roll around on the floor. His crew throws Wrath a dark look as he takes his victory lap around the ring and they drag Irish to the back.

The audience rushes to the betting windows. Teller takes our slips and runs off with Murphy to get our winnings.

Z and Rock have managed to wedge Hope and me between them, keeping us protected from the jostling crowd.

"Prez, we gotta get out of here," Z warns.

No, no, no. We can't leave without Wrath. He promised me he'd find us immediately after the fight. I plant my feet ready to fight if Z tries to make me move. Hope peeks around Rock and bounces up on her toes, making me look in the direction she's looking.

There's Wrath. Half-dressed and moving fast. Wriggling out of Z's hold, I fly into Wrath's arms.

"Whoa, I'm fine." He wraps me up in his arms and I sob against his chest. I can't get a single word out. He kisses the top of my head, right there in front of everyone and I claw at his shirt so he doesn't let me go.

"Wrath, we gotta go," Z urges.

Wrath squeezes me tighter, before releasing me for a second to slip a fitted knit hat on. Then he wraps me in his arms again and we all march to the side exit.

We regroup outside and I can finally breathe. We're going to make it out of this.

Teller and Murphy smile when they see us and give Wrath a quick nod and fist bump. Wrath's big, warm hand envelops mine.

"I'm in a spot around the back," he informs Rock.

Rock turns his head in that direction and then the opposite way. "Fuck. We're in the lot over."

Wrath shrugs. "We'll meet up at the gas station at the bottom of the hill."

The guys agree on that plan and we go our separate ways.

Get me the fuck out of here.

WRATH

Trinity's so quiet. Once the guys take off, we head toward where I parked the bike. When we clear the building and my bike is in sight, I stop and tug her over to the shadows against the brick wall.

I place a hand on either side of her face. "Are you okay?"

Her eyes dart around, wild and unsure. "What are you doing? We have to meet up with them."

"It's going to take them a minute to get through the parking lot. I want to make sure you're all right."

She glances up at me. "Are *you* okay?"

"Yeah, I told you he wouldn't get a shot in."

She takes a deep breath, then chuckles low and soft. "You're nuts."

Something about her laugh unhinges me. To get her here, I told her I'd want to fuck her after the fight. I was lying at the time, but all of a sudden I can't stop myself. We need to get the fuck out of here. A bad feeling about the way people were reacting inside followed me out the door.

But I want her so fucking bad, *right now*. Rationally, I know it's left over adrenaline coursing through me. The fight hadn't lasted nearly long enough.

Tipping her chin up, I slam my mouth over hers. I back her up against the wall, my hands fumble with her jeans.

"Baby, next time please wear a skirt."

She lets out a moan/giggle sound that drives me insane. I keep her pinned to the wall and manage to get one sneaker and one pant leg off her, while she frees my aching cock and rolls a condom down my dick. We're in perfect sync, which is good because this is going to be straight up, hard and fast fucking.

"Trin," I grind out against her mouth. "Tell me you're ready, I don't want to hurt you." Never again. I don't want to ever hurt her again.

She wraps her legs around me tighter. "I'm ready."

I grip her ass, yanking her toward me while at the same time thrusting into her nice and slow. "Watchin' me fight turn you on, Angel Face?" I breathe into her ear, as I pick up the pace.

She shakes her head and a tear rolls down her cheek, halting my frantic thrusts.

"I was so scared," she whispers, clinging to me tighter.

For the first time in my life, I regret a fight. I hate that I rattled her so bad. "I'm okay, baby."

She nods and kisses me. "Fuck me, please," she whispers against my lips.

Jesus Christ. "Hang on to me." Using the wall for leverage, I slip one hand off her ass to play with her clit. I need her to come if it fucking kills me. In the dark, I can't see her very well, but our mouths meet. We kiss slow and deep, reconnecting and reassuring each other. Time stands still as I keep grinding into her until she blows. Fucking hell, she clenches down on my dick so hard, it sends me over the edge right along with her.

"That's it. Good girl. Come hard for me, angel." I gasp as she keeps squeezing the fuck out of my cock.

She babbles uncontrollably—the way she does when she's far gone. As soon as she opens her eyes, I kiss her lips, then set her down. I right myself and help her hop into her pants.

At the bike, I slip a hoodie over her head and get her helmet on. She's quiet but there's a soft smile curving her mouth now. Taking another second we don't have, I run the back of my bruised and aching hand over her cheek. It's on the tip of my tongue to tell her how much I fucking love her.

"Thank you," I say instead.

Her lashes flutter when she kisses my hand. "Let's go."

Yeah, here isn't the place to have our talk. It needs to be special and I know just where I want to take her.

Trinity

Even with our outside quickie, we make it to the gas station before Rock and the others. Wrath passes two SUVs at the pumps, and tucks us into a spot near the exit. He doesn't bother shutting off the bike.

He shouts to me over the rumbling exhaust, "Wanna head to the park?"

"Don't you want to enjoy your victory party?"

"No. We need to talk."

We do? About what?

I don't get to ask, because the roar of our guys approaching drowns out everything. Wrath pulls out ahead of them and leads us out of Ironworks.

Sweet relief sweeps through me when we finally cross into Empire County. Wrath takes us through the winding, country roads and the left over tension from the fight ebbs away.

Teller and Murphy are suddenly on either side of us. Just seeing that they've broken formation is enough to make me tense right back up.

"The fuck?" Wrath shouts.

For a brief second my gaze collides with Teller's and he shakes his head.

The revving of an engine behind us, makes me turn around. There's an SUV bearing down on Z. Rock's only slightly ahead.

Fuck.

Z swerves to the side and lets the SUV pass, but it keeps pressing Rock and Hope to the edge of the road.

"Hold on," Wrath shouts.

The SUV bears down on us. My heart jumps, terrified something happened to Rock.

Something definitely taps our rear tire and we swerve, but Wrath keeps us upright. A scream tears out of me.

"Fuck!"

Glancing down is terrifying. Light glints off the giant SUV bumper bearing down on us. I almost want to reach out and push it away. But at the last second I pull back, knowing that's a good way to lose a hand.

It taps us again, pushing us to the side. The bike jerks to the right. The rear end slides out and I brace for contact with the pavement. Then we're flying through the air and bouncing down the slight hill. I hold my breath as my stomach flips. My arms cling to Wrath as long as possible, but we're thrown from the bike. There's a horrible crunch and snap of metal.

I'm blinking up at the black sky. It's pretty and I wonder if I've fallen asleep outside the clubhouse.

Shots echo in the air and I guess the guys are at the gun range? But that doesn't make any sense because it's dark.

I blink and sit up. The throbbing in my head explodes and I sit there dazed taking in my surroundings.

Ahead of me, I hear Wrath groan.

Okay. Not at the clubhouse.

Woods.

"Trin?"

"I'm here."

I can't stand yet. Nothing's broken, but my knees have turned to jelly. I turn and crawl over the cold, wet ground.

A short, startled scream tears out of me when I find Wrath and scramble to his side.

"Wyatt?"

He groans.

More shots echo through the night.

"Don't move."

Reaching down, I yank the Glock from my ankle holster. Miraculously it stayed put.

"Wrath?" I hate leaving him unprotected, but he's not conscious enough to take the gun.

I get my legs under me and stagger forward.

Ahead there's rustling. I almost sob with relief when I hear Rock's voice. Tears roll over my cheeks when I finally see him.

"Where is he, Trinny?"

My hand jerks behind me. "He's not moving, Rock. It's bad."

More gunfire above us. "Stay low," Rock whispers.

Wrath's groaning when we get to his side and I'm so relieved, I burst into tears.

"Stay quiet, man," Rock says, as he puts a hand on Wrath's chest. He turns and eyes Hope. "Hope, what did you do with the gun?"

"It's in my pocket."

His jaw tightens. "Give it to Trinity."

Before I can open my mouth and say I already have one, Hope's shoving the weapon in my hands. On autopilot, I rack a bullet into the chamber.

"Stay with him," Rock says to both of us.

I glance down at Wrath once more. The best thing I can do right now is keep him safe.

WRATH

What the ever-loving fuck? Loud groaning comes from somewhere nearby. My head throbs. My leg's on goddamn fire. I'm cold. I'm wet. Everything hurts.

The person groaning in pain is *me*.

Someone squeezes my hand, further bringing me awake.

"Shh, honey, it's okay."

Hope?

"My leg."

Something brushes over my face. In the background I hear gunfire and panic tightens my chest.

"Trin!?"

"Right here, Wyatt," she answers.

Thank God.

I need to get to her, but I can't seem to make any of my body parts work. Something presses against my chest keeping me down. I almost laugh when I realize it's Hope.

"Wrath, don't. You could have something broken. Plus, there are still guys shooting at us," she says in a rush.

Fuck. "Prez?"

"He's okay."

Christ, I'm doin' a shit job protecting my president and my girl.

I blink and Hope's anxious face fills my vision. Her hand's wrapped around mine and I squeeze it tighter. "It's gonna be okay, Hope."

She bites her bottom lip and nods, then meets my eyes.

"This is why I been tryin' to push you away, Cinderella. So you don't get hurt."

She tears up. "Wrath," she sighs.

I can't keep my eyes open any longer, but I hang onto her hand. Vaguely, I'm aware of her running her hands over me. Checking for injuries, I guess—seems like an inappropriate time for her to cop a feel.

She touches my leg and I suck down a scream.

"I think it's broken," she chokes out.

"No shit."

Her hand touches whatever stings on my head.

"Ow, fuck. Watch it."

"Sorry," she whispers.

I grab her other hand to keep her from poking at any more injuries.

"I don't know what to do," she sobs and I feel fucking horrible for putting her in danger.

"Just keep holding my hand. My leg really fucking hurts."

"Okay," she answers, so soft I almost don't hear her.

I must black out again. I'm aware that I'm freezing. Something covers my chest. Hope's hands rub over me. Fucking girl has to be terrified, but she hasn't left my side.

Someone else presses against me.

"Honey, you're shivering." I recognize Rock's voice. I try to ask him if he's whole and find out what happened, but I can't force any words out.

"Afraid he's going into shock. He needs an ambulance bad," Hope says.

"A driver stopped. He's calling 911. That's what finally chased those fuckers off."

"His leg, Rock. And his head."

Someone shines a light over my face and pain stabs my eyes.

"Get that outta my face," I mumble.

"Well, his personality is fine," Z jokes. Z. Fuck, I'm thankful he's okay.

"Fuck off," I grumble. He laughs. Fucker.

Sirens. Thank fuck.

I don't have to open my eyes to know my girl's on my other side. "You okay?" I ask.

"Yeah." Thank God. The temperature must be dropping, 'cause I'm fuckin' freezing.

So fucking cold.

Part Three

Our unending
road to love.

CHAPTER TWENTY-ONE

Trinity

Other than what the doctor said was a mild concussion, I'm fine. Wrath's in surgery and no one will tell us a thing. I'm released, with instructions to rest. I don't get far. Rock finds me and leads me to the waiting room.

As soon as Teller spots me, he rushes over. "You all right?" he asks, pulling me against him.

"Yeah," I mumble into his shirt. I'm so frickin' tired.

"Fuck that scared the shit out of me," Teller says. Whether he's talking to Rock or me, I'm not sure. My body sways and Teller grips me tighter.

"Come on. Let's sit down."

The guys sit on either side of me, while Rock and Z talk in the hallway.

"Wrath's bulletproof, Trin. He's gonna be okay," Murphy says, giving my hand a squeeze.

My head bobs up and down, because I think it's expected of me. Rock and Z seem to be finishing up whatever they're talking about, so I wander out to see if they've heard anything.

Rock holds out his arm and I don't hesitate to take shelter against him. He hugs me tight and I inhale a shaky breath. Not only had I been scared for myself, and Wrath, I don't know what I'd do if something happened to Rock. I choke out a sob-snort noise and Rock squeezes me tighter.

"He's gonna be okay, Trinny. He's a fighter down to his marrow," Rock says.

"I know."

The doctor comes over to talk to Rock and he passes me off to Z who hugs me. "Why, Z? Why would someone do that to us?" I sniffle into his shirt.

His hold on me tightens. "I don't fuckin' know, girl."

We are after all, in the middle of the hospital. And even though the only people around are Kings, I keep my voice low. "I get it. But they had to see Hope and—"

"Fucking cowards." He pushes me back and stares me down. "We're gonna handle it, Trin. Promise you that."

I nod. That's how things work in our world. Assaulting one member is an attack on the entire club. Retaliation will be swift and brutal.

"Tonight scared me too, you know. Don't know what I'd do without you. And," he nods at Rock. "You know those two are closer brothers to me than my actual brothers are." He scrubs his hands over his face. "Fuckin' bullshit."

Shit. That's a lot for Z. He's jokes around so much, it's easy to forget he can be serious too.

Rock returns and gives Z a meaningful look before addressing me. "Babe, I want you to go home and get some rest."

I won't be able to rest. What if something— "I need to see him first."

His hands settle on my shoulders. "I just spoke to your doc, he said you need rest. As soon as Wrath wakes up, I'll have one of the guys bring you back. But right now, you need to take care of yourself or you won't be any good to him."

Rock knows the right words to get his way and my mouth curls into a tired smirk.

"Come on, Trin. I'll keep my phone on. If we get word he's up, I'll turn right around and bring you back," Z promises.

I nod and Rock presses a kiss to the top of my head. "Go on."

Z wraps an arm around my shoulder. "Doc said don't let her sleep too long. She can have Tylenol, but make sure she eats something," Rock says to Z as if I'm not standing in between them. I'm so out of it, I don't even care.

They can make me go home. But I won't rest until I know Wyatt's okay.

CHAPTER TWENTY-TWO

WRATH

Ow.

Everything's hazy. I could have sworn I won the fight, but I feel like I've had the shit kicked out of me.

My nose twitches. Antiseptic. Unpleasant. Trin doesn't use crap like that to clean with.

Oddly, that's the thought that pulls me out of my fog.

"Trinity?"

A small, pretty woman smiles down at me. "Welcome back, Mr. Ramsey." Huh. Running my gaze over her, I determine she's a nurse. I'm in a hospital bed. Definitely in a *gown*. What the fuck?

"Where am I?"

"Empire Med. I'll go grab a doctor. And your family's here."

She pats my arm, her hand lingering a little longer than professionally necessary. "My girlfriend, Trinity. Where is she?" Her mouth turns down at the word girlfriend. I may have had the tar beaten out of me, but I know when a woman is interested. Instead of flattered, I'm annoyed.

"Both women that came in were treated and released," she answers before hurrying out of the room.

Good. Now, where is she?

I take a few seconds to look myself over. Leg's in a fucking cast.

Despite the risks I take, I haven't had a broken bone since my dad snapped my arm when I was eight. My head's killing me. Reaching up, I realize they shaved my fucking head.

Before I assess any other damage, a doctor breezes in.

"You're awake sooner than I expected."

"I'm special that way," I grumble and the doctor nods.

"Do you remember what happened?"

Trinity up against a wall. Definitely remember *that*. "Trinity? Where is she?"

He checks his notes. "Everyone else who came in with you is fine."

Thank God. Still, I need to know *my girl's* okay. "The blonde?"

"I didn't treat the others, but no one else was admitted."

Okay. That's good news.

"What else can you remember?"

My mind's still fuzzy. Riding. Getting pushed off the road. *Fuck!* "We were run off the road."

He nods again. "That's what I've been told. There are some police officers who want to talk to you. I told them they had to wait."

Good. Hate pigs. Maybe I should have a lawyer? "Is Hope here?"

He seems confused. "My pres-brother's ol-girlfriend," I clarify remembering at the last second to use words that will make sense to the doc.

"There are a lot of people here for you. I'll go find out."

Two officers slink in after the doc leaves. One's old and chubby, the other young and still has that enthusiastic look about him. Two walking clichés.

"Mr. Ramsey. We need a statement from you."

"My doctor okay with you bein' in here? I don't even know what's fuckin' wrong with me yet."

They share a look. "Do you remember what happened?"

I haven't talked to Rock yet. "No."

"Where were you last night?"

"I don't remember."

"Look, your blood tested clean. We're not looking at you for driving under the influence," young and optimistic informs me.

Chubby gives him the side-eye. I'm guessing his partner went off-script. I never drive impaired, so this isn't really news to me.

"Is it possible your gang was in the middle of handling business, and that's why you can't remember?"

"Gang? What the fuck are you talking about?"

The older one rolls his eyes. "Sorry. Your *club.*"

Out of it or not, I'm not going to give this fuck the satisfaction of rattling me. "No, sir. Best I can recall—with my head injury and all—is riding with my girl and a car running us off the road."

"Okay. Yeah. That's the story the others had too," Chubby says. He seems so disappointed.

"If you remember anything else, call us." The young one flips a card and I slap it on the table next to me.

The doctor returns, not at all pleased to see my visitors. "I did not give you permission to speak to my patient," he snaps. "He has a head injury, for God's sake. You can't question him."

"Yeah, sure, Doc. We're just leaving."

The doc stares the duo down until they shuffle out the door. I kinda like this guy.

"I apologize. They should not have been in here." His mouth settles into a grim line. "What do you remember? Or up until what point?"

Spending the day with Trinity. The fight. Sex with Trinity. My face pulls into a smile at *that* memory. The talk I wanted to have with Trinity. Pulling out of the gas station to meet up with the guys. Teller's anxious face. Crashing. Fear. Failure. Hope holding my hand and taking care of me, even though I've been so mean to her.

"Remember everything I did yesterday."

Doc looks relieved to hear that.

"Remember riding and an SUV bearing down on us. Gettin' pushed off the road. After that it's a bit sketchy."

"Okay. That's good. Very good. I think you're going to be fine, Mr. Ramsey. You're strong. In good health. But that said, you've got a concussion and we're going to keep you to make sure it's not more serious than that."

I groan and he smiles.

"I know. Now, your leg is a tibial shaft fracture. That will take some time to heal. We can discuss it more when you've had some rest."

"Okay. Can I see my brother? Rock? He out there?"

"Yes. I'll send him in." He taps my arm. "You're lucky. Motorcycles are dangerous. Could have been much worse."

My eyes roll and he chuckles. "I know. I'm obligated to say it."

He walks out and I'm not waiting long before Rock pushes the door open. He gapes at me and I'm about to flip him off when I spot Hope.

I hold my hand out to her and she brushes by Rock, hurrying to my side. I take note of the bandages covering her hands and my jaw clenches.

"Oh my gosh! They shaved all your beautiful hair off," she gushes, while gently running her hands over my head.

The girl actually says *gosh* and I almost got her killed last night. "You okay, sweetie?" I feel like fuckin' shit. Never shoulda let Rock talk me into bringing the girls.

"Some scrapes. Nothing. How are you?"

I snort. "I feel like I got run over."

Rock finally steps closer to me. I imagine he's pretty rattled. "You kinda did, brother."

Why is it just the two of them? "Where's Trin? Is she okay?"

Rock nods and runs his hand over the back of his neck. "Yeah, I sent her home with one of the guys to get some rest."

Godfuckingdammit. I don't want her taking comfort anywhere else but with me. The thought of her alone up at the clubhouse with—"Who'd you send her home with?"

Rock takes a deep breath. "Easy, brother. She's on her way back now."

Good.

I turn back to Hope and gently take her hand. "You sure you're okay? That was some bad shit, sweetheart. Thank you for taking care of me like you did."

She seems embarrassed. I understand a little better why Rock's so far gone over her, but I also don't understand how he thinks keeping her in our world is fair. "I didn't do anything useful. I froze. Trinity is the one who went all *Tomb Raider* on us."

I'm real fuckin' happy to hear that. Glad I took Trin to the gun range the day before too. Pain stabs through my head. "Fuck. How long did the doc say I'll be down?"

Rock isn't one to fuck around when it comes to serious shit. "Four to six months."

Jesus Christ that's a long time. Rock doesn't give me a chance to start my bitching. "You're going to follow every damn instruction. If you don't, your leg will heal all fucked up and you'll be a gimpy fuck the rest of your life. So six months is nothing to make sure you're not walking in circles from now on."

This is what makes Rock such a good prez. Always looking out for all us fuckups. Christ. I can't protect the club in this shape. Who do I trust enough to take over for me? Dex? Murphy? Z? *Shit.* "You gotta take my patch, don't ya?"

Rock groans. "Fuck, man. Why are you worried about that now? It's not going anywhere. Z and the others will take care of shi—"

Nope. It don't work like that. "Can't ride. You gotta take my cut, prez."

"Knock it off."

Rock's eyes zero in on the way Hope has her fingers wrapped around mine and I almost laugh out loud. "We know who it was?" I ask to distract him.

"Z has a lead on it. We'll discuss it later."

I want a piece of that. "When they gonna let me out?"

"A day or two. We gotta get you set up on the first floor somewhere—"

"He can stay in my room," Trinity says softly from the doorway.

Thank fucking God. Warmth burns through my chest as I take in every inch of her. My girl's okay. Couldn't stand anything bad happening to her. I hold out my hand and she rushes over to take it.

"You're such a big baby. Don't you know how to drive your bike off a cliff by now?" She's teasing, but I see the tension in her face. Especially the way her hand trembles when I grasp it.

Hope pats my unbroken leg and joins Rock.

He clears his throat. "We're gonna get going. Trin, you need a ride, call me."

"Yeah, okay," I answer without taking my eyes off Trinity.

Her nose is a bit red, but it's her lost little girl expression that makes me want to pick her up and carry her home. Except I can't fucking move with the cast and all this other stuff in my way.

"You okay, angel?"

Her lip quivers, but her voice comes out strong. "Yeah."

"Come sit next to me. Let me hold you."

She hesitates. "That hospital bed's barely big enough for you."

"Eh, we've slept in smaller beds together and survived." Her cheeks flush at the memory.

She finally climbs into the bed, carefully tucking herself against my side. Throwing her arm around me, she lets out a sigh. I brush my fingers through her hair, checking to make sure she's okay.

"Rock said you went home. Get any rest?"

"A little."

"Z take care of you?" The words stick in my throat, but I push 'em out. She laughs softly. "Yeah. Kept waking me up."

Don't like the sound of that. "Why?" I ask trying to keep my voice neutral.

She tips her head up. "Doctors said I had a mild concussion. Not enough to keep me here, but said I shouldn't sleep too long unchecked."

Oh. Well, now I feel like shit.

"I'm so sorry, angel."

"You think I should leave?" she whispers.

"No fucking way. I dare anyone to say a word to me."

She chuckles against my shoulder.

"Close your eyes."

She shifts in my arms. "Am I hurting you?"

"No, babe. Close your eyes."

"Okay," she mumbles before falling asleep.

Overly friendly nurse returns and I prepare to fight her if she tries to wake Trin up. But she smiles, checks on a few things, then leaves.

Next time I wake up, Teller's sitting in the chair next to me and Murphy's pacing at the foot of the bed.

My mouth's so dry, it takes two tries to get any words out. "How long you guys been here?"

"Haven't left yet, brother. Gotta make sure you're protected," Murphy answers as he hands me a bottle of water from a small refrigerator in the corner.

"Thanks."

Teller jerks his chin at Trinity. "She okay?"

"Yeah."

He shakes his head. "You guys scared the fuck outta me. That took some skill, laying your bike down a mountain."

I snort even though I know he's being sincere. He shrugs. "Coulda been a lot worse, bro."

I'm well aware and the thought has been nagging at me, even in my sleep.

Trinity stirs and blinks up at me. "You okay?" she asks.

First thing outta her mouth is asking if I'm okay. Takes me a second to answer her. "Yeah."

Teller stands. "How you feel, Trin?"

She shakes herself awake and sits up, finally noticing Murphy and Teller. "Hey, guys. I'm fine." She flashes a weak smile at Teller.

"Need a ride home?" he asks. My arm tightens on Trin and the corner of her mouth twitches.

"No. I'm staying."

It's awkward for a second or two before the guys hold their fists out. We tap knuckles and they leave.

Trinity struggles to sit up and I panic. "Where you goin'?"

"I need to pee."

"Oh, okay. You can do that."

She smirks and wriggles out of the bed.

While she's gone, a bored-looking girl drops off a tray of what looks like warmed over shit for breakfast.

"What the hell is that?" I ask her.

"Oatmeal. Healthy stuff," she answers with a smirk, like she thinks I sit around drinking beer and eating Pringles all day.

"My girlfriend cooks lots of healthy stuff—it never looks like *that*."

She shrugs and leaves. I poke at the brown slop with a spoon.

Trinity's laughing when she returns. "I caught that whole exchange, you know."

Good. I said it loud enough.

She stretches and glances at the tray. "It can't be that bad."

"By all means." I push the tray toward her. She snags the apple and takes a chunk out of it.

I had planned to have a talk with her last night. After what happened, I can't wait another second.

"Come here, babe."

She hesitates. "You don't want me crowding you again."

"Yeah, I do. Get over here."

She sets the apple down, takes a swig of orange juice, then climbs up and settles against me. My mouth finds her forehead and I press a kiss there. "No more bullshit, babe. You and me. I mean it," I murmur against her cheek.

"Okay."

Although she agreed, I don't think what I said sunk in. I sift my fingers through her hair. "These last few weeks made me real happy." She picks her head up and stares at me. Now she's getting it. "No more going to war with each other, Trinity. You're mad at me, you tell me. If I'm an asshole, just say it. You're feeling bad, take it out my cock. No one else's. No more of this dysfunctional tit-for-tat thing we've been doin' for years."

A deep, ragged sob tears from her throat. Yeah, I finally admitted what we've been doing for way too long. Big fat tears slide down her cheeks. "Wyatt, what are you asking of me?"

"To be my girl and I'll be your man. That's it. Nothing complicated, Angel Face."

"Wy-"

"Hello, kids!" Rock announces as he flings the door open.

Motherfucker has the worst goddamn timing. *Asshole.*

Trinity, of course, jumps up like a scalded cat, cursing a blue streak. She whacks my bad leg in the process.

"Ow, fuck, Trin," I growl at her. I'm so pissed she's leaving.

"Sorry, sorry," she mumbles. "Uh, I'm gonna go." She runs out of the room and I want to choke the living fuck out of Rock.

I also want to tell him what he interrupted. Thought I was about to get somewhere with her. But he's got that smug fucking smile on his face that I just want to punch.

"Knock it off, dick," I grumble as I settle back into the bed.

"Sorry I interrupted cuddle time."

I return his glare. "Fuck you."

My stomach rumbles and I glare at the hospital tray. "You come here to tell me anything useful? Maybe bring me something?" I ask.

"What the hell do you want, balloons and flowers?"

"A fucking magazine would be nice. I'm bored as fuck."

He gestures at the door. "Didn't look bored a minute ago."

Not sure if it's the accident that rattled him or something else, but brother is seriously testing my patience today. More than normal. When I say Rock's like my brother, I mean it in every way—especially the pissing me off until I want to knock him out way. I notice he's by himself and wonder if that's what crawled up his ass.

"Did Hope come with you?"

His jaw clenches. Yup, that's what's bugging him.

"No," he spits out.

"She okay?"

He comes closer and I take notice of his torn up hands. Brother fought someone recently. "I dunno. She. . .You don't realize, but she lost her dad when she was a teenager. Lost her husband young. I think this rattled her."

Poor girl. I knew about her husband, obviously. "Oh, fuck. I didn't know about her dad. That's rough."

"Yeah, and her mom went to shit after, so she basically got abandoned there."

"Okay. Got it." Maybe Hope fits in better with us than I thought.

He rubs the back of his neck like I know he does when he's stressed.

"I'm afraid this brought up bad shit for her. I'm worried she's not dealing with it well."

Probably not. "Not surprising. After getting through that other shit, sounds like she lived a pretty normal life 'til you barged in."

"Thanks," he grumbles back.

Of course he thinks the worst. "I'm not trying to be a dick. I just don't know how you think it's going to work out between the two of you."

"This wasn't exactly normal."

Is he kidding? This kind of shit happens all the time in our world. We've lived through much worse and I can't understand why he'd wanna drag someone as soft as Hope into something so foreign to her. "You know what I mean. Look, I get it, she's a total sweetheart. Treats everyone with respect. She's not stuck up. I like how nice she is to Trinity. Hell, I like her. But I think soon she's going to start dividing your focus. You can't be half in, half out as our President."

Of course he's not ready to listen to reason where his woman's concerned. "You want the gavel?" he snaps.

"Fuck, no, that's not what I'm trying to say. But she doesn't get what we're about—at all. She's too clean for our life. I've tried explaining shit to her, and it goes in one ear and out the other. Don't drag her into it anymore. It's not fair to her."

His eyes narrow and he cocks his head to the side. "What exactly did you try to explain to her?"

"We are *outlaws*. She acts like it's a bedtime story that has nothing to do with you two."

"How many times have I told you to leave that shit to me? I'll tell her things when I think she's ready to hear them."

Which if Rock has his way will be *never*. "Yeah, but by then she'll be so deep in our shit, she'll blow the MC to hell trying to escape."

His eyes close for the briefest second and I know I'm not the smartest fucker in the world, but it hits me in the gut what he's doing. "Rock, you think she's going to fall so far in love with you, she's going to overlook the fact that we're up to our balls in illegal shit?"

I don't need him to answer. The guilt's spelled out all over his face. I shake my head.

"Jesus Christ." Maybe we irritate the shit out of each other, but Rock's a damn good person. The best. Picked my ass up off the street and gave me a home when I was a teenager. Gave me work and brought me into the MC. Saved my life more than once. I know he ain't reeling her in on purpose to be cruel. Doubt he even realized until right this second what he's been doing.

"I love her," he says simply.

"Yeah, got that, brother." After the misery his ex-wife put him through, he deserves to be happy. "We need to do a better job making her understand and keepin' her safe."

The corners of his mouth lift. "Thanks."

I tilt my head in his direction. "You gonna explain why your hands look like you went one round with a brick wall?"

He glances down, opens and closes his hands. "What do you think?"

"Coulda waited for me, brother."

"Z had a tip they weren't gonna be around long."

"Handled?"

"For now."

A different nurse comes in. She's older and doesn't look like she'll put up with any shit. "Out," she barks at Rock. "He needs to rest. And I need to poke him."

"I prefer to do the poking," I say to her with a wink.

That stops her in her tracks and she actually laughs.

"I'll be back later." Rock gives me a fist bump and heads out, leaving me at the mercy of the nurse who seems determined to do things to me I'm not gonna like.

CHAPTER TWENTY-THREE

WRATH

"So, I finally get to see the inside of Trinity Hurst's room. Only took a broken leg to get here."

That earns me a smirk from Trinity. I'm so fuckin' happy to be free from the hospital. Still feel like I got hit by a train, but at least I'm free. As free as I can be with this clunky, fuckin' cast anyway.

"How come your room is so much nicer than our rooms upstairs?" I tease.

"'Cause you're all pigs?" I love the laugh that comes with the words. She'd been so silent and tense the whole way home. Said she was worried about me, but I could tell more than my gimpy condition was on her mind.

"No twin bed?" I ask.

Her startled eyes meet mine. "I ordered a new one," she whispers.

I look around the spacious bedroom. "You had a twin bed? Here too?"

Her chin tilts down and she lifts her shoulders in an embarrassed shrug.

"So, you got this for me?" I jerked my chin at the king-sized bed occupying the entire right corner of the room.

"Well, the club bought it for you." She waves her hand at the bed. "It's one of those adjustable ones, so you can elevate your leg. I want you to be comfortable."

Fuck, I don't even know what to say to that. "Thanks, angel."

She gives me a quick nod, then turns and starts rifling through her dresser drawers. Weary from the day, I throw myself onto the bed. Watching her sends dark questions through my mind.

"What are you doing?" I finally ask.

"Grabbing a few things. I'll stay in your room upstairs."

Like hell. "Why?"

"So you can recover in peace."

"Trinity, spending time with you is the only damn thing I've been looking forward to about this whole mess."

"Oh."

"Yeah, *oh*. Now get your sweet ass over here."

She places the clothes in her hand back in the dresser and shuts the drawer.

Damn straight.

Without hesitation, she takes a few steps until she's standing in front of me. Taking her hand, I press my lips against her fingers.

"I meant what I said in the hospital, Trin."

She tosses her head from side to side. "You were high on painkillers."

"Babe, I ain't ever been high on anything in my life that would make me say that shit if I didn't mean it."

A quick tug and spin gets her ass perched on the thigh of my good leg.

"What did I say in the hospital before Rock interrupted us?"

"You said a lot of stuff," she hedges. Trinity can't help but make this difficult. I understand, I guess. We've been hurting each other for years. Besides that, I have a better understanding of just how damaged she is. That leaves things up to me, and it's not like I'm the poster boy for healthy relationships.

Man, we're so fucked.

Running back over the last few days, I try to recall exactly what I said to her.

"Trinity, I started falling for you eight years ago—"

"Wyatt," she sighs, cutting me off.

"No. No talking. Just listen." I press my hand against her mouth to emphasize the no talking thing.

"I'm sorry about the shit I did in the past. But I want us to move forward. Together. You and me."

She wraps her fingers around mine, and tugs my hand from her mouth. "Can I speak now?"

"Only if you're going to say 'Yes, Wyatt, I understand.'"

One corner of her mouth tugs up. She must think I'm kidding.

"What are you going to do when you get bored with me? Or you're mad at me 'cause you think I looked at one of the guys the wrong way? Or a new club girl shows up and you want to—"

"Hush. In eight years, I ain't been bored of you yet."

"Yeah, but except for getting you ready for the fight, we've barely spent any time together. There's nothing interesting about me. I'm a glorified housekeeper."

"Are you fucking with me right now?"

"Wyatt, I don't know *how* to be in a one-on-one relationship. I've never seen a healthy example of one."

"You think I have?"

She stops and seems to think that over.

I wrap my hand around hers. "Listen, I enjoy being with you."

Her face softens, and she brushes her fingers over my cheek. "I like being with you too."

"Good." I take a deep breath for the next part. "When I'm with you. Really *with* you, I don't *want* to fuck anyone else."

The hand against my cheek trembles and she puts it back in her lap. Her eyes drop down and I slip my fingers under her chin to tip her head back up.

"The thought of you fucking any anyone else sends me into a murderous rage. I'm actually getting rage-y thinking about it right now, Trin."

Her mouth twitches. Mine doesn't and she realizes I'm dead fucking serious.

She doesn't pull away. My words don't scare her. Thank fuck she knows I'd never hurt her. No, my rage I take out on myself and other unsuspecting fighters.

"We've hurt each other a lot over the years, yeah?"

She nods.

"So, how about this. While we're trying this out,"—I have to pause because this next part is sticking in my throat like glue— "if either of us feels like fucking someone else, we talk it out first?"

She snorts, then rolls her eyes. "How's that going to work? One of the girls puts her hand on your dick and offers you a blowjob and you're going to say, 'Hang on, honey, I need to ask Trinity if she minds?' Not fucking likely."

Laughter rumbles out of me so hard, she bounces in my lap. "Yeah, something like that. I need to learn to curb my impulsive behavior anyway. Getting too old for shit that gets me in trouble all the time."

"What are you talking about? You're the most in-control person I've ever known. It's why you're such a good enforcer."

"Yeah, that's the only place my gut instincts serve me well. Everywhere else it just fucks things up."

"Like what?"

"Like eight years ago, when you tried to explain yourself to me and instead of listening, I stormed the fuck outta here. Or like not that long ago when I thought you were hooking up with Z and I took Cherry up to my room to get even with you."

"Oh."

She's silent as she absorbs everything I've laid out. Then, "You want me to be your girl?"

"More than anything."

"Wow." She hesitates and shakes her head. "You want to be my man?"

"Yes." *Your only man*, but I keep that to myself. I think I already made myself clear on this subject. Apparently I'm going for broke today. I force myself to take a deep breath. "I love you so fucking much, Angel Face."

Wary honey eyes stare back at me as her breath stutters and catches. "Wyatt?"

"Say it. Don't say it. I don't care, Trinity. It's true and I need you to know."

Tears run down her cheeks and I suffer some minor guilt. I've laid an awful lot on her, awful fast today.

Her fingers trace over my face, stopping at my chin. "I can't love you, Wrath. It hurts too much."

She's trying to distance herself by using my nick name. Okay. I get it. I can deal with it. I just hold her tighter. I'm surprised by how little her denial bothers me. She may not recognize it or know it, but she loves me. She'll figure it out. I'll spend every day showing her I'm worth the risk.

"Doesn't matter, babe. I love you enough for both of us. I'll prove to you we can do this. We're done hurting each other."

Trinity

255

Along with his clothes and other belongings, Wrath unpacked a lot of heavy feelings in my room today. I don't know what to make of anything he confessed.

He thinks he's in love with me.

Shit. I don't know what love is. Hatred, sure. I have a lot of that stored up inside. Not for Wrath. Not anymore anyway. Maybe never. For myself? Definitely. Sometimes there's so much hatred inside I don't think there's room for anything more.

I'm behind the bar in the front room of the clubhouse. Wrath's in the middle of the room, soaking up the attention of his brothers and other friends who've joined the MC tonight to welcome him home. Each girl who approaches him gets a nod, but nothing more. Even through the crowd, I catch him watching me as I'm slinging drinks.

My gaze skips to Rock who's pacing the room. He's tried to reach Hope a few times and if it wasn't for this being Wrath's welcome home party, I'm pretty sure he'd be banging on her front door right now. When he finally gets her on the phone, the change on his face is visible even from where I'm standing.

Wrath nudges in and takes the phone away from Rock, shouting something at Hope. He gets a thump for his troubles, but laughs it off.

"Your boy is a pain in my ass, Trinny," Rock grumbles as he sits down at the bar.

My boy. Did Wrath talk to Rock already? I need to ask him not to. I'm not ready for that. I mean, it's stupid because the whole house probably knows by now that Wrath and I are shacking up together in my room. But I still have the cover story of it being about him recovering from his injuries. No need to go public with our "relationship" yet. I can't stand the looks of pity I'll get when we blow up.

Because let's face it, we're going to blow the fuck up. No matter what he said earlier, the reality is there's no way Wrath and I will work.

"I hear you, prez. Hasn't been in my room a minute and he's driving me nuts."

"I heard that," Wrath calls from his spot halfway across the room.

"Friggin' bat ears, I swear," I mutter under my breath. Rock snorts. "Hope coming up tonight?"

"Yup. Just talked to her. She's going to bring a few things up. I think you're getting thin back there."

"That's nice of her." I'm surprised because Rock's developed a weird thing about Hope not doing stuff around the MC. Whether it's for my benefit or hers I'm not sure. It *would* be annoying if after all these years his ol' lady came in and took over things, so I'm not complaining. As much as I like Hope, she doesn't strike me as the domestic type.

I keep busy running back and forth to the kitchen. Every time I look up, Wyatt has his eyes on me.

I'm an idiot for pushing him away earlier. But I know how this works. I watched my mother do the ol' lady thing, then the whore thing. The constant heartache and worrying seemed miserable. Never expected to find myself living the same life.

Not quite the same. I'm not saddled with a kid I never wanted and a man who taps club ass behind my back.

Because I *am* the club ass. How does Wrath really think this is going to work? If I give in and admit my feelings for him, I'm the one who stands to lose the most when we break up. Not him.

Why does he think he's in love with me? Sex? Yes. No problems there. Except when he does that weird hot and cold thing that confuses the hell out of me.

My gaze drifts to him again. Still watching me. My mouth turns up.

We've got a full house tonight. Couple members from the downstate charter even came up to celebrate Wrath's return.

Obviously no one learned their lesson from the Inga incident, because I spot a few dancers from CB milling around. I recognize one grubby little gold-digger—Lexi, and I want to kick the shit out of her when she perches her perfectly tight ass in Wrath's lap.

See, this right here is one problem. I don't *want* all my possessive instincts stirred up.

I laugh when Wrath pushes her off his lap and she almost falls because she can't balance herself on her seven-inch fuck-me stilettos.

Strike one.

She stumbles over toward me and leans on the bar. "He's in a worse mood than usual. What's his issue?"

I wasn't aware that we were friends, but I answer anyway, trying to be a good hostess. "Maybe he didn't want you sitting in his lap, with the broken leg and all."

Or maybe he meant what he said earlier.

She glances over her shoulder at him. "Oh yeah. Oops." She giggles and I work on keeping my hand still so I don't smack her. We almost died the other night and he's laid up for the next four months, yeah, it's a real laughfest.

Bitch.

Rock stops by the bar again. "You okay back here?"

"Yup."

"Hey, Rock. We miss you at the club," Lexi coos while running her hand up his arm.

Even though he smiles back, he removes her hand and takes a step away.

Strike two.

"Z and Dex treating you okay?"

"Oh yeah." She lets out the fakest giggle and tosses her hair. I roll my eyes. "But it took two men to fill your shoes."

Good God.

Rock smirks, and turns to me. "I'm gonna be outside waitin' for Hope. She should be here any minute."

"Sounds good. Will you at least let me say hi to her before you tuck her away upstairs?" I respond with a wink.

"I'll do my best." He takes another step from the bar. "Good to see you, Lex."

"Are *any* of these guys DTF?" Lexi bitches at me.

I scan the room. No one here I dislike enough to sic her on.

"Maybe one of the prospects?" I suggest. They never get any ass.

Finally she wobbles away. Just in time too, because Hope breezes in about five seconds later.

"Finally!" I shout and throw my arms around her. She laughs and hugs me back.

"Rock said you were bringing supplies."

She nods at the hallway. "He asked the prospects to unload my car."

I quirk an eyebrow. Just how much did she bring?

"I'll go check. Make sure you give him lots of attention," I say nodding at Wrath.

Her gaze sweeps the room, nose wrinkling at the antics of some of the guys. But her lips curve into a smile when she spots Wrath.

"Hope! You're finally here," Wrath calls out.

She turns to me. "Did the doctor ever tell you how bad his head injury was?"

It takes a second, but I realize she's joking. When I'm finished laughing, I tap the bag in her hand. "What's in there?"

She tilts her head in Wrath's direction. "He asked for Jack Daniels."

"Oh boy, he'll love you forever."

She laughs and crosses the room, shyly handing him the bag. Wrath said she brought him burgers in the hospital. It's cute that they've reached some strange, friendly truce since the accident.

Shaking my head, I walk down to the kitchen to make sure the prospects don't make a mess out of my pantry while they're unloading Hope's car.

When I return, Wrath's over on the couch with Rock and Hope. Without me behind the bar, no one could figure out how to serve themselves, so there's a bit of a line waiting for me. I get most of them taken care of pretty quick. When I glance up, Hope's on her way over, looking dejected and annoyed. My gaze flicks to Wrath and Rock who seem to be having an intense discussion.

"I've been sent away," Hope grumbles as she leans her elbows on the counter.

It doesn't take a genius to figure out why. "Club business?"

"Something about Wrath's gym."

Okay. Furious Fitness isn't exactly top secret, but I feel I should warn Hope should she ever overhear something relating more closely to the MC. Especially as I spot a number of other members from our downstate charter in the room. "Always play dumb when it comes to club business, Hope."

Poor girl reacts like I threw a bucket of ice water in her face. Shit. I should have kept my mouth shut. "I'm sorry, Hope. I didn't mean to sound like I was scolding you. Just if...you know, we were ever around any other clubs or one of our other charters—always act as if you hear nothing."

She pauses then leans back over the bar. "Sorry, Trinity. I know you're just looking out for me."

That's a relief. The last thing I want to do is disrespect Rock by offending his woman. She flashes a pained smile at me. I try to picture myself in her world—wearing a suit, arguing in a courtroom—I'd be completely out of place. And while I'm aware of and understand a woman's place in the MC world, I'm sure it pisses Hope off. "I'm used to it, but I imagine it's weird for you."

She still looks a little forlorn. Even worse, I notice a number of the guys in the room checking her out. Rock's wrapped up in his discussion with Wrath, so he hasn't noticed yet. Only a matter of time before he does and loses his shit.

"FYI, I wouldn't keep standing like that in a room full of bikers. You know how they say men think about sex seventy-five percent of the time? With these guys, it's closer to ninety-nine percent."

She doesn't answer, but she does turn and glance at Rock, who's got his eye on her now.

Z walks up behind her and by the grin on his face, I know he's about to cause trouble. "Hey, Hope. Keep standing like that and you're just begging for a spankin'," Z says, eying her up and down.

Her reaction is pretty funny. She straightens up and yanks her shirt down over her ass. "Told ya," I say through a mouthful of giggles.

"You startled me, you perv!" she yelps, slapping his arm.

Z gives her one of his panty-dropping smiles, but Hope's immune to anyone's charm but Rock's.

Although, if he keeps acting this way, "Rock's gonna kill you," I warn him.

"Nah. Hope's like that hot sister-in-law you got inappropriate feelings for, but wouldn't touch on a dare."

She has no idea what to do with that. "Thanks, I think."

Z winks and I know whatever he's about to say will embarrass me. He's got some sort of agenda tonight and I can't figure it out. "Now you," he says, focusing all his attention on me. "Nothing about my feelings for you are brotherly. What are you doing later?"

Is he fucking kidding? In front of Hope? Why?

"Can I get a Crown and Coke to go, please?" Hope asks.

After she practically runs away with her drink. I turn my glare on Z. "Why would you try to embarrass me in front of her?" Shit, my nose stings and my cheeks feel like I've been standing in front of the oven for too long.

"Give it a second." He glances over his shoulder at Hope, who's now snuggled up against Rock. "I love the girl, but she won't be able to keep her mouth shut."

Sure enough, Wrath's angry gaze swings our way. The scowl on his face deepens when he notices, Z running his fingers over my hand. "You're an ass," I grumble, while snatching my hand away.

A wave of people come in the front door and I'm swamped. Not enough that I miss Wrath slap Z on the back—hard—and tell him Rock's looking for him. Z laughs and ducks away.

Wrath crosses his massive arms over his chest and leans against the wall behind the bar. "You almost done, babe?"

"In a minute."

Out of the corner of my eye, I catch him yanking his phone out his of pocket.

A few minutes later I realize what he did. Hoot nudges me out of the way to take over bar duty. I edge out from behind the bar. A few of the guys ask where I'm going. Bitching about Hoot not being as pretty a bartender.

"What's wrong?" I ask Wrath as I approach.

"Gettin' tired of you waitin' on everyone else. You're supposed to be waitin' on me." He flashes that boyish smile of his that does me in every time.

He bitches about the crutches the whole way to my room and drops them at the foot of the bed as soon as we're inside.

"What was that all about with Z?" he asks.

I can't stop the immediate eye-roll. "Messing with you. Obviously it worked."

"What did he say?"

"I don't know, he made a joke about spanking Hope's ass—"

"Oh, so he's as good as dead," he quips and flings himself onto the bed.

"You need your pain meds?"

His jaw clenches and I know he wants to say no. Wrath's very much a *Real men don't need pain killers* type of guy.

"I probably shouldn't. Had a lot to drink."

I hesitate because this is weird. "Um, I'm going to change."

"Okay," he answers making no move to…what I don't know. Where's he supposed to go? I grab a nightshirt. As my hand closes over the bathroom door, Wrath asks, "Where you going?"

"Uh, in the bathroom to change."

"Why? I've seen you naked."

Yes, that's true. I turn and find him grinning. "What do you expect? A strip show?

"No."

"This is weird," I mutter.

"What?"

I point at him and then myself. "You, me, us, this whole domestic weirdness we're doing."

The smile slides right off his face. "Why? You were staying up in my room before the fight," he says softly. Too softly for Wrath.

"That was different."

"Why? Because I told you I love you?"

Shit. "About that...Can we not tell people about whatever this is just yet?"

He's silent, but his jaw's ticking like crazy. "Tell me why," he finally says.

Why? Because this is never going to work. "Everyone knows you're just staying here because of the cast."

"Trinity, I could have figured something else out. Hell, I could have kicked you out of here and told you to go stay up in my room if I really wanted to."

My throat's so tight I can barely speak. "If this doesn't...if we don't make it this time...I don't want everyone feeling sorry for me." Then there's the biggest reason of all. The one I hate the most because it means I'm only thinking of myself. "I don't want to be kicked out." I hate how pathetic and miserable I sound. Inside I'm ticked he's forcing me to voice my insecurities.

"Shit, baby. Come here." He holds out his hands to me, but I'm rooted to my spot. "Trinity, come here. *Now,*" he says, much louder.

That voice my body responds to, and I find myself in front of him. His hands curl over my hips, holding me in place. "I'd never do that to you." There's no judgment or anger in his voice and I relax a bit. "Besides, you know the club wouldn't survive without you takin' care of us."

I snort and lift my gaze to meet his eyes. Those deep, ocean-eyes, pulling me under. Making me think maybe we have a chance.

WRATH

Did I finally get through to her? It's hard to tell. For fuck's sake, I don't know what the hell I'm doing. What does she need?

To feel secure, wanted, and loved. To be *safe.*

I know I can give her all of that. And more.

She shakes her head and sighs. "You guys would find some other chick to help out."

"Is that what you think? You're replaceable? Fuck without you we'd probably starve to death for one thing." She chuckles and looks away. "We'd definitely be rolling around in our own filth." She laughs a little harder.

"But—" I struggle to come up with the right words. "Even when I've been mad at you, I've needed you in my life, Trin."

The admission seems to startle her, but then her face softens. "I always feel better when you're around," she says.

Hell, that's practically an *I love you* from Trinity. "Even when I'm a jerk?"

"Yeah, then I just fantasize about slitting your throat."

I throw my head back and laugh. "Remind me to chuck my pocketknife." Her mouth quirks. "Okay, will you be more comfortable if we don't go public right now?"

She doesn't even hesitate. "Yes."

"Until the cast comes off?" I ask, because, fuck that's months away.

She nods. "And you're sure you want to be with me?"

"I've never been surer of anything in my life, babe." I run my hand over my head, wincing when I brush over the bandage. "Fuck, that's a long time. Four months?"

Her eyes well up. "I'm sorry. Maybe—"

I press a finger to her lips. "If that's what you need, then that's what we'll do. But in *here*, together. We're doing this for real." I poke my finger at the door. "Any of them—" Fuck, I hate this. "You shut them down, and if they give you shit, send them to me."

"People are going to wonder."

"No one will have the balls to stick their nose in our business. They'll just assume I'm being my regular asshole self."

"That's not fair. I'm sorry." She slides to the floor and grabs for my belt.

"What are you doing?"

She flutters her lashes at me and her lips curve into a smile that I think she intended to be sexy, but it's more sad. "You really have to ask?"

My hand closes over hers and I pull her away. In my shorts, my dick's cursing me out. "No. Not like this."

Her bottom lip juts out. "What? Why?"

"You think I'm mad at you, and that's not what's going on here."

Her smile disappears.

I jerk my chin at the bathroom door. "Go change. I'm exhausted and I bet you are too."

She balances on my good leg and pushes up off the floor. "I'm sorry I'm so fucked up."

"Babe, we're all fucked up in one way or another. One day you'll tell me what your reason is."

Stunned honey eyes stare back at me. What? She thought I wasn't going to want to know every piece of her eventually? "Be surprised all you want, Angel Face. But I intend to be your man in *every single way*."

CHAPTER TWENTY-FOUR

WRATH

Z's the first one at the dining room table the next morning, which is unusual. Still pissed about last night, I grunt at him instead of an actual greeting.

Trinity hurries past me into the kitchen and once again, I'm irritated that my girl's serving everyone breakfast.

Except she's *not* my girl—yet. I'm trying hard to honor her request, but it's annoying the shit out of me.

By the way Z keeps staring, I'm waiting for him to say something.

"Sorry about last night, bro."

Surprised, I raise an eyebrow at him.

He shrugs. "I wanna see you two work your shit out."

"It ain't me, brother."

Z cocks his head, but doesn't seem surprised. "I never...not until she told me a couple weeks ago and then it all clicked...if I'd known you two had something back then...I never—"

Fuck me. "Yeah, I know."

"You gonna claim her or not?"

Z must think this cast is gonna stop me from beating his ass. "She's not ready."

He gives me a *So what?* shrug.

"No. There are some things she needs me to tell her to do, and others..." Yeah, Trinity's been tough to figure out, but I'm learning. Slowly. "Besides, I ain't claimin' an ol' lady who doesn't want me to be her ol' man."

Z nods, and I realize he understands. "She worried about the club?"

My shoulders lift. "I guess. She had a fucked up childhood."

He looks away for a second. "Yeah, I always kinda figured."

My hands clench into fists because I can only guess what made him say that. *Fuck.*

Murphy swaggers in, and I'm overwhelmed with the urge to punch him. Don't know why. Instead of sitting, he curls his hands over the back of one of the chairs and leans over. "Where's Trin at?"

"Why?" I growl at him.

"Need a blowjob," he says with a cocky smirk.

Never hit a brother.

Fuck that shit.

Unless he's earned it.

That comment's definitely grounds for a beating. Cast doesn't slow me down a bit as I jump out of my chair, reach across the table and wrap my fingers around his neck. Z's up so fast his chair clatters to the floor. He slaps his hand over my arm. "Let him go," he says to me with complete calm.

Just one more squeeze and I release the little fuck.

"Seriously, bro?" he asks Murphy.

Murphy leans over and coughs. "Fucking hell." He lifts his wary gaze to me before standing up straight. "What the fuck? I thought you were just staying in her room—"

"Let it fucking go, and watch your mouth, asshole," Z advises as both of us sit back down.

Murphy's got no sense of self-preservation, because he pulls out a chair and drops into it. He runs his hand over his neck, but won't meet my eyes. "Sorry. Fuckin' irritated from seeing Heidi and Axel all over each other last night."

Z cocks his head. "When was she up here?"

He shrugs. "She came up to surprise him. T ended up chasing her home."

I feel for him, but I'm still fuckin' pissed. "From now on, find someone else to work out your Heidi-frustrations."

Murphy doesn't get to respond because Rock and Hope join our tense group. He casts a suspicious glance at each of us before pulling out a chair for Hope. Sweet and oblivious as always, she smiles at everyone, as if we're not a crew of degenerate fuckwits.

Teller joins us next.

"Thought you were home?" Murphy asks.

"Nah, came back after I dropped Heidi off."

Murphy grunts and looks away.

Hope's gaze keeps darting between Z and me. As if she's worried we're gonna kill each other. If only she knew. Murphy's more likely to get the fuck beaten out of him at the moment.

Trinity brings mugs out for everyone, then coffee. Hope chews on her lip as she watches Trinity move around the table.

"Trinity?" she calls.

"You need something, Hope?"

Curious about what she's up to, I wait for Hope's answer.

"Don't you ever eat breakfast?"

"Sure, in the kitchen while I'm getting everyone else's stuff together."

"Oh, no wonder you stay so skinny," Hope answers with a grin.

"Look who's talking," Trin jokes back.

Hope's gaze flicks over each one of us. "Well, I'm kind of on testosterone overload. Would you mind eating breakfast out here today?"

"Sure, I'll be right back."

Hope jumps up and follows Trinity into the kitchen. Girl is persistent, which is good because otherwise Trin will dawdle and find excuses not to return.

I lift my chin at Rock. "What's your woman up to?"

One side of his mouth kicks up and he shrugs. "You heard her. We're boring."

The girls are gone for a while, making it impossible to pay attention to the conversation at the table.

Hope returns first, hands Rock his breakfast and kisses his cheek like it's the most normal thing in the world. Trinity sets plates in front of Z and me, then hesitates. Hope's not going to be deterred though, she taps the chair next to her.

Murphy apparently still needs his ass kicked. "Hey," he mumbles.

Teller turns and scowls at him.

"Birch is coming," Hope explains to the little bitch.

Still shocked at the way this morning's turning out, I must be staring at

Hope. She glances up and pink stains her cheeks. "How do you feel today?" she asks.

"Hung over. Sore. But happy to be home." Happy as fuck to have finally weaseled my way into Trinity's room too. Even if she slapped a bunch of conditions on our arrangement.

"I think everyone is relieved you're home," she says with a chuckle. Her attention turns to Trinity, who hasn't moved. Hope picks up the milk and shoves it at her. "Sorry, didn't mean to hog up the milk, Trin."

It's enough to pull Trinity out of whatever's bothering her. "Thanks, Hope," she mutters.

Thanks is inadequate. She's done more for my girl in five minutes than I've been able to do in five weeks.

"Sucks we're gonna miss the run with Sway's guys down to Virginia," Z says. "Last big run before we're all trapped in cages for winter."

Like I don't feel bad enough about all the shit going on. "Fucking go," I grumble at him.

"No fucking way. We all go, or no one goes," Murphy shoots back. As if loyalty is going to stop me from kicking his ass today.

"We'll do up a big one at the start of the next season for you," Teller adds.

They turn to discussing what upgrades they plan to work on over the winter. It just depresses me because I probably won't be ready to ride at the beginning of the next season. And I sure as fuck ain't in any condition to work out in the garage all winter long.

"Don't you ever get tired of all the boy talk?" Hope whispers, loud enough for all of us to hear.

Nervous laughter tumbles out of Trinity. "Not really."

"What do you like to do, Trin?" Hope asks.

She shrugs. "This place keeps me busy. I can't wait for next spring. The guys are going to put in a garden so I can grow some veggies and stuff here."

Hell yeah. She got so excited about farmers markets and feeding me all that healthy crap during my training. Can't wait to help her out with that, plus it will keep her busy. "We'll get the prospects started on that early, so it's ready for you," I say.

Trin's mouth quirks, but she doesn't respond.

"So gardening? Are you the one who keeps the big Buddha guy looking spiffy?" Hope asks.

Trinity finally smiles and seems less freaked-out. "Yeah, that's me."

"Neat. I've never been able to keep any plants alive for more than a week."

"Sparky helps," Trinity explains. Please. Sparky barely leaves the basement. He ain't much help. Girl's too modest.

"Which one is he?" Hope asks.

That's Rock's cue to interrupt because the answer is, *The mastermind behind our weed-growing operation in the basement, that I've never told you about.*

"Babe, is that all you're gonna eat?" he asks.

She turns and glares at him, making me almost choke on my toast. "Yes, I'm getting fat enough, thanks to you."

Haven't noticed any fat on her. If anything she looks better than she did when she first showed up, looking like a fucking skeleton. But I don't think Rock will appreciate that observation.

"You need more protein," I say instead, pointing at her now-empty bowl.

"Fuck, here we go. Mr. Clean Eating Fighter," Teller interrupts with a roll of his eyes.

I shrug. "Whatever, welterweight."

"Let's go, mountain man. This welterweight will kick your ass," Teller shouts, jumping up and flexing for everyone. Murphy throws him a kidney punch, while Z and I laugh our asses off.

"Sit down before I punt you across the room with my good leg," I warn him.

The girls aren't impressed with our antics.

"What else do you do for fun around here?" Hope asks.

"I read a lot," Trinity answers.

Huh. That's news to me. We've been spending night and day together for weeks and I haven't seen her with a book in her hands yet. Of course, I've been monopolizing all her time, making her take care of me. Between that and all the stuff she does for the house, no wonder she's had no time to do anything for herself. Makes me feel like an asshole.

"I don't know what kind of music you like, but my friend, Sophie, has an extra ticket to see Afterlife on Friday. You think you'd like to go?" Hope asks, nudging Trin's arm.

"Hey," Rock huffs in an offended tone.

"Girls' night," Hope says without turning her head.

After what Rock's told me about Sophie getting drunk and trying to jump him, I can't say Trinity hanging out with her thrills me.

Trinity hasn't answered yet.

Hope, on the other hand—girl only has eyes for Rock. The idea of Trinity spending more time with *her* is very appealing. I like the idea of her having more *girl*friends.

"Come on. You'll probably need a night off from playing nurse to Wrath, right?" she encourages, jerking her chin at me.

My lips quirk up. *Funny girl.* I throw a look at Rock that I want him to read as *Make this happen, motherfucker.*

Trinity looks to me. Silently asking for permission and my chest tightens. I nod and she turns back to Hope.

"Yeah, I like them. Sounds like fun."

Hope acts like a five-year-old on her way to Build-A-Bear. "Cool! You'll like Sophie and Lilly. Hell, they'll probably like you more than me."

"Where's the show, Hope? Not the dive we went to last time?" Z asks. Christ, I wish he'd let that shit with Lilly go.

"No. Downtown at the arena," Hope answers. He and Rock share a look. Hope's nose wrinkles.

That's right Cinderella, you're not taking my girl downtown alone and unprotected.

Trinity

It's such a lovely fall day, after breakfast, I set up an over-sized lounge chair for Wrath outside. He grumbles the whole way through the kitchen and out the back door. He *really* hates me helping him down the back steps. But once I show him the spot I made, his grouchiness disappears.

"How'd you know I was gettin' tired of being inside?"

Because he's like a bear in a cage when he's cooped up for too long. "Just took a guess."

He flops down and I grab his crutches while he stretches out. Before I open my mouth to protest, he pulls me down next to him and tucks me against his side.

Except for the occasional noises from inside the house, the only sounds are some very vocal birds and the wind through the trees. It's peaceful, and for the first time in a long time, I'm content.

"Looking forward to the concert?" he asks after a few quiet minutes.

"A little. You sure you don't mind?"

He tilts his head down, so he can see me. "No. Why would I mind?"

"I don't know."

"It'll be good for you to get to know Hope better."

That's too funny to ignore. "Made your peace with the fact that she's not going anywhere, did ya?"

"Something like that."

He's quiet afterward. Between the breeze, the birds, and the thump of Wrath's heart under my ear, I drift off to sleep.

Wrath is as demanding as a toddler, and I spend my week running him to the gym and doctor appointments. By the time Friday rolls around, I'm eager to get out of the house. Maybe that was his plan all along.

Hope knocks on my door in the afternoon. She's bouncing with excitement. I'm baffled by her eagerness to spend time with me. Did Rock ask her to be my friend? I hope not, because the more I get to know her, the more I like her.

Holding up a traincase of makeup, she bustles into my room, making her the second person who's ever been in my space. "So," she says, "I own a ton of makeup. But every time I use it, I end up looking like a cracked-out clown."

From the bed, Wrath snorts. Hope's cheeks flush pink when she notices him sprawled out. "For a big guy, you blend in awfully well. I thought you were in the garage with the guys."

"Nope, but continue. I want to hear more about this cracked-out clown thing," he says while pointing at her face and twirling his finger in a circle.

Her mouth twitches, but she ignores him and turns back to me. "Since you do eye makeup so well, I was hoping you'd help me out?"

To say I'm surprised is putting it mildly. "Yeah, I can do that."

"Thank you." She glances around the room and back at Wrath. "It's still early, do you want me to come back later?"

"Nah. We can get started now."

I throw a pointed look at Wrath, who doesn't seem to take the hint. "What?"

"Are you planning to stick around for a makeover?"

He curls his lip. "Are you kicking me out?"

Hope giggles and I shrug. "If you really want to stay for this, by all means."

"I'm thinking of wearing a dress? Unless you think it will be too cold?" Hope asks me, dismissing Wrath entirely.

"We're going to be inside."

"Good point, I'll be right back." She drops the traincase on my desk and darts out the door. Wrath shakes his head as he watches her leave.

"You're really going to kick me out?" he asks.

"Yup. Change of scenery will do you good."

"Doctor told me to rest. You were there, you heard him."

"He also told you to move around, so you don't end up with a pulmonary embolism."

He waves his hand and makes a dismissive snort-grunt sort of noise. "I'm perfectly healthy."

"Good, then take your perfectly healthy ass to the living room. Otherwise I'm going to practice my eyelining skills on *you*."

He sits up and gives me one of his devilish smiles. "I might like that, baby."

It's such an unexpected thing for him to say, it takes a minute for it to sink in before laughing.

"Give me a kiss, and I'll go."

I glance at the slightly open door. Hope will be back any minute.

"I know what you're thinking," he says all low and smoky. "Do it anyway."

When I hesitate, he moves to lie back down. "Okay, make sure whatever you pick matches my outfit."

In two steps, I make it to the side of the bed and grab a fistful of his shirt, pulling him to me. That's the extent of my bravery. Wrath takes over from there, gripping my hips and pulling me into his lap. His hand works through my hair, holding me while his mouth seals over mine. My body has a mind of its own and doesn't care that Hope might walk in at any moment. My arms wrap around him and I'm pretty sure I'm grinding my hips into him as well.

He groans and pulls away. "That'll give you something to think about tonight."

"What?" I ask, pulling back.

Fixing his gaze on the door, he won't meet my eyes.

"You don't trust me? You think I'm such a whore, I'll pick up some random while I'm out with Hope?"

"What? No. That's not what I said."

"It's what you meant."

"Are you a mind reader now?"

I can't think with my body plastered against his, so I drag myself out of his lap and take a few steps back.

His hands are balled into fists, his head hanging down. "I don't want to fight with you Trinity. I'm done."

"With me?"

His head snaps up. "Never. You don't get it so I'll say it again. I'll *never* be done with you. But I *am* done arguing with you over bullshit."

Now I feel stupid for overreacting. "Tell me what you meant then?"

"I'm pissed I can't go with you—not because I don't trust you—because I worry about you. I'm a useless invalid right now."

Wow. That's a lot for Wrath to admit. Like we're really a couple and this might last. "You're never useless." I take a step closer and wrap my arms around him. Because he's who he is, he takes the opportunity to nuzzle his face against my boobs. "You're an ass," I tease. When he looks up, I brush my knuckles over his cheek. "Don't worry about me, okay? I can take care of myself. You taught me all those kick-ass self-defense moves, remember?"

He smirks. "Yeah."

"Should I come back later?" Hope asks from the doorway.

"No, I was just leaving." Wrath pushes me back so he can stand, and I hand him his crutches. "Trin threatened to use her eyeliner on me, so I'm outta here."

Hope giggles and opens the door wide for him, standing back so he can pass by.

When he's gone, she breezes in and drops an armful of clothes on my bed. She shakes her head. "Boy do you have your hands full."

Knowing Wrath's worried about me, my safety, tangles up every one of my emotions. "You have no idea."

WRATH

"I can't believe you're letting them do this," I bitch at Rock when I find him in the living room.

Fucker has the nerve to laugh at me. "One doesn't *let* Hope do anything, brother. And I don't think you have much say over Trinny, either."

Like hell I don't.

"Fuck off," I mumble. Pointing down at my cast, I feel the urge to

272

remind him of our recent misadventure. "It's kinda soon after this bullshit to be letting them run around unprotected."

"Z and I took care of those fucks."

True enough. Still bugs me.

Music drifts out from Trin's room. I'm happy she's having fun with Hope, even if I'm annoyed I don't get to watch them dress each other. "It's like backstage at a fashion show down there. Why couldn't they do that shit in your room?"

Rock shrugs. "Who's coming up tonight?" he asks to distract me.

"Fuck if I know," I grumble. I haven't done a damn thing related to my job all week. Rock really should strip my patch.

"You worried about something else?" he asks. When I shrug, he chuckles.

I may have told a small white lie to avoid an argument with Trinity. I trust her, but this relationship stuff is new to her too. Even though I understand where it's coming from, her refusal to acknowledge what we are to the people we're closest to is fucking with me. Having it tied to something I can't control—my broken leg—only makes it worse.

"They're not going out to pick up guys," Rock says.

"I know Hope isn't. But those other two—"

Rock jabs his elbow into my ribs and I shove him back. "I called Blue. He'll make sure they're protected at the show, and Birch will be on their tail. They'll be fine," he assures me.

That's a bit of a relief. Blue's a solid guy. The arena they're going to is in our territory, so they should be fine.

Trying to distract myself with the television is pointless. Rock disappears into the office and I consider asking him if he needs help.

The sound of the girls giggling makes my mouth twitch up. "We're almost ready to go," Hope announces.

Rock pokes his head out of the war room and I about piss my pants laughing at the look on his face when he takes in her outfit.

Trinity's arrival draws my attention away from them. *Fuck me.* Go ahead and call me a fuckin' pansy, but I recognize the dress she's wearing right away.

"Jacket?" Rock asks Trinity.

She holds up a black leather jacket. "Yes, Dad."

"Very funny," he mutters as he snaps a picture of the girls. I assume he's going to send it to Blue. Smart man.

Hope grabs Trin's hand, dragging her to the door before I have a chance to say anything to my girl. "Let's go. I don't like the bossy caveman faces I'm seeing."

"Hey, wait a sec," Rock calls her to him.

I can't get to Trinity fast enough. Thankfully, she meets me half way. Uncertain honey eyes stare up at me.

Leaning over I kiss her cheek. Her soft, sugary scent rushes straight to my head. "You look fuckin' beautiful," I whisper against her hair. Her breath catches. My hands tighten on her waist, holding her still. "I remember the last time you wore this dress."

"You do?" she whispers.

"Yup. Remember every second I've spent with you. Good and bad."

"Wy-"

"Go," I cut her off. "Have fun. I'll be waiting for you when you get back." My hand slides over the curve of her ass. "When you step inside the bedroom later, I want you to take everything but the dress off."

I pull away and look in her eyes to make sure she sees I'm dead fucking serious. Her cheeks flush pink and pretty. "Okay," she whispers.

Fuck, yeah. "Get out of here, before I change my mind and fuck you right now," I grumble at her.

She chuckles and pushes me away. Grabbing Hope's hand, she says, "Let's run before they change their minds."

They head for the door, and I watch them go. Thinking about what I'm going to do to Trinity when she returns has my dick so hard it hurts.

Trinity

By the time we get downtown, I'm ready to go home. I haven't met Hope's friends before but I've heard plenty about them. Sophie's a lawyer like Hope. Lilly has some sort of graduate degree. Considering I barely made it out of high school and couldn't use the college scholarship I was offered, I feel totally out of place. And let's not forget the fact that they all have real jobs while all I am is a housekeeper-whore.

Hope introduces me as her friend, which catches me off-guard. I don't know why. She's too classy to introduce me as "the whore of my boyfriend's club."

In all my years with the Kings, this is the first time I've questioned myself. Compared to the girls that usually hang around up there, I'm pretty damn lucky. Compared to these three, I feel like shit. I concentrate on not tripping in the heeled boots I borrowed from Hope as we walk to the Red Room.

As soon as we place our dinner orders, Lilly pounces. "So, how tight are you with Z?" she asks. I'm not surprised or annoyed. I'd been expecting it, honestly.

Whether he wants to admit it or not, Z really likes this chick. While I want to be nice to her in case we have to spend time together in the future, I'm also not going to let her push me around. "I've known him for a long time," I answer.

Lilly's eyes narrow. "You fuck him?"

Next to me, Hope gasps and slaps Lilly's arm.

Well, at least the bitch is direct. I have no idea what Z's told her, so I answer honestly. "Not lately."

Lilly seems to appreciate honesty. She sits back. "He fuck around your MC a lot?"

"Why are you so curious?"

She fiddles with her napkin for a beat before answering. "We hooked up. He keeps calling. I just want to know if he's worth the effort, or if he's full of shit."

Christ, Z's an asshole. But my loyalty is to the club—including the big manslut—not this chick. I glance at Hope, not sure how much of this she wants to know. "Besides club girls, I've never seen him with the same chick twice. That's all I can really tell you."

Lilly seems satisfied with my answer and the awkwardness surrounding us evaporates.

Sophie proceeds to get drunk on tequila shots. Lilly keeps an eye on her, and doesn't drink anything herself. Lilly and I end up talking—not about Z, thankfully—and I discover she's pretty funny.

When we finally leave for the show, Hope's bouncing up and down like a teenager—even though she didn't have a drop of alcohol—but her excitement is infectious.

Sophie's law firm has box seats. It's a nice set-up and I'm relieved not to be out in the middle of the crowd. Especially since, from our high vantage point, I can see the moshpit is intense and no place on the floor seems to be safe from flying bodies and crowd surfers.

I send Wrath a text letting him know we're okay and safe in the box seats.

Good. He answers back.

After the show, Sophie has connections that get us backstage.

"You okay with this?" Hope asks me outside the band's dressing room.

"Sure. I wouldn't mind meeting Chase. He's fucking hot."

We both giggle. The singer is indeed hot, but Wrath could probably bench press him. The band is nice enough. Their drummer's clearly down-to-fuck, and offers to give me a "tour" of their bus, but I politely put him off. There was definitely a time in my life where attention from a guy like that would have had me on my back in two seconds flat.

Wyatt's your boyfriend now.

Wow, that's weird.

He's waiting at home for you right this second.

When Hope asks if I mind leaving, I'm jumping for joy inside. Lilly shocks me by pulling me in for a hug. "We'll hang out again soon, I'm sure," she says. Huh. Here I thought I'd made a lousy impression.

Hope takes her time saying goodbye to Sophie, who probably won't remember much of their conversation. To get her moving, I walk up and bump her with my hip. "Ready?"

"Yup."

The hallway is about twenty degrees cooler and a welcome relief.

"Hey, Trinity," a thick, rough voice calls from behind us, scaring the shit out of me. Blood pounds through my ears, drowning everything else out for a second.

"Oh, shit. Hey, Blue." Feeling foolish, I throw my hand out in a casual wave.

"Enjoy the show?" he asks as he approaches.

"Oh yeah, it was great. What're you doing here?"

"Working security."

"Cool. Oh, this is Rock's ol' lady, Hope. Hope, Blue used to bounce at CB."

She responds with a shy hello.

"Where you ladies parked?"

"The garage on Second Street."

He nods and gives the backstage area a once-over. "I'll walk you girls out."

"You don't have to do that," Hope protests.

Oh, Hope, you have no idea.

WRATH

Throughout the night, Trinity sends me a bunch of texts. It makes me real fuckin' happy that even though she's out having fun, I'm on her mind. Each message raises my hopes that things between us will finally work.

The last one she sends is my favorite.

On our way home.

The clubhouse's packed. Rock must have gotten irritated with the parade of muffler bunnies bouncing around. He ducked into our office, closed the door and hasn't come out since. I knock before throwing the door open.

"Girls are on their way back."

He glances at the clock behind him. "Earlier than I expected." I can already see him vibrating with excitement at the thought of seeing his girl. Fuck if I don't feel the same damn way.

"Let's go wait outside for them," he suggests.

We push through the crowd and settle on one of the stone benches in the front yard.

"You still in pain?" he asks, nodding at my leg.

I shrug. "Nothing I can't handle."

"You two getting along okay?"

"Yeah. I think so."

"We gonna make an announcement soon?"

My lack of an answer seems to piss him off.

"What the fuck is wrong now?"

"It's not me. She's not comfortable. Thinks I'm only saying I want to be with her because I need her to take care of me or something." I go to run my fingers through my hair and remember it's not there anymore. *Fuck.*

"You're all right with that?"

"No. But that's what she seems to need right now."

Rock raises an eyebrow and stares at me.

"What?"

"Nothing. It's good to see you finally set your ego aside and take care of her."

"Fuck you."

"I didn't mean it as an insult, ya fuck."

"Sure sounded like it."

Rock shakes his head and mutters what sounds like *asshole* under his breath. "She talk to you about her past yet?"

"No. And that's another thing. I want her to tell me herself."

"She doesn't know, you know?"

"No."

Rock seems to think that over. "I feel like I betrayed her—"

"You should have told me a long time ago, asshole."

He looks over at me. "Maybe."

Rock rarely admits to fucking up stuff like that. I guess we're all growing up. "She won't be mad at you, if that's what you're worried about. She fucking idolizes you."

He doesn't get cocky about that. "Pisses you off, doesn't it?"

"It used to," I answer honestly. "I understand why now."

We're silent for a while. The other reason Trinity wants to keep our status a secret springs into my head. "She's afraid if we don't stay together, the club will kick her out."

Rock shakes his head. "Eight fuckin' years. We haven't had to worry about a damn thing around this place for eight years because of her—" He huffs out a deep breath. "Fuck." He flicks a hand at the house. "Our basement-dwelling brothers would be two mummified skeletons if it wasn't for her."

Laughter explodes out of me, because that's absolutely true.

"You want me to talk to her? Explain she ain't goin' anywhere unless she chooses to?"

"Not yet." I stare down at my hands, closing them into fists. "I've been trying to follow your advice. She makes it hard."

He snickers and shakes his head. "I can imagine."

We're interrupted by the crunch of gravel. Trin comes into view first. Hope's not far behind. She ignores me and flings herself into Rock's lap. That's it for them, they won't come up for air anytime soon.

Trinity hangs back, watching them with a smile.

"Hey, angel."

She holds out her hand to me and I grab my crutches.

It's too noisy to talk inside, so we go straight to her room.

"Did you have fun?" I ask as soon as she shuts the door.

She doesn't answer right away and I turn to find her unzipping her boots and sliding her hands under her dress to roll her stockings off.

I'm feeling off after my talk with Rock. "Babe? Tell me about your night first."

She glances up at me in surprise, her lower lip trembling. "Why do you keep doing this to me?" she whispers.

"What?"

"One minute you're hot to fuck and the next you're telling me to keep my clothes on."

"I absolutely did *not* say keep your clothes on." Dropping down on the bed, I prop my crutches against her nightstand. "Come here." She approaches slowly and sits next to me.

I curl my hand over hers. "I meant what I said. I want you to be my girl. *Really* be my girl. That means I want to actually talk to you and hear how your night was."

Her mouth opens and closes and she shakes her head in confusion. "I'm not used to that."

"So get used to it."

She smirks and lets out a soft snort. "I'm trying."

I raise an eyebrow and wait for her to continue. "It was fun. I was worried at first, but it turned out okay." She rolls her eyes and chuckles. "Lilly pumped me for information about Z."

That's fuckin' hilarious.

"Sophie got wasted. And the drummer for the headline band offered to show me the back of their tour bus."

"What?"

She chuckles. "I told him I had a boyfriend."

My mind's still snagged on some—wait, "You did?"

"Yeah."

"Wish I'd been there to beat the piss out of him."

She snorts and covers my hand with hers. "Yeah. You could have snapped him in two."

"The girls were nice, though? Treated you okay?"

"Oh, yeah."

"What else?"

"*Mmm*, Blue walked us to the car. I assume Rock set that up?"

My mouth curls into a smirk. She doesn't really need me to answer that.

"Did you miss me while I was gone?"

Did I ever. Reaching over, I tuck her hair behind her ear and trace her cheek with my finger. "Yeah, I did."

"Me too," she whispers.

To me, this is a huge moment for both of us, but it's quiet and still except for the sounds of our breathing. "I loved all your little texts."

One corner of her mouth lifts. "You weren't annoyed?"

"No. Never."

She ducks her head and my gaze wanders over her. "You look really pretty."

She tilts her head to peek up at me from under her lashes. "Yeah?"

"Yeah. Stand up." She does and I put my hands on her hips to guide her in front of me. "How far did you get?" I ask, tipping my head back so I can see her face. The soft blush that races over her skin flips my switch.

She tilts her head toward the door, where she discarded her boots and tights. "Not far."

"Turn around." She doesn't hesitate. I take my shirt off and ease up from the bed, standing behind her with our bodies barely touching. Her warmth sears my chest and I fight the urge to crush her against me. My hands paw along the back of her dress, searching for the hidden zipper. Leaning down, I whisper in her ear. "This is why I wanted you to leave it on. So *I* could take it off." As I drag the zipper down to her waist, I enjoy the sound of her breathing picking up. "I've thought about getting you naked all night long."

Trinity

"Then do it."

"Don't be so impatient, Trinity."

My dress loosens freeing my torso. I shimmy and it falls to the floor. Behind me, Wyatt groans. "That was sexy, babe. Do it again."

Bending over to pick up the dress, I press my ass into him and wiggle. A growl rips out of him and I barely have time to throw the dress over my desk chair before we're tumbling onto the bed. "That's a dangerous game."

He holds me tighter as I laugh and try to wriggle away. "No fair. I'm injured."

I snort. "You already have a *huge* advantage over me."

His mouth tips up in a filthy grin. Gripping both of my hands in one of his, he pulls them up over my head. "Don't try to get away again."

A sassy comeback lingers on my tongue, but I can't force it out. It probably has something to do with his fingers traveling up my ribs, tracing under the edges of my bra. One of is big hands covers my breast. He nuzzles his way from my neck to my chin working his way to my mouth, kissing me hard and fierce. My ability to think scatters away. I want to put my hands on his face or his neck and hold him close, but he has me pinned. Thinking about how much I love his kisses, keeps any bad thoughts at bay.

He breaks away, staring down at me. His grip on my hands loosens and

I wrap my arms around his neck. "Are you okay?" he asks, concern wrinkling his forehead.

"Yeah. Why'd you stop?"

He runs one hand over my arm. "You were squirmy and not in the good way."

I hadn't realized. He seems so upset, I force a smile and wiggle my eyebrows. "Now I've gotcha." I push and he rolls back, letting me settle on top of him.

His fingers trace over my cheek. "This what you wanted, Angel Face?"

"No, this is." Leaning down, I press my lips to his softly at first, tasting and taking my time. One of his hands holds the back of my head and he deepens our kiss, sweeping his tongue in my mouth, demanding access. Heat from his body seeps through the thin bits of lacy underwear I still have on. My hips circle, grinding against his rigid cock and he draws back.

"You're torturing me."

"What do *you* want, Wyatt?"

Instead of answering, he reaches out and grabs a condom, handing it over. "Get me ready."

I palm the little square and tease my fingers over his chest, over the ridges of his abs, work his belt loose and slip my hand inside. A rough groan comes from his throat.

"You want my cock?"

I bat my lashes and graze him with my fingertips.

"I'm already harder than steel, babe. No extra teasing required." He tucks his arms behind his head, one corner of his mouth lifting in a sexy smirk. "Take my dick out. Show me how bad you want it," he says low and rough.

I work his shorts off and drop them to the floor. When his cock is in my hands, I take my time sliding them up and down. He makes a sharp hissing sound when I press my lips against the head, softly kissing. His body jerks and one of his hands cups my face when I close my mouth around him. "Go ahead, make me yours."

I hum in approval and give him one last lick before ripping the condom open and smoothing it on. A hint of a smile curves his mouth, but his eyes are dark and possessive as they follow me. Whatever control he's handed me, he takes back. Two rough fingers shove my soaked panties to the side. His hands curl over my hips, lifting and lining me up the way he wants, guiding me down. My eyes close and I roll my hips until he grunts every time I slide down.

"Trinity, look at me."

It's almost too much. The fierce way he watches me, eyes glazed with pleasure. He reaches behind my head and draws me down for a kiss. A sweet, unexpected kiss that triggers a devastating orgasm. I cry his name against his mouth and he answers by wrapping his arms around me as he shudders through his own release.

Too spent to move, I burrow my face against his neck letting his scent surround me. The scent of Wrath and risk.

CHAPTER TWENTY-FIVE

WRATH

In the middle of the night, I wake up to find Trinity at the computer.

"Babe?" I croak out.

"Sorry, does the light bother you?"

Sitting up, I scrub a hand over my face. "No. You okay?"

"Mmm-hmm."

She's intently watching the screen, pulling on her lip with her teeth. Her hand's curled over the mouse and she's busy swirling out different patterns. A shake of her head. More lip-chewing. She lets out a large, silent yawn.

"Babe, come to bed."

"Can't. Gotta finish this."

Curious, I haul my ass outta bed. Her worried gaze flicks to me, and I can tell she closes out whatever she was working on.

Now that's going to drive me nuts until I figure out what she's up to.

I stumble past her into the bathroom, and when I return she's tucked in the bed. Before sliding in next to her, I check my phone.

"Honey, it's one o'clock. Weren't you gettin' up at five?"

"Yeah," she whispers.

I pick her phone up and shut off the alarm. My girl needs more sleep, those fuckers can feed themselves.

As soon as I slide in next to her, she snuggles up against me.

Of course I wake up alone. Shutting off her alarm probably gave her an extra hour of sleep—if that.

Fuck, being laid up sucks. I'm so fucking bored. My leg still throbs like a bitch. The only upside is it's neat being in Trinity's space even though I know I'm drivin' her nuts. She's been such a good sport.

Right now, I bet she's somewhere in the house cleaning up. It's bullshit that she's taking care of me and still doing all her household shit.

Maybe I should talk to Rock about it. Except I know it will piss her off. But eventually the club's going to have to figure something else out. Her days of being the maid of the MC are coming to a close.

Curious about what she could have possibly been working on in the middle of the night, I gimp over to her computer and plop my ass down in her chair.

Shit. Z's the tech guy around here. I have no idea what I'm even looking for. I pull up her browser history, figuring that's as good a place to start as any.

Girl spends a lot of time on photo sites. I know from our last visit to Fletcher Park, she has an interest in photography. So I guess that's not odd.

I'm tense sitting there going through her computer, worried she'll catch me any minute.

Christ, I need a fuckin' hobby.

Trinity

Teller followed me into the kitchen to help me load the dishwasher this morning. Something must be on his mind because he's not usually big on helping out in the kitchen.

"Where's your patient?"

Why's he asking? "Wrath? Resting, I hope."

"Is that going okay? You and him in tight quarters, I mean."

Shit.

I'm saved from any other awkward questions Teller has by the man in question storming into the kitchen. The fierce expression fades when he spots me, then twists into something else when he sees Teller standing close. I sigh because we've already done this so many times before.

"Morning."

He settles himself at the kitchen table. "What's up?"

Teller takes a few steps away from me. "Nothing. I was about to butter Trin up to see if she'll bake one of her cakes for Heidi's birthday party."

"Really?" I ask.

"Yeah, do you mind? I know your plate's kinda full right now," he says with a head tilt toward Wrath.

"I'd love to. I'll get some ideas together so we can go over them and you can pick out what you think she'd like. Or I can ask her..." Heidi hates my guts ever since she stopped by Teller's apartment unannounced and unexpected. Finding me sandwiched between her brother and her childhood crush on the living room couch was probably horrifying for her.

"We've got plenty of time to figure it out. After all our family drama, I want to do something nice for her birthday."

"Of course."

He pats my shoulder awkwardly. "Thanks, babe."

He and Wrath talk while I finish up the dishes. As I start taking items out of the fridge to fix Wyatt's breakfast, Teller leaves.

"Babe, you don't have to go to extra trouble, I'm fine. Come here for a second."

"It's no trouble," I tell him as I walk over. He pats his good leg and pulls me into his lap.

"I hate waking up without you," he says, kissing my cheek.

No one would ever believe this giant, frightening man was such a mush. "Sorry. You know I can't sleep much."

"Yeah, I should be doing my job and wearing you out." He wiggles his eyebrows suggestively.

"You've been doing pretty good there, stud. No complaints."

I'm shocked he hasn't had a fit over finding Teller and me alone together in the kitchen. But so far he hasn't said a word.

Holy shit. Are we really making progress here?

Later, I take Wrath to the gym. Jake and Whisper are thrilled to see him. They're watching over a trainer I recognize but can't place.

When the new trainer's done drilling his client, he jogs over to us.

Wrath slaps him on the shoulder harder than seems necessary. "How's it going, Irish?"

My jolt of surprise must have been obvious because Wrath glances down at me and smirks. "Babe, you remember Irish Storm?"

"Uh, yeah. Hi."

The kid looks away before meeting my eyes. "Hi."

"Get back to work," Wrath grunts at him and hustles me into his office.

"Why is he working here?" I ask as soon as he shuts the door.

His lips twitch. Maybe I shouldn't stick my nose in his business.

"Never mind. I shouldn't have said anything."

His hands curl over my shoulder. "Ask me all the questions you want, angel."

"Wasn't his crew responsible for the crash?"

"Yes. And he came to me when I was in the hospital, swore up and down he had nothing to do with it and offered to work here for free until I'm better."

"You trust him?"

"No. But he doesn't have access to anything important. No keys. He's not left unsupervised. Rock, Z, Murphy, and Dex have been taking turns keepin' an eye on him."

"Oh. Why are you sharing this with me? It's not my place to—"

He circles the desk and drops into his chair. I perch in the seat opposite from him. "You my girl?" he asks.

"Yes." Wow, that came out easier than I expected. Wrath must think so too, because his face lights up in a big smile.

"Then why wouldn't I talk to you about this?"

"I—"

"Babe, you been helping me keep things afloat as much as anyone else."

"Really?"

He rolls his eyes and leans across the desk. "Yeah, really."

We spend the rest of the morning going over paperwork. During an afternoon lull, Jake pops in and settles himself in the chair next to me. "Irish is doin' well."

"Good," Wrath answers without looking up.

Jake is a lot like Wrath, in that he doesn't like being ignored. He raps his knuckles against the desk to get Wrath's attention. "Doctor give you the okay to start working out?"

Wrath's jaw drops before answering. "I've got a fucking cast on the lower half of my leg. How the fuck am I supposed to work out, dick?"

A smirk curls the corners of Jake's mouth up. I have to hand it to him, he's brave. "Your arms ain't broken."

"Funny you should mention broken arms—"

Jake laughs, cutting Wrath off. "At the very least, you need to be doing some range-of-motion exercises to keep your joints healthy and prevent blood clots."

I snicker at that, because I basically told him the same thing the other day.

Wrath flicks his gaze at me. "You ganging up on me, angel?"

"Nope."

"You want to maintain those muscles you've worked so hard for, don't you?" Jake persists.

This time Wrath glares at him. "Why you so eager to get your hands on my body, bro?"

I snort and look away.

"Who says I'm not doing stuff at home?"

"Are you?" Jake turns to me. "Is he?"

"Don't drag me into this, boys." Pushing myself out of the chair, I duck into the bathroom so they can work their shit out on their own.

When I return, Wrath's alone. "Jake still alive?" I ask.

Wrath grins back. "Yup."

"You shouldn't be so mean to him. It's nice that he gives a shit about you."

For once he doesn't have a snappy comeback.

WRATH

Trinity and I are actually getting along and it's fuckin' nice for a change. Almost makes the broken leg seem worth it.

I wish things were going as well for everyone else. Contact of ours in the police department calls and lets me know Rock's girl was attacked in her own fuckin' office. Trinity's out shopping with one of the prospects.

Gimping my way downstairs, I find Z in the living room.

"Brother, you heard from Rock?"

"Not in a couple hours, why?"

"Got a call from Gandy. Something went down at Hope's office. A client attacked her or something."

He sits up, running his hands through his hair. "She okay?"

"Yeah. Rock's tied up with the cops though. Think you can go check on them later?"

He makes one of his duh faces, that just begs for a right hook to the jaw. "Yeah."

Being out of commission like this sucks.

I figure Rock's going to be spending some time away taking care of Hope after what happened. His absence doesn't bother me as much as it did a few months ago.

I understand it better now.

Because now that she's finally mine, all I want to do is spend every second with Trinity. She tolerates my clingy ass pretty well too. Although she drew the line at me going to the craft store with her this morning.

Trinity's putting an awful lot of effort into Heidi's birthday party and I doubt the kid will appreciate it. She'll probably be a rude little snot to Trinity. Just thinking about the whole situation pisses me off.

Fuckhole that he is, Teller not only weaseled my girl into making a cake, but getting all the decorations and other shit too. She's been gone all morning and half the afternoon, so I'm eager to see her, even if she is weighed down with a bunch of bags when she comes home. The smile that automatically brightens her face when she sees me? Like a long fist digging between my ribs.

"Have fun?"

"Not really." The delighted expression on her face says otherwise. Spending all this time with her, I've noticed how much she enjoys creative, artistic projects. And she's really good at them.

So even though I think it's a waste of effort on Heidi's behalf, and I'm worried Trinity will end up with her feelings hurt, I make an effort to be enthusiastic about it.

"You gonna bake some test cakes for us to try out?"

Warm laughter spills out of her. "Yeah."

She sets her bags behind the bar and takes a few steps closer. As soon as she's within reach, I yank her tight against me. Sweet, unblinking honey eyes stare up at me. We're out in the open and she's not sayin' a word about me havin' my hands all over her.

"I missed you, Angel Face," I say against her ear.

A hint of a shiver works over her. Her pretty smile disappears. "I missed you too."

Fuck yeah, it feels good to hear her admit that.

Leaning over, I touch my forehead to hers, brush my lips over hers. "Can you fit me into your schedule?"

"Wyatt?" She's breathless even though we're standing perfectly still.

My hand slides down, running over her ass. "Yes?"

She reaches up on tiptoes and kisses me again, then leads me down the hallway.

Pushing inside, she flips the lights on, but I'm right behind her and snap the switch off.

"What are you doing?"

Words are useless. I'd rather show her. I bend down and kiss her gently.

This is fucking awkward with me all gimped up. Keeping hold of her hand I hop over to the bed and sit, pulling her between my knees.

My knuckles run over her cheek. She's so damn soft. Slowly, I work the zipper of her hoodie down and toss it on her desk chair. My hands skim under her T-shirt, tickling her belly and I love the way she laughs low and soft.

She's impatient, because her hands pull at my shirt.

"You want this off?" I tease her.

"Yes."

It's dark, but not so dark I can't see her eyes light up as she takes me in. Fuckin' love that. Blood pounds through my veins. I want to take her hard and fast, but I also want to take my time.

"You have anything else to do today, angel?"

The question seems to startle her. She glances over her shoulder before answering.

"No."

"Good."

Her brows draw down. "Why? What do you want?"

I want everyfuckingthing. I want her to beg for my cock. I want her to scream my name. I want her to admit that she's mine in front of everyone.

My hands go to the button on her jeans, working them open and tugging them down her legs. She kicks off her sneakers and shoves her jeans to the side.

"I never get tired of looking at you." I tell her.

She snorts.

"Don't," I growl. "Get up here."

We end up side by side on the bed and I lean over to kiss her, slowly tasting her lips. She relaxes, moaning softly, giving in to me. Kissing a trail down her neck to her breasts earns me another sigh of pleasure. I peel the cups of her bra down just enough to get my mouth on her rosy nipples.

She wriggles and pants, her hands gently stroking over my shoulders.

"Wyatt?"

I don't want to be interrupted, so I suck harder, rasping my tongue over the stiff tip. Her hips arch up in response. My mouth goes to her other nipple, sucking and teasing.

Her moaning turns to gasping. Wriggling turns to thrashing. Her hips lift again, offering herself.

It would be rude to turn her down.

My hand moves down her body, sneaking under her simple cotton underwear, stopping to tease her clit.

My self-control is about gone.

I fall back against the pillows. "Get those panties off and come sit on my face."

Her shocked gasp almost makes me laugh. Almost.

She sits up, then kneels on the bed. Flushed, hair mussed, bra barely hanging on—she's perfect.

"Don't make me wait, Angel Face. I want to lick, and suck your pretty pussy until you come."

Her eyes widen. My hand reaches out and I trace my fingers down her thigh.

"Hurry."

She finally snaps out of her hesitation and shimmies her panties over her hips and down her legs, dropping them on the floor.

"Good girl, now come here."

It's not as easy as I thought and we tangle and twist until she's giggling uncontrollably with a knee planted on either side of my head. I grip her thighs and her laughter disappears in a gasp. Her heat radiates over my face as she squirms over me.

"I don't want to smother you," she whispers with a nervous giggle.

"Babe, I'd die a happy man smothered by you."

More laughter, then a sharp intake of breath as I move my hands to her ass, positioning her where I need her.

"What are you doing?" she asks.

I squeeze my hand around her ass. "Don't be so impatient, angel. I'm lookin' at your beautiful pussy, tryin' to decide if I want to tongue fuck you or slide my fingers into you first."

The decision's already made in my head. I need to have my mouth on her slick flesh, tongue against her clit until she's desperate to come. It's still fun to tease her though.

Using my big hands on her hips and ass, I guide her to my mouth. She loses her balance and braces herself against the headboard.

"This pussy's all mine."

"Yes."

I wasn't asking, but I like her answer anyway.

The second my tongue licks up against her clit, she cries out and tosses her head back.

"We've barely started, babe," I mumble, but I doubt she heard me.

I go back to lapping and sucking at her, teasing with light strokes, working my way down to dip my tongue into her pussy.

"Wyatt, I need—"

"Relax, angel. I know what you need." I nudge one finger inside. "I know what you like." Her hips buck wildly. I keep licking, sucking, fingering her until she's worked up into a nice frenzy.

"Please, please. Right there, there—"

I'd love to keep teasing her all fucking afternoon, but my dick is desperate to get out of my shorts and into her.

"You wanna come on my tongue or my cock?"

"Uh, I—whatever you want," she cries.

Oh, fuck me, that's fucking hot. "Want both, angel. Want it all."

"Gimmie."

That's new and I love it. My tongue attacks her clit and my fingers slip back inside, pumping hard. This time, actually giving her the friction she needs to get off. She arches and meets my thrusts. Almost there. I don't let up, even when she wraps her hands around my forearms, and digs her nails in.

"Oh! There, Wy—" she cries jerking above me. Coming so hard she has no idea how loud she's yelling my name. Well, half my name.

She shudders and rides it out. Her skin's flushed and pretty when her head drops down to stare at me. She throws herself to the side and lets out a harsh sob. "I never thought I could do that, that way."

"Come on my face?"

She smacks my arm and I laugh.

Pointing to my dick straining through my shorts, I ask if we're finished.

"Hell no," she says, rolling over and attacking the drawstring, pulling the material down. She's careful not to disturb my bad leg, then leans over and takes me in her mouth without warning.

"Shit!"

She hums and nods. I pull her toward me and spank her ass.

"Ow."

"I want you bouncing up and down on my dick in the next five seconds."

She giggles as I reach out and grab a condom from the drawer. "I think I need more than five seconds. You've got a lot going on there," she says as she runs her hand over me.

"You always say the nicest things, Angel Face."

Leaning, over, she brushes her lips against my cheek.

"Trin, you on the pill?"

She pulls away and gives me an uncertain look. "Yeah."

"Think we can stop using these?"

A head tilt. Something's on her mind, but she doesn't want to spit it out. Takes a second, but I finally get it.

"Babe? You want me to go get tested?"

Her mouth opens, cheeks flush pink, but no words come out. After a few beats, she nods.

"Wanna go with me?" I ask gently.

"Okay."

"Cool, now come here."

I'm ready quick. Trinity still hesitates, so I crook my finger at her. "Come. Here," I order.

Finally, she eases over me, planting her knees on either side of my thighs. Palming her hips, I urge her up, angling my cock to graze her hot, wet pussy.

"Feel that? No woman gets me as hard as you."

"Is that supposed to be romantic?" she asks with a hint of a smile.

Rocking forward slowly, she teases me for a moment before I pull her down.

"Yeah, babe. Fucking romantic as hell the way that magic pussy of yours ruined me for life."

Her giggles turn into gasps as she slides down my dick, then raises herself before trying again.

Christ, she consumes me. I settle back against the pillows, keeping my hands around her ribs, so I can tickle the underside of her breasts. She's beautiful and angelic over me, yet still my dirty, playful girl.

"Show me, Angel Face."

Her eyelids flutter shut. I'm torn between thrusting up fast and furiously and letting things slowly play out. She's so pretty, I enjoy watching her ride me for a while. The sighs, moans, noises and the way she bites her bottom lip start to take their toll on my control, though. It takes a lot of determination to hold back.

"Eyes, baby. Let me see them."

Her mouth curves into a dreamy smile before she opens her eyes.

"Aw fuck." Her honey gaze sends a spark of pleasure streaking down my spine. Bracing her hands on my thighs, she leans back just enough to lift her breasts, but tips her chin, so we're still staring at each other. That's the moment I lose it. Her short breaths turn into rough panting moans as she slams down harder, grinding herself against me.

"Fuck, right there, Wyatt, please don't—"

Gripping her hips tighter, holding her in place, I arch up into her. At the last moment, she shudders long, and violently, her eyes falling shut as she slumps against my chest.

It takes me a moment to come back to myself, but I wrap my arms around her, kissing her head.

I don't care about anything but this anymore. Not our pasts, her reservations. None of it. I just want to keep this feeling no matter what.

CHAPTER TWENTY-SIX

WRATH

"Hey," Z calls out as he pounds down the stairs.

"Where you goin' in such a hurry?"

"Rock needs us. Fuckin' GSC wants a meet, like right now."

"Give me a sec."

He cocks his head and gives me a once over. "We got it covered. Stay here."

"Are you fuckin' serious?"

"Bro, what are you gonna do if shit goes sideways?"

"Uh, my fists and trigger finger are fine, ya dick."

"Come on, don't fuckin' do this. Rock wants you to stay here. Dex, Murphy and Bricks are meetin' up at CB. I gotta go."

Motherfucker.

GSC's been getting twitchier and up in our business more than ever. I should be at that meet. That's *my* job; to protect the president. Having him order me to stay here burns my fuckin' ass.

Godfuckingdammit.

It's not that I don't trust Z and the other guys. Not that at all.

Trinity walks in as I'm contemplating redecorating the living room wall with my fists.

"You need help?" she asks.

"No," I snap back. *Shit.* I stop and put my back against the wall. "Come here, babe. Sorry."

Shock sends her eyebrows up into her hairline. I must be some kind of jerk that she's always so damn surprised when I apologize to her.

"What's wrong?" she asks as she approaches.

"Nothin'. Rock's got a meet and I should be there. This fuckin' sucks. That's all."

"Want me to take you?"

That's the last fuckin' thing I want. But I realize she's just trying to be helpful.

"No, babe. Wouldn't be safe. But thanks."

She tries to keep my mind off things by taking me into the kitchen to talk to her while she's trying out a recipe for Heidi's birthday cake.

Is this what I've been reduced to? I'm supposed to be the muscle of the MC. My prez is off meetin' with some little gang punks and I'm stuck in some alternate universe where my big, grumpy ass is baking cakes?

Christ.

Trin keeps me occupied and stuffs me full of cake for the next hour and a half. Every couple minutes I yank out my phone, but nothing. Fed up, I finally dial Z.

"Hey—" he answers.

By all the background noise, I figure they're in the car and have me on speakerphone. I'm fuckin' livid no one bothered to call me sooner. "What the motherfuck, Z? I've been going nuts."

Rock's the one who answers my outburst. "We're good, brother."

I'm still fuckin' pissed at him for having me stay behind. "Rock, you dick. You coulda at least let me ride along."

"And do what, watch if Loco decided to blow us up?"

"Fuck you. I'm not an invalid." Then his words sink in. "What are you talking about? Loco came?"

"Yeah. Wanted to introduce Gunner's replacement."

Yeah, saw that coming. "Knew that little shit wouldn't last long."

"Also wanted to let me know he was onto our Western connection and that he wants it."

That's bad. Real fucking bad. "Fuuuck."

Rock's sigh comes through loud and clear. "Yeah."

"You tell him yes for now?" I ask.

"Of course."

That's something we need to discuss with all the members. "I'll call everyone in for church tomorrow."

"I'll do it, brother. It's my job," Z answers.

I snort out a humorless laugh. Christ, at least let me do the easy shit. "We seem to have flipped jobs, bro, if you haven't noticed."

"Thanks man," Z says.

"You guys comin' back here?" I'll be bouncing off the walls soon if Trinity doesn't find some more cake testers.

Rock hesitates for so long, I figure it's got something to do with Hope. "Fucking bring her with you, Rock. I'm sure Trin wouldn't mind some alternate company."

"Tomorrow, I promise."

"All right. Later."

"Everything okay?" Trin asks when I hang up.

"Yeah, I guess."

Trinity

Heidi did *not* want to get together to pick out her cake. Teller ended up explaining what she wanted, and I hope I got it right.

"Why are we going if she's gonna be a snot to you all afternoon?" Wrath bitches as I slip my shoes on.

I give him a cool look over my shoulder. It appears he has no intention of getting up and ready.

"She's club family. And she has her reasons."

"My woman shouldn't have to suck up to a little brat. Don't give a fuck whose sister she is."

Holy fuck. The way he calls me *his woman* like that sets off sparks of pleasure over my skin. Thankfully he's not looking at me, so he doesn't notice my reaction. "I'm not sucking up to anyone. I'm helping the club out like I always do." Wrath has never asked why Heidi and I don't get along. I'm sure he already suspects and that's what really has him so miffed.

After some brow beating, I get him into clean clothes. He refuses to shave, but I like the mountain-man scruffy look he's got going on, so I don't push my luck.

He's clearly annoyed I need the prospects to load the cake and decorations into my Jeep. When I get in next to him, he's scrubbing his hands over his face.

"I hate this."

Settling my hand on his knee, I squeeze gently until he turns my way. "I know. Is there anything I can do?"

His irritation disappears—for the moment. "No. You really have been an angel. I'd be even more miserable if it wasn't for you."

"Shit, it's hard to imagine you even more obnoxious."

He cracks a smile and gestures at the steering wheel. "Let's go. Don't want to keep the princess waitin'."

We pull up to Rock's house at the same time Murphy does. He ambles over and opens my door.

"You got my box, babe?"

I jerk my head toward the back seat. "Behind me."

I slide down and push Murphy out of the way to grab Wrath's crutches and bring them over to his side. He gives me a look like he wants to take his cast off and beat someone to death with it.

"Murph, help her with the cake and all that other shit."

"Yeah, no problem."

Hope runs over and grabs the bags out of my hands when I walk into the kitchen. "Oh my gosh, the cake you made is so beautiful!" she gushes, and a surge of pride drowns out some of my nerves.

While we're standing there admiring it, she whips out her cell phone to take pictures.

"Crap. I haven't figured out how to use the camera on this thing yet," she grumbles while messing with the phone.

"It's okay. I got some shots of it before we left."

"Got it," she says, as if my words didn't register. "Let me take a picture of you next to it then." Apparently she did hear me.

"No way."

Hope's forceful when she wants to be and positions me where she wants so she can grab her pictures. I stick my tongue out at her the entire time.

Rock, thankfully interrupts our photo session. "What's Wrath's problem today?" Rock asks as he walks into the kitchen.

"How long do you have?"

He chuckles and gives me a quick hug.

"Did you see the cake she made?" Hope asks.

It's odd that she's so impressed by a frickin' cake, but I sense her admiration is genuine and feel a little less out of place. The awful doubts that usually float around in my head recede to a dull murmur.

"Where's Z?" I ask

Rock nods at the back door. "Messin' with the grill."

I grab the platter, tongs and extra-long spatula I brought. "I'll make sure he doesn't set himself on fire."

Hope's chuckles follow me out the door.

Wrath's taken up a seat next to the grill where he can critique Z's technique.

"Did Murphy bring those bigger boxes up?"

Wrath nods to the shady part of the yard, where someone already set up the lawn games I picked up for the younger kids. By the smirk on his face, it must have been Z. Not a surprise since he's pretty much an over-grown kid himself.

"You're welcome," Z says, kissing my cheek.

"Love the apron, bro. Very manly," Wrath snarks.

Z adjusts the apron ties and grins. "Thanks. I thought so too."

"Are the girls here yet?" I ask.

"Axel's bringing them."

"Why the fuck didn't they ride with you?" Murphy grumbles behind me.

Confused, I turn to find Teller and Murphy. Teller rolls his eyes skyward before answering, "Axel took her out this morning, and they weren't back by the time I needed to leave."

Murphy's clearly not satisfied with that answer.

"Poor Axel trapped in a car with three teenage girls," I joke to lighten the mood.

"Please, that woulda been my dream scenario at his age," Z says.

Wrath can only contain himself for so long. "Who're you kidding? It still is."

The conversation rolls downhill from there.

Someone set up a cooler at the corner of the patio. I find it stocked with beer and soda. I grab one of each and set them down next to Wrath before heading back inside.

The girls finally get here, but go straight inside to watch movies. Heidi stops and glances at the cake. "I like purple better, but it's nice," she says.

I don't know if I should cry or scream.

Instead of doing either, I get more food ready to go outside.

"Do you need help?" Hope asks from behind me.

"Nah, I got it. Maybe hang with the girls?" Laughter floats out of the living room as I say it. Hope looks at me as if she'd rather gnaw off her arm than hang with a bunch of seventeen-year-olds.

"You sure you don't want to hang with them? You're closer to their age."

No, thank you.

WRATH

"You makin' progress there, bro?" Z asks once we're alone.

I snort and look away. "Define progress."

He nods. "Give her time."

Time. Fuck, we've wasted eight years already. I ache all over and can't sit still any longer, so I haul myself out of my chair. The weather's perfect. Hate that I can't ride on a day like this. Hate being trapped and dependent on others to get around. All of it.

I'm talking to Rock when Bricks and his brood show up. Seeing him doin' the dad thing somehow makes me feel worse. He and Winter haven't even been together that long and they look like one big happy family. "Hey, brother," I call out.

His two mini-mes—Lisa and Deacon—run right for me and I brace for impact. Thankfully they stop when they take in the crutches.

Lisa plants her fists on her hips. The expression on her face is too funny. "What happened?" she shrieks.

"Broke it."

"I bet it was on your motorcycle. They're dangerous," she sing-songs back.

Rock chuckles and Lisa turns her glare on him. "They *are*, Uncle Rock."

"So I hear."

"What's up with you, little man?" I ask Deacon. It's a miracle the kid ever gets a word out around his sister.

Bricks catches up to them and chases them off before Deacon answers. "His mom pitched a fit when I picked 'em up. He's been quiet all day."

"Sorry, man," Rock answers.

Winter stops long enough to say hello. She's got her fussy toddler on her hip, so she keeps moving to the backyard after she gets a quick kiss from Bricks.

Heidi and her friends race outside. She stops and gives me a big hug.

"I hate seeing you on crutches, Uncle Wrath," she says sincerely.

"Not more than I hate bein' on 'em, Heidi-bug." She doesn't even blink.

I get away with callin' her bug, mainly because I think she's too scared of me to argue.

The rest of the afternoon's a pleasant blur. We eat. The kids play. The family's in one place. Trinity lets me put my arm around her for a whole five seconds.

Heidi finally gets around to opening presents, saving Murphy's for last. Already heard him yap about the black and pink helmet for days, so I know what's in the box.

"It's from me, Heidi-bug," Murphy says with a grin.

"I figured." Heidi rips into the box, shiny paper flying everywhere. "Oh, I love it! Thank you, Blake."

"We'll take our ride in a few, okay?"

Is he fuckin' serious? Axel left the group when Heidi picked up Murphy's present, but he's still within earshot.

"Yeah." Heidi smiles shyly. "I didn't know if we were still doing that."

"Of course, Bug. It's your birthday."

She runs over to her friends. Murphy's gaze follows her across the yard. Jesus Christ. I can smell trouble from a mile away.

"They've been doing that every year on her birthday since she was like eight," Teller says.

I turn and realize Teller's explaining the completely-inappropriate-now ritual to Hope.

The drama's starting to bore me. I'd love to get through Trin's cake, so we can go the fuck home. Instead, Heidi races back and asks Murphy to take her for a ride now.

I raise an eyebrow at him. "We haven't done cake yet." *You know, the one Trin stressed about making all week long?*

Murphy slaps my arm, coming damn close to having his own arm snapped off. "We won't be gone long, bro."

After watching them leave, Hope turns to us and sighs. "Aw, that's sweet that they have a birthday ritual."

She would think that.

Sensing my irritation, she raises an eyebrow. "What?"

Why do I have to spell this shit out for her when Rock's standing right there? "He needs to knock that shit off. It ain't okay anymore."

"Wait, I thought you were team Murphy?"

After that whole exchange I had with Murphy the morning after my welcome home party, I think I'm switching teams. "Axel's a good kid. He cares about her."

"Murphy cares about her."

Did I grow a vagina and no one told me? Why the fuck am I having this conversation with her? "It's not about that. It ain't cool to have another brother's girl on the back of your bike."

Rock taps my shoulder. "We'll worry about it another day. Axel's fine. Teller's fine with it. Let it go."

Yeah, whatever.

"The cake Trin made is pretty kick-ass. She's real excited about it too. Those two better not be gone too long." Just then I hear Murphy's bike. Fucker.

Hope laughs. "You're so cute."

What? "Cute? Sugar, there's absolutely nothing 'cute' about me."

Rock tilts his head like he's worried she's got a screw loose.

Hope struggles to come up with something. "Well, I think it's cute you're all worried about Trinity being disappointed if Heidi doesn't get to see the cake she made for her," she finally babbles out.

I glance over at Rock. *Control your woman, dick.*

Fucker just smirks at me.

"She spent a lot of time on it, that's all, Hope."

She nods like I'm full of shit. "Sure. Okay, Wrath," she says as she backs away.

Rock watches her walk away before laughing his ass off at me. "She so has your number, brother."

"Shut the fuck up," I grumble.

A good hour later, Heidi and Murphy *still* haven't returned. Ice crackles through my veins when a cop car pulls up with lights and sirens. Christ, I hope Murphy didn't take a spill with Heidi at his back. Once I spot Heidi in the back of the cop car, I can breathe. Whatever this is should be interesting.

Hope flings open the garage door I'm standing next to with an irritated Rock right behind her. I can't help laughing.

"Shut up, dick," he snaps at me.

Hope's red-faced, but as soon as she spots the patrol car, she straightens up and marches down to meet them.

"The fuck?" Rock asks.

"Your house, was waiting for you to go deal with it."

"Thanks."

Rock follows Hope to the car. Me, cops, crutches? It's best I wait by the house.

"Can I help you, officers?" she calls out. I don't get much more of the conversation, but a few seconds later, Rock jogs by. "Need Teller out here now."

Teller's already on his way out to see what the commotion is. Trin's right behind him. She walks up and snakes her arm around my waist and tips her head up. "What's going on?"

"No fuckin' clue."

Z joins us and we watch the show.

Hope doesn't hide how pissed she is as she argues with the officers. She doesn't back down either. If anything the cops seem a little afraid of *her*.

The back door opens and Heidi's finally let out. She runs past us, tears and snot running down her face.

Trin glances at the house, then back at me. "I feel like I should talk to her, but don't know if that will make it better or worse."

"Give it a sec."

We watch Murphy step out of the car and the cops uncuff him.

What the fuck happened?

Hope's still arguing with the officers and Trinity snickers. "She's like a little pit bull."

Finally, the cops leave and Murphy ambles up the driveway. The first thing out of his mouth, "Is Heidi okay?"

"She's in the house," Trin explains.

Hope breaks out of Rock's hold. "I'll check on her." She touches Murphy's arm. "You sure you're all right?"

Murphy grins. "Yeah. I'll be better when I get my bike back."

"I'll drive you downtown," Trinity offers.

Uh, what now? Except she's really the only option that makes sense, so I keep my mouth shut. Even though she still won't let me go public, alone together things have been good. I trust my girl.

Rock shakes his head. "Jesus Christ. Never a dull fuckin moment. You wanna explain that shit, Murph?" he asks, clamping his hand on the back of Murpy's neck and walking him up the driveway.

"Empire pigs really got nothing better to do but hassle little girls?" Z spits out.

As a group, we all head inside. There's no sign of Hope or Heidi. Axel's pacing around the living room and glances up as we come in. "They're in the bathroom."

Trinity fidgets in the kitchen and I'm about to tell her it's time to go home when Hope walks in with her arm around Heidi.

We all give her a round of applause.

"It's not funny," she grouches.

"Can we please have some fuckin' cake now?" Z shouts, breaking the tension.

Trin unveils her creation and everyone admires it.

"Holy shit, Trin. You should be on one of those cake decoratin' reality shows or something." Z says.

"Why do you even know something like that exists?" I ask him and he flips me off.

We've barely finished the damn cake before Hope's cleanin' up after us.

"Let's talk," Axel says to Heidi in a lowered voice, that I don't think I was meant to hear. They leave out the back door.

Murphy watches them, then turns to Trinity and raises an eyebrow. "Can we go get my bike now?"

Motherfucker.

Trinity glances at me before answering. "Yeah—"

Hope pats Trin's shoulder. "I've got this, Trinity. Go ahead."

Thank you so much, Hope.

I catch Trinity's eye before she leaves with Murphy and she shrugs.

Godfuckingdammit.

I've got my hands wrapped around a beer bottle, shredding the label, when Hope settles her hand on my shoulder.

"Need anything?" Must look like a real miserable bastard I guess.

Yeah, I need someone else to drive Murphy downtown. "I'm fine. Thanks, babe."

She squeezes my arm and I reach up and pat her hand. I can't fucking believe the way she went after those cops. Stickin' up for one of us the way she did. "You did good tonight, Hope."

Obvious surprise crosses her face. "What do you mean?"

"With the cops. Sticking up for Murphy. Taking care of Heidi."

An uncertain smile curves her lips. "Thanks, Wrath," she answers.

Trinity

"What a birthday party." I can't help laughing while I'm turning the Jeep around in Rock's driveway.

Wrath snorts. "Yeah, not every day the birthday girl gets to ride in a cop car. Murphy tell you what the fuck happened?"

"No more than he said before."

He grunts and asks me a question that surprises me. "He behave himself?"

"What?" Then his meaning sinks in. "No, we stopped for a quickie in front of the police station," I snap.

"Is that what I asked? I asked if *he* behaved *himself.*" Wrath answers calmly.

Yeah, okay. He's right. "Yes, he behaved."

We're quiet for a while and I run over the day. "Heidi apologized to me and told me how much she loved the cake."

"Good, about fucking time she treats you with some respect."

"You know or suspect why she doesn't like me, don't you?" Why am I inviting trouble? But I can't help feeling like if we're doing this couple thing we should come clean with each other.

"It doesn't matter."

"But—"

"Yes," he snaps. "I can put the pieces together. You don't need to draw me a picture."

"Okay. I'm sorry."

His hand reaches over and squeezes my leg. "You don't need to apologize. It's in the past, right?"

"Right."

But for some reason it still feels wrong.

CHAPTER TWENTY-SEVEN

WRATH

Light stings my eyes and soft cursing pulls me out of sleep in the middle of the night.

Trin's at her computer again. This time I don't get up. I just watch her. It's bugging the fuck out of me that I can't figure out what she's up to.

I end up falling asleep going over all the possible scenarios.

In the morning I'm alone. On my way out of the bathroom, my hip knocks her chair, which bumps into the desk.

Her computer screen lights up.

"What the ever-loving fuck?"

A sharp intake of breath behind me turns my head from the screen. "What are you doing?" Trin yelps and runs over to shut the screen off.

"What am *I* doing? What the hell is that?"

She crosses her arms over her chest. "I can't believe you went snooping through my stuff!"

"I didn't snoop." Not today anyway. "I'm a little fuckin' unsteady on my feet and bumped into your desk." Why am I explaining myself? She's the one who has some explaining to do.

Her bottom lip rolls, and she nibbles on it. Fuckin' great, she's tryin' to distract me by being cute.

"Trin?"

She swings her gaze to me and her eyes are all shiny. "Promise you won't laugh?"

"At what? Why you got half-naked guys on your computer, Trin?"

Her chest rises and falls as she takes a deep breath. "It's a book cover. I've been taking these digital art classes. Well, I was. Not since—"

"What?"

"Not since I started helping you prepare for the fight. Because they were Saturday classes and you needed my help."

I'm so fucking confused right now.

I drop down on the bed and motion her over. "Start at the beginning."

Cheeks bright pink, eyes still glassy like she might cry, my poor girl's twisted up in knots. "I started messing around for fun, just doing little digital art pieces. I posted a few on this site I belong to and someone asked if they could use it for a book cover. Then someone else saw my name in that book and contacted me and it went from there. When I realized I needed to learn some better programs and techniques I started taking classes at the art center over in Ironworks—"

"You've been going to Ironworks, by yourself?"

"Yeah. I don't wear anything that identifies me as belonging to the club. I'm allowed to do that."

She's right. Still hate the idea of her being in Viper territory by herself. But at the same time, I admire her determination.

"It's right over the bridge, barely inside their territory," she assures me.

"Okay. Continue."

"That's it. But I'm behind on a few projects which is why I've been working at night."

Because of me. Fuck. "And the classes?"

"I'm going to sign up for a couple of one-day sessions when you're better."

"You dropped out because of me?" Here I was trying to give her something to focus on, but she already had something and I ruined it for her.

"I didn't drop out. They're going to let me use my remaining classes up. It's not like school where I'm getting a certificate or something."

Still doesn't make me feel any better. Something else occurs to me. "So that 'date' you told me about, was an art class?"

She dips her head. "You hurt my feelings, I wanted to make you jealous."

Sharp laughter rushes out of me. "Well, you did."

"I'm sorry."

"No, I deserved it. I was pretty twisted up after that night, seeing you and Tell—"

Her eyes gloss over with tears again, "I'm sorry."

My fingers trace along her jaw, tipping her head up so I can see her eyes. "I'm not trying to make you feel bad. I just wanna explain—"

"I know. Believe me, I know."

Yeah, I guess she does.

"Wait a second. What's with the half-naked dudes, though? What kind of books are these?"

The pink staining her cheeks gets brighter. "Romance books."

Don't laugh. Don't make her feel bad. Don't.

I nod at her computer. "Show me."

She looks downright horrified at the idea. "Come on. Show me how talented my girl is."

"I used the computers at the school for some of the more complex things. My computer doesn't have enough memory to use one of the programs I need." She stations herself in front of the screen and calls up an online bookstore, taps in a few things and brings up a page. There's a line of maybe fifteen or sixteen book covers and she scrolls through them for me.

"They're so small, babe. Can you enlarge them?"

She hesitates, but does it one by one. "This book made a list." She points out a few other details about different ones and I get a little lost, but try to follow her train of thought. Other than our club by-laws, I don't think I've willingly picked up a book since high school. This is a world that's completely foreign to me. But I can't help wanting to know more because she lights the fuck up as she's explaining it to me. I love seeing her so passionate about something—besides sex. She's so animated and excited, it floors me. She explains the work involved in a rush and it's clear how much she loves this. That she trusts me enough to share this, even though I sensed how hard it was for her, twists my insides.

"So what's holding you back?"

A soft blush spreads over her cheeks. "I'm saving up for better equipment. The art center has been nice about letting me use their equipment, but eventually I want my own set up."

Well, fuck me.

The club has always taken care of her expenses and we pay her a small salary for other stuff she might need, but it ain't much. I may not know anything about books, but from ordering tech stuff for the club with Z, I know plenty about computers. Gonna take her an awful lot of time to save up for the kind of shit she's talking about. I'm sure if she asked Rock, he'd get her anything she wanted. Problem is, she'd never ask for anything from the club.

The other problem is I don't want anyone else helping her with this. I need to do a little research.

An idea begins to take shape in my head, but I keep it to myself.

Trinity

Telling Wrath about my hobby leaves me feeling raw and exposed.

But he doesn't make fun of me. He seems genuinely interested.

"I was thinking about asking Hope if she'd help me incorporate. Make it a legit business." I float the idea to see if he'll laugh.

"That's a great idea. I can give it to Glassman's firm—"

"No!" Wrath seems startled and I try to control my voice. "Please don't tell any of the guys."

"Rock doesn't know?"

My heart thumps a few extra panicked beats. "No. Please. I don't want —I'd be mortified."

He tilts his head. "Why? You're obviously talented and really good at it."

I don't have an answer for him.

"You realize with the way Z monitors the internet set up we have here, there's a good chance he knows anyway, right?"

"I don't really picture him sifting through my e-mail."

"He's a big perv, he could be searching for nudes."

I shove him away. "Ugh. I'd never do that."

"No? What about me?"

"You want to send nudes to someone?"

"No. I want you to send them to me."

"We'll see." I don't give myself time to chicken out before asking my next question. "You know, most stock photos aren't very good and they get reused a lot. You'd make a great model for me."

The look on his face is priceless.

"I mean, I could charge more if I had my own original photos," I explain so he understands I'm not just jerking his chain.

"I'm a little old for that, don't you think?"

Is he kidding? "Uh, no. You're all muscle-y-male perfection."

He just keeps staring at me like I'm completely nuts.

Maybe I am.

"I'd only use you from like, the chin down."

"Not my face?"

"No. The idea is to turn women on, not scare them away."

He pins me to the bed, shifting so he's over me. "Think you're funny don't you?"

I'm laughing too hard to answer.

The length of his body presses against mine.

Then I'm not laughing anymore. His fingers slide into my hair; a gentle massaging touch I wouldn't have thought he'd be capable of. "Thank you for confiding in me."

"Thank you for not laughing."

He draws back, blue eyes searching my face. "You're my girl. I wouldn't laugh."

Every awful thing ever said about me when I was a kid—*ugly, disfigured, damaged, whore*—is replaced by two other words. *My girl.* I adore them, yet I'm so afraid they won't last.

CHAPTER TWENTY-EIGHT

WRATH

For once I wake up with Trin still curled up next to me.

Last night fuckin' floored me for many reasons.

If it's possible, I love her even more.

I roll out of bed as gently as possible and get ready to meet the guys in the war room for church. Grudgingly I grab the crutches and make my way down the hall. Fucking doctor keeping me at non-weight-bearing status is gettin' old quick.

By the look on his face and the way Rock's practically vibrating out of his skin, something's going down. If I had to guess, I'd say he wants to take a vote on Hope gettin' a property patch.

Good. I could use some entertainment this morning.

He studies me with concern as I drop into my chair. "You feelin' all right?"

"Yeah. Fuckin' cast is bullshit."

"Slowin' your game?" Z asks from across the table. As if I can't reach over and punch his pretty-boy face.

"Brother's got no game. Trinity's been carrying his balls around in her back pocket for weeks," Dex snarks.

Well, look who reached down and found a sense of humor. I laugh because it's funny *and* true. Girl has my balls, heart and everything in between. Getting tired of pretending otherwise.

Sparky twitches through the entire meeting. Brother can't stand being away from his plants for too long. He's got a crop close to harvest. I'd say that's why he's stressed but honestly, he's like this through every stage the plants go through.

Strip club's doing well. Z and Dex found someone to replace Inga. I can't imagine that was too difficult. There seems to be no shortage of hot, bitchy blondes willing to shed their clothes for cash.

Got a run out to the Devil Demons that's normally mine comin' up. Obviously, I can't go.

"Told ya, take my fuckin' cut."

My offer is met with the usual hostility from my brothers.

"There's an exception in the by-laws for injuries, you fuckhead, so stop offering," Z bitches at me.

It's true. I still feel like a piece of shit for not carrying my weight. Flipping Z off only makes me feel a fraction better.

Rock calls the meeting to a close, but asks the officers to hang back. That's not unusual. He wastes no time getting down to business.

"I want to give Hope a property patch."

Boom! There it is.

Been waitin' a grip now for this to go down.

As always, Z needs it spelled out for him. "You asking for our votes, prez?"

"Yes."

Rock stares everyone down, his steely gaze locking on me last. Just daring me to vote no.

Inside I'm laughing my ass off and gonna enjoy the hell out of messing with him. Outside, I'm indifferent.

"You lay it out for her?" I ask.

"Yes."

Bullshit. "Everything?"

Through clenched teeth, he spits out, "Not quite."

What the fuck you waiting for?

He reads the question loud and clear. "She knows enough. I trust her. You heard her the night of the party. It ain't gonna rattle her."

Yeah, I guess. Still think she should know what she's marrying herself to.

Teller—asskisser that he is—raises his hand like the obnoxious know-it-all I always wanted to punch in grade school. "She's been real good to Heidi. Trinity too. She's got love for the club. Prez is happy. She gets my vote." Big shock there. Teller is a mini-Rock. He ain't ever gonna challenge him on anything.

My teeth grind together when he mentions Trinity's name. I understand why. Still don't fuckin' like it.

Murphy has liked Hope from day one. He's extra sweet on her since she seems to have taken Heidi under her wing. I definitely respect that. But Murphy's another one who'll never challenge Rock. "She's a classy girl. Doesn't give anyone grief. She was ready to rip those cops' heads off after Heidi's party. Abso-fucking-lutely."

Now Z's more interesting because he *will* challenge Rock if he needs to. But he's also guzzled quite a bit of the Hope Koolaid. "She keeps her shit locked down. Took that bullshit the club girls heaped on her with class. Treats Trinity with respect. Never cops an attitude in public, even though I know she gives prez hell when they're alone. Fuck yes."

All good observations.

Rock chuckles and glances down at the table before turning to me. Fucker's actually happy for the first time in years. Maybe for the first time since I've known him. It seems absurd but somehow they fit together. He seems to be figuring out how to balance between her world and ours.

Doesn't mean I won't enjoy fucking with him a bit.

Sitting back, I narrow my eyes and stare him down. "You trust her?"

"You know I do."

"You trust her with your life? Our lives?" I point at every brother at the table. I know Rock's thought this through. He wouldn't have brought it to the table otherwise. But I have to ask.

"Yes, she'd never spill club business." I agree. As clueless as she is, I've never seen her run her mouth. "How much club business you gonna let her in on?" This is important and I wish to fuck he'd straighten this out *before* he patches her.

"She understands but said she doesn't want details in case she ever ends up having to represent one of us in court."

Didn't see that one coming. I should have though. I've actually seen her in the courtroom and she's a fierce little thing. "Okay. You got my yes."

The relief on Rock's face is so obvious, I almost feel bad for messing with him.

Almost.

Trinity

Now that Wrath knows what I've been up to, it's nice to be able to work during the day. While the guys are locked up in the war room for church, I finish one project and send it off.

Church rarely lasts longer than an hour, so I hustle down to the kitchen. To my surprise, Birch already has breakfast started. I grab a cup of coffee, a piece of toast, and try not to freak out about him messing around in my kitchen.

Rowdy voices come from the dining room, prompting me to grab a pot of coffee and head out. But I'm surprised to find only Ravage, Dex, Bricks and Stash sitting around one of the tables.

"Where's everyone else?"

"Rock, kept 'em behind," Dex explains with no other details. Fuck, I hope nothing's wrong.

"Sparky head back downstairs?"

Rav rolls his eyes at me. "What do you think?"

I run back in the kitchen and make up a plate for Sparky, then run it downstairs to him. He barely notices and mumbles a thank you on my way out.

Wrath's definitely wound up when he busts into the dining room. As soon as he sees me, his demeanor changes. He jerks his head toward the hallway.

"What's up?" I ask when we're alone.

"Just wanted to see you. Alone."

"Everything okay?"

Z, Murphy and Teller walk up together but stop when they see us. "Where's Rock?" I ask.

"Halfway to slam-central station by now," Murphy answers with a snicker.

Z glances at him sideways. "What's the matter with you?"

Wrath finally steers me into my room. "Aren't you hungry?" I ask.

"Yeah. But not for food."

"Handling club business with the guys got you worked up?"

"No. Thinking about *you* got me worked up."

"You were thinking about me in church?"

"I think about you all the time."

Shit. I don't know what to do with that. My cheeks burn and I have to look away. "Me too."

When I turn back to face him, he's wearing such a serious expression, I wonder what the hell went down in church. "Everything okay?"

"Yeah. I'm thinking it's time we stop screwing around and announce our relationship." He runs his finger over my cheek. "I want everyone to know you're my girl."

"Wyatt—"

"You realize I don't need your permission?"

Now that pisses me off. "If that's the way you want to go, why tell me at all? Just embrace your inner caveman, like you're dying to do. Maybe you'd like to drag me in there by my hair to really drive it home to everyone."

"You make me fuckin' nuts. You know that? I'm trying so fuckin' hard—"

I catch his hand and hold it until he looks at me. "I know you are. I'm sorry. Don't you think everyone sort of suspects it anyway?"

"I don't care. I want to announce it. I want everyone to hear me say you're my ol' lady."

The enormity of it strikes me in the chest and I stagger over to my desk to sit down.

"Soon okay? Can we stick to the original plan? I thought things were going well?"

"They are." He glances at the door and back at me.

I know better than to ask what went down in church, but it's really bugging me. "What happened in church?" I blurt out.

His face locks down hard and cold. "Club business. You know better."

Yeah, I do.

"I'm gonna go down to the dining room," he says. "You comin'?"

"No. I ate. I've got some stuff to do."

The disappointment on his face shreds me, but he nods and leaves.

I need something. I'm so damn wound up now. Why am I doing this to him? To us? He's been true to his word. Haven't seen him blink in the direction of any of the girls.

I haven't thought about anyone else. Even when he pisses me off.

Thinking about all this has me jumping out of my skin. I change and walk across the hall to see if burning off some energy will help my brain calm down.

I'm still so fuckin' scared if this doesn't work, I'll find myself homeless. Right? That's my reason?

The familiar swirl of insecurity spins through me but I keep pushing.

Maybe if I pound the treadmill hard enough, I can outrun all the bad memories threatening to crush me. Wyatt's a risk I want to take. I *should* take. But I've chosen safety and security over everything else my entire life. And here I am doing it again.

WRATH

Z senses I'm pissed as soon as I sit down.

"Everything okay?"

"Yeah."

"You mad about voting Hope in?"

"Fuck no."

Murphy chuckles. "I think prez was convinced you were gonna down vote her."

I tune out for most of their conversation. Eventually Z and I are the only ones left.

"What's bugging you, man?" he asks without his usual smirk.

"Nothing. I'd just...nothing." I'm annoyed for a whole bunch of reasons. I wasn't lying to Trinity about wanting to make my own announcement. But she's right. We're not ready. It's not about the fucking cast, or her room, or what anyone thinks.

She still hasn't confided in me about her past. I haven't pushed her yet, because I want her to tell me on her own. Because she trusts me.

Z thumps me on the back once before heading out.

Trin catches my eye when I pass the gym. She's burning up the tread-mill. God damn she's cute. Yeah, I use cute to describe Trinity a lot. But I don't have a better word. Fuckin' adorable? Knock-out beautiful. Dick-twitching hot. Yup. She's all of those things too. I gotta stop being so damn hard on her. She's trying, that's all that matters.

She raises her hand to wave and I tell her to take her time. Girl's been waiting on me long enough. She deserves to have at least a minute to herself.

I'm barely in the door, before she comes in. All flushed and sweaty, she wipes our earlier argument clear from my head. Her red cheeks and chest remind me of other things.

"Hey," she says softly.

"Hey."

She disappears into the bathroom but doesn't bother shutting the door, so I stare at her ass while she bends over to wash her face.

She comes out rubbing a towel up and down her arms.

"Babe, don't you got any of those sport bra top things to work out in?" I blurt out. Not that the fitted T-shirts and tight pants don't turn my crank.

She raises an eyebrow. "Don't you see enough tits and ass running around this clubhouse?" she asks, walking closer. Almost within reach of my grabby hands.

"Yeah, but the only tits and ass I wanna see are yours."

She snorts at me. "Please."

Snagging her around the waist, I pull her to me. "Don't act like I'm spewing bullshit at you."

"Aren't you?"

Squeezing her chin between my thumb and forefinger, I turn her to face me. "Why do I gotta keep explaining this to you? You're the most beautiful woman in my fuckin' universe."

"Wrath—"

"Don't fuckin' 'Wrath' me."

"It's hard okay? No one's ever said that to me before."

How is that even possible? "That's hard to believe."

Her head drops, gaze lowering to the floor. "I used to get teased a lot. Called Lizzie." Her hand brushes over her side. "You know, for lizard skin? My mother spent years telling me how ugly and unappealing I was because of my scars. That I'd be lucky if any man ever took an interest in me. And here you are, physical perfection…"

What the ever-loving fuck? "Babe, your mom sounds like a fuckin' bitch. She was probably jealous of you."

She shakes her head.

"Come on. Known plenty of fuckin' women who get jealous when their daughters grow up pretty and all they're doin' is gettin' old. See them at the gym all the time, callin' their daughters fat and shit. Didn't you ever watch Snow White?"

That makes her laugh. I love the way she laughs. Love it when I'm the one to make her laugh.

"What is it with you and Disney movies?"

What an odd question. "What are you talking about?"

"You're always calling Hope, Cinderella."

The stupid colors from that movie flash in my head. An image. Some sort of memory. Crushing guilt.

Without thinking, my mouth opens. "That's all my sister would watch. Princess movies."

Trinity reels back. "I didn't know you have a sister."

Fuck, my chest burns. I haven't thought about Faith in a while now, and that fact brings on a wave of guilt. "Had. She died."

Her mouth drops. She settles her hand on my chest. "Oh my God. How come you've never—"

"Happened so long ago."

She slides out of my hold, sitting next to me on the bed. "Older or younger?"

"Younger."

"What happened?"

I sit up and drag my fingers over the fuzz on my scalp. Last fuckin' thing I want to remember right now. The gentle touch of Trinity's hand on my arm shakes the words out of me. "I fucked up."

"What? How did you fuck up?"

I can't look at her. "I was supposed to watch her. We always played outside. Safer that way. My job to look out for her."

Her hand moves to my face. "You were only a kid."

"Doesn't matter. I was her big brother. Supposed to protect her."

Trinity's still watching me and I can't believe I'm going to admit this to her. Rock knows. Told him shortly after we met when he wanted to know why I was living on the street. Maybe by sharing it with her, she'll finally open up to me.

"Remember those stupid, plastic Big Wheels?"

"Yeah, sure."

"We were riding them outside. Up and down the sidewalk. I didn't realize she rode out into the street. I should have been paying closer attention. A car came. They always drove too fast in our neighborhood." My eyes squeeze shut. "The sound was fucking horrible." I can still hear my sister's scream, the crush of plastic, the squeal of tires. My mother shrieking. Feel the impact of my father's fists. The yank on my arm, burning pain.

"Wyatt?" Trinity's voice pulls me out of the memory. Her touch pushes it back into the past.

"What was her name?"

"Faith," I croak out.

Her hand automatically runs over my side. "Faith is the bird that sings when the dawn is still dark," she whispers. Her eyes meet mine. "I always wondered, but never—"

"You had it memorized?"

She shrugs. "It's pretty." Her fingers tickle over where I have the bird tattooed above the inked words she just quoted. "How old was she?"

"Five. I was eight."

Her lips form a small O of surprise and she inhales sharply. "Wyatt, you were a kid. Your parents had no right to—"

"She trusted me."

"Of course she did."

"She was the sweetest kid. My friends who had little brothers or sisters hated them. Never understood why. Loved Faith from the second they brought her home and handed her off to me."

"I can understand that. I always wanted a sister to do stuff with."

Of course most of my time was spent protecting Faith from my father's drunken rampages. "Hated when I started school and I had to leave her behind."

"Jesus, Wyatt. All these years, I had no idea—"

My twists into a frown. "That I was such a whiny bitch?"

"No." Trinity's a perceptive girl. I suppose she had to be to survive the life she did. She knows there's more to the story. Her hand squeezes my arm again. "What else?"

"What do you mean? There's nothing else."

"Bullshit."

I turn so I can glare at her, but she doesn't back down. "What do you want to hear? That my father turned gettin' drunk into a full-time job and took his anger out on me? That my mother couldn't stand to look at me after I killed her little girl and did jack shit to stop him? That at thirteen my mother took off for good and then things got real interesting at home? Or that at fifteen I decided I'd had enough and living on the streets was a better option?"

The shock on her face is too much. I have to get up and get out of the bedroom.

"Where are you going?" she sounds close to tears, and I can't fucking stand it.

"Outside. I need to be outside."

"Okay."

I don't realize she followed me, until she reaches out and holds the back door open. The idea of navigating over the uneven ground annoys me, so I drop down onto the top step, stretching my leg out in front of me.

Trin perches next to me but doesn't say anything.

After a few minutes of silence, she places her hand on my shoulder. "I'm sorry. I shouldn't have been so pushy."

I can't stand the thought of her feeling a second of guilt. "It's okay."

"What did she look like?" she whispers after a few seconds of silence.

If I close my eyes I can almost picture my sister clearly. "She was so pretty. Big frickin' blue doll eyes. Had this long blonde hair down to her butt." I shake my head. "I was the only one she'd sit still for to brush her hair. Our mother always threatened to shave Faith's head, so I'd make sure it got done."

"Geez. Wow, Wyatt."

Yeah, I'm a giant sappy, puss, I know.

"Do you have any pictures of her?"

"One. Up in my room. I'll show it to you some day."

She nods and squeezes my hand. "I'd like that."

I cover her hand with mine and pull her closer. "I'm sure later I'll feel better about talking about it. Right now I just feel—"

"Exposed?"

"Yes."

"I understand."

And I know that she does.

CHAPTER TWENTY-NINE

WRATH

I'm still sort of raw from all the darkness I revealed to Trinity. She seems to sense it and keeps her distance.

Well, as much as she can when we're sharing her room.

Rock had yet another blow up with Hope. Right after we voted her in. Poor bastard. This time I can't say it's entirely his fault.

He takes off first thing in the morning to work that out. Z and I sort of shake our heads.

"How did he think this was going to turn out different?" he jokes. "He's in for a lifetime of ball-busting." He chuckles in a gleeful way that makes me laugh too. Yesterday we gave Rock our thoughtful advice. Today we heckled him until he got fed up and left.

My fist lands on his bicep. "You're such a dick."

Trin rushes by with a basket of laundry. That situation needs to end real soon. Girl's still behind on her book covers. That's what she should be focusing on. Not laundry. Z stares after her and I swear to fuck if he makes one comment about her ass, he's dead.

"You two okay?" he asks.

"Like to take my own fuckin' vote," I grumble.

"That what's been pissing you off? Why? You don't need our votes. She's practically a member already."

That's where he's wrong. "Fuck that. She deserves the same fuckin' vote as any other old lady."

Z reels back and I swear his cheeks redden a little. Didn't think the fucker had an ounce of shame in him. "You're right. She does. I just meant, we all trust her. No one would say no."

"I know what you meant." It's a nice sentiment. But I still want things done right.

Z's phone buzzes and he yanks it out.

"Shit."

"What?"

He shows me the text from Rock.

At Empire Med with Hope. Bad.

"Jesus Christ. Tell him we'll be right there." I struggle to pull myself up and decide it will save some time if I just yell for Trin.

She comes running. "What? You okay?"

"Yeah. Want you to hang close to the house today. Something's gone down. Rock's at the hospital with Hope."

"Oh my God." She trembles and chews on her thumb. "What happened?"

"Don't know yet, babe. That's why you gotta stay here," Z explains as he heads for the door.

"I'll call you in a bit, okay?"

"Yeah."

Before I step outside, she grabs my arm and leans up to kiss my cheek. "Just be careful."

Navigating the parking at the mammoth hospital is a pain in the ass. Z ends up throwing his truck in some reserved spot.

"Brother, what the fuck?" Z asks when we find Rock in the waiting room.

"I don't know. They haven't fucking told me anything yet."

Rock's covered in blood and I'm afraid to even ask what happened. If it'd been a drive-by you'd think there'd be cops crawling all over the place. My hand brushes over my side, the familiar weight of the Glock holstered there comforting. Any Vipers show up, I've got ten chances to make them think twice.

"What happened?" I finally ask.

"Went down to meet her, like you suggested. Had to wait downstairs for her. When she came out of the elevator, she looked like death. Next thing I knew she fucking fainted."

I let out a breath and fall back against the unforgiving hospital chair. Not a Viper attack. With me out of fighting shape, trouble with them's the last thing we need.

"Uh, we thought she like got shot or something," Z points out.

Rock turns his hands over as if noticing the blood on them for the first time. "No."

Z and I share a look.

"Aw fuck, man," Z says.

Rock sort of stumbles over to the sink in the back corner and scrubs his hands raw. I take out my phone and text Trin.

Bring change of clothes to EM for prez.

Okay.

A nurse walks in and runs her grave gaze over each of us before landing on Rock.

"Mr. North?"

Rock turns so fast, he forgets to shut the water off. "Is she okay?" While he's busy with the nurse, Z gets up and shuts the water off then drops into the chair next to me.

"She's pregnant?" Rock chokes out. *Shit.*

Z glances at me and shakes his head. No words need to be said.

Whatever else the nurse tells him is bad because he stumbles over. As he falls into the chair next to me, I realize he's crying.

I don't think in the twenty or so years I've known Rock, I've ever seen him cry. Not when we lost brothers for no good reason. Not when we discovered we were betrayed by someone we trusted. Not when he was sent to prison for a crime he didn't do. Not even when I went to visit him in prison to explain his ex-wife, Carla cleaned out his apartment out and skipped town.

If Hope doesn't make it through this, it'll destroy him.

He barely stirs when I put my hand on his shoulder. "She's a little spit-fire. She'll be back to busting your balls in no time, brother." I'm trying for upbeat, but I can barely choke out the words. Hope's been a sweetheart from day one and I've been nothin' but mean to her. She tolerated it because she *loves him.*

I'm relieved when Trinity arrives and presses some clean clothes into

Rock's hands. He leaves to change and Z moves down a chair so Trinity can sit next to me.

"What happened?" she whispers.

"Don't really know." I don't need details. Whatever it is has reduced my immune-to-anything best friend into a zombie.

I ain't gonna hold his hand or whisper feel-good shit in his ear. But I ain't leavin' his side either.

It's a relief when one of the nurses finally tells us we can see Hope hours later. We were here so long, Trin ended up running home The hospital chairs have done a number on my back. I send my girl a text and happily haul myself out of the little plastic torture device.

Rock's hovering over his girl and doesn't bother to move, even though the space is tight and not easy for me to navigate. I suffer no guilt bumping him out of the way. I drop into the chair in the far corner, so I'll be out of everyone's way.

"Sugar, you gave us all some scare," I tell Hope.

She bursts into tears. *Shit.* Rock glares at me, but I don't even know what I did.

"What the hell did you say to her, jerk?" Z snaps at me when he walks in and sees her cryin'.

"Nothing."

"It's not you," she says through a bunch of sniffling.

That's a relief. Maybe Rock can stop making murder faces at me now.

"Thanks for staying with Rock, you guys," Hope whispers.

Z glances at me and shrugs. Of course we'd stay.

I shrug and wink at Hope, making her chuckle. *That's better.* I close my eyes while they talk and obviously they think I've fallen asleep.

"Has he been here all night?" Hope whispers.

"Yeah," Rock answers.

"Why?"

Aw shit. She really has to ask? "You're family now, babe," I mumble at her.

Trin returns later with food and ends up driving me home. I'm still zapped. She must be too, because she's silent most of the way.

"I hurt everywhere," I grumble as I jump down from the Jeep.

"I don't think tiny hospital chairs are meant for giant men to sleep in," she says with a laugh. I love the way she pokes fun at me.

Not much rattles me these days. But Rock almost losing his girl? Only reinforces my need to make things work with Trinity.

CHAPTER THIRTY

Trinity

Hope: Please come visit me! I'm so bored!

I laugh at Hope's plea for company and make my way upstairs. After she got out of the hospital, Rock took her to his house to recuperate without everyone in her business. Once they came here, I still didn't get to see her. But now that the guys are all locked up in the war room we should be able to have a minute to catch up.

Hope's poking through her bookshelf when I knock and push the door open.

"Trinity! I'm so happy to see you!"

She gives me a hug, then winces. "You should probably be resting," I tell her as she pulls away.

"Don't start. I'm getting enough of that from Rock."

I chuckle, imagining how he's been hovering over her.

"They're in church at the moment, so you're safe."

"Thank God. If I didn't feel so shitty, I think I'd have run away by now."

"Uh, I'm pretty sure Rock would hunt you down and drag you back."

She laughs. "True."

"Hey, I know this is sort of an inappropriate time, but do you know how to form a corporation and stuff like that?"

She tilts her head and studies me for a second before answering. "What kind of corporation?"

"Just a small business. Like one person."

"Oh, yeah. You'd probably want to do an LLC then. It's really just filling out paperwork, filing it, paying a fee and publishing it in the paper," she says, ticking off each item on her right hand.

The blank look I give her causes her to slow down.

"Yes, that's something I can do. What's the business?"

I'm not ready to share this yet. Because knowing Hope, she'll want to see the book covers and I can't handle having anyone else knowing about my side hobby. I'm saved from answering by Rock's return.

"Hey, Trin," he greets while running his fingers through his hair until it's standing up in all directions. Yup, time for me to go.

I pat Hope's hand. "We'll talk later."

"Okay."

Wrath and Z are in the middle of a heated discussion when I reach the living room, but stop when they see me.

"Everything okay?" I ask before approaching them.

"Yup," Z answers.

"You free, babe?" Wrath asks.

"Yeah." Checking the time I ask, "Ready for the doc?"

"Not unless this fuckin' cast is coming off."

I don't answer. We both know it's not coming off this early.

WRATH

For once, I'm the one who can't sleep. My restlessness finally wakes Trinity and she turns over to snuggle up against my side.

"Good morning."

When I don't answer her, she tries again. "You okay?"

"Yeah."

"Something's bothering you."

"I'm annoyed Rock's gotta take this run out to Kodack. He shouldn't have to leave Hope now."

She flinches when I mention the Demon's territory, but after a minute she says, "I have a feeling she'll be okay with a day or two of peace and quiet."

"Whaddya mean?"

She laughs softly. "Rock's drivin' her nuts."

"Well, she did almost die."

"Yeah."

She's quiet and I assume she's fallen back asleep.

"Wyatt, do you want kids?"

I don't have to think about the answer to that question. "No."

Even though it's dark, she tips her head up, settling her chin on my chest. "Really? You're so good with the ones at the gym."

"Yeah, 'cause they go home after an hour and are someone else's problem."

She makes a *hmm* noise and I take a minute to frame what I want to say. "I always worried with all the fuckin' beatings I took as a kid...all the fuckin' rage inside of me...I didn't want to have a kid and risk doin' that to 'em."

"Oh, Wyatt. You're so...good to the people you care about. I don't think you'd ever—"

"It's not the same."

"But you don't drink like that."

"Are you trying to talk me into something, babe?"

She snorts and shifts away from me. "No. I'm not mother material."

"What are you talkin' about? Look at the way you take care of everyone here."

I'm not even finished speaking and she's shaking her head to disagree. "What would I do? I couldn't raise a kid here hearing how their mom was the club—"

My hand closes over her mouth. "Don't. Don't fuckin' call yourself that ever again. No one would ever say that about you."

She moves my hand away. "Thank you."

"Just the other night Rock and I were talkin' 'bout how Sparky and Stash would have starved to death if it wasn't for you lookin' after 'em."

She snorts. "Someone has to."

After that she falls back to sleep. I get out of bed and make my way to the kitchen. The *weight bearing as tolerated* order the doctor gave me is some bullshit. Largely because, so far, I haven't been able to tolerate it at all.

I find Birch sleeping on top of the bar in the dining room and give him a nice shove. I'm rewarded with a solid *thunk* when he lands on the floor.

"Go make some coffee, prospect," I bark at him.

Fifteen minutes later, I'm sipping my coffee when Rock trudges in.

From the set of his shoulders he's got something weighing him down. Don't we all?

"Can I talk to you for a sec?"

I kick a chair out for him. He takes it and gives me a questioning look.

"You all right?"

"Yeah, just pissed I can't go on the run. You shouldn't have to do it. Shouldn't be leavin' your girl after everything you two just went through."

He sort of cracks a smile. "Something tells me she'd like some space."

"Yeah, you've been overdoing it a little, playin' nurse."

Leaning forward, he gets this serious look about him and I just know whatever he's about to say is gonna piss me off. "Listen, this is stupid, but if anything happens—"

Is he nuts sayin' that shit right before leaving? "No way. Shut that shit down right now, prez."

"Wyatt, I'm serious. Come on. You never know. She fell apart after her husband died. You gotta promise me if something happens—on the run, next year, ten years from now—promise me you'll take care of her."

"Fuck, why you gotta do this to me? Of course I'll take care of her. The club will take care of her. Now, knock it the fuck off. You're drawing bad mojo your way."

He snorts and looks away, clearly debating whether he should say whatever else is on his mind. "One last thing—and I swear to fuck if you make a joke about this, I'm going to break your other leg."

"This should be good."

He stares me down so I know he's serious. "She's still hormonal and stuff, so could you please try not to give her shit. She's liable to either rip your head off or cry. And if you make her cry, I'm going to kick your fuckin' ass."

If I *had* feelings, they'd be hurt that he thinks I'm such a jackass. "I'm not completely stupid. Girl almost died. I'll behave myself."

"Do your best."

I'm about to reassure him that Trinity and I will watch out for Hope while he's gone, when I notice her sneaking up behind him.

I lift my chin at Rock. "Fuck you."

As if I'm not even here, the two of them get each other worked up into a frenzy from a simple good morning.

"You sure you want to get him all horned up, then send him on his way, Hope?" What? I promised Rock I'd play nice *after* he left.

"What's that supposed to mean?" she snaps back.

And there's that *rip your head off* thing Rock mentioned.

"Ignore him, baby doll." Rock pulls her into his lap and they're all over each other again.

"Let's get on the roaaad!" Z shouts as he enters the dining room. Thank God, I was starting think I should throw some cold water on these two.

We engage in some predictable, filthy joking around after Hope goes into the kitchen. Well, Z and I do. Rock's not in a joking mood.

I get mine a few seconds later when Trinity walks by and they razz me. Secretly, I enjoy every second.

"Did you make Trin kick me out?" Hope yells a few minutes later. Girl rarely raises her voice, so her tone's damn funny.

"Get over here," Rock calls to her.

She settles in his lap and then they proceed to do disgusting lovey-dovey shit that no one should have to sit through at the dining room table.

Trin chuckles at them when she sits down and joins us. I take a risk and throw my arm around her. She actually leans into my side, and stays that way while she polishes off her breakfast. It feels really fucking good to touch her out in the open like this. Z glances at us and smiles, then focuses the rest of his heckling on Rock.

Without Rock, Z, and Murphy around, the house is quiet. Hope retreats to Rock's room. Trinity tries to check on her without being annoying.

I'm wrapped up in watching Trin work on her book covers when I get a text from Teller a couple days into Rock's trip.

Hope just dropped Heidi off. Why she out alone?

"Godfuckingdammit!"

Trinity spins around. "What's wrong?"

"I don't know. Teller says Hope just left his house? When the fuck did she sneak out?"

"You know she's a grown woman, right?"

I glance up in time to catch her lip quiver with laughter. "You've been hanging around her too much, that sounds like something she would say." I'm holding back my own laughter as I say it.

She snickers and stands. "I'll run up and check."

"You think Teller's lying?"

"No, I guess not."

"Should take her about an hour to get here. I'll ream her out then."

She shakes her head goes back to what she was working on. "You better not."

After more than an hour goes by, I'm halfway between pissed-off and worried. She just got out of the hospital, what if she runs off the road or something? Stupid, fucking Teller should have driven her home.

Where the fuck are you?

Thankfully she answers right away.

On my way back.

Twenty-five minutes later, she strolls in.

"Where the fuck did you go?"

She drops her gaze to the floor, making me feel like shit for being so sharp. "I, uh, took Heidi out."

Great, now I feel even worse. "You didn't think to tell me? Rock's gonna have my ass."

"I didn't want to bother you." Her gaze bounces around the room.

No, princess, Trinity's not here to save your butt.

"I figured I'd be back before you noticed I was gone," she says with a smile.

"Teller told me."

"That little fucker," she mutters.

I gotta laugh at that. "Agreed. But still, not cool, Hope. You took so long getting here from his house you had me worried."

Her eyes well up and I remember Rock's warning too late. Christ, he really is gonna skin me alive.

"I'm sorry. I stopped by my house to grab a few things."

I work my voice into a gentler tone. "Okay. You need to go anywhere else, though, just tell me."

"I think I'm done. I'm exhausted."

Yeah, she looks pale and I can't believe she risked driving bratty Heidi around in her condition. "Go get some rest, Cinderella."

"Did you properly scold Hope?" Trinity snickers at me when I return to her room.

"Shut up."

I said it with a smile, so she laughs and comes over to hug me. "Poor Wyatt. Responsible for all these pain-in-the-ass females."

I love seeing Trinity in a lighter mood. Grinning down at her, I grab a handful of her ass and squeeze. "I'll show you a pain in the ass."

Pink spreads over her cheeks. "I might like that," she says with a raised eyebrow.

Trinity

329

Wrath's still staring with an intensity that sends a throb of pleasure through me. What I said off the cuff, I realize is true. But I can't figure out how to explain what I want.

There are things in my past I need to talk to him about. He hasn't pushed me to announce that we're a couple, but it's there simmering just below the surface. Every day I feel it getting closer and it's only a matter of time before he either flips out or gives up on me all together.

"How are you doing with your book covers? Are you caught up yet?"

The question surprises me. Wrath has asked me about my work once or twice every day since I came clean with him. At first I thought he was just trying to be nice, but I'm starting to realize he really is interested.

I don't know how to handle that.

"Okay. I'm almost caught up, but I got a few new requests that came in. One of them is super-picky, so I've been back and forth with her a bunch of times about what she wants."

"Anything I can do to help?"

Oh. Wow, that's— "You're awfully sweet for a Wrecking Ball, you know."

His mouth curls up in a sensual smile that makes my panties scream *Take me off now!*

"Only to you, baby."

"Well, you could let me take some photos of you?"

A twitch of amusement flickers over his face. "Seriously?"

"Well…"

"Anything else?"

"You can *not* give me a hard time when I run over to the art center tomorrow for a class."

"Trin—"

"It's a day class. I promise I'll be careful."

"I'll come with you."

"No way. The classes are too small for visitors. Besides, you're more likely to draw attention than I am."

I can see him considering my words. "You asked how you could help me out," I remind him. I consider skipping out of the house tomorrow before he wakes up. But that's not how things work between us.

"What if—"

Using the best weapon at my disposal, I press my body against him and throw my arms around his neck. "If I take you to class with me, none of the women will be able to pay attention," I say in a low, teasing voice. "I'll slap the shit out of any woman eyeing my man. Is that what you want?"

He blinks, his blue eyes deep as the sea. "I love how that sounds coming out of your mouth."

Then he takes my mouth in an almost worshipful kiss, leaving me willing to do anything he asks.

CHAPTER THIRTY-ONE

WRATH

I'm irritated Trin's in Ironworks without me to protect her. One text to Birch asking him to keep a low-profile watch over her only makes me feel a tiny fraction better.

Having her out of the house, though, gives me a chance to make some phone calls without worrying about Trin overhearing me. There are also some items I need to order. Z helps me find a few of the things on my long list. Fucker's surprised and amused when I tell him what I'm after.

Once that's done, I gotta figure out how to get her out of the house again tomorrow.

Like a grumpy bump on a log, I'm hanging out on the couch downstairs, flippin' through channels when Hope joins me.

"Hey," she greets. "How's the leg?"

"Okay."

"You eat breakfast yet?"

It's sweet she wants to take care of me. "I'm fine, thanks."

She heads to the kitchen and I continue flicking the television remote. Why are there so many fuckin' channels but nothing on?

"Where's Trin?" Hope asks when she returns.

In enemy territory. "Out."

Surprisingly, Hope isn't put off by my grumpiness. She tucks herself into the other couch. I glance over at her. She's bundled up more than usual.

"You cold?"

She hugs her knees to her chest. "I'm okay."

After a minute, she blurts out, "Is that Thor's hammer?"

I turn and realize she's been admiring my ink. Like the cocky asshole I am, I hold my arm out so she can take a good look. "Yeah." Running my gaze over her, I ask, "You got any ink, Hope?"

She shakes her head, and I'm not surprised. I take another look at her. Besides being dressed for a nap on an iceberg, she seems stiff.

"Are you still in pain?"

Her lip trembles and she hugs her knees tighter. "A bit. I stopped taking the pain pills because they made me loopy."

Christ, she just had surgery and she's not taking anything at all for the pain. I guess she's tougher than I give her credit for. I haven't spent all this time being part of one of the largest grow operations on the East Coast without knowing some things about pain management. Sparky keeps all of us well-informed on the various medical uses of his marijuana. I lean forward and pull a stash of weed from the coffee table drawer.

I hold up the box to her. "You smoke?"

"No."

Somehow I don't believe she's never even tried it. "Never?"

"You mean weed?"

God damn she's funny. "Yeah."

"I tried it in high school a few times."

"Well, well, you do have a little bit of bad girl in you after all." I nod at the screen. "Come on, *Fight Club* is even better stoned."

She makes a face like there's a hundred other things she'd rather watch before *Fight Club*, but eagerly takes the joint I hand her.

After a few hits she's staring off into space.

"Feel better?" I ask.

She snort-giggles, and rolls to the side. "Feeling no pain."

Oh, good God, what did I unleash?

"Why're you being so nice to me, Wrath?"

Aw, shit. "I been mean to you, sugar?"

More giggle-snorts. "Uh, duh. Yeah."

Shit she's funny like this. I hand off the joint again and try to collect my fuzzy thoughts. "You proved yourself. You got enough love for Rock to accept all this shit. Known him more than twenty years. Went through lotta bad shit together. Never seen him cry once until that day in the hospital when he thought he might lose you."

Fuck, she's tearing up and I can't stand to see it. "Don't you cry. Can't handle females cryin'." I try to say it teasingly, but it comes out a little harsh.

"You think I'm too soft for Rock's life. For the club, I know," she says with a pitiful sniffle.

Shit, how do I even explain the conclusion I've come to? "Yeah, sugar. I ain't gonna lie. You're soft. Took me some time to get it, but that's what Rock likes about you so much. Your softness. Our world is hard most of the time, so I guess he needs that. You give him something he can't find anywhere else."

Her lips curve up into a slight smile.

"Besides, you're a good girl. You've been tough when it counted."

I want her to understand if I've had reservations about her and Rock, it's not because I don't *like* her. It ain't about that at all. "You realize I worry about your safety? You ever got picked up by one of our enemies… I can't even think about it."

"Shit, Wrath," she breathes out. *This* is where Rock's reluctance to explain our world to her really pisses me off. "Hope, we've worked damn fuckin' hard to strike a balance and keep our alliances tight." I stare right at her so she understands how serious I am. "But this life ain't easy on women."

"What about Trinity?"

I'm surprised her first concern is Trinity and not, oh, I don't know, herself. I think of the things Trin's lived through and I want to fuckin' choke someone. "She's been through enough."

Her whole face softens. "You love her, don't you?" she whispers.

Love doesn't quite describe how I feel about Trinity. Madly infatuated? Obsessed? Fucking furious we've wasted so many years hating each other. Frustrated she's not ready to let everyone know she's mine. "That girl's made me work harder than anything in my life."

Hope doesn't seem to know how to respond, which is fine, because I got nothing.

She sniffles. "I miss him."

"Yeah. I know. I'm sorry, sugar. Shoulda been me on that run."

"What is this 'run' anyway? Rock never said."

I roll my eyes at her. She should know better by now. "Club business."

"Ohhhhh." She falls over on her side laughing. "Top secret, big, bad biker stuff. I get it."

"You are soooo fucked up right now."

My phone buzzes against my thigh, and I yank it out of my pocket. Rock. Perfect timing.

"Yo," I answer.

"Hey. Where's Hope? She's not answering her phone. She okay?"

Hello to you too, asshole. "Yeah, she's right here."

"Where's *here*."

I kind of want to fuck with him and say *my bedroom* but I don't. "Living room."

"Doin' what?"

"Gettin' her high."

"What the fuck?! I'm gonna rip your fuckin' head off!"

"Is that Rock?" Hope yelps as she holds out her hands. "Gimmie, please!"

Jesus Christ. I hand over the phone.

"Hey, baby," Hope coos.

Christ, I wish I didn't need the crutches. I'd run the fuck away so I didn't have to listen to this.

"Yes, he's been a perfect gentleman."

Well, now she's just making me look like a pussy.

"Not if I spank you first." Seriously? Is there a bucket around here I can hurl into?

They do their nauseating goodbye thing which takes *forfuckingever*, before finally hanging up and Hope hands me my phone.

"He threatened to kick my ass you know," I inform her.

"I don't ever want to see you two trade punches."

I don't know if I should be flattered or insulted. "He can hold his own."

"I don't doubt it."

We're quiet for a minute or two. Hope's not into the movie. She starts playing with her hair. "I need to get my hair trimmed," she says absently.

Ding! The perfect way to get Trinity out of the house has just been dropped in my lap. *Thank you, Cinderella.* "You and Trin should go out tomorrow. Do some sort of girly salon day thing."

Hope seems to consider the idea. "Does she…? She's not really the girly type."

Just then, the front door slams shut. Speaking of my little angel. "Jesus, it fucking reeks in here!" Trinity sniffs. "Goddammit, Wyatt. Did you get her high? Rock's gonna kill you."

"Yeah, he already chewed me out." I hold out my hands to her, but she sits next to Hope and takes the joint out of her hand.

"Hey!" Hope shouts.

I've got the perfect excuse to get them out of the house tomorrow. "Trin, Hope wants to go get her hair cut. Can you take her tomorrow?" I ask her casually.

Trin nods and glances at Hope's hair. "Sure. Girl I know owns that pin-up salon downtown. She always fits me in. I'll text her later."

Hope wrinkles her nose. "I'm not too nerdy for that place?" she asks, completely serious.

Trinity flashes a grin at her. "No."

Now I just have to pray like fuck they go early enough.

Trinity

Wrath's awfully eager to get us out of the house this morning.

"What time did your friend say she'd get you guys in?"

"Eleven."

"You should probably leave early in case you can't find parking."

My eyes search his face. He's up to something, I just can't figure out what.

No matter how impatient Wrath gets, Hope's impossible to hustle out of the house. "We're going to a salon, you don't need to do your hair," I mutter after watching her mess around for the last fifteen minutes.

"You're right."

Finally.

Wrath catches my hand at the door. "This is for both of you." He presses a wad of cash into my palm.

"Wrath—"

Against my ear he whispers, "Don't argue with me."

The no-bullshit tone and his words spark a shiver of desire and now I don't want to leave. "Yes, Wyatt."

His mouth curls into a sexy, arrogant smirk. "That's my girl."

I swear my legs are wobbly as I walk to the Jeep. Hope's oblivious and chatters away as we head downtown.

We're lucky enough to find a spot in front of the salon. They fit us in right away.

"Krystal, you think you can do one of those dip dyes on the ends of my hair?" I've been wanting to do it forever, and for some reason, I'm feeling brave today.

She runs her fingers through my hair. "Oh yeah. You want to do the peacock blues we talked about last time?"

"Yup."

"Cool, let me go mix up some color. I'll do from here down." Her hand skims over my hair from a spot between my shoulder blades to the ends.

Hope's done way before I am, so she perches in the chair next to me and watches.

"So where did you sneak off to the other day? Wrath flipped his shit." I ask as we wait for the color to soak into my hair.

She blushes and looks away. "I took Heidi out."

"Oh. Nice." Now it's my turn to look away.

"Why do you think she doesn't like you?"

Sometimes I don't think Hope understands what my role in the club is...or was.

"Do you honestly want to know?" I ask.

She shrugs. "If you want to tell me."

When I don't answer right away she surprises me. "I assume it has something to do with Murphy?"

"Sort of."

Her shoulders lift again. "It's really none of my business, Trinity."

I relax a notch. She seems to honestly mean it.

When we're finished, I talk her into the lingerie store next door under the pretense of grabbing something for Rock's return. But really I want to find something to surprise Wyatt with.

Except when I squeeze myself into the black and royal blue, lacy halter bra and matching ruffle trimmed garter skirt. I feel ridiculous instead of sexy. It doesn't help that I can't figure out how to get the damn thing hooked right. Completely mortified, I call Hope in to help.

After closing the door, she stops and stares sat me. "That thing was made for you. It looks gorgeous with your new hair. Wrath's going to flip."

"No, no, it's not—"

She gives me an incredulous look. Why am I even bothering to deny what's so freakin' obvious?

I twist and turn, checking out every angle in the full-length mirror after she leaves. I look silly. Don't I?

My phone buzzes.

How's it goin'?

Wrath checking up on us.

The phone's already in my hands. Do I dare? Before I lose my nerve, I strike an awkward-sexy pose, snap a picture and send it with my reply.

Should I get it?

He responds almost immediately.

Fuck, yeah.

My phone buzzes again.

Don't tease. You better get it.

I don't answer. The wondering will do him some good.

WRATH

Thank fuck the girls finally got the hell out of here. The damn Fed Ex truck pulled up to the gate maybe five minutes after Trinity's car cleared it. I have to call downstairs for Stash and Sparky to come help me carry the boxes into Trinity's room. This invalid shit is getting old.

"Holy fuck, man, what the hell did you get her?" Stash asks after getting a good look at the boxes. Sparky mumbles something about his plants needing him and takes off the minute the boxes hit the ground.

Self-conscious under my brother's stare, my left hand reaches up to rub the back of my neck. "Eh, like a thank you for letting me invade her room, you know?"

Stash isn't buying a word of it.

Once I get everything situated the way I want it on the new desk—facing the door, so it's the first thing she sees when she walks in—I go wait in the living room. I'm so fucking bored. I've never been so inactive for so long in my life. The only good thing has been enjoying all this extra time with Trinity. Getting to know her better. Every second with her has made this shit worth it.

My phone pings with a text from Trinity.

Holyfuckingshit.

I don't know what the hell she and Hope are up to, but there's a half-naked picture of my little angel waiting for me on the screen.

Should I get it?

What kind of fucking question is that?

Fuck yeah.

I fire back.

After seeing that picture, waiting for their return is excruciating. I'm half hard the entire time. Teller and Dex drop by to fill me in on what's going on down at my gym and I struggle to focus on the conversation.

Finally, the girls walk in. Hope's carrying a bunch of bags, but turns to thrust one at Trinity.

"Get anything good?" I ask as casually as a guy trying to hide a boner can.

A sly grin curves Hope's mouth and she dashes to the stairs. Once she hits the landing, she shouts back, "Nothing but some sexwear."

She giggles all the way down the hall.

Something like a growl rips out of my throat and my gaze focuses one hundred percent on Trinity, who's busy edging toward the hallway.

"Whatcha got, Angel Face?"

She shakes her head, drawing my attention to her hair. Grasping the stupid crutches, I pull myself off the couch and swing over to her. I pick up a handful of hair, sifting the silky strands through my fingers. "I like it. Very pretty."

A flush spreads over her cheeks. I love the way my tough-as-nails Trinity blushes.

"Thanks." Her shoulders lift in an embarrassed shrug. "Something different."

"It's beautiful. You're beautiful."

Her cheeks turn even pinker.

I hate that I still have to use these crutches. What I want to do is take her hand as we walk to her room. Or swing her up into my arms, carry her, kick open the door and throw her on the bed. I'm so distracted I briefly forget about the surprise waiting for her inside.

When we reach her door, I'm almost too excited to follow her inside. She stops dead over the threshold, jaw dropping.

"Wyatt, what is this?"

"For you, babe."

The bag in her hand hits the floor with a light thump. Yeah, I haven't forgotten the bag of sexwear. I dip down, pick it up and toss it on the bed, 'cause we're *so* exploring that later.

As if she's approaching a rattlesnake, Trinity inches toward the new set up. Confusion clouds her face as she turns to me. "I don't understand."

"What's to understand? I got you everything you should need for your business."

"How? Why?"

"Uh, how—there's this magical thing called the Internet where you can order things and *poof,* they show up at your door." She's so stunned, she doesn't respond to my teasing. "Why—I want you to have everything you need. It makes you happy and you're good at it. I don't want you to wait."

"Wyatt. It's too much. I can't—"

I cut that off right the fuck away. "Oh yes you can. I've known you eight fucking years. I'm completely ashamed that I've never gotten you a birthday or Christmas present or anything ever. I owe you something big."

Her mouth twitches at the corners a bit. "I hate my birthday, anyway." Something sad and vulnerable makes her voice raw, so I know she's not just making a joke.

Leaning the crutches against the wall, I hop over to the bed and drop down. With the sweetest, awed expression, she approaches her new desk. "God, Wyatt, all of this had to cost you thousands of dollars."

My shoulders jerk up. So fucking what? I live at the clubhouse and stuff pretty much all the money I earn with the club in the bank. My expenses are minimal. The only things that matter to me in this world are the club, my bike, my gym, and Trinity. And not in that order either.

"I got the smaller laptop, so it's easier for you to carry around, but it's got all the upgrades."

More shock. She hadn't noticed the laptop. I'm a little giddy about this whole thing. I've never had anyone I cared enough about to buy presents for. This is fucking fun.

"It's in the backpack," I direct.

She pulls it out and flicks her eyes at me. "Wyatt. Too much."

"Nope."

She glances back at the massive display monitor that came with the desktop set up. "This is just like the one they have at the art school."

I know because I called and asked them what their exact set-up was. I'm not ready to reveal that yet, so I just nod.

Her eyes gloss over with unshed tears.

"Uh, I didn't know what graphic design program you wanted, so I'll leave that to you." I pull out a Visa from my back pocket and hand it to her.

"What's..." Her voice trails off when she sees her name on the card. Questioning honey eyes meet mine. "I want you to be able to order what you need without worrying about it."

"I can't—"

I cut her off with a sharp shake of my head. "You my girl?"

"Yes, but—"

"No. No buts. You're my girl and I want to do this for you. You want to pay the monthly bill for the program fees, that's fine, the rest of it though… *gifts,* and it would really hurt my feelings if you turned them down." Yeah, I'm not above a little guilt to get my way.

"Thank you."

"One last thing." Reaching under the bed, I pull out the last gift. "It's not the fanciest out there, but it's a professional one. It'll get you started."

"Fuck, Wyatt." Tears are running down her cheeks, and I reach up to brush them away.

"I hope those are happy tears, Angel Face."

"Yeah," she sighs.

She takes the bag and looks inside. "Those lenses can be used even if you decide to upgrade in the future." I have no clue about cameras and didn't have much time to figure it out, so basically once I decided on the camera, I picked out one of everything I thought she could use. She looks up and grins. "Jeez, I'll have to take a class just to learn how to use all this stuff."

I love seeing her smile like that. "Good, you must be so bored sitting around with my invalid ass all the time."

She walks over to the desk and sets the bag on top, carefully pushing it away from the edge, then returns to me. "I never get bored of you."

I cock my head at her. "Really?"

"Well, not yet anyway," she teases, running her fingers over my head.

Wrapping my arms around her waist, I tug her down to me. "Did I surprise you?"

"You have no idea."

"You like?"

Tears shimmer in her eyes again. "Yes. I can't even… Yes, Wyatt. I like everything. Thank you so much."

"You're welcome, babe. You're really talented, I know you'll do well."

She sniffles and rolls out of my arms to stare at the ceiling. "You have no idea what that means to me. I felt so freaking stupid sharing that with you."

Rolling over and propping my head on my elbow, I reach out and trace my finger over her cheek, until she looks at me. "Why?"

"I don't know. It seems silly. Insignificant."

"It's not silly if it makes you happy and you enjoy it. *Nothing* about you is insignificant."

CHAPTER THIRTY-TWO

Trinity

Wrath believing in me enough to figure out what I needed and going to the trouble of buying everything for me?

I have no words to explain how grateful I am. For his generosity, yes. But also for his faith in me.

It's mean, but I can't help teasing him a little. "So does that fancy camera mean you're going to be my cover model?"

His eyes go round with surprise, but then his sensual mouth curves into a smile. "Maybe. We'll see if I ever get this cast off."

That was not the answer I expected at all. "You mean it?"

"We'll see," he says again with a teasing laugh. He picks up a chunk of my hair and runs it through his hand. "I really like this."

"Thank you."

As if he suddenly remembered something, he sits up, grabs my shopping bag and hands it to me. "Show me what's in the bag."

I reach in to take the garments out but his hand over mine stops me.

"No. *Show me.*" He raises an eyebrow so I get his meaning.

Heat shoots straight through me. My nipples perk up, my clit throbs.

"Okay," I whisper.

Safely hidden in the bathroom, I take my time getting ready. Just like I did in the store, I can't get one of the hooks. I almost sob in frustration. This is why I don't bother dressing up or wearing sexy things.

Opening the door a crack, I poke my head out. "I need help." This is mortifying.

Wrath's face breaks into a smile and he beckons me closer.

"Close your eyes."

Of course he has to roll his eyes before closing them. Then he sticks his hands in the air, opening and closing like a blind boob-grabber.

As I approach, I grasp his hands and pull them down to my leg. "Hook that for me."

"I need to open my eyes to see what I'm working with."

"Fine."

He keeps silent while he slides the hook into place. "This is so embarrassing. I needed Hope to help me with it—"

"You two were trying these things on together?"

"Well, no. I just—"

"Stop. Please." He holds up his hand and pushes me back. "Let me see you."

I don't realize it, but I'm standing there staring at my feet.

"Trin, look at me."

Slowly, I raise my eyes to meet his stare.

"Turn."

My throat's suddenly so dry. His fingertips graze my thigh as I turn for him. Despite my growing nervousness, that gentle touch is enough to ignite my body.

"You're so pretty, Trinity."

His rough hands slide down my bare back, over my hips, then sneak under the filmy fabric of the garter skirt.

"What made you get this?"

"I—I…" I don't know how to put it into words. "I never do stuff…wear stuff like this for you, so…" I trail off.

Behind me he's silent, setting off my nerves. I take a step and Wrath's hand circles around my wrist.

"Where you going?" His voice, low and heavy with desire tips me from embarrassed to aching with need.

His arm hooks around my waist, pulling me into his lap. My body trembles as he kisses my shoulder, up my neck and then sucks at the tender flesh below my ear. "Every time I look at you, I can't get over how beautiful you are. But I like this too."

"Thank you."

"You were thinking of me?"

"The whole time."

"You my girl?"

I don't even have to think about it. "Yes."

He drags me backward and to the side, until I'm flat on the bed staring up at him. "I love when you say it without hesitating."

"I like saying it," I whisper.

And I mean it.

WRATH

"You awake?"

The contented *mmmmm* sound from her throat totally makes me want to thump my chest with both fists.

The gifts weren't my way of getting laid. Got no complaints there. Knowing I was on her mind while she was buying that sexy, barely-there outfit to tease me with was *my* gift.

After we wore each other out, she brought me a pitcher of ice water, then stripped down and crawled into bed. I'm tired of having her wait on me. Can't wait for this cast to come off, so I can finally take care of her. And while I definitely enjoy playing bucking bronco for her, I've got a long list of other positions I want to fuck her in.

Her head's resting on my chest. My arm's wrapped around her, my thumb stroking her hip. It's nice and from now on I want things to always be this way for us. "Babe, I'm sorry it took us so long to get here," I murmur not really expecting her to hear me or answer.

Her head pops up and she focuses her sweet, honey eyes on me. "What do you mean? Why are you apologizing?"

I can't quite explain. I'm trying hard to work past our history, but the angry toddler in charge of my brain still thinks some of our problems are her fault. Saying that will be the equivalent of dropping a bomb in our nice, cozy nest, so I shove that thought away. "I just wish things had been different."

"You wish I'd never been part of the club, don't you?"

Shit, is that really a secret? "Well, you know that."

"Wyatt, if I thought for a second you were serious back then, I would have done whatever you asked. But we hadn't known each other long enough. If things didn't work out between us, I'd have been tossed out with no protection. I couldn't risk that. I had bad shit going on I needed to hide from."

I know this. She doesn't know I know this. This is the most she's told me about her past yet. It makes me want to push for more. I need to hear all of it from her, because she trusts me. Besides, there's one last thing I don't understand, no matter how hard I try. As gently as possible, I have to ask.

"You didn't have to make yourself available to the club."

Bombs away.

She scrambles into a sitting position and since she's still gloriously naked, I can't help dropping my gaze to her tits. Fuck me, they're perfect.

"Wyatt!" she snaps. "Rock told me it was my choice. But I don't think I really believed him at the time. And I wanted to make that decision myself not have it forced on me later. I knew how MCs treated their women."

"How did you have all that knowledge at twenty-one?"

"I already told you—"

"No, you never really have. Your dad, yeah. But he died when you were little."

"I can't talk about this." She moves to climb over me, but I catch her hand.

"Please, Trinity. I want to understand you. I want to know everything about you."

Something sad passes over her face. I'm pushing her too much. After a second of hesitation though, she settles down beside me and lets out a deep breath.

"Ask."

Shit, she's giving me the green light. I gotta take a sec and organize my questions before she changes her mind.

"Tell me about your dad."

A faint smile ghosts over her lips. "He was great, even though he wasn't around a lot. Club business, you know. His tattoo parlor kept him busy too. But when he was home, he was good to me. I always felt safe and loved."

Considering Rock told me he met Trin's Dad once, and he was a scary-ass motherfucker, it's interesting to hear her version.

"It's weird, because I can't really picture what he looked like anymore without that damn green prison jumpsuit. I cried for days when he went away. Everyone kept saying it would be three to five years, that he'd be out in a year and a half to two years. And that made me happy, because I thought he'd be out by my tenth birthday."

"Why ten?"

She lets out a soft snort. "My dad promised me he'd take me to get my ears pierced for my tenth birthday. He swore he'd be on his best behavior so he'd get out in time to take me."

"I'm sure he tried, honey."

She nods and focuses her gaze on the bedroom door. "He did at first. I think he meant to keep his promise. But the club kept asking him to 'take care of things' inside. In return, they promised to take care of me and my mom." Her mouth twists on those words and I understand why. The club did fuck-all to protect her.

"How did you know this? You were just a kid."

The corners of her mouth turn down. "My mother couldn't be without a man for a fucking day. The day my dad went in, she started trying to snare the president, Tyler Cross." She spits his name out like a swig of spoiled milk.

I hate doing this to her.

"I spent a lot of time at the clubhouse while she was busy servicing the members. Back then, they had thirty patch holders. Because I was little, they'd stick me in the corner and forget about me. As long as I had some books with me, one place was as good as any another. Besides, without the threat of my father coming home at any minute, my mother had no incentive to take care of me. I had to fend for myself if I wanted to eat and get myself to school. At least there was always food at the clubhouse and I could walk to school from there."

"That's awful."

Her shoulders lift, like it never occurred to her things should have been different. "It got worse. She started seeing Tyler seriously. He'd come to our trailer after I went to bed. One night, I must have woken up and walked in on them." She stops and stares down at her hands. Even though I know what's coming, I hold my breath. "She started tying me to my bed after that. I'd cry every night and beg her not to, but..."

"Tyler didn't think that was weird?"

She glances up at me as if she never thought of that. "I don't know."

"Go on," I urge her gently.

"Maybe a week before my tenth birthday, we were told that, not only was my dad not getting released, but he'd had another fifteen years added. I was devastated. My mom would only take me to see him once a month. I cried so hard at that visit, she made me leave early." She swipes at her damp cheeks and I feel like fucking shit for making her do this. But I wait to see if she wants to continue.

"That was the last time I saw him. There was a fire. Our trailer burned down. The smoke woke me up. Of course, tied to my bed, I couldn't get out, so I screamed and screamed. This huge guy I'd never seen before rushed into my room. I wasn't sure what scared me more—him or the fire. He hacked through the ropes but on the way out, my pajama top caught fire." She points at her hip. "That's how my side got burned. He carried me away from the trailer and left me in the grass."

"He just left you? Where the fuck was your mother?"

"I'm not sure. I woke up in the hospital. They kept me there for weeks. There was talk that my mother might not get me back, and I was so fucking happy. I wanted to go into foster care. But the hospital let me go home with her after all."

"Where?"

"To Tyler's house."

"Really? She managed that?"

"Yeah." She shrugs. "It wasn't bad. He was actually nice to me when I first got there. Always buying me stuff and taking me out on his bike. I thought he was pretty cool."

She pulls at her bottom lip with her teeth. All of a sudden, she glances down and seems to remember she's naked. "I can't talk about this like this." She crawls to the end of the bed and leans over, giving me a filthily spectacular view that I can't even admire because I'm so torn up. Plucking my shirt from the floor, she slides it on, then backs up against the wall out of my reach.

"Are you sure you want to hear this?" she asks.

"I want to hear whatever you're comfortable telling me. I wish you weren't so far away though."

She shifts a little farther up the bed. At least now I can reach out and rub the top of her foot. She takes the ends of my shirt and tucks her knees up under it, then wraps her arms around her legs.

A nervous smile flickers over her face. "I developed early. By the time my mother got around to getting me a bra, I was already a C cup." She glances at me, I think to see if I'm going to make some crude comment. When I don't say anything, she continues. "I fucking hated it. All of a sudden, I got attention from boys and men. I was twelve and grown men would say these disgusting things to me. By then, my mother almost never took me to the clubhouse, but she also started disappearing for long stretches, leaving me alone with Tyler."

She glances up again.

"I'm right here, Trin."

"He'd take me out for shopping trips. Buy me whatever I wanted. He'd also pick out these revealing outfits and make me try them on for him. At the time, I thought it was awesome. His attention made me feel pretty instead of scarred. Like the girls at the club that I always admired."

My fists are balling up the sheet as she talks. For a second she focuses on my hands. I reach out and try to touch her foot again, but she jerks it away.

"Please. Don't touch me while I'm telling you this."

I raise my hand in surrender and put it back in my lap.

"You can guess what happened, right? You don't need me to say it. By fourteen he made me his 'girlfriend.' He was very open about it. He'd bring me to the clubhouse and perch me on his lap like a trophy. We'd make out in front of everyone. I thought I was hot shit. The president's girl."

Unfortunately this doesn't surprise me. Run across plenty of MCs that operate this way over the years.

"People knew how old you were?"

"It wasn't a secret. No one was going to tell Tyler to stop. The other girls hated me. It was awful, because the only friend I had was him."

"Where the fuck's your mom?"

She blinks at my sharp tone. "Shacked up with the Devil Demons."

"You're kidding?"

"No. She brought me there a few times when I was little. I didn't understand until later how odd that was." Odd's an understatement. If she was married to an officer in the Saints and fucking around with their enemy, the Demons, behind his back? That's some serious, fucked-upedness in our world.

She pauses, fiddles with the hem of my shirt. "So, from fourteen to sixteen I was in Tyler's bed, on the back of his bike, and thinking I was untouchable. He told me all the time how much he loved me and how he was going to make me his ol' lady when I turned eighteen."

And another piece of the Trinity puzzle falls into place. Why she can't say *I love you* and why the thought of us together publicly freaks her the fuck out.

She sighs and glances around the room. "Somehow, I kept going to school. Tyler was fine with it because he didn't want me to be like all the other 'dumb bitches' who hung out at his club, and it got me out of his hair during the day."

She pauses and I open my mouth to tell her she can stop, but then she continues. "The club planned a sweet sixteen party for me. Cool, right? I thought the girls had finally accepted me a little bit. I got ready for that motherfucking party for hours. Tyler brought me, walked me in holding my hand. I trusted him."

Something painful twists in my chest at the way she says that.

"They had a party ready. Balloons, cake and all sorts of crap. It was nice, I felt welcomed. Grown up. After a couple hours, the girls started leaving."

"Trin, it's okay, you can stop." I was wrong, I can't hear this. Every word shreds me. I can't stand making her relive something she's tried so hard to forget.

"I won't go into details. That's why the night Inga was up here pulling her shit bothered me so much. You can figure out what happened to me, right? I told myself it was okay. That it meant they loved me and accepted me. Even though they fucking hurt me."

I swear I'm so close to losing it. "What did Tyler do?"

"Sometimes he watched. Sometimes he helped hold me down."

"He let them—"

Her fiery gaze burns into me. "He was done with me. I was club property from then on. They passed me around that clubhouse until I graduated from high school." She takes a few deep breaths. "Some of the guys treated me okay. Others not so much. About a week after graduation I discovered I was pregnant."

Aw, fuck.

"There was no fucking way I was raising a kid in that mess. Besides the fact that I had no way of knowing who the fuck the father was, I did *not* want to be a mother at eighteen." She glares at me so fiercely, as if daring me to challenge her. I don't.

How could I?

"I understand," I say softly while holding her gaze.

Reaching over to the nightstand, I grab a glass of water and hand it to her. After finishing it, she passes it back and continues. "I gathered as much money as I could and got the fuck out of there. Headed East because I knew it was Demon territory Saints shouldn't step foot in. I stopped in Corner Grove and lived there for a while, but it wasn't far enough away for my comfort. After a year, I made my way to Empire where it was easier to blend in. I did fine until a week after we met, when one of Tyler's guys, Jug, walked in the bar."

She pauses and I watch as she clenches and unclenches her fists. I'm about to tell her she can stop, but she takes a deep breath and continues. "Jug had always been one of the nastiest ones. Nights he forced me into his room, he'd make me sleep on the floor like a damn dog." She shifts as if reminded of something especially painful.

White spots jab at my eyes. I want to slam my fists into Rock until he tells me where these fucks are buried so I can dig them up and kill them all over again.

Trinity's voice pulls me out of my futile revenge fantasies. "When he spotted me that night, his face split into this evil fucking grin and I was terrified. Whatever he had in store for me was bound to be a thousand times worse than I remembered. Then he dropped the bomb—that Tyler had a fifty thousand dollar bounty out on me. He gave me an ultimatum—come with him quietly, or he'd get backup to take me home forcefully."

"Why didn't you call me?"

"I didn't have that kind of time, Wyatt. You were on a run. I had no idea how far away you were."

"Trin—"

She cuts me off with an angry shake of her head. "I called Rock. He, Dex, and Teller, came to the bar and got me out of there. Rock brought me to the old clubhouse. I told him the story. He had a right to know what he was getting into by giving me shelter. He gave me a room, and asked if I'd want to take care of this place. The club needed someone to clean up, cook, whatever, and they would give me a room and pay any other expenses. You guys had just closed on it. I visited and loved it so much. He gave me this room, told me to get whatever I wanted for it and the rest was up to me."

"Baby, if you had told me this, I would have—"

"What? You would have what?" she snaps. "Laid a claim on me? I didn't want you to look at me differently. I couldn't stand your pity, Wyatt."

"I understand, but—"

"Have you ever noticed at the bigger parties, I always avoid the older guys?"

"Uh, I'm not sure how to answer that."

The corners of her mouth tilt up in a pained smile. "You know Ulfric? I like him. He's a decent guy. He hit on me once and I almost barfed."

"Okay. What does that have to do with anything?"

"Think about it. None of you were more than seven or eight years older than me. You were a small charter, only ten of you. After what I'd been through, I could handle that. Not all the guys were even interested in me, so that was even better. Bricks was married. Dex didn't do club girls. Sparky and Stash never leave the basement. Rock never had any interest in me sexually." She stops to let that last one sink in. In a much lower voice, she continues. "No one pulled trains here. No one roofied me. If I wanted to say no, I did, and I didn't get the shit beaten out of me. All the guys treated me well."

"Everyone except me?" I ask.

"Yup."

"Fuck, Trinny."

"I didn't think you cared about me that much. We hadn't known each other long. I tried to explain, but—"

"I refused to listen?"

"Yeah. I had already left my job and my apartment. I was terrified of being kicked out and having no place to go. Jug found me, I was afraid it was only a matter of time before someone else did."

"But I told you—"

"That you'd get me an apartment, yeah. But for how long? You still would have been gone long stretches leaving me unprotected." She shakes her head and focuses her gaze on her lap. "I was scared," she whispers.

"I wish you had told me."

"I didn't want you to look at me differently or feel sorry for me. Then when you didn't say anything, I figured you didn't care. When I realized how angry you were, I knew I'd made a horrible mistake. I also knew how it worked. Once you jump beds, you're done. I couldn't change it and I didn't know how to fix things between us."

"You couldn't have fixed it, baby. I'm just as responsible for it getting broken."

"After leaving the Saints, I never spent more than one night with a guy until you."

Somehow that's not as comforting as I think she meant it to be. I think she senses it because she tries to explain. "I felt so dirty, I didn't think anyone would ever want to be with me for more than one night."

"Oh, Trinity. You have no idea, do you? Never mind how beautiful you are. You're so fucking sweet and funny. I think I fell for you that first night when you told me you weren't looking for an ol' man."

She chuckles at the memory. "Can I tell you something?"

"You can tell me anything."

"That night I told Hope how Rock and I have never...I'd already explained it to her. I said it again for your benefit."

I snort and look away. "Am I that obvious?"

"Yes."

I pause. "What about your mother?"

"Demons tossed her out. She tried going back to the Saints, but they wouldn't let her in the door. I never found out what happened to her. Don't care honestly."

The worst is over. She's smiling a little.

I open my arms to her. "Can I hold you now?"

She crawls over to me so quick, I'm thrown. Snuggling right up against my side, she lays her head on my chest and wraps her arm around my middle. My arm winds around her back, my hand landing on her hip again. We lay like that quietly for a while.

"Wyatt, do you hate me now?"

"No. Why?"

"You don't think I'm a disgusting whore after—"

"Stop. No, I'd never think that about you. Don't ever say that again."

"But—"

"I've fucked around as much, if not more, than you. Do you think I'm a disgusting whore?"

"Yeah, kinda." I feel her smile against my chest.

"Wench."

While she's busy giggling at me, my hand lifts the hem of her shirt, and lands a nice, crisp smack on her ass.

"Ow!"

I bend down and kiss her forehead. "Baby, your time with them...none of that was your fault."

"No, but everything I did afterward is."

I'm not so sure I agree with that.

She's suddenly serious again. "I like sex."

"Good. So do I."

She scrunches up her face and pulls away from me. "No, I felt ashamed for years because I figured that's why Tyler—"

"Babe, he sounds like a sick fuck who preyed on an innocent girl."

She tips her head forward so that her hair covers most of her face. "I wasn't innocent."

My hand brushes over her leg to get her attention. I want her to look at me. "You were, what? Fourteen?" I'm sick thinking about it. She should have been sneaking around with boys her own age not being molded into what some twisted old fuck wanted her to be.

"I never said no," she whispers.

"Did you feel like you could?"

Finally, she looks up at me. "Not until I came here. The times I tried, didn't end well for me. I ran away once and being on the street was almost worse..."

Christ, no wonder she's so twisted about us.

"Trinity, you know I'd never let that happen."

"But what if we—"

"No. No *what if*. I love you."

"Wyatt, please listen to me. I couldn't go back to all that hostility between us."

Because you love me too. Admit it.

"It would kill me and where would I—"

"Trinity, I'll leave first before I do that to you, okay?"

"No. You couldn't—"

"Yes, for you I would. But it's a non-issue."

"I'm afraid when you get to know the real me, you won't like her very much and realize this was a mistake."

A number of things come to mind. First—that's absurd. Second—I wonder the same thing about myself sometimes. Third—that's never going to happen. I start with number three. "I think I know you pretty well by now."

Her mouth curves up a bit. "Yeah. Probably better than anyone else ever has."

I like the sound of that. "And I love everything about you."

Now her face pulls into a sad smile. "I like everything about you, too. So much it scares me."

"So let's try not to worry about stuff that will never happen."

"I'll try."

I guess that's as good as I'm gonna get right now.

She takes a deep breath and looks in my eyes. "I've never told anyone the whole story."

"Thank you for trusting me." I hold open my arms and she snuggles up against me again.

"Do you remember the night we met?"

"Of course. It's still one of the best nights of my life, Trinity."

She pulls away and stares. "I trusted you. You made me feel safe and comfortable. Even though I was a little nutty that night."

Laughter rumbles out of me. "Yeah, you definitely took me down a peg or two."

"I think I was just freaked out by how much I liked you. The last time I trusted someone like that..."

Yeah, she doesn't need to finish that sentence.

"Trin, about that night. I'm sorry I—"

"No. Don't ruin it. It's still one of the best nights of my life too."

CHAPTER THIRTY-THREE

Trinity

Revealing my past to Wrath doesn't leave me feeling as vulnerable as I thought it would. If anything, I'm relieved to share it with him. Not once did he make me feel bad or ashamed. I fall asleep in his arms and don't wake until morning. Not one nightmare.

"Hey, babe," he greets me in the sexy, morning-rough voice I love so much.

"Were you watching me sleep?"

He runs his hand over his face and yawns. "Yeah, you're pretty."

It's simple but so amazing to hear.

His phone buzzes and he throws his arm out, slapping the nightstand until he finds it. He takes a second to check the screen and smirks. "Guys are on their way back."

My mouth turns up. I know how happy Hope will be to see Rock and I say so.

"Ummm, he said keep it under wraps. He wants to surprise her."

"That's mean. What if she wants to get all dolled up for him?"

Wrath shrugs. "Only one I'm worried about gettin' dolled up is you."

We tease each other like that for a few minutes. Then one hand cups my cheek and he stares into my eyes. "You okay, baby?"

"Yeah."

"I'm sorry I made you—"

"I feel better."

He nods once. "I have a confession to make."

Immediately I assume he's teasing me. "Oh, yeah?"

He runs his thumb over my bottom lip. "The reason I asked you to help me prepare for the fight? I just wanted a way to get close to you again. You blew me off after we—"

My hand reaches for his face. "Oh, Wyatt."

"You *were* a big help to me. Once I came up with the idea, I knew it was a good one."

I work to keep the smile off my face. "So why the confession?"

"I feel guilty you got behind on your book stuff because of me."

Sweet mercy. How is it this man, who could kill someone with his bare hands if he wanted to, is also so fucking sweet? "Yeah, but you got me all my fancy new stuff. I'll be caught up in no time."

"I'm glad. Want you focusing on that. Gonna talk to Rock soon about you handing off your household chores to someone else."

Now wait just a minute. I bolt upright. "What?"

"I don't want my woman being the maid of the MC anymore."

"You said you—"

"That came out wrong. You're my girl. I want you lookin' after me and I want you concentrating on your art."

"Wrath. You know I like taking care of things around here, right? It gives me purpose. I can't explain it."

He looks away. "I get that. Just think about it, okay?"

Think nothing. Now that I'm aware this is in Wrath's head, it's only a matter of time before he takes it to Rock. I'm not sure how I feel about it, although I would like the extra time to make my business more solid.

"I'll think about it."

He leans down and plants a kiss on my forehead. "Thank you."

WRATH

Trinity decided she wouldn't be able to keep a straight face around Hope, so she's in her room. Honestly, I think she couldn't wait to get her hands on her new computer equipment. When I left, she was so into setting things up, she barely glanced at me.

I'm not insulted. Seeing her happy, makes me happy.

Messin' with Hope is also making me happy. She's got no clue her man's coming home any minute now.

"What?" she asks me for probably the tenth time this morning.

"Nothing." I grin at her and she wrinkles her nose.

Her face goes through a complete change when we hear the guys coming up the driveway.

"You're evil! Why didn't you tell me?" she shouts, shooting off the couch.

"Go greet your man." That was pointless. She's already halfway to the door.

After a minute or two Rock carries Hope in. He barely glances at me long enough to nod and then takes her right upstairs.

Murphy drops his bags at the foot of the stairs. "Ain't gonna see them for the rest of the day," he says with a smirk.

"That fucker got her name tatted on him," Z informs me.

"Would you shut the fuck up about it," Murphy gripes.

I grin at both of them. "Calm down children. Maybe if you're good little boys, Daddy will get your names inked on him too."

Z throws himself down next to me. "Look who's chipper. Have fun while we were gone?"

Wrapping my arm around Z's neck I pull him in for a hug-choke and rough him up. "Yeah. Missed you, though, little brother."

He breaks out of the hold, laughing.

Murphy slaps my outstretched hand. "How's the leg, bro?"

"Gettin' there."

"You're back!" Trinity yells from the hallway, rushing out to greet Murphy and Z. She gives both of them a quick hug and the two fucks keep a respectful distance.

"I take it Rock's upstairs?" she asks.

None of us really need to answer that. Trin takes a seat in my lap, which makes me pretty fuckin' happy.

Z smirks at us and heads into the war room. "Got some shit to do, then I'm taking a shower and a nap. Any of you fucks wake me up, I'm kicking some ass."

Murphy laughs at him. "I'm gonna grab something to eat then do the same." He slaps my shoulder and heads into the kitchen. To my delight, Trinity stays put. In fact, she leans back against me.

"Thanks for letting me get some work done," she finally says.

"Sure, babe."

"Want to see what I was working on?"

I tip my head down to take her in. "If you want to show me."

A hint of a smile slips across her face. "I've got a few things to show you."

Now she really has my attention. Sliding out of my lap, she holds her hands out to me. I made it down here without the crutches, but I'm not sure about the walk back. I'm not about to tell her that though. She wraps her arm around my waist, and I lean on her more than I care to admit.

Restless, I leave Trin sleeping. Definitely proud of myself for wearing her out again. If only I could wear myself out.

I find Z, Dex and Murphy yapping in the living room.

"I thought a fucking bomb hit the house," Z finishes saying as I walk in.

"What are you talking about?"

The guys turn and look at me. Murphy smirks. "Z's tender ears were hurt listening to Mom and Dad get it on."

I throw my head back and laugh so hard, I almost lose my balance.

"Fuck both of you," Z snaps.

Dex chuckles. "Keep your mouth shut. That girl embarrasses easy. You upset her, prez will kill you."

Z waves his hand in the air, dismissing Dex's sage advice. "Nah, she loves me."

I shake my head.

Dex and Murphy head out. Z fills me in on the trip.

"Seriously, he didn't look at another chick the entire time," he says.

I shrug. "Is that supposed to be a surprise?"

Z tilts his head and stares at me. "It's fuckin' weird, that's all."

"I thought you liked Hope?"

"I do. What's that got to do with anything?"

I make my *For fuck's sake* face at him.

Z lowers his voice. "Don't tell me on your next trip out there you're not gonna hang with Sha—"

My hand squeezes the back of his neck. "Worry about where you park your own dick, brother."

He slaps my arm away. We're interrupted from further discussion by the couple in question coming down the stairs.

"Hey, porn stars," I call out. Hope's finally wearing her property patch. The sight of it knocks the breath out of me.

Z goes on to do exactly what Dex warned him *not* to do, almost getting an ass-kicking from Rock. I sit back and enjoy not being on Rock's shit list for once.

"Are you still in pain?" Rock asks her after I have to sit through the two of them playing an extended game of tonsil hockey.

"A little." She reaches over and taps my leg. "That's why Wrath offered to get me high."

Thanks for bringing *that* up, Cinderella. "See, I told you I'd take good care of her." I smirk at Rock.

Sparky surfaces and asks for Rock's help. Once they disappear downstairs, Hope turns to me with a sly smile. "Enjoy Trinity's new outfit?"

Well, now. Cinderella came to play. Let's see if she can take it or only dish it out. "I sure did. Heard you got one just like it. That what got prez so worked up?"

Her cheeks turn bright red. Just as I thought. She taps my side with her fist. "Jerk."

"You started it. I'm not sure if you noticed, but no one's sex life is a secret here." Fuck, that's the understatement of the year.

"I'm a bit of a prude, aren't I?"

Well, at least she's self-aware. "We'll work it out of you. Oh, and I gotta tell you, the idea of you and Trin trying that shit on together is going straight into my spank bank."

Her face flushes even redder. "Oh my gosh! It wasn't like that. And ew."

My star patch on the side of her vest catches my eye. On Trinity's vest, the star would be over her heart. Am I ever going to get there with her? I feel like her finally confiding in me last night moved us closer. I'm not jealous of Rock. Not exactly. But Trinity grew up in the life and understands the significance of a property patch. The fact that Hope—who had no fucking clue anything like that existed before she met Rock—is wearing one first, frustrates the fuck out of me.

Rock's gone for a while and I can tell she's getting anxious.

"Wrath?"

"Yes, sugar."

"What's downstairs?"

I chuckle. "*The* club business." She doesn't laugh. *Motherfucker.* "Rock still hasn't told you?"

"Geez, don't tell me it's more strippers," she grumbles.

"No strippers."

"Porn studio?"

"No sugar. Noting like that."

Rock chooses that exact moment to come back upstairs. I turn and glare at him. "Can I have a word with you, brother?"

"Not now, we've got a problem," he answers, dismissing me.

"Why don't you take Hope on a tour of downstairs?"

Rock's jaw sets in a hard line. "Not now.

Hope sits up. "Wrath, it's fine. I—"

"What the fuck you waiting for? You patched her."

Rock clearly wants to knock me the fuck out, but this is getting ridiculous. The girl's here all the time. She should know the risk she's taking.

"Fine. You wanna see what's downstairs, baby doll?" he asks her.

Hope's gaze swings between the two of us. "If you want me to."

"Christ, it's not that big a deal at this point." I say.

"Shut up. Remember, you started this," Rock growls.

He leads her downstairs and I wait for the fallout.

Maybe half an hour later, they return. Hope seems to have survived. Rock looks like he wants to punch something. Probably me.

He keeps going right upstairs even though Hope stops to talk to me. "Rock?" I call out, but he ignores me. Shrugging, I turn to Hope. "What did you think?"

"Pretty cool."

What crawled up Rock's ass then? "You're very unpredictable, Hope."

She pats my arm and takes off after Rock.

They're barely gone a minute, when she comes racing back downstairs. "Hope! What's wrong?"

She's shaking her head and I can tell she's close to tears. Before I can grab her, she darts out the door.

Motherfucker. I'm gonna wrap my hands around Rock's neck and squeeze really hard. How dare he take her on a tour of our entire operation, then piss her off so bad she storms off afterward.

I've been doing better without the crutches, but the stairs are a pain in the fucking ass. I'm livid by the time I reach Rock's door, so I pound on it extra hard. "Rock! Open the fucking door."

After a minute, he opens it wearing a towel.

"What the fuck did you say to her?" I snap at him.

"Who?"

"Hope, you asshole. She just took off in fucking tears."

He glances around the room then back at me. "She's not going to run to the cops, if that's what you're worried about. She thought Sparky and his setup were adorable."

Now I really do want to choke him. I know she isn't gonna run to the police. But we also don't need her sobbing to one of her girlfriends and mentioning our grow house in the process. We do not need is a pissed-off woman who not only knows where our clubhouse is, but what's in our basement running around.

He promises to go talk to her and I hop next door to my room before I really do knock his ass out. No fuckin' way am I making it back downstairs anytime soon.

My room's surprisingly clean and dust free considering I haven't been in it in weeks. I assume that's Trinity's doing.

I roll onto my bed and stare up at the ceiling. Remembering the conversation Trinity and I had about my sister, I reach out and snag the second drawer of my nightstand. My only photo of Faith is tucked into a silver frame. Both of us are actually in the cheesy Sears portrait. I can't stand looking at what a goofy kid I was, but Faith's just as adorable as I remember.

I set the frame on top of the nightstand so I'll remember to bring it back downstairs with me.

Z shoves my door open. "What're you doin' in here?"

"Didn't you ever learn to knock?"

He snorts and steps inside. "You and Trin okay?"

"Yeah. I came up here to choke Rock." We've all been friends for so long, this doesn't phase him.

I give him the concise version and he laughs. "She ain't gonna run her mouth. Even if she's pissed at him, he's got her pretty well dick-whipped."

A harsh laugh explodes out of me. "I'd love to see you say that to her face."

He grins. "I gotta run out. You need anything?"

"Nah. I'll hop back downstairs eventually."

After he leaves, I end up dozing off.

My phone buzzing in my pocket wakes me.

Where are you?

Something about Trinity asking where I am makes me grin like an idiot. I let her know I'm upstairs and dial Rock.

"What?" he snaps. Typical.

"Where are you, dick?"

"At Hope's."

Thank fuck. "She okay?"

"Yes."

"Are you guys okay?"

In the background I hear Hope say, "Awww" and it makes me chuckle.

"Yeah, we're good," Rock answers.

"Are you coming back up tonight?"

"Yeah, we'll be up in a little while," she answers.

"Oh, for fuck's sake, are you going to turn into one of those annoying couples who answers every phone call together?" I snap, but I'm laughing the entire time.

"Bye, Wrath," she says and hangs up on me.

I'm still shaking my head when Trinity knocks on the door.

"You don't have to knock, angel."

She shrugs. "Do I want to know?"

At first I think she's joking, but then I notice how nervous she looks. "I came up here to kick Rock's ass and was too tired to hop back downstairs," I explain.

"Oh."

I pat the bed. "Come sit. I want to show you something."

She rushes over and sits next to me. I pull her down for a kiss. "You're not gettin' rid of me, if that's what you were thinking."

"No?"

"No. Even once you finally let me publicly claim your ass. I think I'd rather stay downstairs with you."

"Really?"

"Yeah, really."

"But—" She stops and looks around my room. "This is a nice room. You earned it, being one of the officers of the club—"

"Trin, look at me." I wait until she does what I ask. "Don't give a fuck about that. I like being away from all the stuff going on up here. Unless you don't want me..."

"No." She glances around again and I can almost hear her thoughts. "I'd like that."

"We can talk about it later."

"Okay. What'd you want to show me?"

Picking up the silver frame, I glance at it one more time before handing it over.

"Oh." Watery honey eyes blink up at me. "She's so pretty, Wyatt."

A smile tugs at the corners of my mouth. "Yeah."

"Look at you. All those blond curls." She chuckles while running her fingers over the glass.

"I look like a doof."

"Oh, no. You're both so sweet together. Can I bring it downstairs with us?"

"Yeah, of course." I shove over to make room for her and pat the bed. "Come here."

Slowly, she lies down next to me so we're both staring at the ceiling. "I used to hate coming in here...before," she says quietly.

"Why?"

She turns her head, staring at me. Hurt crosses her face and I know what she's going to say. "I never knew who or...what I'd find in your bed."

Shit. The idea of her cleaning up after...It probably occurred to me once or twice over the years, but never like this. "I'm sorry."

She shrugs and turns away. "It was my own fault. I deserved it."

"Don't say that, Trinity."

"How many times did you run into me leaving—" She chokes on a sob and finishes her thought by flinging her hand in the direction of the hallway.

"Too many. And I hated it every time."

She laughs and sniffles at the same time. "I guess we're even?"

I catch her hand in mid-air and bring it to my mouth, kissing her fingertips. "We're done hurting each other."

She nods and swipes her cheeks.

"Let's go back downstairs, Angel Face."

CHAPTER THIRTY-FOUR

Trinity

We all knew it was coming. Rock was never going to be satisfied with just the property patch.

On a chilly winter day, he proposed to Hope. Wrath and I were at the clubhouse and celebrated with them.

Somehow I get dragged along to celebrate her engagement with her friends the following Friday.

I chose a simple outfit of jeans and a soft, sparkly sweater. Hope went all-out. She picked a blinding-pink dress, gray tights and shiny heels. Rock got one look at her and we almost didn't make it out of the house.

Wrath pulled me in for a hug right before we left. "Have fun, angel."

I don't know about that. Lilly and Sophie start teasing Hope about her dress almost immediately.

"What? I think it's cute," she says.

"I like it too," Mara says, reaching over to give Hope a quick hug. This is the first time I've met Mara. Supposedly she's married to a judge or something. She seems really sweet and shy though. I don't get to talk to her much because she's at the opposite end of the table.

"Her man almost didn't let her out of the house when he saw her tonight. You're lucky I got her down here," I explain to the girls.

"Seems like a good time to hand you this, then," Mara says, picking up a shiny pink gift bag from the floor.

"I'm scared to open it," Hope jokes.

She should be too. She pulls sex guides, sex toys, lube and finally, a paddle out of the bag. Hope's a good sport. "Really? Have I given any of you the impression we need help in that department?"

Imagining Rock's reaction when Hope tells him her friends think he needs the *Guy's Guide to Going Down* has me falling out of my chair with laughter.

They joke around a little longer. I guess Mara's not so shy after all.

Sophie kills the laughter. "Are you going to take your time planning this wedding?" She waves her hand in the air, almost smacking Lilly. "You and your mother threw the last one together so quick, we all thought you were pregnant."

Hope looks like she was punched in the gut and I have to stop myself from jumping over the table and smacking the shit out of Sophie. Hope just lost a baby. What the fuck is wrong with her friend?

"Fuck, honey. I'm so sorry. I didn't mean... I forgot. Shit, it just happened, and wow, I'm sorry," Sophie mumbles.

Not ten seconds later, Sophie brings up Hope's first wedding again. What the hell is wrong with this chick?

I glance at Lilly. "So, Lilly, are those knockers real?"

Well, that's certainly one way to take the focus off Hope. But I swear to God, if Sophie says one more thing to upset Hope, I really am going to kick her ass.

Eventually, guys show up. More lawyer friends. Adam and Ross. They're nice enough. Then *our* guys show up. Well, Rock and Z do.

Z smirks while Rock gropes his woman in the middle of the bar. Then he pokes me. "Your roommate's waitin' outside."

What the fuck? Why can't he come inside like a normal person? We had this sweet and honest moment the other day. He's been after me to announce our relationship, but he can't even come inside and sit with me?

I'm so irritated, I barely listen to the conversation around me.

When we all get up to leave, I stick with Hope. Wrath's leaning on my Jeep facing the door when we step outside. He glances up and smiles when he sees me.

My heart skips.

"You could have joined us," Hope says.

"Nah, I'm good, Cinderella."

Mara giggles when she hears that, so Hope introduces them. He's actually being civil. So why couldn't he come inside and do that?

He raises an eyebrow at me and I ignore him.

When we're down to just Rock, Hope, Wrath and me, Wrath snags me around the waist and yanks me against him.

"Why you ignoring me, Angel Face?"

"Trin, you okay to drive?" Rock calls out.

"Yup, only had water," I shout back.

He waves and takes off.

"Let's go," I say, wriggling out of his hold and unlocking the car.

Once we get on the highway, Wrath sighs. "How was your night?"

"Fine."

"You mad at me?"

"Nope."

"Yeah, you are. Why?"

My hands tighten on the steering wheel. "Why couldn't you come in and sit with me? You keep saying you want to announce us to everyone, but then you don't want to be seen in public—"

"Trin, what are you, five-seven, a buck twenty-five?" I snort because he's being awfully generous there, but he ignores me. "I'm more than twice your size. You have any idea how uncomfortable those tiny fucking buildings down here are for a guy my size? Got nothing to do with how I feel about you. Fuck I didn't even think my shoulders would fit through the door. Then with the cast, I'm even more clumsy and awkward—"

"Oh." Wow. I feel like total shit. He's always so cocky, and sure of himself, it never occurred to me something like that might bother him.

"You got your issues. I got mine," he says, staring out the window.

He's right. He's so patient with me and all my emotional fuckery.

"I'm sorry," I whisper.

He reaches out and squeezes my leg but doesn't say anything else.

We drive up the long road to the clubhouse behind Rock's vehicle. As I back into my spot, Wrath snorts.

"Looks like Rock has his hands full."

"Aw, he's so sweet."

Wrath glances over at me.

"What? He is."

Rock's trying to juggle carrying Hope and getting the front door unlocked. Wrath chuckles. "It's sad that you gotta keep druggin' your girl to get her up here."

Rock's laughing so hard, I barely make out the "Fuck you" he responds with.

He jerks his head at his car. "Grab her stuff for me?"

I open the front door and as I turn to get the stuff out of the car, I see Wrath already grabbed it. "Nice pink bag."

He grins and lifts it up and down. "What the hell's in it? It's heavy."

How to explain? "Books and sex toys," I answer through giggles.

He raises an eyebrow at Rock who shrugs. "Her friends' idea of an engagement present," he explains.

Of course Wrath takes that as an invitation to start pawing through Hope's stuff. He cracks up when he gets to the paddle.

"Give me that," I snap, snatching the bag out of his trouble-making hands. "I'll drop this in front of your door, prez," I say as I jog up the stairs.

On my way back, Wrath's laughter reaches me before I see him. "Sure, whatever you say, Cinderella."

I guess Hope's awake.

"There's a guy's guide for going down on his girl. You can have that since Rock doesn't need it."

Oh, boy.

Wrath laughs even harder. He gasps. "Trust me, neither do I." As soon as he spots me, I cringe, fearing what he'll say. "Right, babe?"

"What am I agreeing to?" I ask when I reach the living room.

Rock's clearly ready for this conversation to be over. "All right, doll, time for bed," he says, slipping his arm around Hope and tugging her up the stairs.

"I offered him the guide to going down," she yells to me.

Oh, that's hilarious. "No. He doesn't need it."

Wrath's not finished making trouble tonight. "Leave it for Murphy. Brother needs all the help he can get," he calls out.

Hope screeches "Ewwww," which makes Wrath laugh even harder.

I plant my hand on my hip. "Was that necessary?"

Here comes the wide-eyed innocent expression he's so good at. "What? I'm trying to be helpful."

"You're just mad anyone suggested you might need help in that department."

He slings his arm over my shoulder and turns me toward my bedroom. "Babe, the only opinion I'm interested in is yours. You think my skills need improving, by all means, let's practice."

"Oh my God," I say through a bunch of giggles and snorts.

When we get to my door, I point at his leg. "You seem to be doing better. How do you feel?"

"Good. That fuckin' doctor better take the cast off this week."

Pushing the door open with his shoulder, he turns and wraps his arms around my waist. "You really want to talk about that now?" he asks while bumping the door shut with his elbow. "Because I want to explore what kind of sex toys *you've* got."

He opens up my nightstand drawer and starts digging through it. I'm both baffled and amused as I sit on the bed and watch. When his search of the top drawer yields nothing, he opens the second drawer.

"I can stop you right now. You won't find any."

The disappointment on his face makes me chuckle. "Why not?"

"Do you really want me to answer that?"

He narrows his eyes. "Probably not, but tell me anyway."

I shrug and look away. "No need for them." Does he want me to explain that for years I've had a house full of guys ready and willing to get me off whenever I asked?

No he doesn't. "Well, I'll have to order you a nice big box of toys to stash under the bed." He pretends to think something over and taps his chin. "A paddle too. For when my hand gets tired."

My fist lands on his side and he pretends to be injured. "Jerk," I grumble.

His mouth turns up in a wicked grin. "Yeah, baby. But I'm *your* jerk."

WRATH

I'm disturbed from waking Trinity up the way I wanted by my phone going off much too early. Recognizing the number, I sit up and answer.

"Motherfucker!" the president of our downstate charter shouts into the phone.

"'Sup, Sway?" Next to me, Trin stirs, then buries her head under the pillow. Like the happy perv I am, I lift the sheet and run my hand over her naked ass. Fuckin' *love* waking up next to her.

"Can't get hold of your prez. He knee deep in stripper-pussy?"

"No, man. He was out celebrating his engagement last night."

"What the ever-loving fuck? Didn't he learn anything—"

I cut that off quick. "She's nothing like Carla. Trust me. What'd you need him for?"

"Need some of your boys to come down and pay a visit. He can bring his ol' lady if he wants. I'm sure Tawny would like to check her out." My eyes roll at that. Sway's ol' lady is the Queen Bitch. Poor Hope might not survive a visit down there.

"Yeah, okay. When were you thinking?"

"Next weekend. Definitely. I'm thinking of looking into National and maybe Rock wants to back me up."

I highly doubt that, but I promise to have Rock get in touch and hang up.

"Ugh, was that Sway?"

I'm instantly irritated, wondering why Trinity's asking. "Yeah, why?"

She rolls over, tossing her pillow aside. "Nothing. He coming here?"

"No. Needs Rock and some of the others to pay a visit."

She relaxes back against the bed. "Good."

"Why?"

She sighs and glances at me. "Nothing, he's just...handsy."

"You fuck him?" Shit it's way too early to be having this argument...again.

She snaps into a sitting position. "No. Not for lack of trying on his part. Something 'bout fucking a dude with his ol' lady nearby never sat well with me. Even *I* have standards." With that, she stands up, jumps off the end of the bed, and pads into the bathroom, slamming the door behind her.

Why can't I ever keep my mouth shut?

She emerges from the bathroom fully dressed, but no less annoyed. "Anyway. Tawny assumes we've fucked, so she's got no love for my slutty ass. Thank fuck they're not coming here. She'd eat Hope alive."

At breakfast, Rock presses Trinity for information about her night out with Hope. I'd like to discuss business sometime today. "Downstate called. Sway wants you to come pay a visit."

That gets Rock's attention. "Fuck. What for?"

"He said ol' ladies were invited. It's not a bad idea for you to bring Hope. Have her meet Tawny..."

"What's this, your last-ditch effort to scare Hope away?" he asks.

Yeah, he would think that, wouldn't he? But honestly, it's not a bad idea for Hope to meet a typical ol' lady. See the kind of women she'll be expected to interact with if she's gonna stick by prez. Yeah, Trin's gonna be my ol' lady soon—whether she likes it or not—but she's not exactly typical.

"Yeah, man. If Tawny don't scare your girl away, nothing will."

"Don't subject Hope to that bitch on wheels," Z pleads with a headshake.

"What exactly did he want?" Rock asks.

No point sugar-coatin' it. He's gonna be pissed one way or another. "Something about national."

Obviously deciding I can't go, he turns to Z. "I'd rather not," Z answers.

"Take Murphy and Axel," I suggest. Make those two fuckers work together. Murphy's gonna need to drop his bullshit soon, and we might as well see if Axel can handle the club or not.

Rock stares at me like I'm nuts. "Really, Axel? He's a fuckin' kid. Barely been wearing that prospect rocker a month. Bad enough we broke the rule about allowing him up here before his year was up."

I notice he doesn't even bother mentioning the bad blood brewing between Murphy and Axel. Especially after Heidi's birthday party. "It'll do Murph some good. Keep his cocky Irish ass in check. Plus, might as well see if Axel can hang now rather than later."

"That's fine. Hope likes both of them, and I know they'll look out for her."

Dick. Like I wouldn't look out for her?

"Prez, I'll go if you're worried about Hope," Z offers.

Rock waves a hand in the air. "Nah, it'll be fine."

Just picturing Cinderella's face when she steps into Sway's compound is enough to make me laugh. "Man, she thinks this place is the gateway to hell. Wait 'til she sees Sway's setup."

Trinity

Before Hope leaves for this trip downstate, I feel obligated to warn her about what she'll encounter. So when she asks me to come upstairs and help her pack, I'm more than happy to say yes.

The way she plows through her closet amuses me. She must drive Rock nuts with her messiness.

More clothes go sailing out of the closet, landing on the floor and I cover my mouth.

"Have you been there?" she shouts from the depths.

"Long time ago."

"I suppose it will be a bunch of half-naked chicks running around?"

I snicker at that. At least she's prepared. "Pretty much."

She steps out of the closet and gives me an uncertain look. "How many of them are going to tell me they fucked my fiancé?"

I feel bad laughing, but thinking of any of the girls down there giving lip like that, is funny. Tawny would yank their hair out by the roots. "None of them, if they want to keep breathing. Sway's ol' lady runs a tight ship. None of those bitches should backtalk you."

My comments don't seem to reassure her all that much. "I wish you guys were coming. Well, I wish *you* were coming with us."

No thanks. But I laugh anyway. They're only going for the weekend, but it seems longer for some reason. "Hopefully, Wyatt's cast comes off next week."

"That's good. Maybe he'll be less cranky." I know Hope's kidding but it just reminds me that he's going to want to go public soon.

She senses the change in my mood immediately. "What's wrong, Trinity?"

Next thing I know she's sitting next to me. Damn, I'm a mess. "Nothing. I don't know. I'm not sure what happens... next." Should I tell Hope and see what her reaction is? "He wants... Never mind. It's stupid."

Time to shake myself out of my pity party. "You're going to have enough to worry about this weekend. Make sure you call or text me if anything comes up. Even if it's some stupid club question that Rock's not around to answer."

"Why wouldn't he be around?"

Oh, Hope. Still so much to learn. "I guarantee you this visit is more than a social call, Hope. Don't be surprised or hurt if you end up spending most of the trip hanging out with Tawny."

"Okay."

This is what I came for. To warn her about what she's facing this weekend. Not to dump my stupid problems on her.

Z ends up joining the guys for the trip to Sway's place. With most of the guys gone, Wrath and I sort of have the clubhouse to ourselves. It's nice in a weird way.

"How would you feel about building our own house?" Wrath asks me after dinner Saturday night.

"What? Where?"

He jerks his head to the side. "On the property. Rock's got a space measured out for the house he wants to build for Hope."

"You're not happy here?"

"It's fine for now." His hand closes over mine. "But eventually it might be nice."

A house? With Wrath. Wow.

We're interrupted by his cell phone. "Shit. The alarm at the gym's going off."

"Do you need to go down there?"

"Let me call Jake."

When he reaches Jake, he says it was a false alarm. Wrath's still twitchy after they hang up. "You want to run down anyway and see for yourself?" I ask.

"Do you mind?"

"Of course not."

The parking lot's empty when we get there. Wrath runs his flashlight over the door before we go inside. "Wait in my office for me, babe." His tone puts me on edge, but I don't question him.

After fifteen minutes, he opens the door and hobbles in. "Shoulda brought my crutches—"

While he was gone, I used my time to strip down to my underwear, and perch myself on his desk.

"Whatchya doin', Angel Face?"

For a second I hesitate. Maybe this was a bad idea. But the ravenous gleam in his eyes extinguishes any doubts. I lean back, thrusting my chest out, enjoying the way his eyes widen. "I realized, in all the time we spent here, we never re-baptized your desk."

"That's just wrong." The door closes with a soft click and he flips the lock.

I slide down, bare feet touching the carpet, turn and lean over the desk, bracing myself on my arms. My hips sway from side to side and Wyatt runs his hand over his chin. "I like you like this. Tell me what you want," he says as he moves behind me.

"I want you to fuck me over your desk, Wyatt. Then I want to go home with you, like we should have done last time." I close my eyes, waiting for the rejection. Waiting to see what he does next. Why'd I say that and bring up all our fucked-up past when everything has been so nice between us?

Feather-light, his fingers trail down my back, unhooking my bra so I can slip it off. He continues his journey, big hands skimming down smoothing the thin fabric of my underwear over my ass. I ease back, bumping into him and he groans. His hand slips under the elastic. "When did you come up with this plan?"

My shoulders automatically jerk. "While I was waiting for you."

He makes a sexy, hummy sound of approval and continues exploring. I pull in a sharp breath when his fingers find their target. Gently he strokes the wetness between my legs, then up to stroke the tips of his fingers against my clit. Not enough to get me off. Enough to drive me nuts.

"Seems like longer to me, angel." His voice is low and rough, so I know he's as turned on as I am. He slides his fingers down again. Almost to the entrance of my pussy.

"Wyatt, please?"

"That's my girl. Love when you beg for my cock." I attempt an outraged snort, but it sounds more like a needy whimper. I try wiggling my hips again.

"Ask nicely."

"You fucker," I grumble, because I wanted to be the one to shock him with some unexpected office sex, but somehow he turned the tables on me. I get a sharp slap on my ass.

"That's *not* nice. Try again."

I let out a string of curses and get his palm against my ass for each one. "I'm starting to think you just like my hand on your ass." He leans over me, kissing my shoulder and I press back against him. He wraps an arm around my body, reaching for my clit. "Yeah, you definitely like it." There's a twist to his voice, as if he's out of breath.

There's a tug at my waist and my panties slide down my legs I kick them to the side and arch my back. Then his hands are at my hips holding me up while he slams into me hard and fast.

"About fucking time." I end up panting the words. Another sharp crack fills the air as his hand kisses my ass again.

"You're mouthy tonight," he says. "I like it."

He's pulling me into him and pounding into me at the same time. My fingers curl over the edges of the desk. "That's right. Hold on, Trinity."

An unbearable tension builds with every thrust. "Right there, please don't stop, Wyatt..." The rest of my words are lost to frantic moaning and sobbing as I come. Wyatt shouts as he comes, too. He drapes his body over mine, squishing me against the desk. Slick with sweat, my arms give out and we end up dropping to the floor in a sweaty, tangled heap. "Fuck, sorry," he apologizes. "You okay?"

I moan out a yes and he chuckles, then shifts, puling me on top of him.

He palms the back of my head and pulls me to him for a harsh kiss.

He gestures to his leg. "Are you trying to kill me woman?"

I burst out laughing and he joins me. Our moment's cut short by a sound out in the gym. My gaze collides with his. "Wyatt?"

"Shit," he lifts himself off the floor and hands me my clothes. "Get dressed." I can't find my bra or panties in the pile he gave me, but it doesn't matter. As soon as I'm covered, he points behind the desk. "Stay down. I'll be right back."

Before I can assure him or ask him not to go, he's out the door. I crouch behind the desk and wait like he asked. He's not gone long when there's a shout and scuffle.

"Trin, it's okay."

I flip the overhead lights on as I walk into the gym. And stop dead when I see Wrath holding up one of the kids from his training class. Even though he's close to being murdered, he takes the time to leer at me. Heat races across my cheeks, I can only imagine what this kid heard.

"Seems Twitch has been breaking into the place at night. We upgraded the alarm system this week, but he didn't know that."

"You two really should have locked the door. What if I'd been a bad guy," the kid says with a small smirk.

"Shut up," Wrath growls. He turns and grins at me. "Wasn't planning to stay long."

We find out he's been breaking in to sleep here, because he left his house. I get the impression there are details he'd rather not go into in front of me. But his story is enough to convince Wrath not to murder the kid.

"I should have him show Z how he broke into the other system," Wrath says to me.

Obviously the kid can't stay with us and he can't stay at the gym. Since they're still prospects, Hoot and Birch haven't earned a room at the club-house yet. Their apartment is halfway between Crystal Ball and Wrath's gym, and that's where we drop Twitch off.

Wrath's laughing by the time we get on the highway. "Jesus Christ, can you believe that shit?"

"No."

As soon as we're in my bedroom, Wrath wraps his arms around me. "Since we were interrupted at the gym, how 'bout a do over? That filthy mouth of yours was a big fuckin' turn on."

I burst out laughing. "I don't think my ass can take it."

CHAPTER THIRTY-FIVE

Trinity

The rest of our weekend is excitement-free. No more break-ins at Wrath's gym. The group returns on Sunday. Hope seems unimpressed with our downstate charter and I smother a smile when she describes Tawny using a bunch of big words that basically add up to "scary biker bitch."

The guys spend the afternoon unloading the van. Hope runs home, which clearly irritates Rock. I mind my own business on both issues.

Teller calls with news that his grandmother died and wants to know if he can bring Heidi to the clubhouse. I promise to have Rock call him back right away.

Since I'm not sure what the guys are actually doing out in the garage, I call out for Rock instead of going inside.

"What's up, Trinny?" he asks as he marches out to meet me.

"Teller's grandmother died. He wants to bring Heidi up. He asked if you'd call him back."

"Fuck. Yeah of course." He pulls out his own phone and walks way.

Wrath navigates his way to me and I fill him in.

"Poor bug. Kid's had it rough her whole life." I melt at the way he talks about Heidi, even though I know most of the time he thinks she's a brat.

He's wrong about himself, he'd be a great dad.

Heidi won't look or speak to any of us when she gets here. Not even

Murphy cheers her up. Axel also joins us, but she rolls herself into a ball on the couch and sobs.

Rejected for the second time, Murphy storms past me. "She's asking for Hope."

Well, at least it's something.

Hope makes it back quick and Heidi responds to her right away. I'm not jealous. Don't have a motherly bone in my body.

What I *can* do is help Teller make the funeral arrangements. I also call Swan and ask her to come up and give me a hand.

The day of the funeral, Wrath warns me Tawny and Sway are coming up. Just what I need.

While I'm in the kitchen with Hope, I figure I better warn her in case Rock hasn't.

"Heads up—Sway and Tawny are on their way up for the funeral."

"Oh. That's nice of them."

Sometimes I understand why Wrath calls her clueless. "More than likely, he's using it as an excuse to come up for something else."

"Oh. Are you worried?" she asks.

"Not really." I better tell her this now. "I won't be offended if you want to boss me around in front of Tawny."

A harsh chuckle bursts out of her. "Yeah, that's not happening, Trin."

God bless her. "I'm not an ol' lady, Hope."

She pins me with a hard stare. "I don't give a fuck. You're my friend."

My chest burns with so much emotion, I'm going to burst into tears or laughter. "Wow, look at you with the potty mouth," I tease.

"What are you talking about? I swear all the time." She almost sounds insulted.

Our silly discussion is interrupted by Rock and Wrath storming into the kitchen. "You girls okay?" Rock asks, his gaze dashing between the two of us.

"Yeah, Hope's just cussing like a sailor," I tell him.

Rock's eyebrow quirks up.

Wrath shakes his head. "Cinderella."

Rock takes her out of the kitchen and Wrath closes in on me.

"We need to talk."

WRATH

Z and I have to call the guys to church the morning of the funeral.

Even though Teller specifically asked the brothers not to make a fuss, Sway's using the service as an excuse to come visit. What he really wants, is to grab some guns he mistakenly gave us. Rock knows I'm annoyed. About the guns, yeah. That's some stupid, fucked-up shit. But after what Trin told me, I don't want Sway anywhere near her. Tawny either. She tosses any bullshit at Trinity, I'll knock her big-haired ass out.

"Rock, unless you think you need me, I'm going to hang with Trinity." Been to enough fuckin' funerals in my life. Don't need to go to one for a woman I barely know who hates my guts.

"Yeah. That's fine. I gotta give Hope a head's up that Tawny's coming." He runs his hands over his face. "What a pain in the balls."

"No shit."

We find the girls in the kitchen. Rock takes Hope and I corner Trinity. "We need to talk." Reaching out, I brush some hair off her face and her eyes close. "You need some rest, babe."

"I know. Once today's over with."

"Listen, I'm gonna hang with you at the house. I know I'm not much help—"

"But you want to keep Sway away from me?"

Shit. Guess I'm pretty fuckin' obvious. "Yeah."

She sighs. "Thanks, I appreciate it."

I expected her to kick up more of a fuss.

When we get out to the grandmother's house, Teller lets us in. "Thanks so much, guys," he mumbles before taking off.

Trinity

I'm happy to be in charge of providing refreshments to everyone after the funeral. With Wyatt sitting at the kitchen table, keeping a close eye on me, I'm able to organize the unfamiliar space quickly.

Besides a few civilian friends of Heidi and Teller, friends of the grandmother's also show up. It's a weird mix of elderly and bikers.

Wrath comes over and squeezes my arm. His mouth quirks up. But before he says what's on his mind, he gets a text. "Fuck, Rock needs me outside for a sec. You okay in here?"

I haven't seen Tawny or Sway yet, so I nod.

He's not gone five seconds before Tawny sashays into the kitchen like she fuckin' owns it. God, I hate this bitch.

"Don't you have someone you should be servicing?" she says instead of an actual greeting.

"Just doing my job. Can I get you anything?" I ask sweetly.

"I thought your job was getting on your knees when a brother asks. You think you're hot shit because that scary mountain man's panting after you today? That ain't gonna last. None of these guys will take used goods as an old lady."

The fact that I *know* this bitch fucks around behind her husband's back, and yet has the nerve to judge *me*, pisses me off. I'm trying to come up with a clever way to say that when she asks where Hope is.

"She should be taking care of this stuff, not you," she bitches. I almost snort at that. Hope's not particularly domestic.

As if she knew we were talking about her, Hope wanders in. "Hi, Tawny," she says brightly.

The old bitch is all sunshine and unicorns for Hope. "There you are. *The* old lady of the upstate charter."

I throw Hope a thumbs up for distracting Tawny and breathe a sigh of relief when they leave the kitchen.

But her damage is done. The words *used goods* keep banging around in my head and I don't know how to stop them.

WRATH

I want to pump my fist in the air when I get the okay from Rock to have the girls wrap things up at Teller's house.

Get me the fuck outta here. Trin's quiet and I just know Tawny did something to upset my girl. Need to get her alone to figure out what it is so I can fix it.

Sway and Tawny take forever to leave. The whole time I'm making small talk with Sway outside our clubhouse, I want to plant my fist in his throat. Once they leave, I'm on the hunt for my girl. Z stops me right before I get to the kitchen.

"They leave?" he asks.

"Yeah, finally. You seen Trin?"

"No." His mouth turns up. "You shoulda heard Hope this morning, tellin' Rock she ain't gonna treat Trinity bad just to impress Queen Bitch."

"What're you talking about?"

His shoulders lift. "I dunno. Somethin' musta went down when we were visiting. I was busy gettin' shot—"

"Quit your whining."

He just laughs. "Tawny must have told her to boss Trin around or something and Hope told Rock—not happening."

Fuck me. I want to protect Trin, but there's some things...well, I'm real happy she's got someone else in her corner.

I catch up to my girl in the kitchen.

"You avoiding me, Angel Face?" I whisper in her ear.

The tremor that runs through her body gets me hard as fuckin' steel. "You done in here?"

"I guess so."

"Good. I need you to myself."

She gives me a strange look. "You were with me all day."

"Not the same."

I steer her to her room, and close the door behind us. "What's wrong?"

She shakes her head, but something's bothering her. "Tell me."

"Nothing. Tawny just got in my head."

I don't like the sounds of that at all.

"Tell me."

Pain twists her face. "Nothing. Same old shit."

We're sitting side-by-side on her bed but she's staring at her hands in her lap.

"Hey, fuck her." I grab one of her hands until she looks at me.

A smile tips the corners of her mouth up. "You're so sweet for a Wrecking Ball," she teases.

"Only to you." Any more words are lost as she leans over and kisses me.

"Thanks for sticking with me today."

"Obviously I didn't do a good job."

"Yeah, you did."

She stands and slips off the plain, black sweater and dark jeans.

I raise an eyebrow when she pauses to look at me. "Keep going."

Instead of stripping down, she walks forward and presses into me. That's fine. I take the opportunity to run my hands over her bare skin.

Flipping her onto the bed, I lean over her and take her mouth. She stretches, arching her back, arms over her head. Spread out like a playboy fantasy, all for me. I lock down a hard shudder that threatens to work through my body.

"Tell me what you want, Trin."

"You. I want your big, rough hands all over me. I want you to take me. *Hard.*"

My mouth goes dry. "I can do that."

"I know you can." She beckons me closer. "First, come here."

It's awkward, but she gets me in the middle of the bed and strips off my shirt. Slowly, admiring every bit.

She keeps her eyes on mine while she works my shorts off. "Weren't you cold in shorts?" she asks as she tosses them on the floor.

"Nope. I'm always hot when I'm around you."

She laughs at the silly line. I'd laugh too, but she's curled her fingers around my dick and I can't form any sounds. Each slide of her palm shifts my entire world.

Next, she drags her tongue along the head of my cock, unhinging my fucking mind. At my sides, my fists clench and release. I sprawl one hand across the nape of her neck, then back off.

She pulls back and lifts her lips in a sultry smile. "Don't hold back."

CHAPTER THIRTY-SIX

Trinity

After the funeral things return to normal around the clubhouse. I divide my time between helping Wrath out, taking care of the clubhouse, my book covers and planning an engagement party for Hope and Rock.

They haven't set an actual wedding date yet, but we nail down a date for the engagement party and the menu. Hope is oddly impressed with my party planning skills and leaves most of it up to me. I want everything to be perfect for the two of them.

Taking care of Wrath means running him to the gym to oversee things, physical therapy and doctor appointments.

And stopping him from killing the doctor when he says he has to keep the cast on at least another week.

"You said that last week!" he snaps.

The doctor isn't impressed by Wrath's outburst. I can't decide if that makes him brave or stupid.

"I understand, but we want it to heal correctly," he says with the same tone one would use on a rowdy toddler.

Wrath's agitated for more reasons than just the cast. He admits it while we're on our way home. "Sparky's crop is sick. We're fucked."

"Shit."

"Yeah."

"Our connection's been up in our business for weeks now and this is making it worse."

"Anything I can do?"

"No. I just wanted you to be aware. Don't want you going out by yourself."

"You think they'd bother me?"

"No. But I still want you to be careful."

"Okay." I don't press for more details. That's not how our relationship works.

Sure enough, Wrath gets called in for church later that night. He's weary when he returns.

"No one likes it when I play devil's advocate," he sighs as he lies down next to me.

"Aw, poor Wyatt," I tease.

"Damn right."

I'm glad Wrath warned me, because the guys are all on edge. At least I know why. I try to make myself as invisible as possible.

While he says things are fine, I still sense a lot of tension in the club-house. Wrath's more fidgety than normal. I know he's eager to get back to being the muscle for the club.

At his next appointment, the doctor takes another X-ray and spends a lot of time checking Wrath's leg over.

"Okay, Mr. Ramsey, I'm going to call the cast tech in to remove the cast."

Wrath looks so damn hopeful I almost laugh.

"Is it staying off?" he asks.

"Well, I'll do another examination of your leg when it's off, but I think so."

"Thank God."

Butterflies zip and dance around in my stomach.

"You need physical therapy. No driving for another three to six weeks."

I expect Wrath to blow up, but he nods and grabs my hand. "I've gotten used to my chauffeur."

That's sweet and I'm not sure what to say.

As usual, Wrath kicks me out when the cast tech enters the room. "I'm going to see it eventually," I remind him. He smirks and still sends me on my way.

While I wait, I text Rock and Z to give them the good news. I get a smiley face back from Z right away, but nothing from Rock.

When Wrath finally emerges, he's lost both the cast and his cocky grin. He has, however been outfitted with a cane.

I wiggle my eyebrows at him. "Sexy."

One corner of his mouth lifts.

"Are you happy?" I ask once we're on our way home.

"Yes. I've got a long list of positions I need to fuck you in."

My skin simmers with heat. A glance at the dashboard shows that, no, the heat's not on. It's all Wrath and what his dirty words do to me.

"Besides that?" I ask.

He huffs out a low laugh. "Yeah, angel. Pissed I won't be able to ride for a while."

"We'll get you set up with the physical therapist—"

"I know." He reaches over and squeezes my upper thigh. "I'm more concerned with making my announcement."

Why do those words make my skin tingle?

"You…you still want to do that?"

"Fuck yeah, babe."

My heart bangs so hard, it might jump out of my chest.

Z meets us at the front door to give Wrath a big welcome home hug and back slap. "When can we ride, brother?"

"Six to eight weeks," Wrath grumbles.

"Fuck man, really?"

I don't bother correcting Wrath. I figure he has his reasons for giving the wrong time frame and if he wants to tell me, he will.

WRATH

Trinity seemed less than enthused when I reminded her of my plans to announce our relationship.

Too bad. She's the one who said to wait until the cast is off. Well, it's fuckin' off. Nothing's gonna stop me from claiming my girl now.

Rock looks like fuckin' shit the next morning. "What's up with you?" I ask as he drops into the chair across from me.

"Where's Hope?" Z asks. "Second morning without her here. I miss the little ball-buster."

I shoot a look at Z who's apparently completely sincere.

Something's seriously wrong. Rock's got his I'm-going-to-gut-all-of-you face on. He usually saves that one for special occasions.

"We're taking a break," he announces without looking at any of us.

Fuck me.

Z's face darkens. "What the fuck does that mean?" he asks. *Huh.* I never pegged Z for the suicidal type.

Rock tips his head up and drills a murderous look at Z. "It means exactly what I said. What do you need explained?"

Trinity gets up and leaves the table.

"Sorry, brother," I say.

He turns his angry glare on me. "What are you sorry about? Thought you'd be thrilled."

"Come on, man—"

"Can we talk about something else?" It might be phrased as a question, but Rock's done with this conversation.

I get up and shove my chair in. "Talk about whatever you want. I'm gonna check on Trinity."

As I limp my way into the kitchen, I'm fucking furious. Furious that my leg still hurts and furious that Trinity's upset. Okay, and a little furious about whatever Rock did to chase Cinderella away.

Trin's busy banging stuff around the kitchen and doesn't acknowledge me at first.

"You okay, babe?"

"I'm fine."

When she finishes slamming everything into cabinets and drawers she finally faces me. "Why didn't she call me or let me know what happened? I thought we were friends."

Aw, shit. Now I really want to kick Rock's ass. Pulling her into my arms, I squeeze her tight. "I'm sure she's upset. And she thinks your loyalty's to the club. She probably didn't want to make things awkward for you."

She sniffles against my shoulder and pulls away. "You're probably right. Fuck. Poor Rock."

Poor Rock nothing.

Trinity refuses to join us at the table—for breakfast or any other meal —after that; something I blame on Rock. To my surprise, she keeps planning their engagement party. I don't have the heart to tell her a wedding is looking unlikelier by the day.

Our issue with Green Street Crew keeps gettin' worse. If Sparky doesn't figure out the plants soon, we're going to have a big problem on our hands.

What I'm really pissed about though is that I haven't made my announcement yet. With whatever's going on with Rock, I feel it's the wrong time. And because I'm a complete asshole, it bugs me that Trinity's not more upset about the delay.

"That's fine. I understand."

Shit. Does she think I'm using it as an excuse to get out of doing it?

We're in the parking lot behind my gym, so I can test out my reflexes behind the wheel. The weakness in my leg is pissing me the fuck off.

"It hasn't been that long. Give it time. You're in better shape than ninety-nine percent of guys out there. You'll heal quick," Trin reassures me.

"Thanks, babe."

Jake's thrilled to see me out of the cast so he can start abusing me again.

He takes one look at the exercises the physical therapist gave me and grins like the sadistic little bastard he is.

"Go get changed, son."

"You know I'm older than you, right?"

He shrugs. "Stop being a little bitch."

Fucker.

Trin brought her laptop and keeps herself busy in my office.

"Why's she still coming here?" Whisper asks when he sees her.

"Still can't drive," I huff out while pulling myself up on the chin-up bar. I'm pretty pissed about how much I've let myself go the last few months.

"People gonna think she's your ol' lady pretty soon."

Fuck it. I'm tired of pretending otherwise. "Good. People *should* get used to that idea."

Whisper has the nerve to chuckle. "You serious? She's fucked half your club and mine."

Next to me Jake shakes his head. "Dude," he mutters.

I drop down to the mat, too furious to feel anything except how good my fist's gonna feel planted in Whisper's jaw.

Asshole doesn't even see the blow coming. I kneel down next to him on the mat. "Next time you comment about my girl like that, I'll fuckin' kill you."

He moves to get up and I jab my finger in his chest. "Stay down, or I'll knock you the fuck out."

"Fine. Fuck. I'm sorry," he spits out.

"Wyatt? What's wrong?"

Shit. Trin comes running over. "You okay, Whisper?" she asks. As if the fuck deserves her concern.

"Just havin' a conversation with *your man*, sweetheart."

"Shut *up*, dude," Jake mutters under his breath.

I really am gonna have to kill Whisper. Trin's face falls and her eyes skip to me. She's smarter than all three of us combined. I can practically see the gears turning in her head as she stops in her tracks. Her gaze darts between me and Whisper. "Wyatt?"

"It's nothin'. Go pack up, babe. I'm done here."

"Okay." She turns and leaves us.

We hardly speak on the way home. As soon as we're in her room though, she bursts into tears. "I'm sorry."

Pulling her into my hold, I run my hands over her back. "Shhh. About what?"

"That fight with Whisper was about me, wasn't it?"

See? Smart.

"No. It was about him being an asshole."

She shakes her head and pulls away. "How do you ever think this is going to work? I'm too experienced—"

"Yeah, I'm thirty-fucking-six, I'm just dying to be with a virgin."

She shakes off my sarcastic tone. "This will keep happening. You shouldn't have used goods as your ol' lady."

"First, don't ever call yourself that again."

"Wyatt. I've known guys in the life. They want to own their—"

She's not fucking listening again. Cupping her chin in my hand, I give her a gentle squeeze and turn her to face me.

"I am *not* the sick fucks you grew up around. I'm Wyatt Ramsey and I love *you*. And if you think for one second I don't already own your pussy, you're dead fucking wrong."

She sighs. "Wrath—"

Am I mistaken? Is she fighting me so hard because she honestly believes she's no good for me? Or is this her twisted way of letting me down easy?

The idea leaves me cold.

"Babe, I'm not trying to force you into somethin' you don't want." My stomach's churning at the thought.

Her jaw drops, shiny tears fill her eyes and she drops to her knees, laying her head on my thigh, wrapping her arms around my leg. "I'm sorry," she whispers.

It's impossible not to comfort her. My hand runs over her hair. "You're making things so much more complicated than they need to be, angel. Stop trying to second guess everything I tell you."

"I'm sor—"

"Shhh. No more. Don't apologize for who you are."

We're silent for a while. It takes me a second to realize her hand is creeping up near my dick before she starts fiddling with my belt.

My hand wraps over hers stopping her.

"No."

"Wrath," she pleads.

"I said no." I shift, so I can stand. Fuck, having her on her knees in front of me is making this fucking hard, but it needs to be done.

"Get up. Let's go for a walk."

"What? You're rejecting me? After you just said—"

Gripping her arms, I yank her to her feet. "I'm *not* rejecting you. Not now. Not ever. I'm trying to show you that you mean more to me than a couple of holes to stick my dick in. Grab a sweatshirt, and let's go—now."

Trinity

Even though I feel guilty about Wrath limping through the woods, the walk helps clear my head.

We reach the stone amphitheater and I plop down onto one of the low benches. "I thought if Rock and Hope got married on the property, this would be a good spot," I tell Wrath as he sits next to me.

He chuckles. "First time we looked at the place, I figured the cult that owned it must have held virgin sacrifices out here."

"Oh my God." I laugh and shove him away. I think back to what he said in my bedroom. "Did you mean what you said?"

He gestures to the stone structures in front of us. "Fuck yeah, they got an altar and everything."

Shaking my head, I grab his hand and pull it into my lap. "No. What you said in my room."

"Which part? That I already own your pussy? I definitely meant that."

"You're nuts."

"Yeah, but you love it."

I do. Why can't I say it? "It really doesn't bother you?"

"The only thing that bothers me, is how much time we've wasted being pissed at each other." He pauses and his mouth quirks up. Whatever he's about to say will be completely obnoxious. "Besides, think about what a cocky asshole I am. I've got total reassurance I'm the best you've ever had."

How can I not laugh at that? I shove him away. "You're unbelievable." Of course he grins like a fool. "You're right though. You're the only person I've ever pictured spending the rest of my life with." I wave my hand in the air. "Back then...through the years...now." Shit, I feel raw admitting that to him.

He pulls me tight against his chest and runs his hands over me. "Thank you, Trinity."

We stay like that for a while. It's completely peaceful and there's nowhere else I'd rather be.

"Trinity?"

"Yes, Wyatt."

"Would *you* want to get married here?"

Married? His question sets my heart on overdrive.

"Fletcher Park," I blurt out. Because yes, I've allowed myself to be stupid over the years and daydream about such a thing.

"*Hmmm.*" The sound vibrates through me and I feel him nod against my head. "Yeah."

We sit there holding hands a little longer. The wind picks up and I shiver. Wrath glances at me. "Think you'd want to take off to Florida when we're older?"

That's where a lot of retired Kings end up. They usually visit and cause trouble in the summer.

"Sure. I can totally picture you riding down the coast on a nice, big Harley Tri-Glide."

He rolls his eyes at me, then pulls me to my feet. "As long as you're on the back of it."

When we get back to the clubhouse a little later, Z and Rock are standing in front of the television wearing some very unhappy expressions. "Is everything okay?"

They both turn and stare at us and Rock mutes the television. He lifts his chin at Wrath. "Call everyone in for church." Next, his serious gray eyes land on me. "Trin, you need to stay close to the house."

I don't even ask why. Rock wouldn't say it if there wasn't a good reason. "No problem, prez."

Wrath kisses the top of my head and enters the office he shares with Z and Rock.

"Do you need me to do anything?"

Rock glances at the war room, then back at me. "If you can put some coffee on and throw together some sandwiches or something when the guys get here, I'd appreciate it."

"No problem." Over his shoulder I catch the headline scrolling across the screen. *Local Gang Member's Body Dragged From Hudson River.*

Guys stream in all afternoon. A couple of brothers from downstate even show up. Z leaves after church. The situation can't be too dire, because things turn into a party as the night goes on. Someone brings a bunch of girls up. A few I don't recognize and briefly wonder if they're even legal.

Rock disappears upstairs as soon as someone turns the music up. I hate how miserable he's been since Hope left.

As I'm running around bringing out food and drinks, Wrath calls me over.

He's sitting next to Teller. My gaze darts between the two of them, trying to figure out what's up. "Yeah?"

He pats his lap and pulls me down. "I think you're done. Let the prospects take care of things," he says against my ear.

"But—"

A quick shake of his head cuts off any protest. Teller chuckles uncomfortably.

"Who's responsible for bringing up the barely legal crowd?" I ask him, nodding at the two girls putting on a show in the middle of the room.

Teller's mouth twists into a smirk. "They're legal. They go to school with Axel."

Okay. That surprises me. I've never seen Axel's gaze stray a centimeter from Heidi. Then I laugh, wondering if it's his way of distracting Murphy from Heidi. "I thought he was going for diesel mechanics? They got girls in that program?"

He laughs at my question. "No clue. Hot, female, diesel mechanics, though? They'll probably make a fortune."

I roll my eyes.

"You should take them up to visit Rock," Wrath suggests.

I twist to glare at him.

Teller shrugs. "I don't think that's a good idea."

"No, seriously. He's been miserable. Maybe it will help him get his head out of his ass. Or at the very least give him some stress relief."

With another shrug, Teller gets up and talks to the two girls.

"What's the matter with you?" I ask Wrath. His eyebrows shoot up. "Do *not* make your cute *Who me?* face, either, Wyatt. I'm serious. Why would you do that?"

He can't stop laughing long enough to answer.

"You're such a jerk. He'll probably kill Teller and scare the shit out of those poor girls."

Sure enough, a couple minutes later the girls come running back downstairs.

"Let's go to bed, Angel Face. I've had enough excitement for one day."

CHAPTER THIRTY-SEVEN

WRATH

"You know I feel like an epic douche, right?" I grumble as Trinity crouches down to snap another pic.

She flashes a devious grin. "Why, 'cause you just said, 'epic'?"

I grumble some more at that. This is my reward for finally taking my bike out. I wasn't comfortable going too far, so Trinity and I decided Fletcher Park was enough of a ride. I didn't think anything of it when she grabbed all her camera equipment.

Then she reminded me that I said I might let her take some photos of me for her book covers.

"The important word there was *might*, angel."

Somehow she talks me into it.

At first it's not so bad, having her fawning all over me. Snapping photo after photo. Me on my bike, next to my bike, arms crossed over my chest, hands on my hips, nose in my armpit, whatever. The grin on her face keeps me motivated. Until she asks me to strip off my T-shirt and throw my cut back on.

I cock my head at her. "You realize no self-respecting outlaw would ride bare-chested with his cut on, right?"

Her musical laughter relaxes me. I find myself in the ridiculous pose, even though I feel like a complete jackass.

She raises an eyebrow. "Yeah, but think of all the panties you'll melt."

"Only panties I'm worried about melting are yours, babe."

"I'm not wearing any panties, Wyatt."

Fuck me.

"Prove it."

"Uh-uh. We don't have much daylight left."

Bending over she flashes me an eyeful of cleavage. I'm pretty sure she wore the tight, button-up vest shirt for my benefit. It definitely distracted me when she was talking me into this.

Every time she leans over or moves the right way, I get a nice flash of the creamy swells of her breasts spilling out of the top or glimpses of flat stomach when she stands. It's been enough to keep me from complaining so far.

"What the fuck is that for?" I ask as she approaches me with a bottle of baby oil.

"I want to oil you up."

"Are you serious?"

Her bottom lip pushes into that sexy fucking pout that makes me agree to do stupid things. "Fine," I mumble.

Her warm hands feel good rubbing the slippery crap into my skin. She pays extra attention to my arms and chest. When she's finished, she plants a kiss on my cheek and darts away.

"Can you turn away? Look pensive and thoughtful."

"You promised you'd crop my face out," I say as I turn the way she asked.

"I will, I just need you from chin to crotch."

She gives me a bunch more directions, and at a certain point, I realize she's fucking with me.

"Come here, Angel Face."

She must sense my less than honorable intentions, because she carefully packs her camera away and slips one of the straps of the backpack over her shoulder. Towel in hand, she approaches. After wiping the baby oil off, she slips my cut down my arms and hands me my shirt. I give it a quick tug, and she topples into my lap.

"Gotcha." My fingers brush against some loose strands of hair, tucking them behind her ear.

A ghost of a smile touches her lips. "I think I got some great shots. Thank you for doing this for me."

She's suddenly so serious.

"Only you could talk me into this, Trin. That's how much I love you."

My words seem to stress her out, rather than make her happy.

"Thank you."

Am I annoyed that she still can't admit she loves me? Yeah. Am I going to make a big deal out of it and pick a fight? Fuck, no.

She takes a step back, sticks her hand in her pocket and fidgets with something.

"I've, um, been carrying this around for a while now. To give you." She hands over a folded up piece of paper.

"What is it, angel?"

Her eyes gloss over. "I—"

Unfolding it, I see what she's written and my chest tightens.

Shit. I'm actually choked up and can't form any words. Instead, I hold out my arms and she throws herself against me.

"I'm sorry I'm so messed up, Wyatt."

"You're not messed up, baby. Or if you are, you're my kind of messed up."

"Thank you," she mumbles against my shirt.

"You gonna let me claim you now? Tell everyone you're my girl?"

She freezes, then nods. "Yes."

Finally.

"Let's go home."

Trinity

What an afternoon. Like a scared little girl, I finally gave Wrath my note. I'm still stinging from humiliation because I can't just say the words.

But he doesn't press me any further. In his eyes, I see my words affected him. There's a fierce protectiveness mixed with surprising tenderness. It makes me feel safe and vulnerable at the same time.

In my room, his hands travel over the contours of my body. I'm able to push away all thoughts about tomorrow or the announcement Wrath wants to make. My only thoughts are of where his hands are and what I want to do to him.

He lowers his mouth to mine. Our lips meet, the kiss hard and demanding. I need that edge, the possessiveness that my body responds to.

"I love kissing you," he murmurs as he pulls away, trailing kisses down my jaw, nuzzling my neck. "You teased the fuck out of me with this shirt today."

As he says it, his hands work the three buttons loose. I'd hesitated this morning, since it was more revealing than I normally dared, but obviously the shirt was a good choice. My fingers creep under the hem of his shirt. "No fair, you've been looking at me all day," he teases.

He lets me strip it off anyway, and I stop to admire him.

"Love the way you look at me, angel."

"I love looking at you."

"What do you want?"

"I want to taste you," I say as I nudge him over to the bed.

"Trinity—"

"Please?" I beg with a sly grin on my face.

I run my hand down his chest and over the very large bulge in his pants. He groans and I love how his breathing increases. Unzipping his pants, I drop to my knees in front of him.

This has never been my favorite thing. With one or two forced exceptions, I've held fast to my rule. Never on my knees. It's too powerless. Reminds me of a time when I had no control at all. Over anything.

With Wyatt, things have been different from our very first night together. Kneeling before him, I feel invincible, sexy, beautiful, and in complete control. He likes me to keep my eyes on him. Angel eyes he calls them. If anyone else called me that, I'd laugh, but not Wyatt.

He means it.

His deep blue eyes focus on me as I pleasure him. Every lick, suck and flick of my tongue registers across his face. A soft hiss when I take him deep sends a rush of arousal through me. Something I've never experienced while using my mouth on a man. His heavy breathing makes me want to please him, to take him right to the back of my throat. In and out. Salty pre-cum hits my tongue and I lap it up. He's close to blowing and that sends a shudder of pleasure through me.

It's a struggle to keep my eyes up and focused, but I do it because I know how much he enjoys it. I want to sink into the sensation of teasing and tasting him, but this isn't for me. He gasps for air, but keeps his eyes locked on mine. He's frightening in his intensity, but somehow I feel like the one in charge.

"Do you know how beautiful you are?"

Does he expect me to answer? His tone is so serious. Not just sexy talk. I nod once. I do feel pretty under him. He makes me feel a lot of things.

A deep breath lifts his muscled chest. "You're all mine, Angel Face."

Damn, I want to be his. I really do.

"That's right. Taste every part of me. This is the only cock in your mouth and I'm the only man you're fucking from now on." His rough voice surrounds me. The possessive, crude words stir up an ache that only he's ever been able to soothe.

I hum and nod and his cock twitches. Up and down I slide my mouth over him, swirling my tongue over his head, then taking him as far as I can go. With someone else I might feel debased, but his worshipful gaze holds all my usual insecurities and fears at bay. In his eyes I see a promise to protect and cherish me.

My nails dig into the back of his hard thighs. His hands thread through my hair, tightening as he takes control of the pace.

"Get ready." His low, deep voice sounds almost primal. I *love* it.

If anyone else showed me that raw, brutal intensity, I'd probably run screaming from the room. But even when we've been enemies, Wrath has always treated my body—if not my heart—carefully.

"Fuck," he grinds out. His rasping voice has my eyes rolling back in my head.

"Eyes, angel," he pants, too worked up to get out more. "So close."

Above me, he stiffens and lets out a hoarse gasp. His face contorts into something mesmerizing and beautiful. Hot cum fills my mouth and even though I'm expecting it, I jolt in surprise. I work down a hard swallow. A warm rush of arousal sizzles between my thighs. Never have I gotten so turned on giving a guy head. Wyatt's fingers grip my chin, his blue eyes searching mine.

"Thank you."

That he thanks me so honestly, twists my insides. This big, powerful man could hold me down and force me to do whatever he wanted. Yet he's always so gentle with me. Sweet even. A side of him that belongs only to me.

Suddenly, he swings me up into his powerful arms. A giggle works out of me and I kiss his sweaty chest, then lick my way to his neck.

"Give me a second," he groans.

My body hums in anticipation as he lays me out on the bed. I know we're not finished yet.

"Please," I beg. I never thought I'd want someone to do what I'm asking. Or enjoy it so much. But I *need* it.

He kneels between my legs. "Ask me again."

Something dark and urgent sparks in his eyes making me shiver.

"Please put your mouth on my pussy."

"You kill me," he mumbles. His head dips down, tongue licking from my opening to clit. My fingers run through his short, soft hair and he shivers.

Feeling brave, I brush my fingertips over his cheek. "Get to know that pussy well, Wyatt. It's the only one you're getting from now on," I whisper, echoing his earlier words.

He stops and grins up at me. "About fucking time you admit it. Arms over your head, Angel Face. Stretch out your beautiful body for me. Let me see what's mine."

With him, I forget I even have scars. He accepts all of me. Always has. I don't hesitate to do as he asks. We established a long time ago, I'll do anything Wyatt wants. He waits until my fingertips touch the headboard before resuming his sensual torture. First, he works his fingers over my slippery flesh, teasing me with hard pressure, but not entering me or touching my aching clit. He pauses and hooks my legs over his thick shoulders. My body squirms under his intense gaze.

Finally, his tongue's on me. Swirling, tasting, licking.

He lifts his head, grinning at me. "Too much?"

"No."

It is too much though. I'm scared. He has me so wound up, afraid to let go. Afraid I *can't* let go.

He presses soft kisses against my inner thighs, then tongues my outer lips. His hand presses down against my lower stomach, holding me in place, while his tongue drives me crazy. He works into a perfect rhythm of kissing and licking every part of me before finally sucking softly on my clit. I squirm and pant. One finger slips inside and I let out a curse.

"Shhh. Stop fighting me. Relax."

Relax. As if that's possible with his tongue working my clit, his fingers fucking my pussy and his hand pressing me down into the mattress.

"Wy—oh, shit. Wyatt! What are you doing to me?"

"Let go for me, Angel Face."

My eyes screw shut with the unbearable pressure. Sensations pulse behind my eyelids. "I can't," I gasp.

He makes a humming noise against my clit that sends me spiraling higher.

"Yes, come for me."

Words are beyond me, I'm trying so hard to follow what he's doing, to go where he's leading me.

"Stop trying. Relax. Just feel."

Feel? It feels fucking amazing and my body finally unlocks. "Yes."

"Good girl."

I give myself over to the wonderful sensations, fingers pulsing in and out, pressure, his mouth over my clit, sucking, tongue licking. One or all of those things send me over.

"Eyes," he commands.

My eyes pop open right as the orgasm crashes over me. I gasp and cry out, my hips bucking off the mattress. My vision goes white, as his mouth seals over my pussy, licking and sucking everything.

"Holy fuck," I manage to get out.

He climbs up my body with a smug smile on his glistening lips. "Fucking beautiful, Trinity."

My breathing's still ragged. Heart racing. "What did you do to me?"

"Babe, it's really what you did for me. Feeling like a superhero now."

I tap his chest with my fist. "You nut."

"Yup. Come here." He gathers me close, trailing gentle touches over my body. "You're all pink and pretty," he whispers against my neck.

"I don't think I've ever come so hard in my life." I'm still blown away.

He nuzzles and licks at my neck. "Good."

I'm drifting in and out, when Wyatt's arms tighten around me. "You're mine. No more hiding. No more denying. Gonna tell the whole club at church," he whispers against my hair. He says it very matter of fact, as if the commitment he's proposing is the easiest thing in the world. As if it won't cause a shit storm of problems for him.

As a reflex, I start to shake my head, but his arms band around me tighter. "Stop fighting it, Trinity. I'll take care of everything. Promise. You're mine," he says again.

Sweet mercy, I want it to be true. But I'm terrified.

CHAPTER THIRTY-EIGHT

WRATH

My girl's all worn out. I love watching her sleep. Not in a creepy way. In an I-can't-believe-she's-finally-mine way. Having the cast off is newfound freedom. I haven't gotten through half the positions I've been planning to fuck her in yet.

Time for fucking around with our relationship is over.

I slip out the door, making sure to close it as quietly as possible.

Trin's been nervous since I told her I'm making my announcement. Tough. She's had plenty of time to get used to the idea.

"Can we talk?" I ask when I find Rock.

He nods, and we step into the war room.

"Door open or closed?" he asks and I shrug.

"I'm making my announcement at church."

His face breaks into a huge grin. First time I've seen him smile since Hope left. "Thank fuck."

He pulls me in for quick hug, slapping my back.

"I'm sorry. I know with you and Hope, it's shit timing."

"Brother, it's a long fucking time coming. I'm happy for both of you." And I know he genuinely means it.

"Thanks. I want to announce it in front of everyone, then take a vote."

He doesn't need me to explain why. "You got it."

His phone buzzes and his face undergoes a major transformation as he reads the text.

"Everything okay?"

He swallows hard. "It's Hope. She wants to see me."

The optimism in his eyes tells me all I need to know.

"Go bring her home, brother."

He slaps me on the shoulder and is out the door. I barely make it out of the war room before I hear his bike roar to life.

Z walks in shaking his head. "Where's he off to in such a fuckin' hurry?"

"Hope's"

"About fuckin' time."

Trinity meets us in the living room. All groggy and messy-haired from sleep, she's fuckin' beautiful. "Hope's coming back?"

"If not, we all better steer clear of him." No one laughs at my joke.

Trinity's face screws up. "I'm gonna get dressed and run down to Ward's to grab a few things so we can celebrate."

"Take Hoot with you," I say.

"You got it." She leans up and presses a kiss on my cheek.

"Christ, it will be nice to get back to normal," Z says as he throws himself on the couch.

"What's normal around here?"

He shrugs and smirks at the same time. "I dunno. Worrying about dead bodies gettin' pulled out of the Hudson?"

"That ain't funny, bro. I gotta give Whisper a call and see if anyone's ID'd that body yet."

"Yeah, it'd be nice to find out which fuckin' Viper, so we know if it's our problem or not."

"Amen to that, brother."

Murphy thunders down the stairs. "What's up?"

"Nothin'," Z answers. "I gotta take care of a few things. You good?" he asks me.

"Yeah."

Z disappears into our office.

Not much later, Rock returns with his girl.

"First lady!" Murphy shouts as soon as he sees her. "You're back," he says as he picks her up. Rock's so happy he's not even breaking Murphy's arms for touching his woman like that.

"I am," she answers through happy giggles.

She turns her big green eyes on me, and I'll admit, I'm happy to see her. "Missed you, sugar," I say as I drop a kiss on her head.

She gives me a curious look. Whatever she was going to say vanishes. "Your cast is finally off!" she shouts.

"Yup."

I'm stunned when she throws her arms around me for a fierce hug.

Teller pops in out of nowhere. "Glad to see you, Hope. Prez has been miserable without you."

"Fuck off," Rock growls at him.

I should probably feel a little guilty about that whole set up.

"Hey, sweetheart," Z calls as he steps out of the office. They share a hug and Z whispers something in her ear.

"Where's Trinity?" she asks, looking around the room.

Avoiding you. "She ran out for some supplies. She was hoping she'd be back before you got here."

Hope glances at Rock.

"I wasn't fucking around. You were coming back with me one way or another."

"I guess so."

He leans own to whisper in her ear and her cheeks flame pink.

"For fuck's sake, take her upstairs already. We don't need to see this," Z groans.

Rock glares at him. "Prospects should be back with her stuff soon. Tell them to leave it outside our door."

I didn't miss the way he said "our door."

"Got it."

Trinity pulls up maybe five minutes after Rock and Hope go upstairs.

"Well?" she asks, raising an eyebrow.

"They're upstairs. Can guarantee we won't see them for the rest of the night," Z says with a snicker.

"Oh."

I can tell Trinity's a mixture of disappointed and relieved. Not sure how that will play out tomorrow.

We all decide to use the grill out back and barbecue hamburgers for dinner. Not even the scent of burning meat outside his window lures Rock downstairs.

I find Trinity sitting by herself at the edge of the patio staring at her phone.

"What's wrong, babe?"

"Nothing." She shakes her head. "I'm not sure what to say to her."

I'm about to ask who, when I realize she's talking about Hope. "Tell her you've still been planning the engagement party."

The corners of her mouth turn up. "Yeah."

I sit next to her on the low stone wall that surrounds the property. "Tell her," I wrap my arms around her, dragging her into my lap. "If she wants you to be in the wedding, you have to wear a sexy fucking dress I can rip off you later." I punctuate my silliness by growling against her neck until she's giggling and pushing me away.

"That's more like it," I tease as I help her sit up. "Now, I'm starving. Go grab me a burger before Z burns them all."

She huffs and pushes me away. "You're so sweet and then ruin it by being all bossy."

"Yeah, but you love it."

CHAPTER THIRTY-NINE

Trinity

I'm in the gym across from my room at five in the morning and not even ten minutes later, Hope strolls in.

"Hey, Trinity," she greets. "I never got to see you last night."

"Yeah."

She's not dressed to work out, so I don't know why she's down here.

"Can we talk for a minute?" she asks.

"Why?"

She reels back as if I slapped her. I guess my tone was sharp. Maybe I'm still a little pissed.

Taking a few steps farther inside, she pins me with a pained look. "Are you mad at me?"

Dammit. I slow the treadmill down to a crawl and hop off.

"Why would I be mad at you?"

She fiddles with the hem of her shirt. "I missed you."

"Didn't seem like it. I thought we were friends, but I guess not."

Aw shit. Her eyes tear up. Seeing that she's about to cry, makes me want to cry.

"We are. But I didn't think...I know your loyalty is to Rock and the club first. I didn't think you'd want to be friends if we weren't together. And I didn't want to make things weird for you."

402

It's the same thing Wrath said.

"I'm still mad at you," I tell her.

"I don't blame you. I'm mad at myself."

"At least we agree on that," I say and then laugh.

She still looks like she's going to cry, and I can't stand it. "Give me a hug."

"I really did miss you," she says as she squeezes the daylights out of me.

"So why are you up at this ungodly hour?" I ask when we part.

Her shoulders jerk up. "I couldn't sleep. We had this big emotional talk that wore me out, but also gave me nightmares."

"Talk? You're supposed to have makeup sex."

She blushes like crazy and looks away. "We never got to that."

"You better get on that." I give her an evil grin. "Or better yet, get on Rock."

Her cheeks turn an even deeper red. "Oh my," she mumbles. Then shocks the hell out of me. "You're right. Maybe I'll try the wiggle-my-ass-against-him-by-accident move," she says, while demonstrating exactly what she means.

"I'm a big fan of that move myself," Wrath says from the doorway.

Hope jumps about ten feet in the air. "You jerk!" She whips her head around at me. "You need to put bells on him."

Wrath's laughing so hard he can barely talk. "No. Please demonstrate the wiggling your ass thing again."

"I'm out of here."

Wrath watches her go, then grins at me. "I think Z's about to get woken up again."

It's not until breakfast that I get to tell Hope I kept planning the engagement party.

"Trinity—I don't know what to say." Terrific. I made her cry again.

The boys distract her with car talk. After we eat, she follows me into the kitchen.

"Think you can still help me with that business?" I ask her.

"Of course. Are you going to tell me what it is?"

I take a deep breath and explain it. Why was I so nervous? Hope loves it. She claps her hands together. "Oh my gosh, that's amazing. You have to show me."

"I will." I feel like I owe her after Wrath razzed her this morning. "I even got to take some photos of Wrath the other day. He's agreed to be a cover model for me."

Her eyes go round with excitement. "I think I just died of happiness. Can I please make fun of him?"

"Not yet."

Rock interrupts our discussion by barging in the kitchen. "Can we go for a walk, baby doll? I want to show you something."

The corners of her mouth quirk up. "Yeah, sure."

"Stop by when you get back and I'll show you." I give her a quick hug. "Don't say anything to Rock yet, please," I whisper in her ear. She nods against me.

"We won't be gone long, Trin. Got church in an hour." Rock assures me.

"Okay."

Wrath's ready to vibrate out of his chair when I join the guys in the dining room. "What's wrong?"

He glances at me and squeezes my hand. "Nothing, babe."

Z snickers. "I'll give you one guess what those two are up to in the woods."

"Jesus Christ. Will you go get them? Everyone's almost here," Wrath bitches.

"You're excited to get back to being the Wrecking Ball, huh?" I tease him after Z leaves.

"Yeah, something like that."

WRATH

A guy like me can't afford to be nervous. But that's exactly what I am as we sit down at the table. I almost wore a hole in the floor waiting for Rock and Hope to return from their nature walk. While I'm happy they're back together, it's way past time for me to get my own business in order.

I'm not nervous about the regular club business. Everything's good there. "Plants are healing, boss. Yield's lookin' plentiful," Sparky informs the club. He credits Hope with their recovery, which makes me laugh. Crazy bugger is completely smitten with prez's ol' lady.

CB is strong now that we've cleared all the coke-sniffing sluts out.

Rock turns to me next. Not for my announcement. Not yet. "Gym's good. Thinking of keeping the kid on." Rock nods. He's been down there and so far approves of Irish. "Might even be a good prospect one day." Everyone at the table grumbles.

My mouth lifts into a smirk as I remember my conversation with

Whisper yesterday. "Supposedly, Ulfric's all freaked thinkin' you're pissed with him. Might wanna give him a call."

"Jesus Christ, what the fuck is going on with him lately?"

I shake my head. "No clue. But that little discovery was a major fuck-up on his end. He keeps that shit up, they're gonna vote him out."

Rock waves his hand in the air. "Whatever. Not our problem."

Murphy gives some details on a run he's trying to organize over the Fourth of July. Gonna have Trinity on the back of my bike for that and I can't fucking wait.

"Who wants to take the Demon drop with Z?" Rock asks.

I raise my hand right away and Rock nods. "Figured."

"Can we vote on introducing Loco to Sway next?" Rock asks, giving me a weary look. He thinks I'm gonna vote no, but I understand why this needs to happen.

The vote is unanimous.

We briefly discuss patching Hoot and Birch in. Their vote will be a no-brainer. Both of them are hard-working and fit to wear our colors. Axel has, at minimum, another year to go and by the look on Murphy's face, it's going to take some serious convincing to give Axel a seat at the table. It's too bad because he's a loyal kid and would be an asset to the club. Shit with Heidi is going to cause fuckin' trouble real soon and there ain't a whole lot we can do because she's the sister of a patched-in member. An office holder. So yeah, there's a real possibility Axel gets shipped off to a different Lost Kings charter. I wonder if Murphy's thought this through, because if Axel leaves, there's a good chance Heidi goes with him.

"I've got one, maybe two, kids at the gym who might make good prospects," I inform everyone.

Rock nods. "If they're eighteen, start bringing them 'round Crystal Ball when you think they're ready."

Christ, like I wanna hang anywhere near CB. Z smirks like he knows exactly what I'm thinking.

Once club business is out of the way, Rock glances at me. I nod. Hell, yeah motherfucker. Let's do this.

Rock holds one hand up to the group. "Hang tight, everyone. Wrath has an announcement."

I'm glad every brother is here while I deliver my message. "I'm claiming Trinity as my ol' lady. Anyone fucking looks at her with anything other than friendly, respectful intentions will be answering to me." I glance at Rock and see him chuckling at my choice of words.

The responses range from "about fucking time" to "congratulations."

Rock gives everyone a hard stare. "We're all clear on this, fellas?"

No one has an objection. General members are dismissed. Rock motions the officers to stay.

I stare down at my clasped hands on the table. I'm really fucking doing this. Holy shit.

"We're taking a vote on Trinity. Wrath wants to patch her too." Rock doesn't fuck around, getting right to the point.

A whistle. A sharp intake of breath. Why, I'm not sure. It shouldn't be a surprise. Property patch is the next logical step. Trinity and I have wasted way too much time as it is.

Z walks around the table to punch my arm. "All right, brother." He plops down in the empty chair next to me, grinning like an idiot.

Some of the tension drains out of me and one corner of my mouth lifts.

Then Murphy opens his big mouth. "You realize she's fucked everyone at this table, right?"

My eyes snap up at that. Brother apparently didn't learn his lesson. I know he's young and dumb, so this time he needs more than a choking to drive the message home. Rock knows exactly what I'm thinking, because he puts his hand on my arm.

He drills Murphy with a withering stare. "First, that's *not* true. Second, you got a motherfucking death wish, Murphy?"

Murphy looks away. "Sorry," he grumbles. I get why he's so surprised. Club girls *don't* usually become ol' ladies. But he's also known me long enough to know I don't give a fuck about shit like that.

"Get it all out of your systems now, you three." Rock jabs his finger at the closed war room door. "'Cause once we walk out, if one of you dares bring past shit up or makes Trinity uncomfortable in any way, *I* will personally kick your ass before handing you over to Wrath."

"I'm cool, prez." Z reassures us. He taps my shoulder. I turn and give him my full attention. "I'm happy for you, bro. Trinity and me—we've been just friends for a while now. She's a good girl."

I nod. "Thanks, brother."

Teller blows out a breath and I turn to stare at him. Brother can't quite meet my eyes. "Fuck, man. You love her?" He rakes his fingers through his hair. Is he having a hard time with this because he has feelings for my girl? Somehow that bothers me a lot less than if he just saw her as his favorite fuck toy.

Never one to enjoy discussing my emotions, I just grunt. "Yeah."

Teller nods. "She deserves to be happy."

Murphy glances at his best friend like he's got two heads. Guessing he didn't realize Teller's feelings ran deeper than blowjobs and three-ways.

"Anything else you want to add, Murphy?" I ask.

He shakes his head. "No, man. I'm happy for you two."

"Thanks."

Rock sighs and taps the table. "Can we vote now?"

Z, again raises his hand first. "Shoulda made her an honorary member or something years ago for puttin' up with all our bullshit."

I toss a look at my friend. He's obviously got a lot of respect for Trinity to say something like *that*.

"Is that a yes?" Rock grumbles, with a smirk.

"Yes."

Teller and Murphy both give their yeses.

I turn to prez.

"Well, I wouldn't have brought it to the table if I wasn't going to say yes. Jesus Christ, you two have given me fucking gray hairs."

Everyone has a good laugh at that.

Z's the first to get down to logistics. "Need help moving her shit up to your room?"

"No, man. I'm staying right where I am."

A "What?" comes out of everyone, except prez. Even though I hadn't shared this with him yet, I can tell he's not surprised.

I shrug, not really giving a fuck what anyone thinks about our living arrangements. "Her room's bigger and she's not comfortable being in a room where I've fucked a bunch of skanks fifty ways from Sunday." Also, I know I'm the only one who's been in her room. I don't have to say it though, everyone knows.

"Well, at least you'll be closer to the gym. Work some of that flab off you've accumulated sitting around on your ass," Z snarks at me.

"Aw, thanks for worrying about my figure, brother." I give him a quick shove. "Actually, I'm thinking of measuring out a few acres and building a little cabin right next door to you, prez," I say with a completely straight face.

The corner of Rock's mouth twists up into a smirk, but he doesn't comment.

"Copycat," Z jokes.

"So, except for…you know. She gonna do the same stuff around the clubhouse?" Murphy asks.

I don't hesitate. "No."

Rock quirks an eyebrow at me.

My fists clench on the table in front of me. "Fuck, she doesn't want anyone knowing this. She's got this book cover design business started and she's taking art classes. I want her to focus on that."

Rock slowly nods his approval.

Teller's clearly shocked. That's right, brother, we're about more than sex.

Z taps the table to get Murphy's attention, then pins him with a hard stare. "What the fuck you worried about? Learn to clean up after yourself."

I snort out a laugh, then reconsider my blanket *no*. "I'm sure she'll still want to plan the parties. She likes doing that stuff." I nod at Rock. "She's ecstatic about your engagement party, you know."

Rock's mouth twitches. "I'm sure."

"But as far as doing everyone's laundry, and playing housekeeper? No. She's done with that."

"Fair enough. We'll figure it out," Rock says and his word is final.

We break and everyone gets up to leave. Rock stops me before I get out of my chair.

"Books?" he prods when everyone else has cleared the room.

A slow smile spreads over my face. "Yeah, she's good with the art stuff. Real good. She's slowly picking up some authors and making money with it."

I'm not sure what it is, but this look of relief, happiness, and pride flickers over his face. "That's good. You okay with how this went down?" he asks, waving his hand around the table.

I think about it. "Murph fucking pissed me off, but I get it. I'm sure he thinks it's strange. Long as he treats her with respect, we're cool. Teller, though? I think his feelings are more than I realized. Don't know if that's better or worse."

"He won't interfere."

"I know. It's good to know he cared about her more than just a…" Yeah, I don't need to finish that sentence.

"I'm proud of you. You wouldn't have been able to handle that shit a while ago."

"No kidding."

"She know you were doing this?"

"Sort of. I'm not sure she wants it."

"You two have come this far. You'll figure it out. Want Hope to talk to her?"

"I appreciate the offer, but no, we need to figure this out on our own."

Rock pauses and takes a deep breath. Something is weighing on my brother and I wait for him to get it out. "I'm happy for you two." He stops again. "This is the only time I'm ever going to say this, so listen good." Rock closes his eyes for a second, then meets my stare. "I'm sorry for my part in—"

"Don't go there, Rock."

"No. You tried to tell me how you felt. I shoulda sat you both down. I knew her story, but I didn't understand until much, much later what her issues were."

"Jesus, Rock. You were two years out of prison and the new president of an MC that was barely standing on its feet after some serious shit went down. It wasn't your job to play relationship counselor to two fuckups."

His mouth twists and he huffs a bit of a laugh. "I love both of you, you know. It tore me up watching you two rip each other apart, knowing I had a hand in it."

"Let it go. We're good now. I never blamed you." At least I don't think I did.

Rock quirks an eyebrow at me and suddenly I get his meaning. "Uh-uh. Don't go thinking I was mean to Cinder-fuckin-ella 'cause I had some subconscious anger toward you over Trinity. I ain't that deep, prez."

Laughter shades his voice. "Don't underestimate yourself."

CHAPTER FORTY

Trinity

The guys have been giving me strange looks all night. Like they're afraid to talk to me. I can only imagine what went down in church today.

True to her word, Hope came to my room while the guys were in church. She giggled through all of Wrath's photos. "You're so good. He almost looks sexy instead of terrifying. You have to photograph Rock for me."

I can't wait to tell Wrath that little gem.

Wrath has been stuck to me like Velcro all night. Hope keeps glancing at him and snickering. I know it's killing her not to say anything. Rock pulls her away from the crowd eventually and I can relax.

"Is she okay?" Wrath asks.

"She loved your photo shoot," I blurt out.

His jaw drops. "You didn't."

"I had to. She's going to help me incorporate. She needed to know what the business was," I say with a helpless shrug.

He shakes his head. "Great. Can't wait for the guys to start busting my balls over that," he grumbles.

He has to step away to take care of something. Bonfire smoke keeps blowing in my eyes, so I perch myself on a log under a bunch of trees. This way I can watch everyone from a distance.

To my left, Murphy comes out of the shadows.

"Hey, Trin."

I'm not sure how to act. I think Murphy and I are friends, but there's not a lot to our relationship other than Teller and some mutual orgasms.

"Hey."

"Why you over here by yourself?" He sits next to me on the log, keeping a safe distance between us.

"Just quieter."

He stares at the fire for a few minutes before speaking. "Wrath told us today—you two are permanent."

My jaw drops. "He did?"

Suddenly Murphy's alarmed. "He didn't tell you?"

"No."

"Christ, he already wants to kick my fucking ass."

"Why?"

"When he told us, I opened my big mouth and said something nasty." He adds quickly, "I didn't mean it."

I sigh. It will always be this way for us, won't it? Someone will fling my past in both our faces.

"Anyway. I apologized to him. But you're the one I should say sorry to."

"What, why?"

"'Cause I'm a jealous dick?"

"Pfft. I don't think for a second that's true."

"Yeah, I know you don't. But it is." He hesitates. "I'm jealous he can openly claim you." His hand runs through his hair. "Shit, Trin. I'm not good at being friends with girls. But I hope you know I love you and respect you. Always have. If I've ever acted otherwise, I'm sorry."

My hand grasps his. "We're good." It finally dawns on me what he's upset about. "She's gonna be eighteen in a few months, Murphy."

He shakes his head. "Nah. I think it's too late. I don't deserve her anyway."

"Muph—"

"Anyway," he cuts me off. "If I keep my distance for a while, it's not because I'm mad at you. I just got some stuff to work out." He grins at me. "That, and I don't want your man ripping my head off."

"Good plan," Wrath growls from behind us.

Murphy jumps off the log and turns. Wrath comes up behind me and settles his hand in my hair.

Jamming his hands in his pockets, Murphy glances down at me. "Bye, Trin." He flicks his gaze up and nods at Wrath. "Be good to each other."

Wrath straddles the log and turns to face me as soon as Murphy's gone. "What was that about?"

"You really did it?"

WRATH

What the fuck? Did Murphy ruin everything with his big mouth?

Fucking Murphy. I'm going to kill him after all. I let his shitty comments slide, but upsetting my girl won't be forgiven as easily.

"Told them what?"

"That, you and me, we're...together?"

So he *didn't* spill about the vote. I may let him live, depending on what Trin says next.

"Yeah babe. Told you I was taking care of it. What else did he say?"

"I don't know. He apologized. Told me he said something shitty to you at the table and I was really the one he needed to apologize to."

I'm a little stunned. A lot stunned, actually. Murphy has more class and bigger balls than I give him credit for.

"Is it always going to be this way? Not everyone will be as nice as Murphy."

"They will if they want to keep breathing."

"What about when we mix with other clubs or charters? I know that fight with Whisper was about me. People will never forget what I was, Wyatt."

I grip her chin and force her to look at me. "Hey. Listen to me. What you were was a sweet girl who was loyal to her club. What you are now is *my* girl. Anyone has an issue, they can answer to me."

"But—"

"Our business is *our* business. We've worked our issues out. We're putting the past to bed. If other people want to relive it, they'll answer to my fists."

She shakes her head. "Okay."

"I mean it. That goes for club girls too. They give you shit, you tell me. If you're not comfortable with that, tell Hope."

"Wyatt—"

"No. It's not going to be an issue anyway. You'll be wearing my property patch. Anyone dares run their mouth has a death wish I'll be happy to help them fulfill."

Her jaw drops. "What did you say?"

"You heard me."

"Are you asking me, or telling me?"

I cock my head at her, assessing what she needs to hear. "Which one will make you say yes?"

Trinity

Holy shit. Is Wrath really asking what I think he is?

Wait, why is he on his knees?

He takes my hand. "Trin, you remember months ago when I was being a dick, you laid down a challenge for me?"

"What? No. I've never challenged you."

He snorts. "Babe, you've been challenging me since the day we met. But seriously, you said you wouldn't be my ol' lady even if I got down on my knees and begged in front of everyone."

I do remember. And I said it because he hurt my feelings. I didn't mean it. I certainly never meant to have him do something like this. Granted, we're not in front of everyone. But there's definitely enough people around to witness this spectacle.

He wraps his arms around my waist, tugging me against him until we topple onto the ground. His hand threads into my hair and he pulls me down for a kiss.

"Not here. Gonna do it right, babe," he rumbles against my mouth when we part.

Someone whistles. I giggle and roll off him into the damp grass. "Ew, I'm all wet now."

"Yeah, baby," Wrath growls, launching himself at me.

"Get off me," I gasp, but I'm laughing so hard, my words make no sense.

He presses another kiss to my lips, then gets up, pulling me with him. "Let's go to our room, Angel Face," he says low and with so much desire, I shiver.

Once we're tucked away in my room, he spins me around, and pulls me against his chest. His warm breath caresses my neck as I wait to see what he has planned.

"You're my woman now, Trinity. Mine."

My vision clouds with tears. "Yes," I whisper.

"I'm yours."

My entire body trembles under the weight of his words. "Yes."

"Good girl," his low voice stimulates the roughest, most carnal part of me. He strips off my sweatshirt and trails soft kisses across my shoulders.

His arms tighten around my waist holding me tight. "You're mine to protect. Mine to love. Anyone hurts you, I'll kill them." His words dissolve into a possessive growl that rocks down my body, curling my toes.

"Wyatt?"

"Yes, angel?" he asks as he pulls off my pants and sneakers. I'm momentarily disoriented when he picks me up and pins me to the wall. Wyatt's mouth on mine, his tongue licking and tasting me. The heat of his skin burning my flesh.

"I need you spread out in front of me," he mumbles as he carries me to the bed, gently setting me down.

My hands go for his pants, unbuttoning and shoving them down. He takes over. "Lie back for me."

Having someone as perfect as Wrath examine me so closely would have made me squirm before. But he makes me feel beautiful. He hovers over me, settling, his big, warm body against mine, keeping most of his weight balanced on his arms.

His mouth drops to my breast, nipping at my nipple through the silky fabric of my bra.

"You my girl?" he asks.

"Yes."

"Say it."

"I'm yours."

He kisses lower, tickling my ribs with his hot breath. My body freezes when he reaches my scarred side and growls.

Propping his chin on my hip, he glances up at me with a serious expression.

"Want you to get my star tattooed on you, right here." He traces the undamaged skin next to my hip bone. I suck in a deep breath.

"I'd like that," I whisper.

"Good."

He places gentle kisses on the spot in question. "I need to be there when you get it done. No one touches my girl without my supervision." His mouth turns up in a quick smirk, but I know he means it.

"Yes," I agree. I don't ever want another man's hands on me again.

"How do you want me tonight, angel?"

I can't answer, because he lowers the cup of my bra, exposing my nipples for his rough fingers.

He slides up my body, taking one nipple into his hungry mouth.

I stutter and gasp.

Eventually he has mercy. "Tell me," he demands.

"Raw. Hard. Rough. Make me yours." He leans down and runs his teeth over the hard peak of my nipple and my back arches in response. Nudging my legs apart, he pushes a finger inside me and I moan in pleasure.

"Those tests came back negative, baby. You want it raw?"

"Fuck. Yes." I can barely form any words or thoughts with the way his thumb keeps rubbing against my clit. "Please. Please make me come, Wyatt."

He gazes down at me, and I see the war within him. "Don't hold back." I raise my hips and he nods. Without another word, he slides into me. Filling me to the hilt and stopping.

"You with me?"

"Oh, yes."

He withdraws so slow, I'm almost sobbing with relief when he pushes into me once more. My arms and legs wrap around him and I lose myself in the primal, furious motion of him thrusting in and out.

"Are you with me, Trinity?" he asks again. This time I feel the rawness in his voice. For the first time in my life, an honest *emotional* connection overwhelms me, stealing my breath with its intensity.

His lips press against my forehead. "You still want it rough?"

"No. Just like this. Please."

"Whatever my angel wants."

My heart nearly bursts from his words. This man has turned my world upside down. We've hurt and betrayed each other so many times but *this* feels like forgiveness. He captures my mouth. Our tongues tangle as he keeps giving me slow steady strokes. His hips thrust at a slightly different angle and pure bliss flows through me. As I shudder and come undone, he grips my hips, fingers digging in, holding me down for a few more short, intense thrusts.

"Trinity," he whispers. He stills, filling me, falling on top of me. His thick arms wrap around my body, pulling me into him.

Every inch of me still tingles with pleasure.

"Wyatt?"

He stirs, taking some of his weight off me. "Sorry, babe," he mumbles.

"No, I like this." I grasp him to keep him on top of me.

He smiles down at me and kisses my forehead. "I'm going to crush you."

"No, you're not," I whisper, holding tight. The weight of him safe and comforting. I love him so much. Why can't I just say the actual words?

CHAPTER FORTY-ONE

Trinity

Wrath told me I'm not supposed to cook for the house anymore. But honestly, everyone will starve if I don't. I like cooking most of the time and getting things ready for the guys in the morning. With that in mind, I slip out of bed to start the coffee.

Hoot's already in the kitchen, but he's spilled coffee grounds everywhere.

"I got it, kid."

Today he smiles gratefully.

Teller's the first one in the dining room. He's sitting, staring at the mural over the bar.

"Morning," I chirp as I set down a mug and fill it with coffee.

He glances up at me and a hint of a smile curves his mouth. "Sorry I missed the bonfire," he says.

"It's okay."

"You know Wrath told us yesterday?"

"Yeah."

He fists his hands on the table. "I care about you so much, Trinity."

The raw sound of his voice makes it clear his feelings are more than friendly or fuck buddy. I'm utterly floored. I had no idea.

"Teller—"

"No, it's my own fault. I never said anything. I didn't think we could be a possibility, so I just took whatever you would give me. Figured you thought I was too young for you or something. But if I thought there had been a chance, you and me...I would have done it differently."

Shit. The misery in his voice cuts right through me. "I'm sorry."

"Don't be. Wrath had the stones to actually fight for you. He earned you. You deserve someone willing to fight for you. I'm happy for you both, even if I'm sad for myself. He really loves you, you know."

"I know."

"Does he make you happy?"

"He really does. I love him too. Long time now." Oh my God. That came out so easy. Why can't I say it to Wrath's face?

"Fuck," Teller mutters. "All these years, I never...He must *hate* me."

I'd been so wrapped up in my own bullshit. It never occurred to me how my actions might affect their friendship. I pat his shoulder, but it feels awkward and wrong for some reason. "Teller, we'll still be friends."

"I know."

"You'll find the right girl."

He snorts a laugh. "I'll probably just fuck it up again."

"You didn't fuck anything up. I'm sorry I didn't realize—"

"It's not on you, Trin."

I'm so stunned. And ashamed.

All my life I thought I wasn't worthy of love, making the last twenty-four hours utterly confusing. Hell, the last few *months* have been confusing. A sick feeling slithers through me. For years, I've *used* Teller. Many little gestures come to mind. The way he'd fall asleep holding me. I always thought he was teasing when he asked why I took off in the middle of the night. Whenever I thought he was getting too close, I used one of the other guys to push him away.

"Teller, I know we've never talked about this, but I had a really shitty childhood. I didn't think I was worth loving for a long time. It never occurred to me you might feel that way. I'm so sorry."

He wraps one hand over mine. "Honey, you're one of the sweetest people I know. I can't think of anyone who deserves love more than you do. You've nothing to be sorry for. It's on me. You're where you're supposed to be. I'll be fine."

Hot tears threaten to fall. My God. I never knew Teller to be so poetic.

We stare at each other a little longer before I get up.

"Eggs and bacon?"

"That would be awesome. Thank you, Trinity."

WRATH

Waking up alone unnerves me. I declared my feelings in front of the entire club yesterday. From now on, I expect to wake up next to my girl. My breath catches and I hold it, listening for sounds that she's just in the bathroom. Nothing.

Sighing, I throw back the covers and get up to find her. Guilt nags me because I'm thinking maybe it was too much, too soon and Trinity ran from me. Or worse jumped into bed with someone else. I hate myself for thinking that. It's been eight years of us playing sick games with each other though. We still need time to adjust. The guys all sat there and heard me announce my claim on her. Only someone with a death wish would take her to bed after that. I'm sick that I have more faith in my brothers than my girl.

Walking down the hall to the dining room, another thought occurs to me. She's been getting things ready every morning for years. I'm sure me telling her she didn't have to do that anymore didn't sink in. She likes helping out and feeling useful. Nothing I say will change that.

Feeling better about the possibilities, I turn to enter the dining room. Voices reach me and I step back. Teller and Trinity. *Fuck.*

"I care about you so much, Trinity."

You've got to be fucking kidding me.

"Teller—"

The pain in her voice is so clear, I'm ready to slam Teller's face into the table. I just barely manage to stop myself.

"He really loves you, you know."

"I know."

Thank God.

"Does he make you happy?"

I hold in a breath waiting for her answer.

"He really does. I love him too. Long time now."

Blood thunders through my ears and something loosens in my chest. I needed to hear her say this. I know she loves me. And I don't care that she can't say it to my face. Hearing her say it to Teller though? I'm stunned and stupid-happy.

Unfortunately with the relief crashing through me, I missed part of their conversation.

"It's not on you, Trin."

Good boy, Teller.

My poor girl's got so much guilt over something that isn't even her fault. So help me God, if Teller doesn't say the right thing, I'm going to break his face.

"You're where you're supposed to be."

I can live with that. They're saying goodbye in their own way. It's a good thing. Lord knows we don't need tension in the club. I'm proud of my girl. Proud of my brother too. Takes a big man to admit that shit.

I promise myself I won't hassle little welterweight for at least a month.

CHAPTER FORTY-TWO

Trinity

I'm a little bummed this was the last night of my Photoshop class. I can sign up for another one in a few weeks, but I'm not sure if I'll bother. I have a good grasp of things and with all my shiny new equipment waiting for me courtesy of Wyatt, I don't need to keep taking the risk of venturing into Ironworks.

This is exactly what's on my mind as I'm grabbed and thrown face-first against my Jeep in the parking lot. Everyone else in my eight-person class left out the front exit. Stupid me parked in the back.

Keeping silent, I wait to see what my attacker wants before I decide how to handle this. I have the pistol Wrath insisted I carry tucked into a special holster at the small of my back. I also have a knife in the cargo pocket along my right thigh. Neither are accessible at the moment due to the heavy, smelly body pressing me into my car. A wave of panic consumes me. Long-buried memories threaten to leave me quivering and at my tormentor's mercy if I don't get it together.

"You one of LOKI's girls," he finally grates against my ear.

I can't decide if I'm relieved or terrified that this is club business and not a random mugging.

He presses his lips to my ear, and slides his slimy tongue over my skin. My body trembles with revulsion from the contact. The wrongness of any man but Wyatt touching me that way infuriates me, giving me the strength to stay still so I can plan a course of action. "I remember you from the night of the fight. You're with that big blond *pendejo*. Got a lotta nerve being on our turf."

Um, actually, as far as I know, if I'm not sporting club logos or here on club business, I can go wherever the fuck I want. I keep my mouth shut, hoping the silence will unnerve him enough to make a mistake.

"Let's see what *presidente* wants to do with you. He's sick of that *cabrón* president of yours turning his nose up at our business."

Ice floods my veins. Fucking Vipers. There's no way in fucking hell I am getting dragged back to their clubhouse. I did not escape one biker hell only to be kidnapped into another one. I hold no illusions that they'll leave me unmolested while they contact Rock to make their demands.

I'm done with that shit.

The minute my cheek kissed the cold metal of my car, my pulse took off down the highway. I struggle for a lungful of night air and get myself under control. My gaze darts to the bits of surrounding area in my peripheral vision. We're all alone. It's up to me to save myself.

His hand clasps my breast and I squeeze my eyes tight. "Oh you're nice. They'll be real eager to get you back."

Thinking of everything Wyatt has taught me over the last few months, hell, just thinking of *him* and what we finally have together gives me courage. I didn't wait my whole damn life to be happy, only to have it ruined by this asshole.

I almost cry—I've still never told Wrath how much I love him. If I don't survive this, all he has is a stupid, cowardly *note* from me, when what I feel for him is so much more than my scared, scribbled words.

My quiet seems to unnerve him, and he gives me a shake. "You listening, *puta*?

"I hear you, *hijo de puta*," I spit back.

The insult is enough for him to let me go, probably so he can hit me. I drop into a crouch while going for my knife. Sure enough, his fist hits where my head had been seconds ago. My fingers close around the knife about the same time he lets loose with a string of curses. Flicking it open, I thrust my arm back as hard as possible, until the sharp blade sinks into flesh.

My attacker falls back on the ground screaming. Whirling around I see I managed to lodge the knife in his thigh. Not bad considering I'd been throwing blind.

No time to pat myself on the back. He's screaming and rolling around, which is bound to draw unwanted attention soon. His hand flails and brushes against my ankle. Yup, he's still too close for comfort. My foot lashes out, kicking his hand away with a satisfying crack. Good, I hope I broke some fingers.

I'd dropped my keys when he grabbed me, and now I frantically scoop them up. Unlocking the door, I throw myself in, backpack on and all. A quick glance in my side mirror shows him still wailing and thrashing on the pavement.

Throwing the Jeep into reverse, I get the hell out of Ironworks. Once I'm safely over the bridge, I pull over. My hands are shaking so bad I can barely sit forward to slide my backpack off or reach into my pocket to grab my cell phone.

Wyatt's on a run. It's only out to Syracuse, but still, he can't help me.

I need to hear his voice though.

"Hey, angel," he answers.

"Wyatt."

"Trin, what's wrong?"

"I...I got attacked leaving art class. A Viper I think. I got away."

"Jesusfuckingchrist, are you okay?" he shouts back.

"I think so."

"Baby, did he hurt you?"

"Not really. Scared mostly. I sunk my knife into his thigh and got away." In the background I hear Z asking if I'm okay.

While they take a second to talk, I buckle my seatbelt and get back on the road.

"Trin, where are you now?" Wyatt asks.

"Getting on 787."

"Good. Okay. You're probably a half hour from home. Go straight to the clubhouse." He pauses. "You call Rock first?"

"No. I uh, needed to talk to you."

He's silent for a moment. "I'll call Rock and let him know what's going on. You concentrate on driving. We're maybe half an hour from our drop. Shouldn't take more than fifteen minutes, then we're turning around and coming straight back, okay?"

"Okay."

"You did good, Angel Face. I'm proud of you."

"Your training paid off." There's so much more to say. It wasn't the defense exercises he taught me that saved me. It was *him*.

He chuckles and the sound comforts me.

My mouth's dry and I swallow past the lump in my throat to come up with a lighter tone so he doesn't worry. "I lost my damn knife though."

His chuckle gives way to harder laughter. "Babe, I'll buy you another one. Now get home."

WRATH

"Motherfuckingdirtygoatfucker!" Bellows out of my mouth the minute we hang up. My fist flies into the dashboard and I'm so enraged, I don't feel a thing.

"Relax, brother. You heard her, she's okay. She did good," Z reassures me.

This is an easy run, which is why there's only two of us. Thank fuck, because that means there are more brothers at home to take care of whatever shitstorm just blew up.

"Calm down and call prez."

The cloud of rage in my head breaks while I dial. Twice in the time I've known her Trin needed me, and both times I couldn't be there. Both times Rock's gonna be the one to take care of her.

At least this time she called me first.

"S'up brother?" Rock greets me in a lazy voice. I hate that I'm about to ruin his night.

"Trin got attacked leaving her art class tonight. Possibly Viper."

"What?" He explodes on the other end. "Where is she? Is she okay?"

"She's on her way to the clubhouse. She says she's fine, just shaken up. She knifed the guy and got away."

"Fuck. He alive?"

"I think so."

"No cops then."

"She ain't in the system anyway, bro."

Rock's quiet. "I gotta get the story from her before I decide what to do. But trying to kidnap an ol' lady. Man, you know what this means."

War.

Damn fucking right. I'm ready to murder every single Viper with my bare fucking hands.

"We're almost at the drop, then we're turning around and coming right back."

"Good plan. Go ahead and let Stump know what's going on."

"You think we'll pull them in?"

"Never know."

From passing through Demon territory, I've seen Stump with some regularity over the last few years. Only recently did I discover he'd been involved in wiping out the fuckers who harmed Trinity when she was a teenager.

To say I've got a soft spot for the grumpy, old fuck is an understatement.

Stump and his son, the VP of the Demons, Chaser, greet us with handshakes. Stump's delighted with what we've brought. As his guys load it in their van, he invites us to their local support club.

"Can't. We got a situation back home. Bordering MC tried to jack my ol' lady tonight. Gotta get back."

Whether he's surprised by the information or the fact that I have an ol' lady, I'm not sure.

"Who's your ol' lady?"

"Trinity."

A dark look of concern transforms his face. "She all right?"

"Yeah. Knifed him and got away, but I gotta—"

"I understand. I'd do the same. I know Trin from way back. She's a good girl. Glad she's with someone like you now."

"Aw, shit. I remember Trinity from when she was just a lil' kid," Chaser adds.

Not really sure what to say to that, I just nod.

Stump shakes my hand. "That shit ain't right. You let us know if you guys need support."

"Will do."

Without the concern of a crapton of weed in the back of the car in case we get pulled over, Z presses the pedal to the floor.

Trinity

Rock meets me at the door with a hug. "I spoke to Wrath. Guys are all coming in. You okay?"

Pulling out of his embrace, I nod. "Yeah."

All softness vanishes and President Rock is in charge. "While we're waiting for Wrath to get here, tell me what went down," he barks at me as he leads me into the war room. Teller's waiting in a seat on the other side of the table, but he gets up and gives me a hug.

Holding me at arm's length, he peers into my eyes. "You okay?"

I nod and he releases me.

Rock points at Wrath's chair and has me sit.

"Sorry, you're going to end up going over this more than once, sweetheart," Rock apologizes.

It's okay. I tell him word for word everything I can remember.

"This is over me not letting them dip into our territory. Are they fucking nuts?" Rock fumes.

"We're gonna have to call some brothers in to help keep Crystal Ball locked down," Teller mutters.

"Yeah, I'll have Z do it when he gets in. Where the fuck is Murphy?"

"Don't know, Prez. I texted him a bunch. Got no answer yet."

"Fuck, that's all we need."

My head hurts from where I got slammed against the car. Listening to them go back and forth lulls me into a sleep like state. Sometime later, I'm aware of Rock picking me up and laying me down on the leather couch in the back of the war room. A blanket floats over me and I drift out.

Angry voices shake me from sleep a little while later. The guys are assembling around the table. Murphy's here and he smiles at me. Wrath and Z's spots are still empty. My bladder insists I get the fuck up, so I toss off the blanket.

"You okay, Trin?" Rock calls.

Feeling fuzzy, I nod. "Yeah. Gonna run to the bathroom."

Run is overly optimistic. What I do resembles lurching. Instead of using the communal bathroom, I go into my room to clean up. Brushing my teeth unzombifies me a bit, but I'm still exhausted.

Walking back to the war room, I hear car doors slamming outside. I quicken my pace just as the door's thrown open and Wrath storms in. Fierce is the only way to explain his expression. I choke out a startled gasp drawing his attention to me.

"Angel." In three quick strides he crosses the room, and sweeps me into his arms. Only then do the tears start falling.

WRATH

Every sob that wracks my girl's body sends a shiver of rage through me. This is three years ago all over again. Fucking Vipers going after women.

This time, they all fucking die.

Trinity has her arms looped around my neck, face buried against my shoulder, legs wrapped around my waist. I've got my arms banded around her keeping her tight to me, one hand rubbing her back.

"You're okay, baby. I got you. You did good. I'm so proud of you," I keep whispering in her ear.

Rock and Z are standing in the doorway to the war room looking like they've just spotted an alien spaceship in the living room. I pause to flip them off, then go back to calming my girl down.

Every patched brother is at the table as I carry Trinity in and drop into my seat. She adjusts, so her legs are draped over my lap and she's leaning against me. She's stopped crying, but she's definitely still close to the edge. Exhaustion dogs me, but I shake it off.

Rock gives me the story. I'd like to hear it from Trinity's mouth, but she's still silent and I don't want to push her. My brothers are still staring at us like they can't believe what they're seeing. Fucking hell, can't we concentrate on the war that's breathing down our necks instead of my love life?

"He said he remembered me from the night of the fight," Trinity says suddenly.

"Good. Good Trin," Rock reassures her. "Anything else you remember?"

"Uh, he called Wrath a *bandeho.*"

Bricks snorts at that. "Was it a *pendejo*, sweetheart?"

"Yeah."

My eyebrows draw down. "What the fuck is that?"

Bricks shrugs. "Depends where the fucker is from. Could be anything from jackass to coward."

I grind my teeth.

Lowering my voice, I ask her the question I've been dreading the most since I first got her phone call. "He touch you anywhere else, baby?"

She squeezes her eyes tight, her lip quivers, giving me all the answer I need. White spots of rage dot my vision.

"Any other words Bricks can translate?" Rock asks with a smirk to lighten things.

"He called you a cabrón."

"Asshole," Bricks clarifies.

"Called me a *puta*, but I know what that means," Trinity says with a laugh.

I know what that means too, and if my rage intensifies anymore I'm going to disappear in a cloud of smoke.

Trinity sits up and faces the table. I keep my arms around her waist. I know we need to strategize, but all I want to do is take her to our room and make sure she's okay.

"It all happened so fast, guys. I just knew I couldn't let him take me anywhere."

"You kicked ass, Trinny. We're all proud of you," Teller says with a smile. Everyone agrees.

"All right, I'm going to give Ulfric a call. We gotta align ourselves with his pack again. He's been itching to take these fucks out for a while now, and I'm sure this will push him over the edge." Rock doesn't elaborate on why that might be. Trinity shifts in my lap.

"Do you want me to go, prez?"

Rock flicks a glance at my face, which I'm sure is screaming *No fucking way* and shakes his head. "Stay in case I need you to explain any of it to him."

Rock uses a burner to call, but sets the phone on the table on speaker so we can all hear.

"What?" Ulfric snaps.

"It's Rock."

"What up, man?"

"Got a situation. Viper tried to grab one of our ol' ladies tonight as she was leaving class." Rock gets that out right away, because he needs to establish that Trinity hadn't been violating our turf agreement with the Vipers.

"Fuck me. You sure it was a Viper?"

"Pretty sure. Said he recognized her as one of our girls."

We all hear him cover the phone and call for his VP and sergeant-at-arms, then put us on speaker. "I got Merlin and Whisper on now too."

"His beef seemed to be about us not wanting to do business with him, but she didn't get a lot more info than that," Rock continues.

"Whose ol' lady?"

"Mine," I answer. "Wrath."

"Since when you got an ol' lady?" Merlin snickers.

"Who?" Ulfric asks.

"Trinity."

"Fuck, she okay?" Merlin asks.

I find it interesting that Whisper didn't spill to his brothers why I gave him a split lip a couple weeks ago.

"I'm okay," Trinity answers.

There's a bit of silence as I'm sure they're absorbing the fact that one, Trinity belongs to me now, and two, we're letting her sit in on club business.

"Tell me the story from the beginning," Ulfric asks.

Trinity sits up, her voice much clearer and recounts everything.

"Damn girl. Your man trained you well. Nice job," Merlin praises her.

Hearing her tell the whole story from the beginning leaves me shaking with murderous rage by the time she finishes.

CHAPTER FORTY-THREE

WRATH

"No fuckin' way, prez. You ain't shuttin' me out this time."

Rock drags his hand through his hair. "I'm not. There's nothing we can do right this second. We need to plan and organize before we take action. You need to take care of your girl." He glances at Trinity, who's curled up in the couch staring at nothing.

"You're right."

Rock's eyes widen. Guess he figured I'd be more stubborn about it. "I promise I'll come get you as soon as I've got something."

"Okay."

He smiles and slaps me on the back. "Take care of your girl."

Trin doesn't even look up as I approach.

"Come here, angel," I whisper as I scoop her into my arms.

She clings to me, but remains silent.

I drop her carefully onto the bed and shut the door. She lies there while I strip her down. "Come on. Sit up for me," I urge so I can slip a nightshirt over her head.

I take off my cut, shirt and shoes and slide into bed with her. Gathering her in my arms, I kiss her forehead.

"Wyatt?"

"I'm here."

"I love you."

My heart stops.

She slicks her tongue over her bottom lip. "For a second tonight, I thought I might die, and I was so angry with myself for not saying it to you. Only giving you that stupid note...I'm sorry. Please don't think the only reason I'm saying it now—"

"Please stop." I yank my wallet out. Flipping it open, I pull out the note she gave me and hold it out to her. "It's the sweetest thing anyone's ever given me. Keep it with me so I can look at it whenever I miss you."

She gasps and cries even harder. "Shhh." I wrap her in my arms and after tucking her note away, toss my wallet on the night stand. "Come on, let's get some rest."

I've got a splitting headache when my phone wakes me up. Completely disoriented, I roll over and answer, noticing it's one in the afternoon.

"What?"

"We got a meet with Ransom's crew in two hours."

Scrubbing my hand over my face, I nod, then realize Rock can't see that over the phone. "Yeah. I'm up. Give me ten."

"Hope's downstairs, waiting for Trinity."

Fuck. I can only imagine how well *that* conversation went. "Thanks."

Trin settles her hand on my back. "Wyatt?" She crawls over until she's sitting on top of me. From the look on her face, sex is the last thing on her mind. "Please don't do this."

"What?"

"Go after them. I don't want to be the cause of another war between—"

Cupping her face between my hands, I stare into those honey eyes I love so much. "You *know* that's not how things work, Trinity. They touched what's mine. They pay."

"I—we just got things figured out. I don't want anything to happen to you."

Aw, shit. "I promise I'll be careful. But you know this can't stand. What if they went after Hope next? You think she'd get away like you did? Or Swan? Or even Heidi?"

Understanding flares in her eyes and she nods. She rolls to the side and sits up next to me.

"Well, with the mouth on her, they'd probably give Heidi back right away," she jokes.

I'm happy she's able to laugh, considering how grave the situation is. "That's my girl."

Following the noise in the hallway leads us to the dining room. Hoot, Birch and Swan are busy running back and forth taking care of things. Everyone's here.

As soon as she spots us, Hope runs over and pulls Trinity into a hug. Rock whistles to get everyone's attention.

"Members and prospects to the war room. Everyone else stays on the property until further notice."

I have just enough time for Swan to shove a cup of coffee and a sandwich in my hands before I follow everyone down the hall. Z catches up with me. "She okay?"

"Yeah. Better."

"Good. Real fuckin' proud of her for gettin' away like that."

My mouth quirks up. Me too.

Once we're seated, Rock remains standing and takes a look at everyone. I spot two members from downstate and give them a nod.

"I know some of you have only gotten bits and pieces, so I want to make sure everyone's on the same page. Trinity, a long time asset to our club, and Wrath's ol' lady, was attacked last night in downtown Ironworks."

One of the guys from downstate—Steer—raises his hand. Rock cuts him off with a shake of his head. "Our agreement with the Vipers is, associates, family, ol' ladies are all allowed in their territory as long as they're not on club business or wearing club colors. Trinity was there for class and no way would she wear colors in their territory. She knows better."

That seems to answer whatever Steer was planning to ask.

"Trinity managed to knife the guy—" Rock's interrupted by the room breaking out into applause, shouts and whistles, which makes me chuckle.

"Yeah, we're all proud of Wrath's girl," Rock says with a smirk. It's probably an inappropriate time to notice, but I really like how *Wrath's girl* sounds coming out of my president's mouth in front of everyone.

"Trin was able to identify the guy as Viper based on what he said to her. I've spoken to one of our local allies, and they're ready to back us."

I raise my hand quick and Rock nods at me. "We also got an offer of support from the Devil Demons MC."

"Why ain't you callin' either of them in?" Bull—also from downstate —asks.

Now, *my* answer would be *Shut the fuck up* or *Because I fucking said so,* something along those lines.

"Until we know what we're dealing with, I'd rather keep this in-house. No reason to use a blowtorch if a match works," Rock explains as if he's talking to a two-year-old.

That's why he's the prez, and I'm not.

"I also needed to let the local guys know to keep a closer eye on their women."

Bull nods as if that hadn't occurred to him. As his name suggests, he's dumb as an ox. That's why he's the sergeant-at-arms downstate and not the prez.

"I've been in touch with Ransom, the Viper's current president. At first he denied any knowledge of the attack. Said he didn't authorize it and assured me there would have been no issue with Trinity being down there for class."

This is all new information. Seems Rock was busy while I was napping the morning away.

"I got a call back from him a little while ago. They say they tracked the guy down. One of their hang-a-rounds, trying to impress the club. They're holding him for us so we can verify. Now, I trust a Viper about as far as I can throw one—"

"Which ain't far, they're a bunch of fat fucks," Z blurts out for a little comic relief. Rock shakes his head.

"This could be a trap or they could be sincere. I want to go in heavy enough so they know we're not fucking around but not so many guys it looks like a threat. I also need to make sure CB has adequate coverage—just in case. And I need guys here at the house." Rock levels a stern look at each of us. "These are the assignments. Do *not* question me unless you have a very good reason. And it better be stellar, so think it through before opening your mouth."

I'm not worried at all. I know exactly where I'm going.

"Wrath, Z, Murphy, Bull, and Ravage—you guys are with me. We'll take two vehicles. Ravage, Bull, and Murphy will wait outside and stay alert for trouble."

No one opens their mouth to complain.

"Dex, Steer, and Birch—I want you at Crystal Ball. We open at four. I want you down there checking things over by three o'clock."

"Teller, Axel, Bricks, Stash, Sparky, and Hoot—I want you at the house. Sparky and Stash, I need you two upstairs and alert."

"Got it, boss," Sparky assures him. For once he actually looks sober.

"Bricks, you know the security set up, so I want you on that."

"You got it."

Rock addresses the guys staying at the house. "Trin's got the combination to both gun safes and she's proficient with just about every weapon we have. Don't hesitate to have her help out." Rock sighs and his mouth turns up in a tired smirk. "Hope's been to the range, but she's not confident."

I think Rock's message is to use Hope as a last resort, which isn't quite fair. Cinderella's a good shot—once you load the weapon for her and show her where to point it.

Teller pipes up. "Heidi's good with a couple different weapons."

Rock nods. "That's it. We're all clear?" Everyone says yes. Rock calls Bull and Steer up to the front of the table. "I think no matter how this goes down, I'd rather have some extra muscle at CB this week, you two up for it?"

They don't have to think about it. Hanging out in our strip club all week isn't exactly a hardship for these guys. "Hell, yeah."

Rock slaps their shoulders. "Thanks."

Steer heads out with the CB crowd. Ravage joins us.

"Prez, you really want me outside?" Murphy asks.

"Did you miss something?" Rock asks.

Murphy shakes his head. Rock's feeling more generous than I am, 'cause I woulda kicked Murphy's ass for that. Instead he slaps Murphy on the back and pulls him close. "Vipers blow the three of us away, you and Teller will have to fight it out for my seat."

Murphy finally understands why he's being asked to wait outside. "Sorry, prez." He glances at me. "I'd take his job anyway."

Yeah, I'd like to kick Murphy's ass on a regular basis—for lots of reasons—but I'd be comfortable with that. Not that it matters if I'm dead.

Z's jumping around ready to go. "I hope they give us a fuckin' reason."

"Hey," Rock snaps. "Simmer the fuck down. He looks over the five of us. "Everyone suited up?"

Shit. "I gotta run upstairs, Rock."

He nods at me. "Yeah. Meet us at the front door."

Trinity intercepts me at the staircase. "Everything okay?"

"Yeah, I gotta grab something from my room. Come with?"

She follows behind me and watches me get ready. "They think they found the guy." I press a cell phone into her hand. "Check this later. I may send you a picture."

"Okay. Was it Viper?"

"Right now they're saying it was some hang-a-round."

She seems to think that over. "That makes more sense. Probably thought taking me would help him get his prospect rocker."

"Yeah, well the fucker better have come up with that on his own."

My leg's aching like a bitch on our way downstairs, but I gotta push the pain down and focus.

Rock, Z and I ride together.

Murphy, Bull, and Ravage stay right behind us the entire way. We left our cuts at home. Fuckin' hate entering Ironworks. "Was that Trinity's last class?" Z asks from the backseat.

"Yeah."

"Good timing."

No shit. No fuckin' way is she coming near Ironworks again. She needs more art classes, I'll send her anywhere else she wants to go.

The Viper's clubhouse looks like a fuckin' crack den. It's right on Second Avenue in what's known as South Ironworks. South of Satan's toilet is more accurate.

If the eight-foot chain link fence doesn't scream *gangster hideout*, the four pit bulls who attack the fence when we get out of our vehicles certainly do. The two houses on either side have blacked-out windows and some strange ventilation choices.

Z catches my eye and subtly tilts his head at the four different video cameras facing the street.

The stench of cat piss permeates the entire area.

We wait on the sidewalk for someone to come get us. It's a respect thing. Walking up and ringing their doorbell would not be respectful.

"Guess they've moved their cooking in-house," I mutter to Rock.

He nods once.

How they feel comfortable having their operation in plain sight smack in the middle of Ironworks, is beyond me. Ironworks PD must be shadier or lazier than I thought.

Murphy, Bull and Ravage stand behind us but move farther back when Ransom himself comes out to meet us.

He shakes Rock's hand. "I ain't even gonna check you for weapons. This is how much I want to make it clear we're not tryin' to start trouble."

"Appreciate it," Rock answers.

Ransom motions for us to follow. I slip on a pair of leather gloves as I walk behind Rock. Now the inside is surprisingly nice and clean, considering what outside looks like. The usual half-naked chicks are running around. What's unusual is how many of them look underage.

I know that's not why we're here, but it pisses me off anyway.

Ransom gets right down to business and takes us downstairs into their basement. "Murder room" is a better description. It's been outfitted with epoxy-coated cement and large drainage holes for easy wash downs. Hooks and eye-bolts to house multiple "guests." The current guest is tied to a chair that's bolted to the floor.

"Eduardo, say hello to our friends," Ransom prods the barely breathing prisoner.

"You got a 'before' picture, we can send to our girl to I.D. him?" Rock asks. "Don't know if she'll recognize him in this condition."

Ransom grins and pulls something out of his pocket. Next to me, Z tenses up, but otherwise doesn't move. "Recognize this?" Ransom asks, holding out a bloody knife.

Rock motions for me to take it. I recognize it right away. "Yeah, that's hers."

"We took it out of his leg," Ransom says, pointing to the guy's bloody pants. He's got a hole in the upper thigh that fits what Trinity described.

I nod at Rock.

Ransom kicks the chair. "Sit up," he barks as he pushes the guy forward. "No ink. He ain't Viper."

Well, he's got ink. But not the back piece every patched-in Viper sports. Ransom texts a "before" photo to me and I send it to Trin.

Walking up to the guy, I kick his leg. "You touch my girl?"

"Didn't know..." he trails off.

"Eduardo, right?" Ransom nods at me. "I know that's not true. You told her you recognized her from the fight a couple months back."

He's got no answer. He does piss himself. Geez. Here I've been so calm and mild-mannered.

Trin replies to me.

I'm pretty sure that's him.

"She's not one hundred percent," I tell Rock. My gaze shifts to Ransom. "She didn't stop to get a good look, with her being attacked and all."

He holds up his hands. "I understand. I'll wait outside if you want to question him."

Ransom steps out. I don't think for a second we're not being monitored.

Crouching down, I poke at Eduardo until he meets my eyes. "Someone put you up to it?"

He shakes his head then jerks it toward the door. "Mary."

"What?"

"Mary-ella."

I glance at Rock. "Who the fuck is that?"

"How would I know?"

"My girl's name is Trinity. The blonde. Why'd you go after her?"

He shakes and drools.

"He's fuckin' useless, Rock," Z mutters.

Rock settles his hand on my shoulder. "You good?"

"No. But there's not much more to be done here. There's no justice in killing a half-dead fucker who can't defend himself." I'm still not entirely sure this pathetic fuck had anything to do with Trinity's attack. I may be a thug, but even I won't cross certain lines.

He shakes his head. Before we make another move, Ransom and his sergeant-at-arms, Killa, pop back in the room.

Ransom raises his eyebrows at us.

"We're good." Good as we're going to be considering these assholes robbed me of the payback I'd been looking for.

He smiles as if this isn't a fucking disgusting, shitty situation and nods at Rock. "Can we talk business before you go?"

"Sure." Rock sounds neutral, but I know him well enough to know he'd rather do anything but.

He leads us upstairs. Rock steps into the living room and a girl who's eighteen if she's a fuckin' day takes one look at us, lets out a short scream, and runs into the kitchen.

"Finish it," Ransom says behind us. Few seconds later, there's a muffled shot from the basement.

At least that's one less body on *my* conscience. I'm still not convinced this wasn't some sort of initiation suggested by Ransom or one of his officers. I'll happily wipe each one of them off the face of the planet. Eduardo got the idea that shit was okay from *somewhere*.

"You can call your other guys in, Rock," Ransom suggests. Yeah, just what we need.

Ransom and Rock sit down together at the kitchen table. I take up the space behind Rock's back and keep my eye on the room. Killa stands behind Ransom and keeps his eyes on our crew.

I'm not insulted. I'm doing the same.

"I got customers who want some green, but I can't touch any in this area," Ransom starts off. He doesn't fuck around with small talk, something I know Rock appreciates.

"GSC won't sell to you?"

Ransom snorts. "Not without a hefty mark-up."

Rock glances over at Z, who took up the seat to Rock's left, before answering. "I'll be honest, we're tapped out right now. How much are you looking for and how often?"

Ransom names an absurd amount and Rock immediately shakes his head. "We can do maybe a quarter of that, but not for three to four months." Rock holds up his hand. "And that wouldn't change our agreement. No fuckin' meth in Empire."

Ransom shrugs. "There ain't much of a market for it anymore, anyway."

Normally I'd say that's good news. Except Ransom's lying through his teeth. The two meth labs he's got set up on either side of this building suggest business is booming.

"There's no decent clubs left in the area, you know," Ransom says. I guess we've moved on to his other topic of conversation. "I got two girls who'd like to work a Crystal Ball—"

"Open a club out here." Rock says, cutting that idea off.

"You know everyone crosses the bridge for that shit."

Rock shrugs. "Open one closer to Vermont."

"Got no juice for zoning."

"What do you want me to say? Last time your girls worked there, they were turning tricks. That shit doesn't go on in our club."

Ransom's face doesn't change much, but he's clearly pissed. "First, that was under our old leadership. Second, you know damn well that shit goes on all the time."

"Any of our girls get caught, they get canned. I don't need Vice sticking their nose in our business. Same for drugs."

Ransom cocks his head like he thinks Rock's full of shit.

Z pipes up. "We just did extensive drug-testing and fired a bunch of people."

"My girls are clean. I'll send them for whatever tests you want."

Rock turns to Z. "We need any new girls?"

Z shrugs. "We can always use fresh talent."

"Your girls dancin' 'cause they want to or you forcing them to?" Rock's tone borders on disrespectful and Killa raises an eyebrow.

Don't even think about it, cocksucker.

Ransom doesn't seem to care one way or another. "Gabby's got a kid to support. Her ol' man's locked up." Club should be supportin' her and the kid if he's locked up over something he did for them, but whatever. No one asked for my opinion.

"Mariella just wants to save up for a BMW," Ransom says with a chuckle.

Mariella. None of us show it, but I know each one of us reacted to hearing the name.

"You sure you're okay with that, Rock?" Z asks when we're back on the road.

"No, I'm not fuckin' all right with it. I'm trying to keep the fuckin' peace, though. We keep callin' him a liar ain't helpful." Rock stops his rant long enough to glance at Z in the rear view. "You okay with it? You're the one who's gonna have to keep an eye on them." This is Rock's not-so-subtle way of telling Z he's not spending any more time at CB than he needs to.

"Yeah. Only giving them one or two afternoon shifts. I ain't bumping our regular girls to make room for these two."

Rock inclines his head my way. "You satisfied with how this went down?"

"No. Not at all. Something's off about the whole thing. The way he already had the guy beat half to death. The way he was all prepared to talk business after." I shake my head. "Feel like we got lured down here and bent over. Sure as fuck not happy about letting their girls in our club. You know if Loco gets wind of us selling our weed to Vipers, he'll go ballistic."

Rock sighs and grips the steering wheel tighter. "You're right on all counts. We need more bodies. Bull and Steer said they'd both stick around for the week and help out at CB, but I can't see Sway lettin' two of his officers hang here indefinitely."

"Call some nomads in. Iron Jim's had interest for a while now," I suggest. He's a scary fuck. Perfect to station down at CB.

"Yeah, okay."

Z's phone buzzes and he taps me on the shoulder. "Trin's patch won't be ready for two weeks."

I turn and face him. "Are you fuckin' kidding me?" Haven't I waited long enough?

"No. Patty had a heart attack. Her daughter came up to take over the shop, but she's backed up."

"Yeah, well why don't you take your pretty-boy face down there and charm her into moving your favorite brother to the top of her list?"

He screws his face into mock-disgust. "Have you seen Patty's daughter?"

"No."

"For you and Trin, I'll take the hit," he says, shaking his head.

"Thanks."

He gets another text and chuckles. "Hey, Bronze is renting a chair at Dirty's place for a bit."

Rock raises an eyebrow. "Oh yeah?"

"That who tatted Hope's name on you?" I ask.

Rock lifts the corner of his mouth in a smirk. "Z just can't keep his mouth shut, can he?"

From the back, Z snickers.

"I think his feelings are just hurt, prez. He always thought you'd ink his name on you first."

Not at all insulted, Z laughs even harder.

"When's he gettin' into town?" I ask Z.

"Says he's already here. Looking to set up appointments this week if we know of anyone."

Perfect timing.

Trinity

At least I heard from Wrath once, so I know he's okay.

Of course it was to identify my attacker. I'm still upset that I couldn't be one hundred percent sure.

"Are you okay?" Hope asks for the tenth time.

"Yeah," I answer because I know she's scared out of her mind. She checks her phone, probably upset she hasn't heard from Rock.

"He won't text you while they're handling this, Hope. He's probably got a burner on him."

She seems confused. Isn't she a lawyer? "If they ever got arrested, he wouldn't want the cops to make the connection to you so easily," I explain.

"Oh."

She looks like she's going to be sick.

I hold up the little flip phone in my hand. "Burner to burner," I explain.

"Oh," she says again.

A little later I get another text.

Wrath: On our way home.

Thank God.

The guys are either weary or fired-up when they return. No one's covered in blood, so I take that as a positive sign. Rock squeezes my shoulder and nods at me before taking Hope upstairs.

None of us explained the situation to Heidi, so she's not sure what to make of all the guys storming in. We haven't had a semi-lockdown situation like this since she was a kid and I doubt she remembers much of it. She's in Axel's lap, talking, when Murphy comes in. She glances up and waves hello.

My attention is drawn to Wrath and I immediately get up and run to him.

He catches me, and lifts me into his arms. "You okay, angel?"

"Better now."

He presses a kiss to my lips. Quick, but full of affection. "Rock go upstairs?"

"Yup."

"We're gonna have church later when the CB guys return."

"Okay. Need me to do anything?"

"No, baby." His gaze strays to somewhere behind me and I turn to see Murphy talking quietly with Heidi and Axel. He seems to be behaving himself and I wonder if this is part of the *working things out* he mentioned the night of the bonfire.

"You got plans this week?" Wrath asks as we walk down to our room.

"Nothing special. Some things I need to do around here...why?"

He leans against the wall while I open the door, and follows me inside. "Just want to take you somewhere."

"Okay."

Wrath's on some sort of mission. He keeps talking, but he's stripping me out of my clothes at the same time. Then he's stripping off his own clothes and leading us into the shower.

He leans down and nips my ear. "Miss me?"

Shivers ripple over my skin. Both from desire and all the fear I felt earlier. "Yes."

"Worried?"

"Very."

He straightens up, finishes washing me and hands me the shower gel. "I think things are okay for now. I still don't want you running around alone or unarmed. Prospects know they're supposed to keep an eye on you and Hope. Think you can talk to her, so she's not giving them a hard time?"

"Yeah, of course."

He turns and I take my time washing his back, digging my fingers into his tight muscles, admiring every inch of him.

"Your ass is a perfect blank canvas, if you ever want to get my name tatted on it," I tease, giving him a soft smack.

He laughs and turns, snapping off the water. Yanking me against him, he stares down into my face. "Funny you should mention that."

CHAPTER 43

WRATH

Clean Ink is exactly as the name implies. Sterile. It's funny because the owner has been called Dirty for longer than I've known him. This is where I take Trinity Tuesday afternoon as a surprise.

She glances at the parlor and smirks. "Who are we here for, you or me?"

"Both."

"Oh, really?"

"Yup."

"Do I get a say in this?"

That stops me. "You said you wanted to get my star on you."

"Oh." Her face softens. "You really meant that?"

"Of course I did." Reaching out, I tickle her side. "Except now I'm thinking instead of your hip, maybe on your forehead."

She slaps my hand away. "I love you, but that's definitely not happening."

Fuck. I grab her around the waist and haul her against me. "Say it again."

"What?" Her eyes search my face for a second, then her fingers trace my cheek. "I love you, Wyatt."

We're standing on the sidewalk in the middle of downtown Empire in broad daylight. I still need to kiss her long and hard.

Bells jingle and something bangs into my leg, breaking our kiss. "Ow."

"Shit, sorry." The guy looks up. "Wrath? The fuck, man? You coming in or not?"

"Hey, Bronze." Trinity slides out of my grasp and takes my hand. We follow Bronze inside. The place is empty except for us.

"Where's Dirty?"

"Vegas."

We take a minute to catch up before I pull out the drawings I brought.

Trinity frowns at the two pieces of paper. "I only agreed to one," she says with a teasing smile.

"The other's mine."

She raises an eyebrow. "I was only joking. I don't want you to get my name on your ass."

Bronze breaks out laughing. "Thank God. I don't need to see his pasty white ass."

I hand her the drawing.

Her breath catches as she stares at it. "A Triquetra?"

"Yeah. A Trinity Knot. For our past, present, and future."

"Oh, wow." She looks around and finally drops into a chair.

"Trin, you okay?"

"Yeah. I just—you sure?"

"Fuck, yeah."

Bronze is staring at us a little too intently.

"Give us a minute." Crouching down in front of Trinity, I take her hands in mine. "You okay?"

"Where?"

Don't even have to think about it. "Right here, babe," I answer, tapping my chest. "You've owned my heart since the night we met. I think it's finally time to put your name over it."

"My name?"

"Yeah, baby." Gently, I pull the drawing out of her hands and show it to her again.

"Trinity's Man." She sniffles and swipes under her eyes. "You really want my name on you?"

"Yes." I'm starting to wonder if I should have done it on my own and surprised her with it. "We can come back for yours another time if it's too much for you, babe."

She drops her head, and pushes out of the chair. "Yeah, sure."

"I'm getting mine now. You can wait if you're not ready," I clarify because she seems to have misunderstood.

While she nods at me, I still don't think she gets what's about to happen. I take her hand and pull her toward the back. "Bronze, we're ready."

"'Bout time." He takes us into a side room and points at the table. "Who's going first?"

Don't even have to think about it. "I am."

He motions to me with his hand. "Whip it off."

My eyes roll, but I take off my shirt and hand it to Trinity. The blush that colors her cheeks as she takes me in makes me want to kick Bronze out and put his table to other uses.

Bronze lifts his chin at Trinity. "You holdin' his hand, darlin'?"

Finally the corners of her mouth turn up. "Looks like it."

I do hold her hand. Not because the needle hurts—I've certainly done this enough—but because I *like* holding her hand.

Bronze is thorough and it takes a few hours to get it done.

Leaning over, I plant a kiss on Trinity's cheek. "Your turn."

She definitely looks more excited than when we got here. "I like it," she whispers as I sit up. I'm sore and it will be a few days before I can get a good look at it, but I trust Bronze.

"Now I know why you told me to wear loose pants," she teases as she settles in. Her lips twitch. "I'm keeping my shirt on," she says.

"Hell yeah you are."

"You're just a lovely blank canvas to me, darlin'," Bronze mutters as he messes around with the drawing. "Wrath's Girl," he mutters. "You two are so sweet my teeth hurt."

Nervous laughter bubbles out of Trinity at the tired joke.

"Ugh, now I remember why I only have the one," she says about thirty minutes later.

Bronze nods. "Some people don't get the endorphin rush."

She squeezes my hand a little harder and I feel shitty about forcing her into this. "We can stop, baby. I'll bring you back another day."

"No, I want to get it all done today if we can." She flicks her gaze to Bronze, who's so wrapped up in his work, I doubt he even heard our conversation.

TRINITY

I'm trying really hard to find the numbness most people say they experience getting inked. But all I feel is pain. A lot of it. Every stroke of the needle fucking hurts. Figures my body can't even produce endorphins or adrenaline or whatever the fuck would make this less painful.

Besides the pain, I'm a crazy whirlwind of happy, excited and so fucking *in love* I can't wait to show Wrath's star off. I'm proud he wants it on me permanently. I can't even think of what it means that he wanted my name on him. Even though most of them insisted on inking their names on their ol' ladies, few of the guys I grew up around returned the favor.

Wrath's phone goes off and he very unhappily leaves the room to take the call. Bronze keeps right on working. I concentrate on moving as little as possible and not crying.

When Wrath returns, he appears stressed. "Babe, I need to run over to CB for a bit and help out with something."

Bronze sets the needle down and I almost scream with relief. He lifts his chin at Wrath. "You guys were my last customers, I can run her over there when we're done."

Wrath's gaze skips to me, then back to Bronze. "Can you give us a minute?"

He nods, rolls off his gloves and shuts the door behind him.

"I'm sorry, angel. You know I wouldn't go if I didn't have to."

While I'm not thrilled, I don't want to stress him out more. "Wyatt, it's fine. I understand. I'll be okay. I trust Bronze."

He hesitates and glances at the door. "Yeah. Known him a long time. I trust him too. You sure you're okay?"

"I just want to get it done with. I'm afraid if I quit now, I won't come back."

Soft laughter rumbles out of him. "I'm hoping this won't take too long. Maybe I'll be back before you're done."

Unlikely, but I nod anyway. He leans in for a long kiss and touches his forehead to mine. "Thank you for this. I can't wait to see it on you every day."

My throat tightens. I can't swallow or get any words out, so I bob my head.

Bronze rubs his hands together, evil-genius style, when he returns. "Ready for round two?"

Wrath kisses my forehead and stands. I close my eyes and sit back.

"Here, this should cover both of us. If it's light let me know, and I'll settle up when you drop her off."

Behind me, paper rustles. "I think there's more than enough here, bro. We're good."

The more I try to force my body to relax, the tenser I get. Bronze entertains me with a couple jokes. "Relax, Trinity. You're doin' great."

"My dad had his own shop when I was little. I used to daydream about all the tattoos I was going to get when I was older." I have to stop and laugh thinking about it now. "Then when I got the one, I was like 'hell no' and haven't tried again."

Bronze laughs with me. "Where's the other one?"

At the last minute, I remember to stay still. "My back."

"Mmmm…spine's painful," he mumbles. He seems to be lost in his work so I stay quiet. Eventually, the feeling of being repeatedly scratched by an angry alley cat lulls me into a semi-conscious, semi-painful state.

"Okay. All done. It looks good, but I'd like you to keep it covered for two to three days at least. It should be presentable in about two weeks. Don't hesitate to call me if it needs touching up or something."

I can't believe I'm going to ask my next question. "How long would it take to get, um, like a name inked?" I tap my right ear. "Behind my ear."

Bronze tilts his head. "You haven't had enough today?"

"Well—it's just…I want to surprise—"

His lips curve into a knowing smile. "Let me guess, you want to get *Wrath* inked there?"

"Not quite."

WRATH

Of course the "emergency" at Crystal Ball is the kind that means my ass is stuck here for the rest of the night. When Bronze drops Trinity off, she takes one look inside the darkened club before her pleading eyes meet mine. We end up staying outside behind the club, where I can keep the back door open and listen for trouble.

As much as I'd love to ask her to stick around, I know she'll be miserable. "I'll call Birch to give you a ride home."

Relief softens her face. "Thanks. Everything okay?"

"Yeah, one of the bouncers got roughed up and it's a stupid mess. Nothing major." It's not major which is why I'm so fucking irritated I gotta hang out here for the rest of the night, instead of going home with my girl. "No reason to make you suffer with me."

That makes her laugh.

"It go okay after I left?" I ask. "Bronze behave himself?"

Her lips curve into a sly smile. "Oh, yeah."

"I can't wait to see it later. Between the ink, my patch and the ring I'm planning to put on your finger, there'll be no doubt who owns your ass."

She gasps and pulls away from me. "Ring?"

Of all the things that came out of my mouth, ring's the one that freaks her out?

"Yeah. You said you'd want to get married at Fletcher Park."

"I...uh—"

"What? You want to do it up at the property instead?"

"One thing at a time, Wyatt."

"Oh, no. You've made me wait all this time. Wrap your head around it now."

"You're kind of taking all the romance out of it."

I run my gaze over her face. The corners of her mouth twitch—the sign she's fucking with me. "I'll make it romantic. Don't you worry."

"Yeah, but now you ruined the surprise."

I snort out a laugh. "There's no mystery, Angel Face. This is happening. I'm yours and you're mine."

She flings herself at me, wrapping her arms around my neck and I lift her up. Over and over she presses soft kisses to my forehead, cheeks, finally landing on my mouth. My hand threads into her hair, keeping her still for my exploring tongue.

We're in the back parking lot of Crystal Ball, but it's still daylight and there's a road that runs right behind the building. Someone whistles and Trinity pulls away.

"You're lucky I'm not some crazy bridezilla." She rests her palm on my cheek. "All I want is you."

"Be as crazy as you want, babe. You're still mine."

After Trinity leaves, I take up a position with my back to the bar so I can see the whole room. I'm getting old and jaded because the whole scene bores me. Not even the endless parade of flawless, glittered skin and perfect tits on the stage cheer me up. I'd much rather be home with my girl, inspecting her fresh ink.

Closing time can't come fast enough.

Rock stops in with Hope, which is a surprise. She doesn't wrinkle her nose or react to the half-naked chicks strutting around the bar. Nope, she hops onto the stool next to me and grins. "Having fun?"

"Not at all," I answer, glaring at Rock.

Fucker just laughs. "Sorry. We're spread thin. Last time I'll ask for a while."

"Yeah. It better be." I'm still grumpy I had to send Trinity home.

"Geez, I figured a bunch of horny bikers would fight to the death for the honor of hanging out here all night," Hope teases me.

Dear God, this woman comes up with some funny shit. "Nah. The younger guys, the prospects, think it's the greatest thing ever," I say, when I finally stop laughing.

"You've seen enough?" Hope asks with a knowing smile.

"Something like that."

Rock's still shaking with laughter as he curls his arms around Hope's waist and pulls her against him. "Problem is, the younger guys are too busy watching the naked ladies instead of doing their job. Can't have that."

"Oh." She twists and turns toward the stage where Lexi is busy doing obscene things to the pole. "Yeah, that makes sense."

I raise an eyebrow at Rock and he shrugs. "I'm gonna grab something out of the office. You good?" he asks.

"Yup." Didn't escape my notice the way he says *the* office instead of *his* office. Hope grabs the hand he holds out and follows him to the back of the club.

Two a.m. takes forever to get here. I stay until all the girls have finished and tipped out. Each one gets walked to their car before I finally head home.

I'm rewarded for my miserable night by finding Trinity awake and waiting for me. She kneels up on the bed and holds out her arms as soon as I step inside our room. I'm momentarily distracted by the skimpy tank top and underwear she's wearing.

Her lips push into a fake-pout. "Poor Wyatt. Were the strippers mean to you?" she asks while laughing at me.

"No," I grouch. "They know better." She squeezes me tight, but doesn't sniff me or check me over for stray pieces of glitter. It feels good knowing she trusts me.

"Can I see?" I ask, rubbing her side.

"Which one?"

Takes me a second to realize what she said. "What do you mean?"

"I got a secret one after you left," she whisper-giggles.

Part of me is turned the fuck on, part of me is not happy Bronze

449

touched my girl anywhere else. "It better not be in any of the spots your tiny outfit's hiding."

"It's not."

Huh. "Stand up."

She jumps off the bed and spins.

"Where, angel?"

She wiggles her butt at me. "Find it."

Not under her clothes. I gather her hair in my hands and hold it up to inspect the back of her neck.

Nothing.

Even so, I brush my mouth over the spot and enjoy her shivers.

Bingo.

"Behind your ear?"

"*Mmm-hmmm.*"

"Does it hurt? Can I see?"

"Go ahead."

As carefully as possible, I expose her skin.

Wyatt

I'm knocked fucking sideways. "My name?"

She turns and her hair falls out of my hand. "Yeah. You're always nipping that ear. Figured you should have your name there."

"I am?"

Her laughter is the sweetest sound of the day. "Yeah." Her hand lifts her tank top and brushes over the plastic covering the ink on her lower stomach/hip. "Do you want to see how this turned out?"

Yes I do. Kneeling in front of her, I carefully peel the plastic away.

Wrath's Girl

I can't fucking wait until it's healed and I can see it on her every day. I lean in and press my lips against her hip and her hand runs over my head.

"I love you, Wyatt."

"Love you too, Angel Face."

She hesitates. "You don't think 'girl' is silly?" she asks, pointing to the tattoo.

My arms wrap around her legs, squeezing her tight until she looks down and meets my eyes.

"Fuck no, Trinity. When we're old and gray, and you're on the back of my Tri-Glide, you'll still be *my girl.*"

Are you ready for Rock and Hope's wedding? You know it won't be an easy road to the altar for the attorney and the outlaw.
Wrath and Trinity's story also continues in
White Heat (Lost Kings MC #5).

NOTES FROM THE AUTHOR

Wrath and Trinity's story was long and complicated. But I have more in store for them in the future. Once or twice I snickered to my husband that after 145,000 words, Trinity still isn't patched or married at the end. I told him I was worried you guys would hunt me down. If you've read me before you know that I'm not a big fan of conventional HEAs. My thought on that is that unless you want to read about a couple until the day they *die*, all of it is HFN (Happy for Now). Maybe I shouldn't put that in writing. I'll get my RWA membership revoked!

I was blown away by all the notes and messages I got after *Strength From Loyalty*. Every day for weeks I woke up to messages or posts describing how much someone loved the book and what it meant to them. Since it was hard to express my happiness and gratitude without sounding crazy or using a dozen smiley faces, I started using what I call the "Snoopy-dance picture". That's basically what I look like every time I get one of your messages, so it seemed fitting.

Expectations for Wrath's book were so high, I was convinced all the way through I'd screw it up. Probably a dozen times I said "fuck it, I can't do this." Thankfully I have my husband, crit partners, and writing partners who kept reminding me that no matter what, I can't please everyone and to just write the story the way **I** felt it needed to be written. So that's what I did.

That's how the threesome scene ended up staying. Wow. I've never gone back and forth about a scene the way I did the Teller-Murphy-Trinity threesome. It was risky and something I think you can only get away with in MC Romances and Indie publishing. I know readers are always harder on the heroine and I hate that double standard (no one suggested I take Wrath's couch blow job out). But I was writing about a club girl and I wanted to be honest. I got such 50/50 feedback on that scene. Some of my betas said "you have to take it out" some said "it's hot, leave it in there" (which was funny because I thought I wrote it pretty dispassionately). I needed to get two things from that scene, but with some rewriting, I could get them without the actual sex part. At one point, I ended up taking most of it out. I discussed it some more and ultimately decided it was necessary to show how the guys respected Trinity's boundaries. So then I wrote most of it back in. There were a couple other scenes that got similar rewrites, but that one gave me the most angst.

You see, I'm an obstinate sort. I hate the notion in a lot of romances that the man can have all the sex he wants and the woman…can't. I also can't stand what I call the "golden vagina" heroine. The woman the hero falls in love with and treats like gold. But all the "other" women, club girls, whatever, are treated like trash for no reason other than they don't possess the golden vagina. There's nothing sexy or "alpha" about that to me.

But my guys are still MC guys so their feminist streaks only run so deep. Even though my series is a romanticized, less gritty MC, Hope and Trinity won't be getting a seat at the Lost Kings table. Not that either of them want one.

Tattered was a challenge because I had the time line from the first three books to follow. While I was committed to keeping the time line straight and I knew what their story was, a lot of Hope and Rock crept into Wrath and Trinity's story. Thanks to my crit partners and editor, I have an endless pile of deleted and heavily rewritten scenes that put the focus back where it belonged.

Wrath's story came about in an interesting way. Last year when my betas were going through what became Slow Burn, he was one of their favorites. I couldn't understand why, since he was usually a jerk. I think around that time I also took a class on Goals, Motivation, and Conflict and it got me thinking about *why* he was such a jerk. Once Wrath had my attention, he wouldn't shut up!

Since no two people experience the same event the same way, I really liked the idea of exploring the same situations from another character's perspective. I also realized if I rewrote word for word every single thing from the first three books in Wrath and Trinity's POV it was going to be a long and boring ride. I tried to pick and choose the most important events that moved Wrath and Trin's story forward.

I've heard from people who want more from Rock and Hope in the future. They felt there was unfinished business of some sort? If you were one of those readers then you'll be happy with Book #5. If you're tired of Rock, Hope, and Wrath, then you'll probably want to skip *White Heat (Lost Kings MC #5)*. Rock and Hope will have their wedding...I just need to torture them a little bit first. Oh, and you read that right. It will be Rock, Hope and Wrath. No, they're not having a threesome. You'll just have to wait and see.

I always assumed Z's story would be next. But I've been bombarded with questions about Heidi and Murphy. I'm shocked by how many people are team Murphy. Like, *passionately* Team Murphy. Don't get me wrong, I love Murphy too, but *wow*. Axel has some fans too (Mr. Lake being one of them) but not the way Murphy does. I laughed when people were arguing team Murphy or team Axel while I was writing Tattered, because I knew Murphy was a bit of a dick in this book.

With some help from my crit partners I have a good idea of what Murphy, Heidi and Axel's story is. *More Than Miles (Lost Kings MC #6)* is complicated and will take me some time to figure out and get right. I have a few other projects I'm working on as well, but the Lost Kings are still my first priority.

I'm lucky to have some amazing readers who kept after me, very gently nudging me and prodding me about when Wrath's book would be finished. I hope you know how much I appreciate it. I'm planning to attend at least two signings in 2016, so I hope I get to say hello to some of you in person.

If I left you with unanswered questions, you know by now I did it on purpose.

Thank you!

Autumn

THE LOST KINGS MC® WORLD

By Autumn Jones Lake

Sometimes I'm asked where the stand alone books fit into the Lost Kings MC World. This is a loose, chronological reading order that might help!

Suggested Chronological Reading Order

1. Kickstart My Heart (Hollywood Demons #1)
2. Blow My Fuse (Hollywood Demons #2)
3. Wheels of Fire (Hollywood Demons #3)
4. Renegade Path
5. Slow Burn (Lost Kings MC #1)
6. Corrupting Cinderella (Lost Kings MC #2)
7. Three Kings, One Night (Lost Kings MC #2.5)
8. Strength From Loyalty (Lost Kings MC #3)
9. Tattered on My Sleeve (Lost Kings MC #4)
10. White Heat (Lost Kings MC #5)
11. Between Embers (Lost Kings MC #5.5)
12. Bullets & Bonfires (Standalone)
13. More Than Miles (Lost Kings MC #6)
14. Warnings & Wildfires (Standalone)
15. White Knuckles (Lost Kings MC #7)
16. Beyond Reckless (Lost Kings MC #8)
17. Beyond Reason (Lost Kings MC #9)

18. One Empire Night (Lost Kings MC #9.5)
19. After Burn (Lost Kings MC #10)
20. After Glow (Lost Kings MC #11)
21. Zero Hour (Lost Kings MC #11.5)
22. Zero Tolerance (Lost Kings MC #12)
23. Zero Regret (Lost Kings MC #13)
24. Zero Apologies (Lost Kings MC #14)
25. Swagger and Sass (Lost Kings MC #14.5)
26. White Lies (Lost Kings MC #15)
27. Rhythm of the Road (Lost Kings MC #16)
28. Lyrics on the Wind (Lost Kings MC #17)
29. Diamond in the Dust (Lost Kings MC #18)
30. Crown of Ghosts (Lost Kings MC #19)
31. Throne of Scars (Lost Kings MC #20)
32. Reckless Truths (Lost Kings MC #21)
33. Rust or Ride (Lost Kings MC #22)

...and many more books to come!